BLINDING PASSION

Morgana stared speechlessly into the hard, unrelenting features of the man who had just saved her reputation from ruin. A flicker of unidentifiable emotion moved across his face, and Morgana suddenly found herself enfolded in a strong, comforting embrace.

"Come on, darlin', no more tears." Smiling encouragingly, Devon lowered his head to press light kisses across the clear skin of her forehead.

Her lips were full, appealing, drawing him, crying for his consolation, and he moved to cover them lightly, gently with his own. With supreme gentleness, he kissed her again and again, his mouth moving to cover hers more fully each time until his kiss was deep and searing.

Gasping at the unknown emotions sweeping her senses, Morgana surrendered herself completely to his embrace. She was overwhelmed by a kaleidoscope of l....... iridescent hues that eliminated all but the m........... man who held her in his arms. . . .

SWEET TORMENT
ELAINE BARBIERI

ZEBRA BOOKS
KENSINGTON PUBLISHING CORP.

ZEBRA BOOKS

are published by

Kensington Publishing Corp.
475 Park Avenue South
New York, N.Y. 10016

First printing: June, 1984

Printed in the United States of America

To my parents, who prove the basic truth
that love can endure for a lifetime

Quickly surveying the teeming scene around her, Morgana adjusted her grip on the small bag she carried, took a deep breath, lifted her chin, and started forward. In the months since her father's death she had not yielded to fear, and she did not intend to start now. She had her father and Aggie to thank for an education far above that of the ordinary woman of her time. She was, after all, fluent in Spanish and French, and at least conversant in German; was extremely well read in the classics; had a knowledgeable appreciation of art and music; and played the piano very well. She was confident she would be able to compensate Tía Isabella in some way for her generosity. If nothing else, Aggie's strict Scottish upbringing had instilled in her a firm sense of responsibility to a commitment made in good faith. Yes, she had written Tía Isabella accepting her generous offer, and she was going on to Mexico, with or without Aggie!

Fastening uncertain doe-shaped eyes on the steamboat *Hercules*, Morgana squared her small frame and continued briskly forward. The disorder of the docks was staggering. A melée of arriving carriages, anxious passengers, shouting sailors, and carts loaded with barter of all sorts appeared to block her path at every turn. Abruptly feeling a small, insignificant part of the almost chaotic scene being enacted before her eyes, Morgana slowed her step in an attempt to chart the best path.

The March wind was brisk and biting. A sudden gust lifted the folds of her grey velvet cape to flap chillingly against her. Adjusting the wide bonnet that dwarfed her face, she gathered the undulating garment around her, allowing herself one last glance at the tall, grey-haired woman who still stood woodenly in the spot in which she had alighted from the carriage. Anger at Aggie's unexpected, painful mutiny flushing her with a new determination, Morgana turned sharply forward. With a rapid step, she started across the street in the direction she had mentally charted.

With startling abruptness, the loud clatter of horses' hooves was frighteningly near. Her head snapping to the side in a moment of paralyzing fear, Morgana saw two huge horses almost upon her! The screech of braking wheels

9

against the ground grated in her ears in the same moment her mind registered the panic on the face of the driver of the careening wagon as he strove to rein it to a halt. Warning shouts sounded, echoing in her mind along with her own silent scream in the moment before a sudden, brutal grip swept her from her feet, jerking her roughly from the path of the crushing hooves.

Abruptly she was safe, shuddering within a bruisingly powerful grip, supported against a hard, heaving chest as she struggled to regain her stability. Dizzy and disoriented from the rapidity of the terrifying sequence of events, Morgana swayed unsteadily in the binding embrace, her eyes moving upward dazedly to finally focus on a dark, angry face almost as intimidating as the fate she had narrowly escaped. Suddenly she was thrust an arm's length from the haven of the hard chest that supported her. Merciless hands dug into the soft flesh of her upper arms, as a deep voice demanded harshly, "What are you tryin' to do, kill yourself? Don't you have the sense to look where you're goin'?"

His eyes darting around the immediate area to no avail, the man turned back to continue harshly, "Where's the rest of your party? Damn it, answer me! You can't be here alone. . . ."

The startling blue eyes moving over her white face sent little tremors down her spine. The agitated heaving of the broad chest so near her was slowly subsiding, but the fury in the man's glance did not lessen as he impatiently awaited her response.

"Morgana! Are you all right?" Aggie's breathless inquiry succeeded in penetrating the bemused state the angry blue eyes had evoked, causing Morgana to snap her head toward the familiar voice.

"Y . . . yes, I'm . . . I'm all right, Aggie. . . ."

The crushing grip left her arms abruptly, the unexpected release almost unbalancing her as the tall, dark-haired man turned the full force of his anger on the frightened woman who had rushed to their side.

"Are you with this young woman?" At Aggie's silent, shaken acknowledgment, he continued heatedly, "Damn it,

10

woman, where were you when you were needed? This young woman needs more than a chaperone! She needs a keeper! That wagon came on in full view and this fool walked right out in front of it!'' When still there was no response from either woman, the angry eyes raked Aggie's flushed face. ''The least you could do, woman, is to keep a close eye on her if she can't find the way to crossin' the street safely by herself!''

Outrage flooded Morgana's senses.

How dare this man harangue Aggie in such a heartless manner? How dare he insult her own intelligence because of one careless moment! How dare he intimate that she was incapable of taking care of herself! The past six months had proved her far more mature than her eighteen years, and she would not suffer the arrogant boor's insulting remarks, no matter the depth of her debt! Ignoring the trembling that still beset her limbs, Morgana pulled herself to her full, meager height, anger flooding her white face with color. Startled at the tone of her own vehement exclamation, she cut into the man's heated tirade.

''Sir!'' The angry face turned in her direction as she continued haughtily, ''Although I must concede you have done me a great service, your actions do *not* entitle you to become offensive!''

A small, contemptuous snort escaped the man's lips, revealing white, well shaped teeth that contrasted vividly with the sun-darkened color of his face. ''Yes, the truth *can* be offensive at times, can't it!''

''The *truth* is, sir,'' Morgana interrupted sharply, returning strength lending emphasis to her cutting retort, ''I *did* act in an extremely careless manner in crossing the street. That is a fact I cannot deny. But I am *not* a fool, and certainly not helpless in any way! *And,* although your actions today were . . . timely . . . I do not appreciate your supercilious remarks! Despite my short, unfortunate lapse a few minutes ago, you may rest assured I am an extremely capable woman! You need not bother yourself that I will need *your* or anyone else's assistance again!''

Her temporary satisfaction as the man's brows drew to-

11

gether in an intensifying frown was fleeting as he replied in a low, cutting drawl, "The *truth* is, *ma'am,* I don't really *care* one way or another!"

"The *truth,* sir," Morgana interrupted, barely controlling the fury that flushed her face a deep scarlet, "The *truth* is that despite the fact that you *were* instrumental in saving me, you are *not* a gentleman!"

Turning stiffly on still wobbling legs, Morgana retrieved her bag and started haughtily toward the ship. Another flash of rage swept her, quickening her step at the sound of Aggie's low voice behind her.

"I should like to thank you, sir, for your quick action. Morgana is upset and . . ."

Mercifully, within moments the deep male voice in reply was beyond her range of hearing. Her thoughts still filled with the stranger's audacious words, Morgana maintained a quick step, unaware of the well-dressed man who approached her until his voice startled her from her thoughts.

"Excuse me, miss."

Morgana's eyes jerked upward, meeting the glance of pale grey eyes in an unlined, extremely handsome and unfamiliar face.

"I didn't mean to startle you, but I saw your near accident just now. You must still be rather shaken. Might I carry your bag for you? You're heading for the *Hercules,* are you not?" When still she did not respond but remained staring blankly into his face, the fellow carefully took the bag from her hand, smiling as her fingers surrendered it to him. Cupping her elbow in a smooth, practiced manner, he urged her forward, his voice low and soothing to her frazzled nerves.

"My name is Edgar Morrison. I'm on my way to Havana. I'm pleased to say we'll be shipmates during the voyage."

Making a modest effort at a smile for the first time that day, Morgana replied softly, the small tremor in her voice revealing the trauma of the past few minutes, "Thank you, Mr. Morrison. You . . . you are too kind."

Walking briskly toward the gangplank, Morgana could not see the deepening scowl on the face of the arrogant stranger or Aggie's concerned expression the moment before she abruptly concluded their conversation and, turning, followed silently in Morgana's footsteps.

Taking a deep breath, Morgana placed her bag on the floor at the foot of the narrow bunk. Her eyes moving around the small cabin. Having passed the narrows, the passengers had transferred from the *Hercules* to the sailing ship *Helga,* on which they were to make their voyage to Havana. Now, standing within the dreary four walls she was to inhabit until they reached their destination, Morgana suddenly did not find the prospect at all appealing. Having found the cabin with considerable difficulty a few minutes before, she had stepped into the small, temporary abode she and Aggie were to share, the full impact of her decision to go to Tía Isabella . . . to leave the country of her birth . . . hitting her for the first time.

A small sound behind drew her eyes to Aggie's erect, impervious figure as she systematically eyed the soundness of the bunks. Dressed in the nondescript dark attire that had been her uniform since the time of Morgana's first recollection, she drew a small smile to Morgana's lips. The sharply arched brows raised over large, wide-set eyes imparted the same owlish, all-knowing appearance that had more often than not intimidated her into confessing her childhood transgressions without the need for a single word of threat. The hair framing the square, rather flat face, had greyed over the years, and a network of fine lines had begun to mark Aggie's sober features, but her general appearance had changed little over the years. Her devotion to the young, motherless girl whose care she had assumed over twelve years before had been constant and, despite her own attempts to assert her new maturity, Morgana realized she was extremely grateful for the security of the familiar, imposing figure. Her eyes misting lightly, Morgana felt a thickness in her throat. Her slender lips twitching revealingly, she took two quick strides forward to throw her arms unexpectedly around the woman's well-laced proportions.

"Oh, Aggie, I'm so glad you decided to come with me."

Her natural reserve coming to the forefront despite the suspicious brightness in her brown eyes, Aggie responded briskly, "You certainly didn't expect me to leave you to face those revolutions alone, did you, Morgana?" Her tone precluding the necessity for a reply, she patted her lightly on the cheek before continuing quietly, "It's best we settle ourselves in now, Morgana, before the voyage progresses any further."

Nodding her head as she swallowed hard against the lump in her throat, Morgana responded in a lighter tone, "That would be a good idea, Aggie, if our luggage had been delivered to the cabin, but it seems to be nowhere in sight." Her eyes moving over the small room in which the two bunks, situated one over the other, seemed to take up the majority of the space allotted, she continued in a low mutter, "And when they do arrive, I just wonder where we'll put them!"

Sweeping off the cumbersome cape and bonnet, Morgana turned to watch as Aggie placed her bag carefully on the floor beside hers. Precise, considerate, loving Aggie. She was as close as true family to her . . . almost all she had left. . . . Angry at the tears that again sprang into her eyes, Morgana turned away. She had no time for morbid meanderings. She was on her way to a new life . . . new experiences . . . She had no doubt she would . . .

The dull thud as the door to the cabin abruptly jerked open to bang against the wall snapped Morgana from her thoughts, her eyes flying wide as the stranger from the docks stood in the doorway. He was glowering in her direction, and Morgana found herself wondering if indeed that broad, well-shaped mouth ever did crease into a smile.

Stealing the very words that sprang to her lips, he demanded sharply, "What are you doing in my cabin?"

A flash of temper widened her eyes further, igniting glittering flecks of gold into a fiery blaze as Morgana echoed disbelievingly, "*Your* cabin! You are mistaken, sir! This cabin is ours . . . Aggie's and mine! *You* are the trespasser here, not I!"

Entering the room in a slow, self-possessed manner that

14

seemed to sum up his personality, the man gradually lowered his bag to the floor, his eyes trained on her face with an intensity that was effective in raising her color to a point of discomfort. Forcing herself to remain still, apparently unaffected, Morgana clamped her teeth tightly shut, her lips pressed together in a fine, straight line as the light eyes surveyed her openly. Showing a trace of something other than anger, they flashed over the slender length of her, dwelling for the briefest second on the swells of the full, rounded breasts pressed against the modest forest-green gown before sliding upwards to move to the soft chestnut brown hair parted modestly in the center. The scrutinizing gaze followed the severe upward sweep of the gleaming strands to the back of her head where they were secured tightly in a cluster of shining ringlets. The touch of his glance was almost physical in intensity as it moved over her high, clear forehead; touched lightly on her thin, winged brows; lingered to mentally reckon the length of extraordinarily thick brown lashes fringing doe-shaped eyes before continuing to trace the splendid contour of her cheek and fine line of her profile. His glance came to rest at last on her full, pink lips, which suddenly trembled under his heady scrutiny.

"And now that you're finished with your assessment," Morgana demanded sharply, "you will leave my cabin, sir!"

Total silence followed as Morgana's command reverberated on the air in the small cabin. Her words had emerged with unintentioned arrogance, stimulating a flash of anger in the cerulean eyes intent on her face. A knot of fear tightening in her stomach, she saw his sharply etched features stiffen as his eyes raked her flushed face for long tension-filled moments. When he finally spoke his voice was a low, threatening purr.

"Darlin', this is my cabin, and you know it well. There's no need for this playactin'. If you're so intent on gaining my notice, you'd be better off findin' a less irritatin' way. As it is, my first inclination is to turn you over my knee .. and my second . . ." His eyes dropping to her mouth finished the sentence more eloquently than words.

Astounded by his boldness, Morgana was momentarily at

15

a loss for a response, her mouth dropping open even as her eyes rapidly narrowed in escalating indignation.

"How dare . . . how *dare* you insinuate that I've gone out of my way to bring myself to your attention! Quite the contrary, *you're* the one who has invaded *my* privacy . . . has come breaking into *my* cabin! You may take my words as gospel, Mr. . . . whatever your name is, when I tell you I find you the most presumptuously arrogant man I have ever met or ever hope to meet again! And you will please vacate my cabin imm . . . steward!" Her eye catching on the white-coated steward as he flashed past the doorway, Morgana called again, "Steward!"

Within moments her urgent summons had brought the slender Mexican to the doorway.

"*Sí*, señorita. There is something you wish?"

"Yes, there is! My name is Morgana Pierce. I am traveling with my companion, Agatha MacWhorter. I would appreciate your telling this . . . gentleman . . . that this is my cabin, and that I want him out of it immediately!"

The startled steward's hesitation started the first prickle of apprehension down her spine. Her discomfort grew more intense by the moment as his small brown eyes jerked to the tall stranger, only to return uncomfortably back to hers.

"I am sorry, señorita. I, myself, directed Señor Howard to this cabin a few minutes ago." Quickly withdrawing a folded piece of paper from the pocket of his well-worn coat, he pointed anxiously to the crude markings on squares drawn to represent the cabins on their deck. "See, señorita, Señor Howard is in this cabin, and Señorita Pierce and Señora MacWhorter are in the bigger cabin at the end of the passageway."

"It is *Señorita* MacWhorter!"

Ignoring Aggie's quick admonition, Morgana felt a new flush of color transfuse her cheeks. Summoning the full power of her will, she forced herself to meet the knowing glance fastened so mercilessly on her face, her back stiffening with resentment at the necessity for her next statement. Barely able to get the words past her lips, she said tightly, "I . . . it seems I owe you somewhat of an apology, Mr. . . .

Howard. Since this is your cabin, Aggie and I will vacate it immediately, with my regrets for having . . . having . . .''

". . . made a fool of yourself?" His glance direct and un-flinching, Devon Howard continued darkly, "Yes, you did."

Her face flaming, unable to stand another moment of the man's blatant self-righteousness, Morgana bent to snatch at her cape and bonnet. Darting Aggie a quick look that sent her to picking up their two bags without delay, Morgana turned to the flustered steward.

"If you will conduct us to our cabin, steward, we will leave Mr. . . . Howard to his privacy!"

Barely controlling the urge to slap the arrogant expression from Devon Howard's face, Morgana turned with all the dignity she could muster and left the room, the heat of fury still burning her cheeks as she walked regally down the passageway.

Pitching and tossing . . . pitching and tossing . . . the heavy, undulating rhythm had done its work well. The deck was all but deserted, allowing Morgana the respite of well-appreciated solitude. The first two days of the voyage had not proved a pleasant experience, and now, the morning of the third, the sky was again a dull grey, the wind unabating. The retreating view to which Aggie and she had treated themselves as they had left the harbor had been an extremely saddening experience, despite the beauties of the bay. The shores, covered to the water's edge with stark skeletons of trees, still naked from winter's onslaught; the white houses on Staten Island; the pilot leaving to break the last link with land; the mountains of Navesink; the lighthouse of Sandy Hook . . . all gradually fading from view, seemed yet another farewell for which they had been ill prepared. She had also been ill prepared for the conditions on the packet on which they were bound for Havana. Cabins with little or no air, seasick passengers everywhere, and the steady rise and fall of the swells that continued to keep most of the passengers in the very lowest physical state.

17

The passenger list of the *Helga* was small, limiting the number of people to whom she would be exposed during her hopefully brief stay on the uncomfortable vessel: Señor and Señora Acosta, a wealthy Cuban and his wife; Mrs. Belva Tate, a young widow, and her aunt, Mrs. Hortense Martin; Mr. and Mrs. Herman Wollett and their two embarrassingly foolish, man-hungry daughters; several Spaniards whom she had not yet and secretly cared little to meet; two American businessmen apparently interested in the sugar trade; the despicable Devon Howard; and last, and life-savingly attentive, Edgar Morrison.

But the weather had held her contact with her fellow passengers to occasional glimpses of all, with the exception of the seemingly invincible Devon Howard, and, most thankfully, Edgar Morrison. Moreover, the sorry conditions of the passengers had transformed the passageways into caverns of odious sounds and odors that had made it a relief to escape to the fresh air on deck, despite the chill of the day. Spontaneously pulling her cape a little tighter against her, Morgana raised her hand to adjust her hood against the wind. So far she had been fortunate enough to escape the ills shared by so many, which accounted for her unusual freedom on deck. Poor Aggie! Had she not been laid so terribly low, she would have objected strenuously to her solitary sojourns, but even Aggie's stiff Scottish upbringing was no match for the ceaseless undulation of the *Helga*.

But that man . . . Devon Howard! Grinding her teeth in frustration, Morgana fought against the image that once again invaded her mind. The features were hard, strong, sharp, their impact increased dramatically by skin colored and lined by the sun, taut over prominent cheekbones and the contour of a strong chin. The light eyes under heavy brown brows mocked her; the generous curve of his mouth curled in a knowing, insolent smile that drew her despite the anger it evoked. The low, maddening drawl still rang in her ears. Southern gentlemen! Hah! That was a joke! Surely no *Northern* gentleman would take the liberties with his glance of which that *Southern* ''gentleman'' had availed himself so insultingly. Recalling the slow sweep of his eyes as they had

18

traveled her body, Morgana again felt a flush suffuse her cheeks. Anxious for his company . . . indeed! The man obviously had a colossal ego! He was no doubt the type of man described as a womanizer! She would certainly make it her business to avoid any contact with him on this voyage.

But, her mind countered, judging from the reaction of the few available women on the ship to his appearance, he would not be lacking for female company if that was what he desired. Despite her "bereavement," the sultry widow Belva Tate had cast openly appreciative glances in his direction; and the Wollett sisters seemed to be reduced to batting eyelashes and simpering sighs whenever he appeared on deck. Whatever they saw in him was truly hard to conceive! He was tall . . . but not overly so, and contrary to her first impression when he had supported her so heavyhandedly after her near accident on the dock, other than for the broad width of his shoulders, he was not outstandingly muscular in build. Rather, he was lean . . . rangy . . . his carriage casual. His clothes were adequately fashionable, but did not disguise the air of outdoors he managed to convey. Exposure to the elements was apparent in many physical details: the sun-bleached streaking of his heavy brown hair; the telltale lines fanning from the corners of those damned, seeking eyes; the darkened color of his skin; the sharp honing of his physique, tight muscular tone, narrow waist, the thrust of powerful thighs apparent in the body-hugging cut of his trousers. But something far more subtle, almost indefinable, marked a difference instantly discernible between Devon Howard and all the other men with whom she had ever come into contact. It was a strange, unique air he exuded, complete mastery over himself and, she suspected, over any situation in which he might become involved. His eyes were alert, his glance disturbing. He moved with the stealthy grace of a lean, powerful animal, his physical strength and prowess indisputable in his instinctive actions on the dock. She remembered still the feeling of those strong arms around her. . . .

In any case, she had heard he was a Texan, and she could far more easily perceive him as a man who had spent many hours each day on horseback than she could believe the talk that he had been in New York on some political mission of sorts that was now taking him to Mexico City. No, she was certain it was not his handsomeness that drew women's eyes, as much as it was the innately virile appeal of that slow, knowing glance he used so effectively, or the light that flared in his clear eyes . . . as when they had touched on her lips. . . .

What was she doing? Annoyed at the path her thoughts had taken, Morgana shook her head. She wanted no part of a man like that! She had had little experience with men past a casual flirtation and a stolen adolescent kiss. She had no time now, in her new, perhaps precarious position, for matters of that sort. Even if she did, it would be far better if she concentrated on a man like Edgar Morrison. *He* was a true gentleman, and although obviously a man of the world, had been courteous and attentive beyond reproach, filling the long hours of the last two days most amicably, while Devon Howard had contented himself with contemptuous glances in her direction. Even Edgar's small wink when he had mentioned his good fortune in being able to enjoy her company without Aggie's constant presence did not carry a note of threat. And he was certainly far more handsome than Devon Howard! Counting herself one of the more fortunate women on board in enjoying his full attention, she recalled to mind his tall, broadly muscular physique. With gold, curly hair, pale grey eyes, and fine, regular features, he was almost pretty though without a trace of effeminacy . . . truly a beautiful man! So why, Morgana questioned angrily, did not his glance send the same tremors of anticipation up her spine that another perusal so easily induced? So why did . . .

The sound of a familiar step behind her interrupted her thoughts, turning her around as a smooth, cultured voice offered softly, "Now I'm certain it will be a beautiful day. Any day begun with a glimpse of your lovely face can be no more than perfect, Morgana."

Flushing at Edgar's extravagant compliment, Morgana turned to meet his appreciative gaze. "Edgar, you are far too generous."

His hand moving to squeeze her shoulder intimately, he

whispered softly in response, "No, I think not, Morgana. I must confess to a very long, restless night last night while thoughts of you plagued me relentlessly." His hand moving caressingly on her shoulder sent a short tremor of unease down her spine. There was a strange light in his pale eyes as he continued softly, "I'm afraid I'm becoming far more fond of you than I had dreamed possible in our short acquaintance, and the thought of another day in your company fills me with—"

"Good mornin', ma'am . . . Mr. Morrison."

A low, purposeful drawl unexpectedly close behind them caused Morgana's face to flame as Edgar's hand dropped quickly to his side. Annoyed at her spontaneous coloring, Morgana replied tartly, "Oh, I think most of the passengers on this packet would disagree with your assessment of the day, Mr. Howard. Aside from the fact that the air is sharp and penetrating, the sun hidden behind a thick cloud cover, and the wind blowing contrary to the direction in which we hope to travel, the sea is decidedly rough and a source of supreme discomfort to many. No . . . I don't think it is a particularly 'good morning.' "

"Yes, you may be right, ma'am." His brow raising slightly, he directed an amused glance toward Edgar Morrison's hand where it lay at his side. "With the weather so contrary, and the deck almost deserted this mornin', it might actually be considered unsafe for an unchaperoned young lady like yourself to be up here." Completely ignoring the angry tightening of her lips, he raised his eyes to speak his next words levelly into Edgar Morrison's eyes. "Perhaps it might be wise if you did go inside for breakfast now and socialized with a few of the other passengers."

Aware of the tension between the two men as their glances met and held, Morgana stared incredulously for a few long moments. Devon's glance remained trained intently on the face of the tall, blond man behind Morgana as she exclaimed indignantly, "Very honestly, Mr. Howard, I don't think whatever I do is any of your conc—"

"Oh, Mr. Howard . . . Mr. Howard. . . !" A sickening blend of simpering female voices followed by what

21

sounded like a chorus of idiotic giggles interrupted Morgana's speech. There was no need to turn to identify the voices as the two fawning Wollett sisters closed around Devon Howard's rangy frame, each boldly attaching herself to a strong arm. Margaret, the older of the two, smiled flirtatiously into his eyes as she continued breathlessly, "We're so happy to find you on deck this morning, Mr. Howard. Mama and Papa are indisposed this morning and unable to accompany us to breakfast. We would so appreciate your escorting us." Batting her eyelashes in a thoroughly ridiculous manner, she continued sweetly, "We are unaccustomed to being without the protection of a strong man at any time."

Barely able to suppress a groan at the girl's artless manner, Morgana injected insidiously, "Oh, yes, Mr. Howard. A big, strong man like you is just what these ladies need right now! Edgar and I will most certainly excuse you to perform this gentlemanly act of courtesy."

Realizing from the darkness of his glance that he was not amused, Morgana felt a sudden tightening in her throat. His features stiffening warningly, Devon Howard responded politely, "It will be my pleasure, ladies." Raising his eyes, he looked with an almost deadly stare into Edgar's face, his voice a low, ominous purr. "After you, Mr. Morrison."

Holding his glance, Edgar replied with a menace of his own, "I think Morgana and I will wait a few minutes before going in to breakfast."

Devon Howard stood his ground stiffly, his face was blankly unrevealing, the twitching of a small muscle in his cheek the only change in his demeanor. "I don't think that would be a good idea."

Realizing incredulously that the conversation between the two men had abruptly reached a volatile stage, Morgana reached out to take Edgar's arm. "I . . . I do think I would like some breakfast now, Edgar. I'm really . . . far hungrier than I realized."

Freezing her with his glance the moment after he broke contact with Howard's stare, Edgar looked down into her face, a small smile finally warming his countenance as he replied hesitantly, "In that case, Morgana, of course, we'll go in to breakfast now."

His expression stiff and relentless, Devon Howard waited until Edgar turned and started toward the dining room with Morgana on his arm before following carefully a step behind.

Leaning casually at the rail in a posture that belied his angry thoughts, Devon Howard squinted into a horizon that dipped and swayed with the motion of the ship. He was restless, the muscles in his arms and legs stiff from lack of exercise. Running a broad, calloused hand through his heavy brown hair, he took a firmer grip on his slowly dissipating patience and gritted his teeth. He despised this inactivity . . . the time wasted on a voyage that was progressing poorly, thanks to a steadfast contrary wind and rough seas. Now, eight days out, they still had not passed the Bahama banks. The weather had turned considerably warmer, eliminating the need for a topcoat, and indeed, he was a bit uncomfortable in the light coat he wore over the fashionable satin vest he had purchased during his obligatory stay in New York. How much he would have preferred to be dressed in a light, homespun shirt and breeches well worn to a point of comfort, seated on his horse, moving through a rolling sea of tall grass. Hell, he had been away from Texas for months, during which time he had wooed the industrial wealth of New York to the cause of the Anglo-American colony in Texas, without supporting a break with the Mexican government to which they had sworn allegiance. But affairs had reached a dangerous point in the Mexican state of Texas.

Shaking his head, Devon reminded himself that the Mexican state of Texas truly existed only in his mind. The decree forming the joint Mexican state of Coahuila and Texas merely contained a provision to the effect that Texas could petition the general congress in Mexico City for separation from Coahuila when it possessed the necessary elements to form a separate state. In his mind and in the minds of those of his fellow Texans, the time had come. They had long since tired of inadequate representation in the state congress, and of the propensity of the Mexican government to favor the Spanish-inhabited province of Coahuila over its heavily Anglo-American counterpart. In no respect were the needs of the two provinces similar. The geographical position of Coahuila excluded it from maritime trade, whereas Texas possessed great natural advantages for the development of an extensive commercial business with foreign countries. Climates and industrial pursuits were also markedly dissimilar. Pastoral and mining occupations prevailed in Coahuila, whereas Texas was essentially an agricultural country, with cotton, sugar, and cereals being cultivated, all with most flattering prospects. The remoteness of the higher judicial courts also made the process of law tedious, causing delays that tended to defeat the ends of justice. And only the year before a state law had been enacted allowing only Mexicans to become impresarios in the future, lowering the price of lands to Mexican purchasers, while excluding natives of the United States from settling within their province. Clearly, the time had come to split with Coahuila. In April of the previous year a convention had assembled to frame a constitution for the state of Texas, and to draw up a petition requesting the general government in Mexico City to grant separation of Texas from Coahuila.

Smiling, Devon remembered the enthusiastic convening of Texas patriots. Stephen Austin, whose father had obtained the original charter for the Anglo-American settlement; Branch Archer, David Burnett, Sam Houston; and the many lesser-known Texans who formed the backbone of the assembly. Together they had painstakingly drawn up a constitution, thoroughly republican in form, modeled on the Constitution of the United States, but modified to adapt to the conditions of the Mexican federation.

David Burnett had drawn up the actual memorial to the central government in Mexico, setting forth the position of Texas and its request for separation from Coahuila. Startled by their choice of himself, Devon had halfheartedly accepted the position of delegate to the northeastern United States to solicit the financial support of sympathetic Americans—if only for the reason that no one better than he and his fellow

24

Texans realized the danger in their present lack of working capital. Their wealth, unfortunately, lay almost entirely in their land. But of the three delegates appointed to proceed to the city of Mexico, only Stephen Austin had actually made the journey.

A new flush of rage suffusing his strong features, Devon again struggled against his anger at the despicable events that had followed. Stephen Austin . . . honesty and integrity inherent and deeply ingrained in his character . . . accused of treason by the Mexican government! It was incredible! Loyal to the commitment signed to the supreme government in Mexico, and dedicated to his task of petitioning for the separation of Texas and Coahuila, Austin had arrived to have their petition all but ignored for long months while the turmoil between the contending parties in the capital raged on. Having finally met with Santa Anna successfully in November, Austin was at last traveling home, only to be arrested for treason at Saltillo and returned to the city of Mexico where he was incarcerated in the dungeon of an old inquisition building. There he still remained, in close confinement, purportedly treated with harshness demeaning to a man of his political and personal stature.

Word had reached Devon of Stephen Austin's dire circumstances just a few weeks before, along with instructions from the delegates of the convention to proceed immediately to the city of Mexico to speak with Santa Anna in Austin's behalf. Ascertaining Santa Anna's whereabouts had been a considerable feat, owing to the wily Mexican's frequent change of venue consistent with the fortunes of his native country. The *Helga* had been the first packet available to Devon's destination, and, frustrated with the numerous delays in starting his mission, he had arranged for last minute passage on the miserable vessel. But once again he found himself frustrated by delays . . . this time against which he was totally helpless. Eight days out . . . and not yet at the Bahama banks. . . . Considering the traveling time involved—once they reached Havana, they would board another ship for Veracruz and begin an overland journey into Mexico itself—he doubted the wisdom of the council's sending him on this mission. But, no doubt, their decision had lain in the fact that he was personally acquainted with President Santa Anna. Both he and Stephen Austin had met the man on several occasions, and although he did not share Austin's high regard for him, there was no doubt in the minds of the council that Devon was the man for the job of convincing Santa Anna to put his weight into having Austin released. Facing him was the unpleasant task of presenting a diplomatic face to a man whom he secretly believed to be manipulative and self-serving in all his dealings in behalf of Mexico. A small snort escaping his lips, he mused that, indeed, were Santa Anna able to read his mind, Devon himself would soon follow Stephen Austin into the dungeon . . . never to see the light of day again!

A ripple of soft, feminine laughter reached his ears, interrupting his thoughts and bringing a low oath to his lips. Damned fool girl! He did not need to turn his head to see the picture that would present itself at the rail a considerable distance away. A small, elegantly shaped face framed by a halo of bright chestnut curls; clear, unlined skin a bit more golden than the first day aboard, despite the almost total absence of sun; glorious russet eyes sparking with laughter; slender, perfect lips spread wide in a smile that dimpled one smooth cheek. . . . With the change in temperature and the shedding of the voluminous cape that had shielded Morgana Pierce from the piercing wind, he was now all too aware of the dainty feminine appeal of her small frame; the gentle slope of her shoulders; the graceful movements of her slender arms and beautifully shaped hands; the full curve of her breast and the incredibly small expanse of waist apparent in the fashionable pink cotton frock that so added to the charm of her delicate coloring. Morgana Pierce . . . fragile . . . delicate as a China doll, with a subtle sexual appeal that ravaged his senses.

A sense of aversion momentarily overwhelming the devastating allure of her femininity, he painstakingly recounted to himself the blatant weaknesses in her character that had so enraged him from the start. He needed no one to tell him Morgana Pierce's background was wealth. She was typical of the spoiled, rich children with whom he had become all too familiar during his short sojourn in New York. Aside from the luxury of the clothes she wore so casually, it was apparent in the manner in which she carried herself . . . head high, glance disdainful . . . as if she owned the ground on which she walked; and in her imperious tone, her supreme arrogance. She had not demonstrated a speck of gratitude for a kind fate that had saved her from the hooves of that team of horses; had shown no sign that she fully realized how close she had come to losing her life. Indeed, she had displayed instead an innate hauteur, an infinite smugness that accepted without question that fate had not *dared* interrupt the course she had set for herself. Once again returning to the moment of near tragedy in his mind, Devon was, perversely, almost overcome by the desire to stride forward and forcibly remove Edgar Morrison from her side, then take Morgana Pierce into his arms . . . to hold her protectively against him, safe from harm, close to his heart.

What was the hold that defiant young woman had gained over his senses? Was it that flash of vulnerability he had glimpsed so briefly, that flicker that had disappeared so quickly as to make him doubt that he had actually witnessed its presence in the frightened eyes raised to his? Instead, if it had ever existed, that vulnerability had disappeared to be replaced by a hauteur that had only deepened his spontaneous anger at the carelessness which had nearly taken her life. The horror of that last thought causing a convulsive shudder to pass over his stalwart frame, he experienced a new surge of resentment at the power the irresponsible young woman had so effortlessly obtained over his emotions.

In all honesty, he had to admit she had made no effort toward further contact between them after that first day aboard. Contrary to the pattern of the spoiled young rich girls he had been exposed to in New York—who had had no compunctions about using any manner of outrageous ruse in their blatant attempts to attract "that interesting Texan" —surprisingly, having failed with her initial exploratory ruse in invading his cabin, she seemed content to spend the remainder of the voyage tantalizing the cooperative Edgar

Morrison. Even the elements seemed to bow to the wishes of the impudent little twit! Realizing from the watchfulness of Aggie MacWhorter's glance that the observant Scotswoman normally kept a close eye on her charge, he knew instinctively that she would have provided an obstacle to Morgana's alternative plan for the conquest of Edgar Morrison had not the austere Scotswoman become a victim of the rolling seas. Yes, the arrogant little rich girl was having it all her own way again, and most certainly neither needed nor desired his protection. So, his mind questioned, why did he still feel this strong sense of involvement where she was concerned?

His own eyes moving unseen over the questioning tilt of her head, he marked the seductive swoop of her heavy brown lashes as she whispered a response to the remark that had caused her jocularity a few moments previous, and the artful momentary pursing of her warm, pink lips before they spread into a full, truly glorious smile. Cognizant of a deepening of the frustration that had marked his observance of Morgana Pierce since the inception of the voyage, he uttered a low curse under his breath, abruptly furious that he allowed the little witch to monopolize his thoughts so completely. Hell! He was twenty-eight years old, and a veteran of countless encounters with the opposite sex in which, in truth, he had rarely been truly affected, aside from the physical gratifications involved. So how had this foolish, spoiled girl succeeded so well in getting under his skin? Why was it that the fresh, sweet scent of her in those few moments he had held her against him still lingered in his nostrils; the glory of gold-flecked russet eyes lifted to his still stirred his senses? Why did his glance automatically seek her out, only to have his frustration compounded by her blatant flirtation with Edgar Morrison?

Damn! She was nothing more than a willful, self-indulgent child! He would not concern himself any longer with her welfare, despite the ominous gossip that had abounded in wealthy circles about this young bachelor from Havana with whom she now amused herself. The son of a family that had gained enormous wealth in Cuban trade, Edgar Morrison had purportedly displayed intense interest in the fiery mulatto women of Havana before his visit to New York, filling his time between liaisons with bored planters' wives, two of whom had actually come to blows over his attentions. It was rumored that he had sired a mulatto child with one of his former mistresses in Havana, and, after treating her shamefully, had left them both destitute. But, ironically, either because of the perversity of women's natures or a fatal charm the fellow seemed to hold for the opposite sex, his escapades had not hindered his social life in New York in the slightest. And, if he was to believe the gossip at numerous social gatherings he had been forced to attend before leaving that city, where Edgar Morrison was a cherished guest, the man's reputation had only enhanced his popularity with the opposite sex.

His ire rising at yet another low ripple of laughter as Morgana leaned forward to grasp Edgar's arm companionably, Devon's expression darkened. Glancing up at that particular moment, Morgana caught and held his glance, an indignant flush suffusing her cheeks the second before she turned her eyes back to Edgar Morrison. Was it his imagination, or did she take a step closer to the lecherous ass? Oh, hell, what did he care anyway? It meant nothing to him if she threw herself at Morrison's head! She was as shallow as he . . . indulged and pampered to a point past redemption. Raised for indolence, she was probably incapable of a thought, much less a concerted effort that did not have her own welfare at heart. She was obviously out for another conquest, and they probably deserved each other.

Devon forced aside the thought that he himself might have been the man looking down into that glowing smile right now had he not expressed his opinion of her irresponsible behavior so clearly at the start. He could not help but wonder whether the diversion she would have provided would have been a buffer against the frustration he suffered at the voyage's unexpected delays, or whether she merely would have compounded the problem.

The next round of laughter was more than he could stand, Devon turned away with a disgusted snort and walked rapidly in the opposite direction, determined to force the precocious little flirt from his mind.

More aware of his presence than she cared to admit, Morgana followed Devon's exit from the corner of her eye, her heart hammering unnervingly.

"Well, has your watchdog finally left?"

Startled at Edgar's abrupt remark, Morgana stammered ineffectually, "My . . . my watchdog? I don't know what you mean, Edgar."

A small sneer twisting his lips, Edgar lifted his hand to familiarly caress her shoulder. "Oh, come now, Morgana. Howard hasn't taken his eyes off us since this voyage began. If I didn't know better, I'd think someone had commissioned him as your bodyguard! Or, maybe," he continued, a thread of annoyance noticeable in his tone as his grip tightened unexpectedly, ". . . maybe he's jealous!"

"That's ridiculous, Edgar!" Not at all certain she liked the facet of Edgar's personality he was presently displaying, Morgana continued emphatically, "The man all but called me an idiot, and I expect he . . ."

". . . he's regretting it now," Edgar finished insistently, his tone softening to a quiet intimacy. "At any rate, it's too late. I claim you completely for the duration of the voyage, Morgana, and at the rate we're progressing toward Havana, we'll have enough time to get to know each other quite well before it's over. I look forward to that time with avid anticipation, my dear."

Sensing a veiled innuendo in his words and in the heat of his direct, unfaltering stare, Morgana was still unprepared for the quick movement of his hand as it slipped to the back of her neck to hold her fast. Unexpectedly, Edgar lowered his mouth to cover hers. The sensation of his warm lips pressed against hers was startling, but not unpleasant, and, intrigued by the experience, Morgana allowed herself to be drawn into a close embrace. It was then that the first spark of apprehension touched her senses, stiffening her against the hand that moved familiarly over her back, pressing her into intense contact with the intimate mystery of his male physique and the abruptly thrusting tongue that invaded her mouth.

Jerking herself strenuously from his embrace, Morgana

saw a momentary flash of annoyance cross his features before they abruptly changed to reflect open penitence.

"Morgana, dear, I'm sorry if I frightened you. But you're so beautiful . . . so very desirable. . . . You aren't angry with me, are you?"

Truly uncertain what she felt at that moment, Morgana hesitated. Suddenly anxious to get away, to go below to the reassurance of Aggie's familiar, if somewhat pale face, she responded slowly, "No, I suppose I must accept your apology, since it is so sincerely given, Edgar, but I do think I'll go below now. I really must check on Aggie. She was feeling rather poorly this morning."

But you will join me for dinner tonight, Morgana? I would be truly desolate if you were to hold my brief lapse against me."

"Yes, I'll join you for dinner, Edgar." The open sincerity in the light eyes looking directly into hers certainly could not be feigned. "Perhaps I can even convince Aggie to join us. In any case, I'll see you in a few hours."

Uncertain about the true reason for her abrupt departure, Morgana turned quickly toward the steps leading below deck, unaware that Edgar's heated angry gaze followed her lightly swaying figure as it moved away.

Completely lost in her thoughts, Morgana stepped down onto the berth deck and turned up the passageway toward her cabin. She was disturbed by Edgar's actions and was abruptly grateful that the owner of the mocking gaze that had followed her since the inception of the voyage had not witnessed the embarrassing course of events that had transpired topside. In truth, she was terribly confused.

She had been lovingly protected from all unpleasantness in life until the time of her father's unexpected death. Having had little exposure to young men her age, she was inclined to behave in a thoroughly spontaneous manner—which, she saw now, was obviously not feasible. In truth, she was not truly certain what she had done to cause Edgar's unexpected advances. Perhaps she should . . .

31

The sudden opening of a door to her right interrupted her thoughts, jerking her around to Devon Howard's contemptuous gaze. She was unprepared for the hostility reflected in his eyes and the quiet sarcasm in his low drawl.

"Well, comin' below so early in the day? Figure you dealt that fellow all he can handle for the afternoon, darlin'? Reckon you'll give him some time to cool off before you start on him again tonight? You play a damned dangerous game, little girl." At the growing imperiousness of her gaze, the azure eyes hardened icily. "But you probably know exactly what you're doin', and exactly where it'll lead, don't you?"

Her face flaming at the coolly contemptuous remarks, Morgana stared speechlessly up into his mocking smile. Enraging her even more than his words was her own body's treachery . . . its instinctive reaction to the stimulus of his presence . . . the trembling weakness that began deep inside the moment his gaze touched on her face; the strange breathlessness with which she was afflicted; the intense awareness of the clean, masculine scent she remembered so well.

The infuriating realization that she was helplessly drawn to a man who showed her nothing but contempt endowed her with a strength she had not realized she possessed. And Morgana hesitated only momentarily before shoving hard at the firm chest blocking her passage. Unsettling the taut strength of him enough to squeeze past, she shot him a scathing glance before turning to march imperiously down the passageway toward her cabin. His low, knowing laugh echoed in her mind long after she had loudly slammed the door closed behind her.

The long, low ridge of hills on the English salt island of Eleuthera were finally behind them; the charitable revolving radiance of Abaco's lighthouse was just a memory. The Berry Islands . . . thinking of the tale of the enterprising black man who had bought one of the small islands for fifty dollars and, along with his wife and children and many black slaves of his own, had established a kingdom on the desolate island where he raised produce to sell to passing ships, Morgana smiled. How her father would have cheered the man's ingenious undertaking and applauded his success, however modest it might be.

The smile still lingering on her lips, Morgana glanced up at the cloudless afternoon sky, unmindful of the stirring picture she presented as she lounged against the rail, the glory of a tropical sky the backdrop for her own stirring beauty. With the heady profusion of chestnut ringlets swept back from her small, magnificently sculptured, pensive face, she was exquisitely lovely. Large, almond-shaped eyes, the exact color of the curling spirals that bobbed at her hairline, swept the tranquil scene before her. The heavy fringe of lashes brushed the velvet skin of her cheek as she allowed her gaze to slip to the rippling whitecaps caressing the sides of the ship. The deepening of her smile at the antics of a small school of fish directly beneath them brought a fascinating dimple to play in her cheek; the slender, perfectly shaped lips spreading breathtakingly to reveal small, white teeth. The graceful column of her throat and the rise of firm, white breasts were displayed modestly in the scooped neckline of the simple cotton frock she wore. Its soft blue shade was reminiscent of the color of the afternoon sky, complementing the compelling natural beauty of her flawless complexion as it followed the contours of her dainty frame.

Raising her eyes, Morgana experienced a new wave of thankfulness for the sinking sun that still warmed her back, and the stiff breeze that filled the sails overhead. Surely it would be hard to imagine a more beautiful evening than this one that would soon be upon them. The first silver sprinkling of stars had just begun to fill the sky. The last crimson point of the sun was slowly setting beneath the waves, staining the sky in rainbow-hues, deep crimson tinged with bright silver, melting away into pale grey vapor, a prelude to the glory of the tropical night soon to come. Beneath them the water was still a brilliant turquoise blue covered with a light milky froth . . . so clear that the big black sponges on the bottom of the sea were visible to the naked eye.

The chanting song of the sailor was constant now as he

heaved lead with methodic percision at intervals of a minute.

"By the mark three."

"By the mark, three, less a quarter."

"By the mark twain and a half."

Fifteen feet, the vessel drawing thirteen . . . two feet between the *Helga* and the bottom. The watch was constant now, the low steady chant reassuring. Soothed by its constancy, Morgana turned to direct a short glance to the lounge chair behind her.

With the advent of balmier weather, pale, unsteady passengers had begun to emerge from isolation, and now, on the twelfth day of the voyage, the deck was generously populated with fairly animated, relieved passengers. Once again on her feet, Aggie had almost returned to her old self, taking to spending many hours in her deck chair, quietly observing Edgar Morrison's persistent attentions to Morgana, reservation clearly marked in her manner.

Exhibiting an obvious impatience with Aggie's close scrutiny, Edgar had begun to display a sharp edge to his personality in the past few days that made Morgana distinctly uneasy. A small frown drawing together her slender winged brows, Morgana glanced to the man at her side, concerned by his morose expression. Gently placing her hand on the arm Edgar leaned on the rail as he gazed silently out to sea, she was startled by the frustration apparent in the pale grey eyes snapped in her direction.

"What is it, Edgar? What's wrong? You've not been yourself the past few days. Is the extended duration of the voyage making you tense?"

Staring silently into her eyes for long moments, Edgar hesitated before replying, a deep, unexpected resentment present in his tone.

"You must be joking, Morgana! Surely you realize the reason for my frustration!"

Startled by his gruffness, Morgana replied quietly, "If I knew the answer to the questions I've just asked you, Edgar, I would not have wasted both our time in asking them. But, of course, you are right to be annoyed. It is certainly not a matter of my concern why you are disturbed. It is your own business and I . . .''

His hand moving to cover hers warmly, Edgar's expression changed so quickly that Morgana was startled into silence.

"Morgana, dear." Lowering his face as close to hers as he dared under Aggie's watchful eye, Edgar replied intently, "With barely two more days left on our voyage, I find myself chafing at the lack of privacy we are allowed. I had hoped to spend some time with you under circumstances that would allow us to get to know each other better."

Affected by Edgar's obviously disturbed state, Morgana responded haltingly, "I'm . . . I'm truly sorry, Edgar. I've so enjoyed your company, but I'm as helpless as you against . . ."

"Then come with me now, Morgana." He clutched her arm lightly, and his voice was urgent, tinged with a thread of emotion that set her pulse to hammering in her throat. Morgana listened silently to his earnest plea. "Dear Morgana, come . . . take a walk with me now . . . somewhere away from these . . . prying eyes that follow us. I find myself extremely inhibited by such intense scrutiny, and I do so want to talk to you with our old spontaneous intimacy."

Touched by his obvious plight, Morgana responded sincerely, "Of course, I'll walk with you. Aggie could have no objection to our walking together. And indeed," she added, "although I must admit I do not share your discomfort with 'prying eyes,' I also admit I do not enjoy seeing you distressed." A small smile lifting the corners of her mouth, she continued softly, "So, if you can find a place on this ship where we may now arrange to walk in privacy, I most certainly will accompany you."

The expression of smug satisfaction that flashed momentarily in the grey eyes looking avidly into hers gave her a short moment's discomfort before a broad smile covered his face. "Then come, Morgana. You may depend upon me to find a spot for us."

Allowing Edgar to tuck her arm snugly under his, Morgana nodded lightly at Aggie as they began an apparent leisurely stroll around the deck. Startled at the abrupt hastening of Edgar's step once they had gotten out of Aggie's line of vision, she suddenly felt herself propelled to the staircase leading below deck.

"Edgar, what are you doing? Where are we going?"

Turning toward her with an endearing smile as he urged her down the steps, Edgar replied reassuringly, "If we must stroll the passageways in order to find a little privacy, then so be it, dearest Morgana."

Within a few moments they had reached the isolation of the berth deck, and, pulling her unexpectedly into the alcove beneath the staircase, Edgar took her roughly into his arms, his mouth seeking hers with an eagerness that set her pulse to racing. Holding her tightly against him, he ground his mouth tightly into hers, his ardor increasing as her lips separated under the pressure of his bruising kiss. His hands roamed her back in broad, sweeping caresses that set off a warning bell in the back of her mind. Abruptly he released her, taking her a few feet further down the passageway before sweeping her into his arms once again to cover her face with moist, heated kisses. Startled by the sudden explosion of Edgar's passion, Morgana was confused, unable to perceive a way to stop the advance of his violent emotions without an abrupt dismissal that would wound him seriously. But she could not allow this madness to go on. Edgar's kisses became bolder, his caresses more insistent. Abruptly, he stopped again, taking her hand to pull her a few feet more down the passageway. Stopping in a shadow, he again swept her into his arms. This time his attentions were more persistent, his kisses deeper, more searching; his hands seeking and taking liberties that inflamed Morgana's sensibilities. Suddenly she was struggling against the hands that sought out the fullness of her breasts, squeezing and fondling roughly even as his mouth slipped to her throat to trail moist, anxious kisses against the white, gleaming flesh exposed in her décolletage. Abruptly, he returned to roughly recapture her mouth with his. Unexpectedly Morgana felt herself being dragged through the door Edgar had opened to the side of them. Tearing her mouth from his in supreme effort, Morgana gasped breathlessly, "Edgar, what are you doing? Let me go!''

Realizing they stood in the doorway to Edgar's cabin, Morgana struggled all the harder, her protests bringing a hard, angry look to the features that had moments before been filled with passion.

"Damn you, Morgana!" Edgar's voice was a low, angry snarl. "You've been teasing me senseless for twelve days now, and I'll be damned if I'll let you get away now. We only have about two days left on this voyage, and I intend to use every minute!" His mouth clamping down hard over hers muffled her violent protest, even as he lifted her from her feet and dragged her struggling form through the open doorway. Her eyes wide with fear as the door began to close behind them, Morgana attempted to free herself from the wet, punishing mouth that ground so brutally into hers, but she was helpless against the power of the man, who easily overwhelmed her.

In a flash of movement so quick that she was hardly conscious of its advent, the door snapped open behind them. Startled into immobility as she was ripped from the imprisoning embrace, Morgana watched with widening eyes as Devon Howard's broad fist arced through the air to connect squarely with Edgar Morrison's jaw. A loud crack echoed in the cramped quarters of the small cabin, the power of the blow sending Edgar sprawling across the room into senseless oblivion.

Her body quaking visibly, Morgana was unable to move, her gaze fixed on the inert body of the man who had taken her in so completely with his sincere manner.

"Morgana!"

The deep, harsh summons caused her wide, gold-flecked eyes to jump to Devon Howard's flushed face. The cold fury reflected there was more frightening than the abusive attack of the man who lay dazedly a few feet away. She swallowed hard against the paralyzing tightness in her throat.

"Damn it, Morgana! Don't stand there like a fool! If you want to save your reputation, such as it is, you'll have to get out of here now, before someone sees you!"

"But . . . but what about Edgar? He . . ."

37

"Don't worry about him, Morgana. He'll be all right in a few minutes, and he won't tell anyone what went on in here tonight. He'd never admit to it!"

His broad hand enveloping hers, Morgana felt herself being jerked from the cabin. A supreme sense of relief inundating her senses at the sound of the cabin door's closing behind them, Morgana followed Devon wordlessly as he pulled her back down the passageway. The sound of voices on the staircase stopped them both in their tracks. The low, sultry tones of Belva Tate, and her aunt's high, nasal reply lifted her glance to Devon's face in panic. Her own cabin was on the opposite end of the passageway . . . beyond the staircase. . . . She could not allow those women to see her in this condition . . . hair in disarray, face streaked with tears, Devon Howard dragging her misleadingly by the hand. . . . Glancing down, she realized that the sleeve of her dress was torn, and she felt a true wave of panic overwhelm her. She could not go to Tía Isabella with a fresh scandal following her! Tía Isabella's position was too vulnerable . . . her husband was an associate of President Santa Anna himself! Tía Isabella would be humiliated by the inevitable talk that would follow. . . .

The horror of her thoughts was reflected clearly in her expression. Azure eyes narrowing, Devon hesitated only a moment before abruptly pulling her into motion once again. Jerking open a door just a few feet away, he had just succeeded in pulling her clear of the doorway and closing it behind them when the light tread of the two conversing women touched down in the passageway.

Her eyes moving quickly around the small room, Morgana realized she was in Devon's cabin, the same one in which she had faced him once before when he had expressed so clearly his poor opinion of her. Remembering her abusive conduct that morning and her behavior toward him in the time since, she was suddenly ashamed. He was right . . . she was a fool . . . a fool to have trusted Edgar . . . a fool to think she could handle him so easily . . . a fool . . . a fool . . . a fool . . .

Her silent appraisal of her own actions showing only too

clearly on her expressive face, Morgana stared speechlessly into the hard, unrelenting features of the man who had just saved her reputation from ruin. A flicker of an unidentifiable emotion moved across his face, and Morgana suddenly found herself enfolded in a strong, comforting embrace. She did not realize tears were streaming down her face until hard, jerking sobs from deep within her began shaking her body. She had been so frightened by Edgar . . . so terribly frightened.

"Shhhh, Morgana, quiet now. The walls are thin. Someone will hear you, and all our efforts will be for naught." The deep, resonant tones that a few minutes before had harangued her sincerely were now soft and comforting. The broad hand raised to her hair was gentle as he smoothed back the curling wisps that adhered to her temples.

Raising her tear-streaked face to his, Morgana attempted to speak, to express her gratitude for his rescue, but fear and humiliation had stolen her voice. Instead, her russet eyes flecked with gold overflowed, her gaze remaining trained on his face as he gently stroked the tears from her cheeks.

"Come on, darlin', no more tears." Smiling encouragingly, Devon lowered his head to press a light kiss against the clear skin of her forehead. "You needn't be afraid anymore."

But she was still trembling, the tears still spilling down her cheeks unchecked, and, making a sincere attempt at control, Morgana closed her eyes and bit down hard on her lower lip to still its quivering. The gentle, consoling kisses continued across the tear-dampened lids of her eyes, along the contour of her cheek, the soothing words slowly stilling the intermittent quaking in her limbs.

She was shaken, small and vulnerable in his arms. The pressure of her slender body against his chest sweet to his senses, Devon unconsciously tightened his arms, pulling her closer still. That bastard had proved true to his reputation. But the depth of his own rage at the scene he had interrupted only moments before had been startling. Had the situation not been so pressing, he would not have been content to leave the room until he had beaten Edgar Morrison bloody. The necessity of getting Morgana out of Morrison's cabin as quickly as possible had been the only thing that had held him back from doing just that. A knot of emotion tightening in his throat, he watched as the glorious, tear-stained face raised to his. God, she was beautiful! He could not recall ever having seen a woman more glorious than she! She struggled to speak, but could not, and he was possessed by a deep desire to protect her, to hold her close against him, safe from harm.

"Come on, darlin', no more tears."

Obviously striving to control her emotions, she had allowed her heavily fringed, almost transparent lids to drop over her tear-filled eyes as she bit down on her quivering lower lip. Tenderness overwhelmed him, and, longing desperately to comfort her, Devon pressed light kisses across the delicate lids, his lips following a trail to the damp velvet of her cheek. He could taste the salt of her tears, could smell the sweet scent of her skin. Moving his hand to tangle in the silken mass of chestnut curls, he marveled at the supreme texture of the shining ringlets that curled around his fingers. His lips traveled gently to the pink shell of her ear, pressing light kisses on it between whispered words of comfort. He felt the swell of an unfamiliar emotion inside him as her trembling began to subside. He continued his mumbled words of comfort, no longer conscious of the words he spoke as he pulled her closer against the breadth of his chest, his mouth following the soft contour of her chin to the corner of her mouth. Her lips were no longer quivering. They were still, and slightly parted as he moved to press a light, fleeting kiss on their full, generous beauty. Gradually, without his knowledge, his words came to a halt, but she remained silent and still within his arms, her face lifted to his, the supreme beauty of her flawless countenance turned up to his like a flower to the sun. Her lips were full, appealing, drawing him, crying for his consolation, and he moved to cover them lightly, gently with his own. But the taste was too sweet, too beautiful to withdraw. With supreme gentleness, he kissed her again and again, his mouth moving to cover hers more fully each time until his kiss was deep and searing, searching out the intimate reaches of her mouth for which he had so longed since he had first held her in his arms.

He strained her tighter against him, the pliant molding of her slender frame in his arms sending a wave of exultation over his senses. Tightening his hand in the shining ringlets, he strained her closer still, his tongue moving into the mouth she surrendered so completely to his tender invasion. Gently he probed the innate sweetness of her mouth, coaxing her into a passionate play, his broad palms moving the slender breadth of her back as the urge to consume her devoured his senses. She moved lightly against him, her body so in tune to his own that the simple movement stirred a searing ecstasy deep within his soul.

Gasping at the unknown emotions sweeping her senses, Morgana surrendered her mouth completely to the fondling caress of his tongue. Lifted to a plane of swelling elation, she was no longer in the small cabin, but in a world of surging, breathtaking colors, each touch, each caress lending another shade, another tint, until, tantalized by the magic of Devon's lovemaking, she was overwhelmed by a kaleidoscope of blinding, iridescent hues that eliminated all but the moment and the man who held her in his arms.

No longer conscious of time or space, existing in a world of rioting sensations, Morgana was not conscious of the strong arms that lifted her gently, or the firm bed beneath her back. Instead, she felt only the pressure of Devon's strong male body upon hers, and welcomed it, her arms stealing around his neck to hold his mouth fast against hers. Conscious only of his tantalizing touch, she did not feel the delicate fabric of her bodice fall away from her body, or the shell of her chemise succumb to his featherlike touch. His low, hoarse gasp bringing her slowly to her senses, she raised heavy, passion-drugged lids to Devon's wonder-filled face. His hands moving slowly, worshipfully over the soft perfection of her breasts, he whispered softly, "Morgana, darlin', you're the most beautiful woman I've ever seen. Darlin' . . . little darlin' . . ."

Unable to take her eyes from his face, Morgana watched as Devon slowly lowered his mouth to the pink, waiting crest, a sharp gasp escaping her own lips as his mouth covered it completely, his tongue working to fondle the tender nipple even as his mouth held it safe and secure within its moist confines. Clasping his head tightly to her breasts, Morgana gloried in the beauty of his tender ministrations, her emotions lifting on brilliant, effervescent wings that sent a soaring rapture through her veins. Devon was right . . . it was beautiful . . . so beautiful. She didn't want it to stop. She . . .

An abrupt, harsh knock on the door froze the beauty of their lovemaking into a silent tableau. Raising his head from her breast, Devon paused to place a light kiss against the pink crest he had abandoned before responding slowly, "Yes, what is it?"

The low ripple of giggles that preceded the response sent the hackles rising on Morgana's spine even before Margaret Wollett's cloying voice sounded quietly. "My sister and I are about to go on deck for a walk, and are sadly in need of an escort, Mr. Howard. We were wondering if you could oblige us."

A dark flush suffusing his face, Devon closed his eyes, straining for control. His response a short moment later was soft and to the point. "I'm sorry, ladies. I find I'm indisposed this evenin'. If I might take you up on your offer tomorrow, I should take it very kindly."

Disappointment was apparent in the mumbled, "Oh, I'm sorry. Yes, of course . . . tomorrow . . . good evening." Within a few moments the sound of footsteps could be heard moving down the passageway.

For Morgana, the interruption had been a startlingly rude awakening from the enraptured state to which she had ascended in response to Devon's expert lovemaking. A flush of color moving across her face, she was suddenly embarrassed by her partial nudity and clutched at the bodice of her dress, awkwardly attempting to adjust it to cover the white, gleaming swells whose taut crests still declared bold invitation.

A pained expression on his face, Devon whispered softly, "Morgana, darlin', please don't . . . nothin' has changed. Let me love you. . . ."

"Ev . . . everything has changed!" Morgana pushed

hard at the male strength of him that still held her captive with its weight. "I . . . I must have been crazy to trust you . . . to come in here with you! You . . . you're no better than Edgar! You . . ."

The tenderness present only a few moments before in the blue eyes looking into hers abruptly vanished. In its place a familiar hardness slipped over the features of the man whose mouth was still only inches from hers.

"No, Morgana. Don't put me in the same category as Edgar Morrison! I didn't force you into this cabin. You followed me willin'ly! I didn't force you onto this bed. You were sighin', groanin' your desire . . . hell! I would've been less than a man if I hadn't responded to the encouragement you gave me!"

"How . . . how dare you say . . ."

Stopping the outraged, wide-eyed response with a short, angry growl, Devon snapped, "I *dare* because it's true!"

Suddenly he was on his feet beside the bed. Reaching down, he jerked her to her feet, compounding her embarrassment by watching her intently as she awkwardly adjusted the bodice of her dress to cover her breasts. When she was sufficiently covered, he turned and pulled her roughly by the arm to the door. Opening it slightly, he looked up and down the passageway. Before Morgana could take a breath, he opened the door wider and jerked her into the passageway behind him.

"No, please . . ." Her hand moving to her disheveled hair, Morgana felt herself pulled along the passageway behind him until she stood before the door to her own cabin. Pushing open the unlocked door, his face livid with anger, Devon hissed ominously, "The next time you want to play games, little girl, remember tonight! And you're damned lucky we're here on this ship and not on my home ground, Morgana Pierce, or the situation would've had a much different conclusion than this tonight!" His chest heaving with emotion, Devon paused to rake her white face with a heated glance before rasping in a low, tight voice, "And now, you teasin' little bitch, I warn you. Stay out of my sight!"

In a quick, efficient movement, Devon pushed her firmly

43

through the open doorway and pulled the door shut behind her, leaving Morgana staring numbly at the closed door as the sound of his footsteps echoed down the passageway.

CHAPTER TWO

Supreme relief moving over her strained expression, Morgana stared at the imposing outline of Morro Castle. Black and frowning, its foundations embedded in solid rock, its towers and battlements of dark grey stone, it glared in silent warning from its position as guardian of the beautiful bay of Havana. In startling contrast, feathery cocoas stood, light and graceful amidst the thick herbage that covered the area surrounding it. A short distance away, occupying a considerable expanse of ground, the fortress of Ganaño stood regally, a brilliant rose in color, with bastions of gleaming white that seemed to smile in a welcome that did not quite negate the effective warning glower of the Morro. Extremely grateful for Aggie's sturdy presence beside her at the rail, Morgana felt her thoughts of the past two days began to still, the beauty of the bay mercifully driving from her mind the dark, accusing glance that haunted her, and the memory of the searing touch that still had the power to leave her weak and shaken. Her eyes followed the movements of the soldiers of the garrison, their uniforms bright spots of color against the light stone, touched on the ominous presence of the prison built by General Tacón, and moved curiously over the irregularly shaped houses painted red and pale blue, noting their cool, uninhabited look—probably suggested by the absence of glass in their windows. Listening silently to the words of the Spaniard at the rail beside her, she picked out the palace of the captain-general—large but lacking in outstanding architectural detail—and the palace of the commandant.

The *Helga* gradually emerged from the narrow entrance to the bay, revealing an astounding number of merchant ships and large men-of-war at tranquil rest on the brilliant, undulating blue swells. Vessels from every port in the commercial world were represented, with little boats with snow-white sails gliding gracefully amongst them. Her eyes moving to the wharves, Morgana saw that they were populated predominantly by black people. The ambiance of the area was totally foreign to her eye.

Behind her the noise and bustle on the deck became more marked as they approached the wharf, but, refusing to turn her head toward the source of the sounds, Morgana kept her eyes fixed on the nearing land. She no longer sought to evade Edgar's heated glances, for just the day before she had chosen to accept his humble apology. His grey eyes sad and appealing, the small bruise on his jaw hardly noticeable, he had laid the blame for his rash behavior on his capitulation to her charms. Although she had believed not a word he uttered, she had smiled and magnanimously agreed to forgive him. Silently fearing the danger in having a man with his family's influence as an enemy in her vulnerable position, she outwardly dismissed the hostility she inwardly harbored against him.

But Devon Howard . . . that was a different matter! Mortified by her own body's wild response to his persuasively gentle lovemaking, she had relived again and again the humiliation she had suffered in his cabin, needing only to feel the touch of the man's eyes on her person to again experience the breathless trembling that she fought desperately to overcome. But he thoroughly despised her now, of that she was certain. His attentions to the ridiculous Wollett sisters were more marked than before, and he allowed her only occasional glances of cool disdain, which had begun to foster within her a hatred that grew with each additional encoun-

46

ter. Stay out of his sight, indeed! She wanted nothing more now than to be out of his sight forever, and to have the luxury of never seeing his infuriating face again!

Startled from her thoughts by an unexpected touch on her shoulder, Morgana turned to Edgar's handsome, smiling face.

"I should like to share your first view of Havana with you, Morgana, and I would consider it a privilege if you would allow me to show you my adopted home during your short stay."

Smiling politely, Morgana obligingly made room for Edgar beside her at the rail, catching a contemptuous azure-eyed glance out of the corner of her eye that only succeeded in brightening her smile. "I expect my stay in Havana will be short, Edgar, perhaps only a day. In any case, I will be leaving on the first ship for Veracruz. But I do appreciate your offer. Now, please," turning back toward the fast-approaching shoreline, she continued lightly, "do point out the places of interest we can see from here. I am so anxious to learn about your city."

Unaware of the dark stare that raked her slender figure unmercifully, Morgana turned her full attention to the city of Havana as it came fully into view.

Unconscious of the oppressive heat of the port of Havana, Morgana stared disbelievingly at the short, meticulously dressed Mexican who stood a short distance away. Having anchored in the bay, the *Helga* had begun to accept the first of the steady stream of small boats from shore which were to welcome and transport the passengers to the wharf. Noting that a small entourage of three very official-looking Mexican gentlemen had been directed to her by the captain, Morgana watched them approach. Although aware of the appreciative glances they flicked over her body and her frothy green cotton dress—that gave her the appearance of a cool confection for the eyes—she was truly oblivious to the fact that her own compelling beauty had added immeasurably to their warmth of manner. Representatives of her uncle, General Manuel

47

Escobar, they informed her that her uncle had arranged for her accommodations in the home of a friend that evening, and that her passage was booked on a ship bound for Veracruz in midafternoon of the following day. Her aunt and uncle, she was told, awaited her arrival at Manga de Clavo, the country home of President Santa Anna himself, and after the voyage, which would last approximately seven days, she would be met in Veracruz. In Veracruz she would spend the night at the home of another friend of her uncle's and would set out the following day by diligence for the estate of the president. Smilingly acknowledging her approval of the arrangements made in her behalf, the very agreeable Señor Grivera, spokesman for the three, then turned and requested to be directed to Señor Devon Howard!

Listening with horrified disbelief to the conversation that had then progressed between the polite Mexican gentleman and Devon Howard, she heard the recitation of the very same accommodations that had been made for Aggie and herself!

So it was true! Devon Howard was on a political mission to President Santa Anna himself, and it was her damned, incredible luck to be forced to travel with him for the better part of the next two weeks! No! The situation was impossible! She could not bear the heavy weight of his disapproval . . . his contempt . . . for two more weeks! She could not!

"Señorita Pierce."

Her mind snapping from her panicked thoughts back to the present moment, Morgana shot Aggie a short, helpless look before accepting the hand held out to her by the smiling Señor Grivera. Stepping forward to the rail with a weak smile, she watched as her luggage was lowered over the side to the waiting boat and the chair readied to lower Aggie and herself down. Extremely conscious of the fact that the tall, rangy Texan had stepped casually forward to await his turn to follow, Morgana's heart raced as he took a step closer. Taking a short, quick breath to still the quaking that had inevitably begun inside her, she closed her eyes for the briefest second as she strained for control.

Slowly lifting steady, russet eyes moments later, Morgana

graciously accepted the guiding hand of Señor Grivera, her slow, self-possessed smile belying the silent, incredulous protest of her mind.

"Aggie, I cannot . . . I cannot possibly sleep here . . . not even for one night!"

Careful to keep her voice low, Morgana directed her words of protest into the sober face that regarded her steadily as they stood uncertainly in the quarters assigned to Morgana for the night.

"I'm afraid you have no recourse, Morgana." A note of censure becoming apparent, Aggie continued stiffly, "You did insist upon coming to this foreign land to reside, and you shall have to abide by its customs! In this case, you shall have to forsake your sensibilities for the night."

"But . . . Aggie—" Her words trailing away at the unsympathetic expression on Aggie's face, Morgana absent-mindedly marveled at the coolly dignified appearance the large, heavy woman managed to project in the simple black dress that seemed to adapt to any climate in which it was worn. Her grey-streaked hair in a familiar tidy bun, Aggie appeared impervious to the humidity that Morgana herself felt difficult to bear even in her cool cotton. Realizing it was useless to protest to the sternly unrelenting woman, Morgana turned away and gave her head a short, disbelieving shake, recalling her first glimpse just a short hour before of the handsome home of the Ariverra family where her uncle had arranged her accommodations. A home of considerable size, it formed a great square in shape. In the center was a main courtyard, around which were the offices, the rooms for the black servants, coal-house, bathroom, etc., and in the middle of which stood the volantes in which they had been transported through the city. Looking up, she had seen a large gallery, which ran all around the house. Upon mounting the staircase, she had arrived at the gallery and passed into the sala, a large, cool apartment with handsome cane-bottomed chairs, low tables, and comfortable chaise longues scattered around the room. Drawn to the window through

49

which wafted a brisk, refreshing breeze, she had gasped her enchantment with the wide, unfettered view of the bay that sprawled out before her. Her admiration had brought a bright flush of pleasure to the face of her gracious silver-haired host. But her delight had been short-lived, as the entrance of Devon Howard into the room at that moment and the quick deprecating glance her enthusiasm obviously inspired in him were, sufficient to dampen her spontaneity. Infuriating her even further was his abrupt change of manner when the lovely daughter of Señor Ariverra entered the sala, and the slow, sensual smile with which he acknowledged the introduction to the obviously flustered young woman. Damn him! He had *never* smiled at her like that . . . not once! But that was all right with her! She didn't need Devon Howard's approval or his attentions! And, hopefully, she would be free of the need to even look on his disagreeable face within another week's time . . . if only she could last that long without slapping that look *from* his face! With that uncertain thought in mind, she had turned to the advancing step of her hostess and forced a smile.

But only minutes later, having been shown to her quarters, she had found it difficult to conceal her horror at the lack of privacy so casually accepted in the household! Granted, the oppressive heat and humidity of the climate demanded that a free flow of air move unrestricted through the house in order to afford the inhabitants any semblance of comfort, but how could she be expected to accept draperies of white muslin and shaded silk as the only walls separating her bedroom from the sala? And, indeed, as they moved from one room to the other around the gallery, she saw that similar muslin and silk walls separated each of the remaining bedrooms. But there it was in front of her, as incredible as it seemed—a handsome French bed . . . blue silk drapery with blue silk coverlets and clear mosquito curtains, fringed sheets, fine lace and embroidered pillowcases; and yet another drapery that divided her room from the other guest chamber, to be inhabited by none other than Devon Howard!

Turning back to Aggie's unflinching glance, she pleaded

her hopeless cause.

"But how can I be expected to . . ."

"You must remember, Morgana," Aggie's tone was unrelenting, "that you are in a foreign country with foreign customs. If you are to make a sincere effort to function to your aunt and uncle's benefit, you will have to learn to accept the differences between these countries and yours with grace and affability."

Hours later, having made only one requested for a change in her sleeping arrangements—that of having a small cot installed in her own area to support Aggie's weary bones for the night—Morgana had prepared for bed. Having discovered a sliding door that provided some semblance of privacy, she had changed into her night rail. But she had soon discovered that the closing of the door had shut her and Aggie into an airless cubicle without benefit of a window, which, in the humid heat of the city, was beyond enduring. Softly instructing Aggie to open the door once again, she had slipped into her bed, desperately hoping the absence of light would render her all but invisible to the man who slept on the other side of the flimsy diaphanous partition.

But sleep had not come. Conscious of the low, steady pattern of Aggie's breathing, Morgana realized the durable Scotswoman was not having the same problem as she, and, feeling a flash of annoyance, she twisted restlessly in her bed. Unconsciously, her eyes strayed to the still figure reclining on the other side of the incredible swaying wall. Damn! What was her preoccupation with Devon Howard? Why did she allow him to invade her thoughts, why did she entertain the memory of his kiss against her lips, his warm body against her, his mouth searing the flesh of her breasts? Why did she allow thoughts of him to plague her? No! She would think of him no longer . . . would dismiss the thoughts of the hands that had caressed her gently, the abject tenderness that had softened his harsh features, turned the ice in his eyes to warm, blue velvet.

Abruptly exasperated by the course her wayward thoughts were taking, Morgana turned sharply on her side, away from the reclining figure that haunted her . . . gave her no peace . . .

Straining to remain still, to present an appearance of deep sleep, Devon turned his face slowly, unnoticeably, toward the bed on the other side of the tantalizing curtain. Morgana was a small, unmoving rise against the starkness of the white sheets. With the aid of sharp, vivid recall, he filled in the picture that the darkness did not allow him to see. Long, riotously curly hair lay streaming across the pillow, gleaming in a faint shaft of moonlight, framing a small, flawless face with skin unforgettably soft to the touch, incredibly sweet to the taste. Graceful curling lashes rested against the delicate contours of her cheek, emphasizing the provocative slant of her amazingly brilliant eyes and slender, winged brows. The brief closing of the door had undoubtedly allowed her the opportunity to change into a nightrail, surely a light, almost transparent wisp appropriate to the humid heat of the night. A small tremor passing over his body, he despised the weakness that made that thought almost more than he could bear.

She was so close, and he remembered so well the velvet softness of her skin beneath his fingers . . . the gently sloping contour of her shoulders, the soft rise of her breasts . . . the intoxicating fullness of those breasts beneath his lips. But, most of all, he remembered the tenderness the incredibly lovely Morgana had awakened in him, her instinctive response to his touch, the tremors that had shaken that slender, glorious body when his lips had touched her flesh. Her eyes had glowed with passion, the small, golden flecks flaring into a brilliant golden blaze that lit a similar fire deep in his soul . . . one that he had not yet, despite his greatest efforts, been able to extinguish. And damned if the little bitch didn't know exactly how to fan the embers of the blaze!

Oh, she had heeded his warning, outwardly, at least. She had stayed clear of him for the remaining two days of the voyage. Yes, she had done that! She had stayed far away from him and had allowed that bastard who had almost raped her back into her good graces! Stupid little bitch . . .

allowing that nauseating ladies' man to devour her with his eyes, to drool lecherously into her face. . . .

And now, tonight, as if the circumstances of their accommodations were not difficult enough, she made certain to twist and turn on that broad, inviting bed, calling his attention to her sleeplessness, inviting him to see that she could not rest with him so near. But he would be damned if he would allow her to see how well she disturbed his rest . . . how very close he was to stealing silently past the billowing, transparent barriers that stood between them. Aggie . . . the stalwart old Scotswoman . . . her loud snores proclaimed all too clearly for his own peace of mind the fact that she would be an ineffectual deterrent to a quiet invasion of the large blue and white French bed.

Damn that Morgana! She was so close . . . so very close . . . In a few, short, silent seconds he could be lying beside her on that great, inviting bed, stroking the softness of her flesh, tasting the sweetness of her lips, loving her. . . . God! How very much he wanted her . . . wanted to feel her softness under him again, this time more intimately than before. He wanted . . . he wanted . . .

A quick, restless movement on the wide bed, tauntingly visible to his eyes, sent a convulsive shudder down his spine. Hell, he was trembling like an untried boy! Overcome with self-disgust, Devon raked an impatient hand through his heavy brown hair, suddenly realizing he was covered with perspiration that was not the result of the heavy humidity of the night. He was breathless with desire, his chest heaving violently as he fought to control the urge that grew stronger with each moment. Damn her . . . damn her . . . he would not let her break him down!

Slowly, in a movement calculated to feign sleep, Devon rolled over on his side, presenting his back to the small, restless figure that tantalized him mercilessly. Carefully, deliberately, he slowed his breathing to deep, even breaths, his only measure of satisfaction in the small feat the fact that Morgana squirmed restlessly yet again. Was that a low moan he heard coming from the broad French bed? Experiencing a responsive tightening in his groin, he caught his breath.

Damned little bitch . . .

Would this voyage ever end? Slapping the uninteresting
novel down on the desk beside her, Morgana shot a quick
glance toward the bunk nearby. Well, at least Aggie was
sleeping. Poor Aggie . . . After four days out, three of which
had subjected the *Estrellita* to the cruel "balances" that had
been a true test of Morgana's seamanship, the sober Scotswoman had confided quietly that she strongly suspected she
would not survive the voyage! Although she was in far from a
festive mood, Morgana had experienced a startled, perverse
amusement in the woman's sober declaration, which she had
been hard-pressed to subdue. Stricken with guilt at her blatant lack of sympathy for Aggie's low state, she had patted
the wide, clammy hand and made an excuse to go up on
deck. After all, seasickness was not a laughing matter, and
she had been convinced Aggie would ill appreciate her levity.
   But, now, back in the cabin, she reflected that there had
been little to laugh about on this voyage so far. Shaking her
head, Morgana allowed her eyes to move around the dingy,
foul-smelling cabin. Incredibly uncomfortable bunk beds,
arranged one over the other, dominated the room. A much
abused night table of sorts stood nearby. Its chipped, travel-
worn appearance inspired inordinate gratitude in her mind
for the brackets that attached it to the wall, eliminating the
otherwise distinct possibility that it would collapse to the
floor, taking the small number of personal articles it supported crashing down with it. An equally ancient washstand
stood a few feet away, its mirror darkened with a stain that
distorted her features abominably. Completing the fur-
nishing of their cabin was the hard chair on which she sat,
and a scarred desk that faced the inside wall. Swaying over it,
lending its inadequate light to that which filtered through
their single porthole, was a large, smoke-marked lantern,
which had doubtless seen countless voyages without benefit
of cleaning. In another corner their bags lay in an ungainly
pile, and Morgana had yet to acquire enough nerve to question the steward about the area in which her trunk was

stored, hoping desperately it was at least adequately protected against the wet.

Compared to the *Estrellita,* the *Helga* had been a luxury ship fit for royalty! And on this ship she did not even have the luxury of interesting company to fill the endless hours! Captain Moreno, short, slender, was admittedly a charming man, typically Spanish and gallant, but his endless duties allowed him little time for his unanticipated passengers. The officers of the small ship held little appeal. The first mate was a gentlemanly, good-natured fellow who obviously felt undue attention to the young American woman who spent so much time unchaperoned on deck would reflect adversely on his intentions; the second mate was a large fellow, far more broad than tall, seeming more interested in the galley than in the few passengers on the ship. The other officers—a short, scraggly-haired fellow with several missing teeth, and a rather handsome young man of medium height, with a look in his eye far too reminiscent of Edgar Morrison's to make her comfortable—appeared to complete the unimpressive roster, with the exception of the efficient sailors who kept hard at their tasks under their captain's watchful eye. Yes, with each moment that passed she became more anxious for the port of Veracruz.

Adding to her chagrin was the fact that she, Aggie, and the odious Devon Howard were the only passengers on a merchant ship that, she had decided, had been built with far greater thought to the storage of cargo than the comfort of passengers. But, she supposed she should be thankful that Tío Manuel had arranged such quick connections in her journey, for she realized that any more time spent waiting in Havana would have been too horrendous to endure.

Her mind slipping to the events of the day before, Morgana felt a spasmatic tightening in her stomach. Well, as much as she despised the indolent boredom of the voyage, she had begun to believe it preferable to a day such as she had spent yesterday. In direct antithesis to the grey sky visible through the small porthole on the far wall, the previous day had been glorious. A brilliant tropical sun had turned the turquoise water to a sea of sparkling jewels that had delighted

55

the eye. The wind had calmed to a fair, brisk breeze that had propelled the *Estrellita* smoothly forward without the dips and churns that had been so hazardous to Aggie's fragile stomach. So encouraged had Aggie been that she had actually ventured up on deck for the first time since the inception of the voyage. Considering that effort all she could manage with her depleted strength, she had collapsed on one of the deck lounges, which Morgana suspected had been installed for their convenience, and had promptly fallen asleep. Abandoned once again to her own devices, Morgana had plopped herself down on the lounge at Aggie's side, thoroughly disgusted at the enforced inactivity of her near captive state. Then, abruptly conscious of vigorous activity progressing on the opposite side of the deck, Morgana had realized with a start that the ship had stopped moving!

Moving hastily to her feet, she had swallowed hard against the lump of fear in her throat and walked rapidly in the direction of the increasing furor on the opposite deck. A bit startled by the scene that met her eye, Morgana had stopped still, her questioning gaze moving over the sailors milling in small, laughing groups as they prepared lines and poles and fussed with buckets that smelled suspiciously like fish. Her eyes widening in surprise, she had heard a softly accented voice at her side.

"*Si*, Señorita Pierce, we have paused in our voyage to allow the men some time for fishing." At her questioning glance, Captain Moreno had continued with a small smile. "This entertainment fills a double purpose, señorita . . . the enjoyment of the men and the provision of fresh fish for our table."

Unable to hide her annoyance at yet another delay, Morgana's voice lacked the enthusiasm apparent in everyone else's demeanor. "But surely, captain, our voyage will not be of so long a duration that the men are in need of this recreation and our supplies in need of bolstering. . . ."

"On the contrary, señorita, although we have been fortunate in experiencing good weather today, our instruments indicate foul weather to come, which may indeed lengthen our voyage by several days, perhaps as much as a week. My experience has proved that it is far wiser to prepare in advance for approaching emergencies than to wait until they appear and attempt to adjust our actions accordingly.''

His sober statement, delivered with quiet authority, had been effective in quelling any further objections she had considered. Cognizant of her acceptance of his statement, Captain Moreno had smiled, diplomatically taking her arm as he had urged her forward toward the rail. ''Come, if you have not experienced the wonder of fishing in the sea before, you may find it amusing as well as educational. If I do not miss my guess, señorita, yours is a very inquiring mind.''

Uncertain how to take his last statement, Morgana had glanced up sharply, only to see a benevolent smile that removed any possible implications from his statement. Flashing him a small smile in return, Morgana had allowed herself to be led to the rail, her eyes on the lines that had already been cast over the side. Following the direction of the lines as they dropped into the water, Morgana was amazed to see the water was so clear that she could see the fish rush and seize the bait as soon as it was tossed in. Frowning as the men jerked out the lines and hastened to bait the hooks once again, Morgana could not suppress the thought that this was indeed more slaughter than sport, and were it not for the spectacle it provided, she would not have remained as a witness. But still, it was fascinating, the preposterous numbers of fish that flocked to the vicinity of the lines . . . small fish, large fish . . . some of immense size . . . she had never seen such a dazzling array of . . .

A loud chorus of greetings from the sailors at the rail had interrupted her mental meanderings, bringing her head up to the approach of Devon Howard. Unaware of her presence, his attention turned toward the men who chided his unorthodox appearance in rapid Spanish, he had laughed at their well-meaning jokes, trading comments in a Spanish almost as rapid as their own. Realizing he had forsaken all pretense at formal attire since the inception of the voyage, having witnessed his appearance in shirt sleeves even during mealtimes, Morgana had still been unprepared for the specter that approached the rail in a rapid stride. The tall, virile form

57

that stood almost a head above the other men was unclothed to the waist, the broad expanse of shoulder and chest revealed in all its masculine wonder. And a wonder it was . . . strong, muscled shoulders; long, tightly corded muscular arms; darkly tanned skin stretched across a broad chest lightly matted with a curling mass of dark hair that disappeared in an ever diminishing line at his narrow, flat waist. His slim hips, emphasized by the bared contrast above, were even more erotically stirring than before, the appeal of his well-muscled thighs apparent in the cut of his britches, completing a picture of blatant masculinity that was virtually breathtaking. A pole in one hand, he continued a rapid stride toward the rail. Bending to scoop up a pail of bait, his eye caught the hem of her light blue dress. His eyes, jerking up to meet her openly assessing gaze, narrowed, his previously easy manner vanishing as he offered formally, "Good mornin', Miss Pierce. I hadn't expected you to join our recreation, or I would've dressed more formally."

Flushing at the knowing intensity of his gaze, Morgana had been certain he could read her reaction to his state of partial undress on her face, and, cursing herself for her vulnerability to the masculine aura he exuded so effortlessly, she had offered stiffly, "I'm here at Captain Moreno's invitation, Mr. Howard, and you may rest assured that your manner of dress concerns me not in the least."

His silent expression of obvious disbelief his only response, Devon had rudely turned his back and baited his hook. Her face flaming, she had returned her attention to the sea below, silently vowing she would remain at the rail until the last fish was caught. She had decided she would not allow Devon Howard to send her scuttling back to her lounge chair like an embarrassed child, as was so obviously his intention.

Nodding silently to Captain Moreno's narration, Morgana had done her best to ignore the tall, brawny form at the rail a few feet away. Forcing her attention to the colorful array of fish that continued to flock to the bait, she had soon become engrossed in the melee of swarming fish, jerking lines and the shouted victorious squeals as a few fish of incredible size were hauled on deck.

". . . and these, Señorita Pierce, they are called cherna . . . and those, pargo . . . delectable eating, as I am sure you will agree after supper tonight. And over there, you see . . . *caramba!*" His leisurely narration jerking to a halt, Captain Moreno pointed anxiously to the large, rapidly moving fish that had entered the active swarming below.

"Tiburón! Cuidado, hombres!"

Her eyes following the rapid movement of the large, vicious-looking shark, Morgana had felt a jerk of fear as it effortlessly snapped a large fish in two, and, turning, prepared to make another lunge through the panicking schools. Following its greedy second run from the rail, Morgana had watched with widening eyes as it snapped up another large fish, catching itself on the same hook that had been in the fish he had devoured. Thrashing about in a fearsome rage, the shark jerked and pulled at the line, the sheer power of his desperation bending the pole until it appeared it would break in two. Raising her eyes to the deck, Morgana had seen that it was Devon who strained to retain the grip on the frantic shark. Grimacing with the strain of the battle, Devon had slowly reeled in the thrashing body until it was close enough to the side of the ship for the men to drop their nets to aid in bringing it aboard. And still the fight raged on, Devon maintaining a taut line despite the pressure exerted against him. Fascinated at the intensity of concentration reflected on his face, Morgana had allowed her eyes to move slowly over the taut, sharply angled planes. The dark brows were drawn together in an intense frown, blue eyes bright with subdued excitement; powerful muscles in his arms and chest corded with strain. A light sheen of perspiration had covered the rippling skin, causing it to glisten in the bright midday sun. A thick shock of heavy brown hair had slipped to his forehead, striking a strange note of vulnerability quite out of tune with the exhibition of power being enacted before her eyes. So caught up had she become in the man that she had not realized the shark had at least been captured in the nets lowered to secure its thrashing body.

Immediately dropping his pole, Devon had lent the support of his considerable brawn to the tangle of men who hauled and heaved until their catch was over the side and on deck. For the briefest of seconds the shark had lain motionless at their feet before beginning a wild scrambling motion, its sharp rows of tearing teeth seeking the legs of the men who had been responsible for its capture.

Her heart leaping into her throat, Morgana had watched as a vicious lunge grazed Devon's legs, her short agonized cry, "Devon!" lost in the scramble of stamping feet and warning shouts that had followed the lightning-quick attack.

But suddenly it was over, as the butt end of a harpoon shoved down the hungry throat had put an end to the violent display. Swallowing against the fear that had brought the sharp taste of bile to her throat, Morgana had closed her eyes, gripping the rail for support against the weakness that had abruptly accosted her. Opening her eyes a brief second later, she had seen Devon kneeling at the side of the motionless shark, his eyes trained on her face. The dark intensity of his glance had burned into hers, had been more than she could bear. Had he heard her call out his name . . . had he been aware of the fear that had paralyzed her soul with the thought that he might be hurt? Her heart still pounding in her ears, her body beset with a trembling she could not control, Morgana had been unable to take any more.

With a supreme effort, Morgana had jerked her gaze from the mesmerizing glance, and, rapidly, wordlessly, had walked away.

Now, in retrospect, Morgana was certain she had just reacted violently to the stimulus of the moment. Certainly it was nothing more than that, nothing . . . because in the time since, she had renewed the conviction in her mind that Devon Howard's conceited arrogance was more than she could bear!

"Damn!" Muttering low under her breath, Morgana felt the swell of the stomach discomfort that had been teasing her for the past few hours. Not accustomed to the excesses of Mexican food, she had found that afternoon's offering, of which she had not dared ask the name, definitely abusive to her tender stomach. Most certainly, it could not be the rough seas that were causing her this growing nausea. She had

60

proved herself a good sailor, had she not? While most of the passengers of the *Helga* had lain in their cabins groaning their despair, she had been vigorously walking the decks with Edgar Morrison. But, then, why this sudden preoccupation with the dip and tilt of the cabin floor, and the musty odor of the airless room? Why this sudden weakness in the pit of her stomach . . . the suspicious quaking of her knees as she attempted to stand . . . the perspiration abruptly appearing on her forehead and the palms of her hands? No! She would not give in to her weakness! She was allowing this small discomfort to grow out of proportion. All she needed was a little air . . . yes, some time on deck and some fresh air in her lungs.

Standing shakily, deliberately ignoring the lurching sensation that accompanied her movement, Morgana took a last look at the bunk. Satisfied that Aggie was still asleep, she walked unsteadily to the doorway, her step hesitant as she stepped into the passageway, and continued up the staircase onto the deck.

Taking her first step onto the deck, which was dipping far more deeply than earlier in the day, Morgana remembered the reason for her return to the dank quarters she had just abandoned. The sky was a dull grey in color, the air heavy and oppressive. Although it appeared the ship's progress was in no way hindered by the wind that buffeted her or the choppy sea now visible to her eye, the weather was definitely disagreeable. Taking a deep breath to still the jerking spasms that had just begun in her stomach, Morgana walked to the rail. It was simply mind over matter . . . that's what it was . . . she would have to control her preoccupation with the steady rhythmic undulation of the waves and concentrate on the overcast sky. But somehow the dipping horizon seemed to get in her way, recording in her mind, even more clearly than the relentless waves, the increased pitching of the ship as it made its way up and down, cutting the sea toward Veracruz.

Up and down . . . up and down . . . Tasting the abrupt bitterness of bile in her throat, Morgana quickly shut her eyes, clutching hard at the rail for stability. No, she could not give in to the sickness making rapid strides against her will. She would not! She would concentrate on something pleasant. . . . But even the darkness against her closed lids seemed to reel before her as an uncontrollable trembling began to shake her limbs. Oh, Lord, she was going to be sick . . . very sick. Feeling the heat of tears slipping from beneath her closed lids, Morgana fought a silent war for control of her heaving stomach.

"Morgana, what is it? What's wrong?"

Russet eyes snapping wide in a small, pale face, Morgana turned slowly toward the voice, her mind registering the concern in Devon Howard's expression as he took a step closer. Strangely, all resentment disappeared in the onslaught of her foul condition, and, hardly recognizing her own voice, Morgana muttered weakly, "I'm . . . I'm sick, Devon. . . ."

Abruptly, to her supreme horror and embarrassment, the battle was lost as Morgana's heaving stomach assumed control. The convulsive spasms seemed endless as she bent low over the rail, the pain of the violent, extended abuse sorely testing her strength as she swayed weakly against the sturdy bar. But a strong arm slipped around her waist to support her, a wide palm moved to her forehead to hold her head, which had been too heavy to support any longer. The revolting spasms concluded, Morgana felt herself taken to rest against a white broadcloth shirt, the fresh scent of the fabric welcome to her outraged senses. Comforting arms closed around her, supporting her as her breathing returned to normal; and within a few moments a fresh handkerchief was mopping the perspiration from her brow. But she was too weak to stir . . . too frightened that the slightest movement on her part would stimulate a renewal of the ghastly convulsions of a few minutes before. Her eyes still closed against harsh reality, she abruptly felt herself lifted high into strong arms, held tightly against a firm chest. Gradually opening her eyes, she looked up into Devon Howard's unrevealing expression the moment before she was carefully placed on one of the low chaises on that portion of the deck. In a moment he was gone, but, too shaken to give his sudden disappearance much thought, Morgana again closed her eyes, her

62

shaking hand moving to shield a face still pale from her recent ordeal.

Unexpectedly a warm, wide hand curled around hers, gently drawing her hand from her face the moment before a cool, wet cloth touched her cheek. Her eyes springing open, Morgana remained motionless under Devon Howard's gentle ministrations, inwardly marveling at the depth of the man's unexpected consideration.

His eyes moving slowly over the white face turned up to his, Devon gently swabbed the perspiration from Morgana's forehead before running the cloth over the fragile, almost transparent lids that fluttered closed under his soothing hand, the short, slender nose, the pale cheeks, and, finally, over the appealing lips that trembled under his gaze. Carefully prolonging his self-appointed task, he still held tight to the small hand he had drawn from her face a few moments before, noting that Morgana made no attempt to either withdraw her hand or resist his attentions.

As reluctant as he was to admit it, he had been desperate to touch her. The fear on her face after the incident with the shark had stirred in him an almost overwhelming need to comfort her . . . take her into his arms, the extreme vulnerability in her eyes in the moment their glances had touched having set off a reaction within him that was difficult to explain, even to himself.

Just now, the brief sensation of holding her in his arms had been intoxicating; her docile submission to his ministrations stirring anew the wildly protective instinct so new to his experience. She was a fragile, wounded bird, completely open to him for the first time . . . momentarily helpless in her need . . . small . . . vulnerable . . . and so damned beautiful that he ached with the sight of her. He gloried in her need, however fleeting it might be, unwilling to pay heed to the whispers in his own mind beginning to signal his own need for her. No, his mind countered, there was no need present inside him, only desire. He had felt desire for many woman in the past, had he not? But, admittedly, he had never felt it so compellingly, with such urgency, and never with such tenderness. . . .

63

Touching the pale skin of her cheek lightly with the tips of his fingers, Devon whispered softly, "You'll be all right in a few minutes, Morgana. I have to admit cherna doesn't quite live up to its reputation. It didn't set well on my stomach, either." Noting that her eyes dropped embarrassedly from his, he gently raised her chin with his fingertips, until her gaze met his own. The small smile that hovered at the corners of his mouth was warm with understanding, encouraging the tentative smile that flickered across the pink lips that so fascinated him. Suppressing the urge to take her into his arms and hold her consolingly against him, stroking her, comforting her, he whispered huskily, "Just close your eyes and relax for a few minutes, and you'll be all right. That's it . . ." His hand moved to tenderly caress her cheek for a few, short moments as her lids dropped obediently over her eyes, raising in him a swell of soul-shaking tenderness. His grip tightening on the small hand curved inside his, he suppressed the desire to touch the gleaming tendrils that had succeeded in escaping her upswept coiffure to appealingly frame the splendid countours of her cheeks. Adjusting the chaise beside hers, he sat quietly on the edge, indulging himself as he silently perused the lovely woman exposed to his glance.

It was mystery to him what it was about Morgana Pierce that was so unique . . . so successful in penetrating his defenses. She was far from the type of woman who had always appealed to him in the past. His upbringing on the raw frontier of Texas had instilled in him an admiration for the capable, hard-working, hard-loving women that Texas seemed to produce in abundance. He had been thoroughly sickened by the pampered wealthy daughters of New York society, finding it hard to control his impatience with their pretentions. But, cut from the same mold, Morgana was yet another thing. To his irritation, thoughts of her far too often took precedence over thoughts of the political situation of his native state, which should have been his first order of business. And, within a few weeks' time, she would no longer be a part of his life. . . . That thought striking a discordant note, Devon abandoned the route his mind was taking, allowing him respite from his nagging confusion. Morgana was here with him now. She needed him, and he would allow himself the enjoyment of her presence.

Yes, he was certain he had never seen a complexion so soft and fair as hers. Even the light color she had acquired in the intermittent sun had succeeded in deepening its creamy, flawless appeal. Certainly the high, clear brow added to her air of patrician appeal, the curling spirals bobbing against it adding a note of vulnerability that was irrestible. What would it be like to see that gleaming chestnut mass down full over her shoulders . . . caressing creamy white skin . . . brushing against the full, well-shaped breasts he remembered so well? Unless he missed his guess, the stubborn tresses once freed would form curling spirals that would tighten with the warmth of a man's hand, stroke his palm with their brilliance. He could remember the silkiness of their touch tantalizing him. . . . His eyes, moving slowly over her face, found their way unerringly to the pink fullness of her lips. There was a raging need inside him to taste them again.

Unconsciously moving closer, Devon brushed his lips against her forehead, a small smile moving across his mouth as Morgana's eyes fluttered open to hold his with a questioning expression.

"The best think you can do right now, Morgana, is to lie back and rest until your stomach calms down."

Appearing to consider his words, Morgana finally whispered in a shaky voice, "I believe you're right, Devon. In any case, I'm not up to much else right now."

Her faltering words seeming to have spent the last of her strength, Morgana allowed her eyes to fall closed. No, she could not afford to think right now. The abrupt rise and fall of the sea was still having too great an impact on her senses. She would not wonder at the abrupt softening of Devon Howard's harsh mask, or the incredible gentleness of his touch. She would not think of anything . . . anything at all.

A gentle rocking motion interrupted the warm safety of her dreams. She did not wish to awaken . . . the delicious,

65

rosy warmth was too comfortable to forsake for reality. But the motion became more intense, jarring her serenity. A small frown creasing her forehead even before her heavy lids began to flutter awake, Morgana heard a low, familiar voice drawl softly, "You'd better wake up now, Morgana. The steward has just announced dinner. Come on now, darlin'."

The sound of the low drawl so close to her ear snapped her eyes obediently open. A responsive tightening began in her stomach at the moment she met Devon's warm, cerulean gaze, and her frown darkened.

A small flash of amusement flicked across Devon's face. "Well, that's not the usual reaction I get when a young lady wakes up and sees me beside her, little darlin', but nothin' about you seems to follow the usual pattern, does it?" When she did not respond, choosing to remain silent, he continued quietly, "How do you feel now, Morgana?"

Memory flashing back with painful vividness brought a light flush to her face. Her eyes dropping from his, Morgana responded hesitantly, "I'm . . . I'm fine now, Devon." Her automatic use of his given name was more revealing than she would have wished, and she continued unevenly, "I . . . I apologize for foisting myself on you like this. I would have been far wiser if I had remained in my cabin and entertained my distress in private. But I was certain if I came on deck I would be able to fight off the nausea."

Ignoring her apology, Devon cupped her chin in his calloused palm, firmly raising it to meet his eyes. "There's nothin' to apologize for, Morgana. But since you're feelin' better now, I think it would be best if you got up and ate somethin'."

"Oh, no!" Her eyes closing momentarily in reaction to the distasteful thought, Morgana took a deep breath and continued quietly, "I just couldn't, Devon. I mean . . . well, I don't think I could bear to eat anything right now."

"You said you felt better. . . ."

"Yes, but . . ."

Directing a firm glance into her eyes, Devon interrupted with quiet insistence, "The best medicine for your affliction, darlin', is a full stomach."

Gritting her teeth against the light wave of nausea that greeted the thought, Morgana grated tightly, "I said I don't want to eat anything, Devon."

The spontaneous flash of anger in the light eyes so close to hers brought a flush of the same emotion to her own face. Devon had been very kind to her, but that did not give him the right to dictate what she would or would not do! Preparing herself for his cutting retort, Morgana was startled at his coaxing tone when he responded softly, "You trusted me a little while ago, and I took care of you, didn't I, Morgana?"

Taken off guard by the simple truth of that statement, Morgana nodded silently, steeling herself as her russet eyes watched him cautiously.

"Well, then just trust me one more time. If you don't eat now, you'll probably spend the rest of the voyage in the same condition in which you passed the last few hours."

Pausing, Devon allowed his eyes to move assessingly over her face. Morgana was looking at him consideringly in return, her slender brows drawn into a small frown. Her long, sweeping lashes lightly dusted the graceful arches while her huge, doe-shaped eyes reflected her careful scrutiny of his words. Unaccountably, he felt a strange tightening in his throat. She was so damned adorable . . . like a small, wary kitten, uncertain whether to take that first, venturesome step. He ached to take her comfortingly into his arms, to stroke her gently, to whisper softly into her ear until she relaxed completely . . . trustingly. But he had to keep in mind that this kitten had claws. He had already felt their sharpness.

An unfathomable spark in the light eyes watching her so intently caused her heartbeat to quicken unexpectedly, and, annoyed at her own reaction to the enigmatic man at her side, Morgana frowned. Her voice was a little less confident than she would have wished. "I'm sorry, Devon. I wouldn't be able to hold anything down and . . ."

Not allowing her to conclude her statement, Devon purposely took her hand, urging her to her feet. "Come on, darlin'. Dinner is waitin'. . . ."

The strength of Morgana's conviction left her the moment

she was set firmly on her feet and a tightly muscled arm moved around her waist. Was it his intensely masculine aura that stole her breath . . . his intoxicating nearness that left her weak? No! Firmly taking herself in hand, Morgana made a last futile effort to protest, only to have Devon lower his head breathtakingly close to hers and whisper confidentially in her ear, "Don't worry, sweet. If you get sick again, I'll hold your head. . . ."

The reminder of his gentle care during her embarrassing lapse a few hours before succeeded in silencing her protests where all else had failed. Chuckling low in his throat at the light flush that stained her cheeks, Devon lowered his head to press a light kiss against her windblown chestnut curls. The sensation of holding Morgana proprietarily close being more heady than he cared to admit, Devon opened the door and led her silently into the dining room.

Her eyes dancing, Morgana looked up into the amused expression of the man at her side. Even in her merriment, Morgana's sense of wonder was acute. If anyone had told her a few days ago . . . a few hours ago . . . that she would be thoroughly enjoying Devon Howard's company, she would have called him a liar! But, incredible as it was, it was true!

Having entered the dining room of the *Estrellita* under duress only a short time before, she had found herself charmed, entertained and effectively cajoled into eating and enjoying her supper by a Devon Howard she had not known existed! Eating with extreme caution at first, she had suddenly found herself ravenously hungry. Now, a few hours later, walking the deck beside him, her arm tucked firmly under his, she began to suspect that the best medicine for her condition had been Devon Howard himself!

Taking a deep, rapturous breath, Morgana stopped at the rail for a few short minutes. Even the night had conformed to her unexpected mood. A sky that had been overcast and dreary had abruptly cleared to reveal a myriad of twinkling stars in a backdrop of infinite black velvet. A brilliant moon cast a shimmering silver path across gently rippling waves, a glowing invitation to bask in the magic of its beauty. The heavy mantle of heat that had oppressed the ship relentlessly had been lifted by the setting sun, and even the wind had calmed to a pleasant breeze that rocked the *Estrellita* gently. Listening absent-mindedly as Devon's low drawl rambled quietly beside her, Morgana smiled full up into his face. How was it she had dismissed so lightly the appeal of this man's subtle, understated humor . . . the quick wit so startlingly contrasting with his soft drawl? And how was it that she had insisted to herself that he was not handsome? Or was it simply that the relaxing of his manner toward her had accomplished all this, turning the chill in his gaze to the warm glow so effective in stirring her senses? She could no longer deny the appeal of his dark, tanned skin stretched tightly over his sharply chisled features, when that harshness was so effectively negated by the supreme magnetism of Devon's slow, devastating smile. Her hand was resting lightly on his arm, and she was intensely aware of the tightly muscled strength beneath her fingers. Even in the darkly conservative clothing he had worn at the inception of the voyage, he had been intensely masculine. She could remember with unbelievable clarity the feeling of the hard strength of him pressed flush against her. She remembered the touch of his lips against hers, their soft persuasion. . . . Her eyes, dropping from his, considered those lips again. Firm, sensuously full, drawn back into a smile that revealed strong, straight teeth. She longed to touch those lips with her fingertips . . . trace their outline . . . But his smile was dropping away. . . .

Unconscious of the fact that the slow drawl had ceased several moments before, Morgana was abruptly aware of the hoarse quality of the voice that whispered softly, ''Morgana, darlin', I think it's only fair to warn you that it isn't safe to look at me that way.''

Morgana heard his words, but she was no more capable of withdrawing her gaze from his lips than she was of resisting the hand that moved up to caress her cheek. There was magic in his touch, the coarse skin of his fingertips eliciting an erotic sensation as they traced her cheekbone tenderly.

Devon's voice was a low, wondering whisper. "I don't think I've ever felt skin as soft as yours, Morgana . . . or as smooth." Lowering his head, he ran his lips across the path his fingertips had traced only moments before. "I love to feel your skin against my mouth. . . ." Moving to her temple, Devon pressed fleeting kisses against the delicate pulse throbbing gently there, sliding to the lids that fluttered closed under the caress of his lips. Cupping her face in his hands, Devon lifted her mouth to his, circling her trembling lips with light, butterfly kisses, until she groaned her agony at his taunting caress. Then his mouth was on hers, the first touch startling to her senses in the sheer power of its glory. Unconscious of her eager arms' stealing around his neck, Morgana was aware only of the searing lips that moved sensuously against hers, the broad hands that pulled her close, the hard, strong body that met hers, took her in . . . but the tender conquest was not complete. Slowly separating the barrier of her teeth, Devon's tongue penetrated the warm, honeyed confines of her mouth.

Overwhelmed by the magnificence of the feelings inundating her senses, Morgana abandoned herself to his searching tongue, reveling in its gentle play, thrilling to the searing quest that grew steadily more demanding. She could feel the heavy pounding of Devon's heart against her breast . . . or was that her own? She could feel the trembling in the strong, unyielding frame, and the fact of her power over his senses was exhilarating. There was so much beauty in Devon's arms . . . more beauty than she had realized existed. She wanted him to hold her closer, kiss her more deeply, to go on kissing her, never to stop. . . . There was a raging need inside her that fed on the fury of Devon's lovemaking, inspired in her a desire to taste its beauty more fully. She wanted . . . she wanted . . .

". . . and I am so relieved at the change in the weather, captain. I do thank you for escorting me upstairs. I had not realized how weak one may become in such a short time."

Jerking herself away from Devon's embrace, Morgana shot a glance in the direction in which the low Stottish burr sounded. Within seconds Aggie's broad, unsteady frame rounded the corner of the deck, accompanied by the slender, erect form of Captain Moreno.

"Morgana! There you are! I became worried when you didn't return to the cabin, and I asked the captain to accompany me topside."

The darkness of night spared Morgana the accusing glance she was certain had accompanied that speech, and, grateful the same darkness also hid the bright flush that suffused her cheeks, Morgana replied hesitantly, "I . . . I didn't feel well this afternoon either, Aggie. Mr. Howard has been inordinately considerate of my discomfort. . . ."

Extremely mindful of the broad hand that had refused to relinquish the smooth contour of her back, but continued to caress it gently under the cover of the night, Morgana shot Devon a pleading glance. Taking a step away, Morgana abruptly turned and closed the distance between Aggie and herself, uncertain whether it was her conscience or her bemusement that made her suddenly long to escape the omnipotent power of Devon Howard's touch.

"I . . . I do thank you for your consideration, Mr. Howard, but I do think I should take Aggie back to our cabin now so we may both retire for the night."

The low drawl that responded was unrevealing in the darkness of the night. "It was my pleasure, Miss Pierce. I enjoy bein' of service."

Nodding a quick goodnight to the captain, Morgana took Aggie's arm and ushered her steadily toward the staircase, bracing herself for the lecture that began as soon as they were out of earshot of the two men they had left at the rail.

"Morgana Pierce, where have you been all day! I should think a person with your upbringing would have the sense to realize the conclusions to which the officers and crew of this ship would jump if you had spent any more time on the deck in the darkness . . . unchaperoned, with Mr. Howard. You must remember, Morgana, your aunt has an important position in society. You are, after all, going to the home of the president of Mexico himself! It would not do to have gossip

71

follow you, for it would plague you endlessly. If there is one thing that is common in all societies, it is the propensity to gossip, and I will not have you . . ."

Aggie's voice droned on, fading from Morgana's hearing as she managed dutifully to nod her concurrence with Aggie's concerned harangue. But she could think of nothing save the velvet touch of soft lips against her face, the merging of eager, seeking mouths, the soft persuasion of Devon's tongue as it caressed hers tenderly, coaxingly. Her body was sensitized to exquisite pain by his touch, the memory of his hard, male body pressed so tightly against hers causing a weakness in her knees so severe that she looked toward her cabin door and the relief of her bunk with avid appreciation. What was wrong with her? Edgar's first kiss had been pleasant enough, but the intensifying of his lovemaking had merely produced an instinctive revulsion inside her . . . an eagerness to escape. With Devon there was no desire to escape. Instead there was a desire to . . .

No! She must gain control of herself! Obviously, Devon's tenderness during her brief illness had inspired in her a gratitude far stronger than she had realized. And Aggie was right. Of all things, she could not afford to go to Tía Isabella with a stain on her reputation, or even the slightest blemish! The events of the past few weeks had merely left her feeling a bit more vulnerable than normal, that was all. She would feel differently tomorrow . . . yes . . . she would feel quite differently in the light of day. . . .

With a short, inner groan, Morgana gave a futile glance at the sky overhead. Oh, it was hopeless! The brilliant cerulean cover was unmarked by a single cloud! The tropical sun was blazing relentlessly, its intense heat regulated to a point of comfort by the brisk breeze that filled the sails overhead, hastening the *Estrellita* with unbelievable speed toward Veracruz. Damn! Where before she had been certain the voyage could not end quickly enough for her, she now felt an inexplicable need to prolong the sun-drenched days . . . to extend the time she spent with the stirring Devon Howard at her side. She had even begun to resent Aggie's intrusion . . . had begun to secretly yearn for the return of the active swells that would necessitate her return to the cabin. And, strangely, where prior to the voyage her days had been spent in silent apprehension of the new life that awaited her, she was now unable to think past the present and her own shameless desire to feel Devon's strong arms around her.

Overcome by a wave of guilt, Morgana turned to shoot Aggie a brief smile before turning to catch and hold the light-eyed gaze that only too clearly echoed her own longing. The slow smile beginning at the corners of his mouth grew gradually to heart-stopping proportions as Devon bent to whisper, in a voice meant for her ears alone, "Aggie's in damnable good health these past two days, isn't she, darlin'? I must be in considerable disfavor with the Almighty, because all my prayers for some good, churning waves have produced two days of sea as smooth as glass. At this rate, we'll be in Veracruz within a day or so. . . ."

Allowing his words to drift off, Devon experienced a surge of guilt at his own traitorous words. Hell, two weeks ago he couldn't get to Manga de Clavo fast enough! With the fate of an innocent man depending on his persuasive powers with Antonio Santa Anna, each day lost in bad sailing weather had been like another weight added to his shoulders. And now . . . taking a moment to allow his eyes to wander over the beautiful face turned up to his, he struggled anew with the agonizing frustration that was so effective against his peace of mind. Hell, he wasn't really sure what was happening to him! All he knew was that the small, chestnut-haired beauty leaning casually at the rail at his side was, temporarily, at least, the foremost thought on his mind. And he was extremely frustrated by Aggie's constant attendance, which had thwarted every attempt he had made to take up where he and Morgana had left off in the moonlight two nights before. Tearing even more effectively at his control was his certainty that Morgana's thoughts were running in the same vein. It was obvious in the way the gold sparks in those incredible sienna-colored eyes came to life when they met his glance, and in the small shudder that passed over her fragile frame when his glance moved to her mouth. He had actually reached the point where he could think of nothing but the unbelievably sweet taste of her; the fragrance of her velvet-soft skin; the sweet singing in his veins when he held her in his arms. Crist! If he kept up like this, he'd be a madman by the time he reached Veracruz!

Tearing his eyes from the source of his bemusement, Devon frowned into the horizon. He had been to Manga de Clavo before. There would certainly be no privacy for Morgana and himself to find there. He'd be lucky if he was able to see her other than at mealtimes. And, as if that wasn't bad enough, Morgana had informed him she was the niece of none other than General Manuel Escobar, the most stringent anti-Anglo-Texan of all Santa Anna's generals! With General Escobar in attendance, he would undoubtedly have an even more difficult job convincing Santa Anna to speak for Steve Austin's release; and he knew, sure as hell, that the general would keep his beautiful niece as far away as possible from his company. Damn it, all he needed was another day of "balances," and Aggie would be flat on her back and Morgana would be in his arms. Maybe then the fire in his blood would cool and he would be able to devote his thoughts to more important matters. As it was now, he daren't even touch her, and he was pretty near wild with the need. Especially when she looked at him the way she was looking at him now.

Unable to stand the subtle torture any longer, Devon pushed himself from the rail, making an attempt at a casual tone as he said loudly enough for Aggie's sharp ears, "I could use a little exercise, Morgana. What do you say to a brisk walk around the deck?"

Absurdly grateful for the opportunity to be out of Aggie's sight for a few minutes, Morgana brightened, her smile deepening the small dimple that winked in her cheek as she took his arm. "Yes, I'd like that, Devon."

And I'd like much more than that, his mind echoed in return as the touch of Morgana's hand on his arm set off a new series of charges shooting through his already tortured body.

Almost breathless at the pace Devon began as they started

around the deck under Aggie's watchful eye, Morgana shot him a puzzled glance. Practically running to keep up with his long-legged stride, she began tentatively as they turned the corner away from Aggie's keen sight, "Devon, please slow down. It's very difficult for me to keep up with . . ."

But she did not have the opportunity to finish her plea as Devon turned to pull her behind the cover of some water-proofed cargo before taking her into his arms in a great hungry swoop. There was no sweet persuasion in the mouth that met and covered hers, hungrily seeking to make up for the hours suffered in frustration. His lips were hot, searing, burning into hers with a fire that consumed any thoughts she might have entertained even briefly of denying him. Aware only of the seeking quest of his mouth, Morgana was once again caught up in a careening world of searing sensation. The broad palms against her body stoked the fire to a blazing inferno, forcing her closer and closer to the heat she craved. Her arms wrapped tightly around his neck as he strained her against the long, lean length of him. Her heart thundering in her ears, Morgana allowed the plunder of her mouth, reveling in the glory of emotions sweeping her higher and higher into a world of which she had only had a brief, rapturous glimpse. She could not get close enough to the strong maleness that pressed so tightly against her, could not get enough of the hands that moved up her back to clamp tightly on the bright chestnut curls, almost causing her pain in their overwhelming desire to possess her completely. She was soaring, moving high in the realm of burning awareness and need when she was suddenly jerked back to earth as Devon tore his mouth abruptly from hers, his body stiffening. A small inadvertent groan issuing from her throat at the suddenness of her deprivation, she saw the flash of pain in Devon's eyes the moment before he whispered, "Someone's comin'."

Slipping her arm quickly through his, Devon stepped forward to continue the stroll they had started only minutes before. Turning to look down at Morgana, he saw tears sparkling in the long, dark lashes dropped cautiously over the great russet orbs, and he gently squeezed the hand that

75

clutched his arm so tightly. God, he wanted her. . . . He needed a storm . . . a good, rolling storm. . . .

A low groan echoed lightly in her dreams, causing a jarring note she could not quite rationalize even in that vague nether world. The second groan brought her blinking from her sleep to a cabin that was flooded with the grey light of morning. There was no sun coming through the porthole, and the floor was rocking in a familiar dipping pattern that signaled the advent of rough weather. Sitting up abruptly, Morgana felt a surge of conscience as Aggie's low moan cut into her momentary elation. "Morgana, you're a selfish wretch," she mumbled under her breath as she scrambled from her upper bunk to look at Aggie's rapidly whitening face.

"Has the weather gotten to your stomach again, Aggie?" Feeling very much the hypocrite as she waited sympathetically for her answer, Morgana soon realized Aggie was not even up to a vocal response. Making a last valiant attempt to convince Aggie of a fact that had forcefully been brought home to her only a few days before, she offered hesitantly, "I told you, Aggie. The only effective treatment for seasickness is a full stomach. If you eat something light, you'll forestall some of this discomfort."

A slight rolling of her eyes was Aggie's only response to Morgana's suggestion. Morgana shrugged helplessly. Well, she had done her best, and she knew from the experience of the past month that there was little else she could do for Aggie other than ready the bucket and leave her to her misery. Slightly ashamed of the lightness rapidly overcoming her senses, Morgana turned to the washstand and prepared her toilette. Her heart beating rapidly, she splashed cold water on her face and dried it carefully before continuing her meticulous ablutions. Somehow it was important that she look especially nice today.

Realizing by the low tone of her breathing that Aggie had again fallen off to sleep, Morgana walked quietly to the corner where she had hung her yellow gown the day before. It had been folded in her case since the inception of the voyage and she had been worried that the creases would mar the simple lines of the dress, forcing her to wear one of the three cottons she had been alternating during that time. But no! The heavy humidity of the climate had worked its magic again, leaving the dress practically wrinkle free overnight! Feeling her spirits lift, Morgana slipped into a fresh chemise and stockings and anxiously pulled the bright garment over her head. Moving quickly back to the mirror on the washstand, she grimaced at the dark stain that partially distorted her reflection. Today would undoubtedly be their last day aboard the *Estrellita,* and although she was truly sorry for Aggie's discomfort, she was immensely glad Devon and she would be able to spend some time away from her watchful eyes.

A heady chill moving up her spine, Morgana flushed at the reminder of Devon's aborted kiss the day before. Telling herself she merely wanted an opportunity for some uninhibited conversation, Morgana began brushing furiously at the long chestnut locks that hung over her shoulders. Damn! The humidity had done its work again! Curls, curls, curls! A great admirer of the smooth hairdos that were the fashion, she had found since experiencing the heavy tropical air that she had to content herself with the gleaming tangle of curling spirals that were her lot in life. How she despised the springing chestnut curls that reflected back from the dingy mirrored surface. They gave her such a hopelessly frivolous appearance and robbed her face of the maturity she tried so endlessly to reflect. After all, she was eighteen years old . . . a woman, but one more swipe of the brush convinced her that she would have to find some other way to reflect the image she sought as her stubborn hair refused to do more than spring back into its original glistening coils. Finally losing all patience, Morgana parted it in the center and swept the gleaming mass up and away from her face with several combs, allowing her hair the latitude to behave in the manner that suited it best. She had learned that any attempt to confine it only ended up in coiffuric disaster. Moving carefully to the bunk, Morgana slipped into her soft leather slippers and came back for one last check before the mottled glass.

Damn! How could she appraise her appearance effectively when the glass gave her the look of a distorted monster! Trying desperately to adjust her position so she might see herself in the unstained portion of the mirror, Morgana leaned forward. So upset was she by the gleaming spirals bobbing at her neck that she was oblivious to the marvelous planes of the face reflected therein, the smooth, flawless complexion, the perfect cameolike profile; the delicate, but determined chin that bespoke inherent stubbornness. Instead, she viewed herself with a severely critical eye. The demure neckline of her gown rested comfortably on her gently sloping shoulders, framing them in a sheer white pelerine edged with a fine lace. Hanging low over a frilled half sleeve, the floating ruffle added a grace of movement to the simple dress that pleased her immensely. Her eyes followed the close-fitting bodice to a minute waist encircled with a wide white ribbon sash. Backing up, she attempted to follow the graceful gathered skirt to the floor, where it was edged with a wide white satin ribbon, but she was thwarted once again by the vastly inadequate size of her glass. Staring almost disconsolately at her mirrored image, she sighed at the certainty of fabric limp without the support of a stiffly starched petticoat, but she had not been able to find a suitable undergarment in the poorly organized traveling boxes stacked in the corner of their small cabin.

Steeped in disappointment at not being able to achieve the image she sought, Morgana failed to take into account the startling contrast of her curling chestnut spirals against the brilliant yellow of her gown. Nor did she note that the vibrant color reflected the sparks of floating gold in her enchanting doe-shaped eyes, to lend a glow to a naturally magnificent countenance that was close to breathtaking. Aware that the gown was an extremely good fit, having been made to her specific measurements, she was surprisingly unaware that the simple lines made the most of a deceptively fragile bone structure, cupping the soft curves of her shoulders with ultimate grace, exposing the smooth column of her throat and just enough of her slender, graceful arms to allow a glimpse of their unerring appeal. A bit embarrassed by the rise of her breast ever so modestly exposed in her decolletage, she attempted to adjust the neckline to allow more modesty, finally giving up when her twisting and pulling had availed her nothing but discomfort.

Turning in an attempt to see the rear of her gown, Morgana groaned her realization that the attempt was an exercise in frustration. With a soft sigh she turned to the door, secretly hoping Devon would see the more positive aspects of her appearance before he noticed its faults. Not stopping to question her need to appear especially pleasing to Devon's eyes this last day aboard, Morgana took one last look at Aggie's sleeping face, and, moving quietly to the door, stepped into the passageway.

Moving as quickly to the staircase as the dip and sway of the deck would allow, Morgana climbed the steps, her first glimpse of the overcast day lending a surprising lightness to her mood. The angry crack of the sails overhead rent the air as the strong gusts of warm, heavy air molded the fine fabric of her gown against her slender figure revealingly, but, unmindful of all but her rising spirits, Morgana made her way carefully to the rail. Thankful she had not wasted her time in an elaborate coiffure that would have already been a shambles, she looked into the grey horizon. Rough whitecaps slapped angrily at the *Estrellita's* sides as she rose and plunged relentlessly forward, and Morgana realized from the position of the well-concealed sun that, despite the rough waters, the wind was blowing them briskly in a direct path toward Veracruz. They would indeed arrive tomorrow at their present rate. Startled at the somber feelings that thought evoked, Morgana wondered at her own contrariness.

Turning unseeing eyes from the dull horizon at the sound of approaching footsteps, Morgana smiled in spontaneous welcome at the man who dominated her thoughts. Watching as he approached, his harsh, unsmiling countenance softening into a slow, sensuous smile that sent her heart to racing, she flushed at the thought that Aggie had never told her that the warm glow of azure eyes could cause a strange breathlessness that left her weak and uncertain, despite the strict, clinical observations of her mind. Aggie had never told her what she should do now. . . .

In his casual attire Devon's innate sensuality was even more disturbing. The white broadcloth shirt, open at the neck, contrasted vividly with the deepening brown of his skin. His casual posture and slow effortless stride were immensely deceiving, masking a powerful, driving force at which it only hinted. Steeling herself against the trembling his sweeping glance evoked, she dismissed her ineffectual attempt at clinical observance.

The last light of day had waned from a sky still overcast and threatening. Leaning casually at the rail, Devon watched the play of emotions across Morgana's expressive face as Juan Alverez, the *Estrellita's* most talented sailor, spun his inevitable tales of peasants and kings, knights and princesses and damsels in distress. Having spent the first few days of the voyage as a spectator to Juan's frequent entertainment of the crew, Devon had inadvertently mentioned Juan's unusual storytelling ability to Morgana. Quite contrary to his own preferences, he had found himself consenting to accompany Morgana to the informal session, and here he stood, frustration welling even deeper inside than it had with the buffer of Aggie's presence.

The entire day that had begun so promisingly had been fraught with frustration. Awakening to a badly rocking ship, he had been instantly grateful to a kind fate that had seen fit to allow him one last opportunity to purge Morgana Pierce from his system in the only possible way. He had promised himself that he would allow no interruptions to thwart him this time . . . would allow no excuses. But in truth, he had not expected Morgana's resistance to be too difficult to overcome. His own driving fascination with Morgana was echoed too clearly in her eyes. She wanted him as much as he wanted her, and if he did not miss his guess, a lifetime of always having her desires gratified by permissive, wealthy parents had set the perfect groundwork. Obviously brought up a child who was indulged and cosseted, she was now a woman who would expect the same from her adult experiences in life. And yes, he had determined to indulge her . . . to her heart's and his content . . . until he managed to free his mind of the sweet perfection of her face, the sultry doe-shaped eyes sparked with gold, and the full, ripe mouth that haunted his dreams.

But now, a long ten hours later on the final day remaining on their voyage, he was no closer to fulfillment than in the early morning hours. Suspicion had begun to put his temper on edge. Was Aggie's physical condition truly so dire that Morgana's frequent trips below were prompted by necessity, or were they prompted simply by a desire on Morgana's part to prolong the game while teasing his emotions to the break-ing point? He was certain only of one thing. He was past the point of reasoning with his driving desire for her. He needed to possess Morgana Pierce completely, to sate his body in the only way remaining to him. He needed it for his peace of mind, before he would be able to oust her completely from his thoughts. His mission was too important . . . the conse-quences of failure too dire. The fate and lives of too many rested on his ability to maneuver the wily Santa Anna to his way of thinking, and he would not be able to accomplish his job with Morgana Pierce haunting his thoughts. Yes, it would be tonight . . . he would have her tonight. . . .

Recognizing the familiar pattern in Juan's colorful recita-tion, Devon moved a step closer behind Morgana where she stood on the outside of the circle formed around the small, unobtrusive sailor. Slipping his arm around her waist, he drew her back against the hard length of him, repeating into her ear the words Juan had spoken in conclusion: "To each person there is a place in time, unforseeable, inescapable, or-dained by God, fulfilled by man. Destiny . . ."

Suddenly certain that the wizened old sailor had spoken those words expressly for them, Devon curled his palm around Morgana's cheek, turning her face to his until their eyes met. He saw the confirmation he sought in the glance slowly lifted to his. Sliding his arm around her shoulder, he turned her toward him, urging her from the group. Walking with undisguised haste, he waited only until a deep shadow

81

afforded them the anonymity he desired before taking her quickly into his arms. Oh, yes, this was what he wanted . . . what he had waited for since his first waking moment this day. Oh, God, Morgana . . .

The old man's poetic words echoing in her mind, Morgana turned full into the strong arms closing around her. Yes, surely this was her place in time . . . their place. She could no more fight this inevitability than she could keep the sun from rising. The demanding mouth that covered hers was hungry, seeking, devouring with an insatiability that echoed her own. A low groan escaping her throat, she abandoned the warm moistness of her mouth to his plundering tongue, allowing the deep ripples of pleasure to sweep her senses. His breathing labored, Devon tore his mouth from hers to crush her pliant form against his burgeoning maleness as he trailed heated kisses to the fragile shell of her ear. Sharing the tremor that shook his strong body as he tasted the ear warmly, Morgana moaned again, the soft sound provoking a new heat in his loving assault. The passionate nips on her throat and shoulders became more intense; the hand that sought the wonder of her errant curls tightened painfully, drawing back her head to expose more clearly the graceful column of her throat and the gleaming swells beneath that heaved with emotion. But it was a sweet, loving pain, endured with heightening passion as the wide, calloused palm slipped from the silken locks to warmly trail the column of her throat, her gleaming shoulder, finding at last the rounded curves of her breast. Gasping at his first intimate touch, Morgana's lids then dropped languorously as he found the blossoming crest, fondling it erotically with his thumb to transport her past conscious thought to a world where searing sensation ruled her mind.

His broad hand still caressing the mounds of her breasts, he covered her mouth with his again, coaxing, loving, draining the last remaining shreds of resistance from her aching, tortured body. Reluctantly tearing his mouth from hers, he mumbled softly through the light, fleeting kisses he spread across her fluttering lashes, the throbbing pulse at her temple, the velvet softness of her cheek.

"This isn't enough for me, Morgana, or for you. We need to be alone, darlin' . . . in our own little world. Let me take you there . . . let me take you there now . . . will you come with me, Morgana?"

Uncertain what he would do if she refused him, Devon watched as the heavy fan of lashes lifted from her cheeks. The glittering flecks of gold in their depths reflected the pale light of the rising moon as she looked directly into his eyes, her lips moving slowly to emit a soft whisper.

"Yes, Devon, I'll come with you."

Exultation flushing his body, Devon cupped the smooth, beautiful face in his hands, hesitating only a moment to drink in her beauty before covering her love-bruised lips with his own. Releasing her only seconds later, he enclosed her small, trembling hand in his broad palm and silently pulled her along beside him.

Her eyes on Devon's broad back as he led her firmly down the staircase to the berth deck, Morgana felt only the slightest twinge when he opened the door to his cabin and gently took her inside. The light of the full moon streaming through the single porthole held Devon in a shadow that eliminated the familiarity of the warm eyes that caressed her, the tender curve of his mouth. Suddenly the man who held her in his arms was no longer Devon but a faceless shadow, and Morgana stiffened with fear.

Sensing her anxiety, Devon pulled her close against him, the tenderness in the deep tone of his drawl against her cheek stilling the mindless fear that had begun to take possession of her senses.

"Don't be afraid, sweet. We're here, where we both want to be . . . together . . ."

The soothing tone healed. The mouth that covered hers gently worked magic on her senses, caressing her trembling lips until they clung to the precious warmth, responding with a growing need of their own. Pulling her flush against the full length of him, Devon slid his hand leisurely down her back, cupping her firm buttocks with his hand to hold her close against the growing heat of his passion.

With breathtaking abruptness, Morgana was scooped up

high against Devon's broad, heaving chest, only to be lowered again moments later against the firm surface of the bunk. There was no time for realization or regrets. The surface of the bunk dipped with Devon's weight as he lowered himself beside her. Turning himself on his side, Devon pulled her toward him until her face was even with his on the pillow. Slipping his arm around her, conscious of her trembling, he held her close against him as he ran his tongue lightly across her parted lips. The answering quake deep inside her stirring a deep tenderness for the beautiful woman in his arms, Devon whispered hoarsely, "I love the taste of you, Morgana. You taste sweet . . . better than anythin' I've ever known in my life."

Running the tip of his tongue across her cheek, Devon fondled the delicate hollows of her ear, dipping and tasting until Morgana groaned with the pleasure assailing her senses. Taking the small lobe between his lips, he sucked it gently, aware that a new level of trembling had begun inside the woman he held so tightly in his arms.

Sliding his mouth along the line of her chin, Devon trailed the slender column of her throat, the curving line of her shoulder, the hand that held her pressed tight against him working the buttons on the back of her bodice until it was freed of her slender form. Releasing her slightly, he slipped the dress from her shoulders and lowered the delicate chemise to expose the full, rounded globes of her breasts to his view. Firm and white, the tender flesh gleamed in the slender thread of moonlight moving through the porthole, stealing his breath with their perfection. Pressing her gently to her back, Devon adjusted his position until his long, hard body lay atop hers. Raising himself on his elbows, he stopped to indulge himself . . . to bask in her beauty.

Slowly removing the confining combs from her hair, he spread the silken mass across the pillow, his voice low and shaken as he whispered in the silence, "I love your hair, Morgana. It's so soft . . . warm . . . it curls around my hand with a life of its own . . . just the way you've curled yourself around my heart. . . ." Lowering his head, he pressed light, fleeting kisses on the silken strands. His lips following the course of his muted ramblings, he continued softly, "And I love your eyes . . . the way you look at me . . . I love your nose and its sweet insolence . . . and, God . . ." his voice breaking, he continued in a low, muttered gasp, "I love your mouth . . ."

Breathless with the wonder of his lovemaking, Morgana surrendered herself to the myriad of sensations assaulting her senses. Abandoning herself to his searing, probing kiss, she moaned in protest against his temporary abandonment, drawing in a quick breath as he continued the line of his heady assault in a direct, searing path to her breasts. Tangling her fingers in the cool weight of his hair, she held him against her as his tongue tasted the gleaming swells, traveling the soft, virgin flesh, skirting the round, pink aureoles that invited his kiss. Kissing, tasting, loving, he circled the waiting crests, withholding his ultimate caress until she was mad with longing. Abruptly, the tender clinging mouth covered the aching bud of her breasts, enclosing it in its warmth, drawing tightly again and again from its beauty, until she was ablaze with the delirious emotions accosting her senses.

"Devon . . . please . . ." Gasping to catch her breath, her heart thundering in her ears, Morgana struggled to speak. "Please, Devon, I can stand no more. . . ."

Lifting himself to his knees, Devon roughly stripped off his shirt, the tremor in his voice bespeaking the depth of his passion as he lowered himself against her once again. "But there is more, darlin' . . . so much more I want to give you . . . and for you to give me . . . so much more . . ."

Devon's kiss seared her mouth once again, the tightly curling hairs on his chest brushing the tortured flesh of her breasts, teasing her to new heights of passionate splendor. Wrapping her arms tightly around Devon's neck, Morgana moved her soft palms along the line of his shoulders, delighting in the feel of his rippling muscles beneath her hand, smoothing and caressing, indulging herself as she familiarized her touch with the strongly muscled shoulders and back she had so longed to touch the first time the brawny strength of him had been bared to her view.

But he was moving away from her again, taking his mouth from hers. She didn't want him to leave her, even for a moment . . . but suddenly a new, delicious sensation had assumed control, tearing her mind from her deprivation as the broad, knowing hands stripped away her dress, tossing it into the darkness beside the bunk. Within a few seconds the wisp of her chemise fell away as well. Suddenly realizing her body was totally bared to his eyes, Morgana felt a moment of sharp discomfort as she searched to ascertain his expression in the dim light of the small cabin. Beginning to tremble as he kneeled motionlessly above her, Morgana raised her hand to his face, her fingers tracing the lines on his cheeks, the curve of his mouth. Was he smiling . . . frowning . . . were his eyes still the soft azure that touched her heart with their warmth?

Turning his mouth into the palm of her hand, Devon kissed it warmly, holding it against his lips for a few moments longer as he whispered raggedly, "You are so beautiful, Morgana . . . more beautiful than I believed in my wildest dreams." Releasing her hand, he placed his own hands on her shoulders, his fingers suddenly splaying wide as he moved them in a wide, sweeping caresses across her breasts, the slender width of her ribs, over her stomach and the rounded curves of her hips. His fingers finally finding and tightening in the shining triangle of dark chestnut curls, he moaned softly, the low, throaty sound sending a tremor over her already shaken body as he whispered, "I've wanted this for so long, Morgana. Our time is so short. I had begun to think . . ."

The slamming of the door farther down the corridor jerked Devon into silence, the voices moving gradually up the passageway stiffening him to attention.

"I do thank you, Captain Moreno. You may rest assured I will post a letter to your superiors relating your graciousness during this voyage. Now that the sea has calmed, I do appreciate the opportunity to take some fresh air into my lungs. I may even join Morgana. She tells me you have an excellent storyteller among your crew and I am always anxious to experience the native tales of different countries. We Scots have many legends of our own which are passed on from generation . . ."

Aggie's distinctive burr was beginning to fade from their hearing when Morgana moved for the first time. Scrambling to be freed from the imprisoning weight of Devon's body, she exclaimed in a panic-stricken voice. "Devon, please, let me up! I must not be found here. If Aggie knew . . . if someone were to find out . . ."

"No!" Rough hands clamping down on her shoulders held her fast against the surface of the bed. "No, not this time, Morgana! You won't leave me again this time!"

Startled by the agitation in Devon's voice, Morgana exclaimed softly, "Be reasonable, Devon! I can't be found here! My reputation . . . We can be together again some other time . . . when we reach Manga de Clavo."

"There will be no 'other time,' Morgana. I expect to be in Manga de Clavo for no more than a few days, at most. Since you seem to be ignorant of conditions in a Spanish household, you will be surprised to learn you will be strictly supervised . . . not allowed the freedoms you are obviously accustomed to. . . ."

A coldness beginning to replace the warmth that had enveloped her senses, Morgana listened to Devon's harsh recitation with startled disbelief. Was this the same man who moments before had been speaking tender words of love . . . loving her?

Her voice choking in her throat, Morgana whispered hoarsely, "Do you mean . . . are you telling me that our time together, our 'destiny' was to be merely a stolen few minutes . . . that you intended all along to leave . . . that it meant nothing more to you than . . ."

Her voice trailing off, Morgana was suddenly grateful for the semidarkness of the room that hid the flaming color of her face as shame filled her being. So she meant nothing to Devon after all . . . nothing more than a fleeting physical attraction that would be satisfied with one night of meaningless passion. And she had thought . . . she had hoped . . .

Suffused with a heated rage, Morgana pushed hard at the broad shoulders bent over her, a deep shame at her nakedness bringing a coldness to her voice as she demanded in a low tone, "Let me up!"

"No, not this time, Morgana! You're not goin' to get away with this again! You're not goin' to run out and leave me. . . ."

"I said let me up, damn you!" Sheer power of will controlling the tears that had sprung into her eyes, Morgana hissed, "Do you think I care about your petty frustrations? It is *my* reputation that concerns me! It is *my* reputation that will be damaged, *my* future that will be ruined if I'm discovered here in your cabin! Any chance for a successful marriage would be destroyed, while you would merely be given a pat on the shoulder and congratulated on your masculine prowess! And tell me, Devon," her whisper dropped to a new, scathing low, "Does it really matter that much to you . . . aside from a slight bruising of your ego? We will doubtless dock tomorrow. Even if you are frustrated this night, it will not be difficult to find another woman on whom to slake your passions. In truth, does it really make a difference to you if it is she or I?" Driven by a raging desire to deliver a cutting blow to his masculine pride so he might suffer a portion of the pain that wracked her being, Morgana added venomously, "And you may rest assured I'll also find someone to sate the primitive instincts you've aroused in me . . . despite the watchful conditions in a Spanish household! I'm a very capable person, Devon. But next time I'll be discerning enough to choose a man on the same level of society as that into which I am entering, not an ignorant Texan with the instincts and finesse of a rutting bull!"

Her senses keenly attuned to the reactions of the man whose body hovered so intimately close to hers, Morgana felt the stiffening of his frame at her words. She experienced for the first time a true rush of fear at the coldness in the voice that stated flatly in return, "There's no need for either of us to go searchin' for satisfaction, Morgana. I'm perfectly adept at providin' a quick conclusion to this night's work. . . ."

A blinding flash of rage overcame her senses as Devon coldly began to work at the closure on his trousers while attempting to separate her thighs with his knee. A whore! He thinks of me as a whore to be used and satisfied . . . nothing more!

Responding instinctively to the thoughts that demeaned her so shamefully, Morgana raised her hand to bring it crashing against his cheek with all her strength. The force of the blow snapped Devon's head to the side, echoing in the small cabin. Her breast heaving in agitation, Morgana watched him slowly turn back toward her once again and in a slow, calculated movement, raise his broad palm to deliver a stinging blow to her cheek in return.

Getting quickly to his feet beside the bunk without a word, he grasped her by the shoulder and jerked her to a standing position. His contemptuous sneer clearly visible in the semidarkness, he grated harshly, "Get dressed, bitch!" Bending down, he snatched her gown from the darkness of the floor and threw it against her naked body. "We must save your reputation so you may catch yourself a wealthy husband, mustn't we, Mistress Pierce!"

Watching as she struggled into her gown, Devon laughed softly in a sound devoid of mirth. Waiting until she had managed to close the buttons on the back of her dress, he bent to pull her flimsy chemise from the shadowed floor. Tossing it against her as she struggled to slip into her slippers, he taunted heartlessly, "You must try to remember not to leave your undergarments behind, Mistress Pierce. It could prove to be very embarrassing."

Grabbing her roughly by the arm, Devon pulled her the few steps to the door. His voice a low, angry growl, he gripped her tightly by the shoulders, forcing her to meet the cold fury reflected in his expression.

"Now I'll repeat what I told you one time before. Stay away from me, you teasin' little bitch! Stay far away, because the next time I won't allow my baser instincts to be governed by contempt!"

Jerking open the door, Devon pushed her outside unceremoniously, scorn clearly visible in his eyes as he slammed the door in her face.

Thoroughly humiliated, her cheek still smarting from his blow, Morgana walked quickly in the direction of her cabin.

Releasing her breath only after she had closed the door softly behind her, she realized she still clutched her wrinkled chemise in her hand. Feeling the heat of tears under her lids, she threw it to the bunk in disgust. Never! Never again would she give Devon Howard or any man the opportunity to humiliate her like that! Abruptly realizing that she must arrange to be abed before Aggie returned, she hastened to unbutton the dress she had buttoned only minutes before. She was in no mood for Aggie's questions. No, she had already determined that she would put tonight from her mind . . . forget it . . . strike it and the despicable Devon Howard from her thoughts . . . if she was able. . . .

CHAPTER THREE

The first silver shaft of dawn had yielded to the golden light of morning, illuminating the interior of the diligence that bumped and swayed steadily along the road toward Manga de Clavo. Having arisen by candlelight at two o'clock that morning, the traveling party of three had wearily boarded the awkward carriage drawn by an extremely unlikely team of mules, and begun their journey. Firmly refusing to allow her eyes to touch, even briefly, on the tall Texan who sprawled dozing on the seat across from her, Morgana was nonetheless acutely aware of his presence. Having shed his coat and hat in deference to the rising heat of morning, he was clad in shirt sleeves, the fine lawn unbuttoned casually at the neck, exposing the tanned column of his throat and a trace of the rough mat of dark hair that peppered his chest. How well she remembered the warmth of his throat against her lips when he had held her close; the thrilling sensation of that dark mat of hair moving against her bared breasts. She knew, even without looking, that the thick, stubby lashes were resting against the sharply chiseled line of his cheekbone. His face in repose, however, was devoid of the harshness that wakefulness brought to his features. She also vividly remembered the complete transformation wrought on those stern features with the slow magic of his smile. His blatant masculinity was omnipotent within the small confines of the diligence, wreaking havoc on her senses.

No! She would not think anymore!

Shooting a quick glance to the seat beside her, Morgana felt a sharp twinge of impatience. Aggie was dozing also! Was it only she who found the jolt and jar of the diligence too great a discomfort to permit sleep? Or was it merely the tension of being forced to share close traveling accommodations with Devon Howard that had unnerved her? Not a word had been spoken between them since their last heated encounter in his cabin two days before, and despite her desire to put the entire incident from her mind, the pain of her disillusionment remained strong within her. She had managed to fend off Aggie's persistent inquiries as to her whereabouts when she had awakened the morning following the shattering incident in Devon's cabin. She had ignored the piercing, owlish perusal, fully realizing that Aggie would note the hostility between Devon and herself and would draw her own conclusions. Well, it was just as well. The whole horrendous journey would soon be over, and within a few days Devon Howard would no longer be present to agitate her peace of mind.

The day before, Morgana had gotten her first glimpse of Veracruz in all its ugliness as it had loomed on the horizon. A more melancholy and forlorn sight she had not considered possible! The fort of San Juan de Ulúa with its black and red walls on one side, and the miserable, black-looking city of Veracruz on the other, they had sailed into the harbor, witness to a huge flock of *zopilotes* hovering heavily over the city, while another feasted visibly on rotting carrion on the outskirts. To the sides and the rear, completely surrounding the city, huge hills of red sand loomed barren and uninviting.

They had left through the gates of that city several hours before, ploughing their way through the very same barren hills of sand she had seen from the ship, enroute to Manga de Clavo. Hours later, the landscape had gradually begun to show signs of change. Vegetation had begun to appear; occasional palm trees and flowers showing beside the road. By the time they had reached the small Indian village of Santa Fe, the light had broken through, and they had appeared to have been suddenly transported, as if by enchantment, from a desert to a colorful garden! A picturesque tapestry had greeted their eyes: small huts of bamboo, roofs thatched with palm leaves; Indian women with long black hair standing at the doors with their little half-naked children; mules rolling themselves on the ground in their favorite fashion; snow-white goats browsing amongst the palm trees. The air had been soft and balmy in the fresh breath of morning, the dew-drops still glittering on the broad leaves of the banana and palm trees, and all around, silent, cool stillness. The huts had been poor, but clean, and, having procured some tumblers of milk, they had changed mules and continued their journey.

Gradually they had reached a countryside where there were no longer hills of sand but land that was fertile and flat, with an abundance of trees and flowers that were silent testimony to the good soil.

It could not be much longer now. Surely Manga de Clavo was not much farther. She would not have to bear the humiliation of Devon Howard's presence and his obvious disregard for the intimacy they had almost shared. Yes, surely it could not be much longer.

Raising an exploratory hand to her hair, Morgana patted her carefully arranged coiffure, her first tentative touch confirming her suspicions. The irritating curls had again escaped their confines to hang in clinging spirals at her neck and forehead, in a familiar appearance of deshabille that Morgana had begun to think was her norm. Groaning inwardly, she let out a small sigh. She had so wanted to present a sober, mature appearance to the aunt and uncle who had not seen her since childhood. Touching the straw bonnet at her side, she nodded lightly. Yes, she would again present the appearance she sought when the sedate bonnet covered her errant curls. She had been most careful in selecting her apparel, hoping to make the best impression possible on Tía Isabella, Tío Manuel and President Santa Anna. Her stomach knotting tightly, she realized the extreme peril of the situation she had entered into so trustingly that last night on the

Estrellita. Had she been discovered, she would have put her aunt and uncle in a very unfavorable light, as well as left her reputation in shreds. Blinking back the heat of tears, Morgana absent-mindedly smoothed the soft silk of her skirt, and straightened her posture as she adjusted the demure rounded décolletage so that it sat more squarely on her shoulders. A pale beige in color, the gown was trimmed with dark brown ribbon at the neck and around the ruffled three-quarter-length sleeves. It was cut in a line that followed her slender form tightly to the waist, flaring to her ankles, where it was trimmed around the hem in wide white lace. A narrow row of the same white lace edged her neckline to lie gracefully against the barest hint of white swells beneath. Yes, she was certain she presented the serious, adult appearance she sought, and she hoped desperately that her discomfort at the presence of the man dozing so easily across from her was not apparent. Closing her eyes for the briefest second as she struggled with her inner resolve, Morgana then turned her head resolutely to the side and directed her gaze and thoughts to the landscape.

Watching covertly from beneath slitted lids as Morgana turned her glance to the countryside moving past the carriage window, Devon felt a familiar tightening in the pit of his stomach that he had begun to associate solely with his reaction to Morgana Pierce. Damn the little bitch! She was still capable of tying him up in knots! For the first time in his life he was incapable of understanding his own reaction to a woman. Woman! That was a vast misstatement! Morgana Pierce was little more than a selfish child who played at being a woman! And knowing that full well, he was still incapable of putting her from his mind. Eating voraciously at his insides was the realization that Morgana had adjusted perfectly to the change in their association, seeming to have the power to drive from her mind at will the spontaneous passion he had felt in her response.

His eyes traced the perfect cameo of her profile etched against the growing brilliance of the landscape, and Devon subdued the rage that simmered just below his surface calm. But his rage was directed at himself . . . at his own susceptibility to the slender young woman seated across from him. Damn! What was it about Morgana Pierce that affected him so violently? He had known many beautiful women before; a few more beautiful than she. No . . . that was not quite true. He had known women with more flamboyance . . . more glittering appeal, but he had never known a woman with greater perfection of feature than Morgana. He had never felt skin as soft and smooth as hers, had never touched hair as lustrously soft . . . silken . . . had never seen a mouth more appealing, had never known a woman who fit more perfectly in his arms. And the scent of her skin . . . the taste of her . . . they were still strong in his mind, despite his most stringent attempts to rid himself of the memory. He remembered vividly the feel of her slenderness lying beneath him. She was so small . . . fragile . . .

A new tension entering his mind, he acknowledged silently that she would do very well in Mexico. In a country of dark-haired, dark-skinned women, Morgana would instantly draw the eye. He had no doubt that once her position in society was established, she would have her choice of men from amongst the most eligible Mexico had to offer. And, knowing her as well as he did now, he realized she would play them well. Had she not told him with her own lips that she intended to choose a man from a higher level of society than he in her next romantic endeavor? Well, he pitied the man who finally took that selfish witch to wife! A woman like her would be utterly useless on the frontier. A real Texan woman would put her to shame . . . would show her up as the shallow, self-centered bitch she truly was withing a minute! Morgana Pierce was a useless China doll who would be physically incapable of functioning without the convenience and luxury in which she was raised, those luxuries that were doubtless necessities to her now. She was nothing more than a beautiful shell of a woman. He knew that well . . . he had no illusions about Morgana Pierce. So, damn it all to hell, why did he still want her so badly?

Uncertain whether the heavy hammering of her heart was

due to expectation or apprehension, Morgana attempted to still the trembling of her hands as the carriage drew to a halt at Manga de Clavo. The renowned hacienda of the president of Mexico was startling to her eye in its simplicity and lack of pretension. A sprawling, graceful building one story high, it was whitewashed a clean, bright white that was appealing in the lushness of its surroundings. The tile roof and window boxes ablaze with riotous blossoms beneath finely grilled windows were the only sparks of color enlivening its almost sterile appearance. Moving her gaze around the immediate area, she saw a picturesque stone wall about thirty feet away, approximately five feet high, with graceful arched gates that permitted entrance to what appeared to be a combination pasture and orchard, where fruit trees of many types lent their fragrance to the spring morning. Behind that area were long, low outbuildings that obviously housed the mechanics of the peaceful hacienda, which grew more lovely to her with each intriguing glimpse.

The heavy clumping of booted feet turned her attention from perusal of her surroundings to the group of three men approaching the diligence. One, a man in uniform, obviously an aide-de-camp, judging from his cool, almost clerical appearance, approached the carriage in a quick step, a polite smile of welcome forming on his pale, olive-skinned face.

Pulling open the door to the carriage without hesitation, he exclaimed in a well-modulated voice, "Señorita Pierce, I am Lieutenant Amante, aide to General Escobar. *Bienvenidas* a Manga de Clavo!" Extending his hand, he helped her graciously from the diligence as the two men at his sides hastened to unload the luggage. "General *y* Señora Escobar await you in the sala." Turning his attention to Aggie, whose stern presence loomed in the doorway of the carriage behind her, he extended his smile and a helping hand. "And Señorita MacWhorter, welcome." His professional smile not dimming in the slightest, the well-trained soldier waited until the tall Texan had touched down on the ground behind the two women before he repeated his greeting. "And Señor Howard, welcome. Presidente Santa Anna has been awaiting your arrival with great interest."

Graciously acknowledging their return greetings, the efficient soldier led the visitors in a quick step up the four wide front steps and through the broad tiled entrance of the hacienda. Ushering them into a large, cool, uncarpeted room with little furniture, he smiled, turning at the sound of a quick step from the hallway.

Tears springing into her eyes, Morgana spied the small, petite figure of Tía Isabella hastening toward her. Still slender as a girl, her dark hair only lightly touched with grey, her pleasant face was creased in a brilliant smile of welcome that warmed Morgana's heart. Moving quickly into the arms held out to her, Morgana could do no more for a few emotional moments than nod her response to the softly lilting voice in her ear, "Morgana . . . *querida mía, bienvenidas!*"

Gently extricating herself from her aunt's loving embrace, Morgana stepped back, swallowing tightly against the lump in her throat as she mumbled almost inaudibly., "*Grácias . . . grácias,* Tía Isabella." Her eyes moving immediately to the grey-haired stately man who stood a few feet away watching the exchange with a soft smile, his strict military bearing attesting years of service to his country more clearly than the vastly decorated uniform he wore, Morgana took an unhesitant step forward into her uncle's warm embrace.

Whispering a few choked words in response to her uncle's brief, sincere welcome, Morgana stepped back to notice for the first time the lithe, athletically built man who had entered the room immediately behind her aunt and uncle. Turning from his sober greeting of Devon Howard, he awaited an introduction, a gleam of interest lighting his handsome, Latin face.

Eyes streaming with unembarrassed tears, Tía Isabella slid her slender arm around Morgana's narrow waist, her voice bearing a distinctly proud inflection as she said brightly, "This, Antonio, this lovely young woman you see here, is my niece, Morgana Pierce. To you, Morgana, I should like to present *el Presidente de Méjico*, Antonio Lopez de Santa Anna."

Morgana was startled, hardly able to hide her surprise at the appearance of the man before her. Certainly he was too

97

young . . . far too young to be the man of whom she had heard such varied, vastly contradictory stories! This man had spent more years in service of his country than she had lived, and yet he looked not of an age that could have allowed such a personal history! He was tall, surprisingly so for his race of people. The figure he presented was that of an actively healthy man with an athletic build void of even the slightest trace of spare flesh. His hair was a true black; his eyes large, equally black, set in a pale face only lightly lined by the years. He had a rather melancholy countenance at first glance, and she thought that he could easily have been mistaken for a scholar or philosopher in genteel retirement, until he spoke. His voice possessed a marvelously modulated tone, which Morgana could easily imagine capable of charming diplomatically and of inspiring intense loyalty.

Taking her hand, he raised it gracefully to his lips, his smile warm as he responded gallantly, "It is my pleasure to meet you, Señorita Pierce. Isabella has been speaking of no one but you for the past three days, and I must admit to wondering at the young woman who could incite such anticipation. My curiosity was almost as great as her eagerness, but I must concede that the reward is by far worth the wait."

Turning back to Tía Isabella with an air of pleasant concession, he responded softly, "Yes, Isabella, I do agree. Your niece is indeed a very lovely young woman."

Watching from his position a few feet away, Devon Howard felt his stomach churn with an emotion he dared not name. Yes, of course, the damned wily Mexican was delighted to meet Morgana! He had never lost his taste for young women, despite his marriage of nine years' duration. His wife had been a mere fourteen years old when he had married her, hadn't she? Fourteen to his thirty-one years . . . Snorting inwardly at the thought, Devon felt the heat of anger rise inside him. Santa Anna professed great respect for his wife, Doña Ines. Yes, he supposed Santa Anna should respect the woman who had come to him with a dowry of six thousand pesos from a Spanish family of considerable renown, who, while being considered a classic example of Veracruz womanhood, was still content to remain at his country retreat while he moved in the exciting circles of the country's capital, functioning in various official capacities, the most prestigious of which was as its president. The poor woman, she . . .

His eyes snapping to the doorway behind the softly conversing group, Devon noted the entrance of the tall, thin woman about whom he had been thinking. Walking directly toward her, he offered politely, "Doña Ines, it is a pleasure to see you once again. It is good of you to have me in your home."

Her stiff expression loosening only slightly, Doña Ines responded uneasily, "Señor Howard, *bienvenidas*. My husband's friends and associates are always welcome at Manga de Clavo."

His wife's discomfort unnoticed, Santa Anna turned to take her hand, drawing her to stand beside him as he spoke, "Ines, you have finally finished dressing! Let me introduce you to our lovely house guest, Señorita Morgana Pierce and her chaperone, Señorita MacWhorter. Dear ladies, may I present Señora Ines Garcia Lopez de Santa Anna."

Acknowledging the introduction with a polite smile, Morgana was hard pressed to contain her amazement for the second time that morning. The second of two surprises, Señora de Santa Anna's appearance was equally startling as her husband's, but for a different reason. Tall, far too thin for her height, Señora Santa Anna could not, even with great generosity, be called attractive. She was indeed homely! Her pale coloring was bland, fading into insignificance, her face lean, surprisingly lined. Her features were not particularly irregular or displeasing, but they blended somehow to a total that was just short of ugly. She was dressed in a short white dress trimmed with a blond fichu, white stockings, and white satin shoes, the sum of which created the impression of a lifeless, unappealing woman, next to whom the handsome vibrant man standing beside her looked distressingly out of place. Managing a smile that she hoped did not reveal her thoughts, Morgana accepted the thin hand extended toward hers with a brief acknowledgment, noticing the huge diamond ring sparkling on Doña Ines's finger, and the other huge stones

99

that hung from the señora's ears and sparkled from a large brooch that rested on her flat bosom. But the high, thin voice that welcomed her was extremely civil, if a bit lacking in warmth, and, distressed at her own reaction to the woman who was to be her hostess for an undetermined length of time, Morgana made a stringent attempt to shake off her bewilderment. Her eyes moving inadvertently to the tall, dark figure standing just a fraction out of the way of the conversing group, Morgana noted that Devon's knowing glance moved between Señora Santa Anna and herself. The flash of contempt that crossed the hard features as his glance returned momentarily to meet hers sent a bright flush rising to her cheeks. Damn! Could the man read her mind? Did he know how lacking she had personally found the wife of Mexico's president, while finding Presidente Santa Anna so very impressive at the same time? Damn him! When was he leaving, anyway? She did not really believe she could bear his presence much longer!

Suddenly feeling a gentle pressure on her elbow, Morgana snapped her mind back to the conversation directed at her, catching it in midstream as her aunt continued lightly, ". . . and after you are finished, we will spend several hours together, just you and I, so you may tell me all that has progressed since dear Arnold's passing."

Realizing her aunt waited for her response, Morgana offered feebly, "I'm sorry, Tía Isabella. I'm afraid I did not hear . . ."

An expression of regret passed across her aunt's pleasant face. "No, it is I who must apologize, *querida*. In my happiness to see you once again, I completely overlooked the exhaustion both you and Aggie must be suffering after your long journey. And your voyage, it was exceedingly rough, was it not? You must have found the experience thoroughly disheartening."

Experiencing a flash of guilt at her aunt's concern, Morgana responded spontaneously, "No, Tía Isabella. Although Aggie suffered inordinately from the rough seas, I myself was unaffected. It is not that part of the voyage about which I feel the deepest regrets." Abruptly realizing her quiet sober statement had caught the attention of the others present, who waited for clarification of her statement, Morgana felt a flush of heat rising to her face. Stammering, she concluded lamely, "Rather . . . it . . . it was the extended duration of the voyage I found the most disconcerting, Tía Isabella. I am vastly relieved to be with you at last."

"No more relieved than we are to have you with us, Morgana. Come." Urging her toward the doorway, Tía Isabella continued warmly, "The gentlemen will excuse us now, and Ines and I will show you to your room."

Shooting a quick smile to the men, Morgana gratefully allowed herself to be led in the direction her aunt urged, her mind registering the brief flash in Devon's eyes the moment of their brief contact with hers. Yes . . . it is true, her mind whispered in response to their searing challenge as she walked out of the room, "I do most certainly have my regrets."

"But you see, my friend, I am not in a position to do our mutual friend, Colonel Austin, very much good at present. As I am sure you are aware, I surrendered my powers as president to Gómez Farías in December, and came here to Manga de Clavo for my health. Although I do maintain contact with the government in Mexico City, unfortunately, I have little to say about the present state of affairs in Mexico."

Hoping his complete mistrust of the man sitting across from him behind the wide mahogany desk was not reflected in his face, Devon sat back in the comfortable leather chair. Stopping to take a deep puff from the long, slender cigar that Antonio Santa Anna had lit for him only minutes before, he used the time to seek a carefully guarded response. He had been ushered into Santa Anna's study only a short time before and was acutely aware that the tone of this first meeting was extremely important . . . that he would have to tread lightly in order to manipulate the crafty Mexican into putting the weight of his position into Stephen Austin's release. When he spoke, his tone was low, reflecting the magnitude of

101

the situation he addressed. "I am aware of the state of affairs in your country now, Antonio, but I also know that you met with Stephen in November last year, just prior to surrendering your office, and at that time . . ."

"*Sí,* at that time I convoked a special meeting of ministers to consider the question of Texas's separation from the state of Coahuila and Texas. I believe you are aware of my thoughts on that subject, my friend. I believe I made them very clear. At that time I stated that I do not feel Texas is yet ready for separation, but I did acknowledge many of the grievances our friend Colonel Austin presented and took steps to correct them."

"Such as . . . ?"

"Such as my suggestion that the state government of Texas and Coahuila adopt measures of reform which would procure for its people the enjoyment of just rights in civil and criminal matters, an area that is sadly lacking now, I am informed. I made suggestions as to means to be employed for convenient administration of justice and the establishment of a jury system."

"There was another area, Antonio . . ."

"Yes, Devon, a matter of great concern to your Anglo colony, I understand." A small smile lighting his expressive face, Santa Anna continued benevolently, "I also abrogated Article Eleven, which prohibited the further colonization of Texas by Anglo-Americans."

A light frown slipping over Devon's hard features, he considered the man in front of him with a skepticism that was reflected in his expression. "Well, if that is so, Antonio, if Steve's petitions were handled in such a satisfactory manner and Stephen and the council parted so amicably, then why was he arrested in Saltillo on the way home?"

"Ah, my friend, that is the crux of the matter, the area that has left me in some confusion. As I told you, in December of last year, just a few weeks after meeting with Colonel Austin, I turned the government over to Gómez Farías, and from that point on explanations for the course of events become less than clear in my mind. According to communications I have received from Gómez, prior to our meeting in

November of last year, Colonel Austin dispatched a letter to the city government of San Antonio de Bejar in which he recommended that that municipality lose no time in communicating with all the other corporations of Texas, and exhorted them to concur in the organization of a local government, independent of Coahuila, even if our general government should refuse its consent. My dear friend,'' Santa Anna's expressive eyes demanded his concurrence, ''that written statement was certainly treasonable in tone, and sufficient to cause Colonel Austin's arrest.''

''But surely you realize, Antonio, the frustration Colonel Austin had suffered, havin' presented his petition to the council in July, and not havin' received any communication with regard to the matter by October, despite the stringent pressin' of his claims. Your meetin' in November satisfied his protests . . . you must have been aware of his gratification with the outcome of the meetin'.''

''Yes, of course, Devon. But I'm afraid I was not in a position to dispute the decision of the acting president of Mexico without full knowledge of the events.''

''But now, Antonio, now you are aware . . .''

''Not entirely, Devon. I have only a general knowledge. I have not read the official reports with regard to Colonel Austin's arrest. . . .''

''. . . and imprisonment under extremely stringent circumstances, sir. I have reliable information which states Colonel Austin is bein' held in the dungeon of the old inquisition buildin' in close confinement. He isn't allowed to communicate with anyone, or permitted the use of books or writin' materials. Surely, Antonio, this treatment is not befittin' a man whose loyalty to the Mexican government until this questionable episode was unblemished. He was often criticized in the Anglo-American community for his motto, of which I am sure you are acquainted, 'Fidelity to Mexico and opposition to violent men or measures.' Certainly these new charges are contradictory to the disposition of a man who at times was vilified for bein' 'too Mexican' in sympathies.''

''Please, my friend, say no more. I am unable to respond to your statements. I am ignorant of the official proceedings in the matter.'' Noting the flush of anger that suffused Devon Howard's face at his statement, Santa Anna continued placatingly, ''But since Colonel Austin's case does seem to bear severe contradictions, I will attempt to settle the matter to both your and my satisfaction. But you must be patient, my friend. It will involve prolonging your stay at Manga de Clavo for several days . . . perhaps more, until I may dispatch a communication to Mexico City and am able to receive one in return. Will the delay inconvenience you, Devon?''

Truly uncertain whether the flash of relief that rushed across his senses was entirely related to Santa Anna's promise to promptly investigate the matter of Austin's arrest or to the mere fact that his stay at Manga de Clavo was extended by necessity, Devon responded noncommittally, ''I am anxious to see Colonel Austin free to return to Texas, Antonio. I do not consider time spent in pursuit of justice an inconvenience.''

''Well spoken, Devon.'' Rising to his feet, Santa Anna came around the desk to stand beside him. Reaching up, he clamped Devon familiarly by the shoulder before continuing amicably, ''And now if you will allow me time to prepare a communication, I will have it ready by morning.'' His dark eyes shining with sincerity, he continued quietly, ''I, too, am interested in seeing justice served.''

Nodding in response to his request, Devon turned wordlessly on his heel, and within a few moments the door of the study clicked closed behind him.

The benevolent smile dropping from his lips as the study door closed behind Devon Howard, Santa Anna's countenance at once set in a frown of concentration. A ticklish situation that needed to be handled with extreme care. Armed with the knowledge that Devon Howard did not possess the distinctly gullible personality of his compatriot, Colonel Stephen Austin, he made the immediate decision to handle this man carefully. For surely, he could not afford to have his plans go astray now, when everything was going so well.

A small smile returning to his full, well-shaped mouth, Santa Anna congratulated himself mentally on the success of his plans. If there was one thing that could be said of him, it was that he was flexible. Having assumed the presidency as a liberal, he had been immediately aware of the reaction of the people to the policies of reform. Early in his term as president, liberal policies had proceeded to strip power from the military, and from the Church, and the grumblings had begun to swell to a roar. Sensitive to the first low mutterings of protest, he had surrendered his office of president until he "might regain his health," and had sat back as Gómez Farías put the reforms into action. Absolved from blame for the unpopular measures instituted by his vice president at his secret request, he observed the progress of events from Manga de Clavo, and, quite according to plan, was the recipient of ardent pleas to return to the office of president so he might still the alarm and confusion within his country. But he had ascertained that the time was not yet right. He would hold his ground a little longer. He needed more time to conclude his strategy with the conservative element within the government. Having been in constant contact with the military and the clergy since his retirement to Manga de Clavo, he was certain of their support, but he needed yet a bit more time to elapse until the country would be in a position to accept him in the status in which he wished to return to Mexico City. Simple presidential powers would not suit him this time. He had long since determined that when he returned to Mexico City the next time, he would return with dictatorial powers.

With regard to the enigmatic Texan who had just left his study . . . well, he would have to handle the man with care. Colonel Austin's incarceration played an important part in his plans for the control of the disgruntled Anglo-Americans in the state of Texas and Coahuila. He had been aware of the grumblings within the colony for a long time. Colonel Austin's unfortunate letter had come to Gómez's attention at an opportune time, and he was very aware of the power Austin's incarceration gave the central government. Certainly the Anglo-American contingent would dare no adverse moves while the fate of Colonel Stephen Austin, the founder of the

Anglo-American colony, lay in the balance. Yes, the sincere but gullible Colonel Austin was an extremely potent hostage for the good conduct of the Anglo-Americans, but he dared not allow his strategy to become too apparent to the perceptive Devon Howard. Yes, he would have to institute some action to satisfy the man while delaying him a little longer. All he needed was a little more time. . . .

And he was confident the task would not be too difficult. In the interim he intended to fully enjoy the time remaining at Manga de Clavo. The arrival of Manuel Escobar's niece certainly added an intriguing spice to a stay that had begun to bore him. He had begun to tire of his vigorous daily rides and the testing of his fine stable of horses that had so stimulated him early after his arrival at Manga de Clavo. He had even begun to find a seed of disenchantment with his fighting cocks, of which he was extremely proud. As for his wife, yes, Ines was a capable, honest woman who had brought great honor to his name. She managed his estate frugally and was extremely devoted to him. It was unfortunate that she was deficient in physical beauty and that her confidence had been so severely affected. But he had come to terms with the fact that Ines would never shine in the capital because of her self-consciousness among the haughty, condescending dames of that society. Well, if she was content to spend her time working at Manga de Clavo, he was also content with the situation that allowed him time to indulge himself in any manner he sought, as long as he was discreet.

His mind returning, as it had many times since her arrival, to the image of the lovely Morgana Pierce, he moved to the buffet and poured himself a small glass of wine. Sipping it slowly, he felt the stirring of a familiar emotion. Yes, she was indeed a beautiful young woman. Her shade of hair was quite unusual, a sort of chestnut brown that gleamed with red highlights, but far more appealing were the wide, sparkling eyes that glowed with peculiarly startling golden sparks. Her complexion was flawless, like white porcelain, and her features were fine to a point of perfection. But most beguiling of all was the softly curving mouth, which was certainly made for a man's kiss.

She obviously found him as intriguing as he found her. He had become accustomed to his effect on women, but he was nonetheless gratified that this particular young woman was not immune to his appeal. Yes, he expected that he would fully enjoy the remainder of his stay at Manga de Clavo, and was also content in the realization that when the time came for him to leave, his close associate, General Manuel Escobar, would travel with him. And with Manuel would travel his entire entourage, which now included the vivacious Morgana Pierce. Yes, his future looked to be decidedly brighter with each passing minute.

Careful to keep her voice low as she worked vigorously to fasten the buttons on the back of Morgana's dress, Aggie repeated in a tone with which Morgana was all too familiar, ''I do not see where you can afford to indulge your likes or dislikes at this point, Morgana. Whatever your feelings, or the *cause* for your feelings about Mr. Howard, it is essential that you treat him in the same manner as you do any other man in this household.''

Morgana's slender lips tightened stubbornly. She was in no mood for Aggie's sermon. Having been introduced to her quarters at Manga de Clavo upon arrival, Morgana had spent several hours with Tía Isabella while the concerned, patient woman had carefully extracted from her all the painful details of her father's death and his penniless state of affairs. The stirring of those distressing memories had left Morgana physically depleted, and even Tía Isabella's fervent reassurances that her future was now secure had done little to restore her spirits. Noting her exhaustion, Tía Isabella had insisted that she take a short nap, and, abruptly anxious to be alone, Morgana had consented without protest.

Now, after having spent several restless hours tossing and turning on her surprisingly comfortable bed, she was preparing for dinner, only to be beset by Aggie's unwelcome instructions concerning her behavior.

Turning slowly to face Aggie's unrelenting gaze when the

last button had been secured, Morgana lost the battle with her self-control and returned sharply, "Please, Aggie, don't bother me with your petty concerns. I do not see where this particular matter is any of your business in the first place! But in any case, I will not . . ."

"But you *will* listen to me, Mistress Morgana Pierce!" Interrupting Morgana's cutting retort with startling vehemence, Aggie continued in a harsh whisper. "It was *your* choice, not mine, that we come to a backward country plagued with unrest! But now that you're here, and have consented to live in your Tía Isabella's household and to become a part of the family she presents to the world, you cannot afford to behave in a manner that will reflect poorly on her or on General Escobar! Your poor mother would turn over in her grave if you were to disgrace . . ."

"Disgrace! It is not a matter of disgrace if I choose not to speak to Devon Howard! It is merely a matter . . ."

"But that is where you are wrong, Morgana! We have had a long, arduous journey, the major portion of which was spent in Mr. Howard's company. Were you to display an aversion to his company at this date, you would leave yourself open to speculation as to the *cause* for your distaste."

Attempting to avoid the owlish stare fastened on her face, Morgana turned to look into the full-length glass in front of which she stood. Raising her hand to secure a few wisps already disengaged from her upswept coiffure, she mumbled almost inaudibly, "It is just that I find Mr. Howard lacking in the usual . . ."

"Morgana." Aggie's short, flat pronouncement of her name snapped Morgana's head in her direction, all pretense of inattention gone as Aggie continued solemnly, "I do not know what happened that last night on the *Estrellita* between you and Mr. Howard to turn you so adamantly against him. And," she continued, her words pronounced in a short, halting manner that effectively emphasized their meaning, "Neither do I care to know! You are a young woman now, and entitled to your privacy. I do not expect to intrude upon it. But what I do intend to do is fulfill my function to the best of my ability, and in order for me to do that, Morgana, you will have to take me at my word when I tell you that differential treatment of any kind toward Mr. Howard will only call attention to you. As General Escobar's niece you will be entering a close-knit society that is doubtless similar to societies of its type around the world, if only in one way. Its propensity to gossip! It would not do to give eager tongues something with which they may lay your reputation to waste!"

Flushing brightly at Aggie's last remark, Morgana turned her attention back to the mirror. Her intense scrutiny of her gown was a ruse that would not fool Aggie's discerning eye, but taking advantage of the time it allowed for consideration of a suitable response, Morgana fingered the white lace that edged her bare shoulders. When she raised her eyes at last, she looked directly into the intense perusal of the woman who awaited her response.

Striving for a casual tone, Morgana replied evenly, "Well, perhaps you're right, Aggie. An open display of my dislike for Devon Howard would only be a disservice to myself. At any rate, I do not believe Mr. Howard's stay will be overly long. His visit is, after all, purely a political matter which I do not expect will necessitate a prolonged stay. I expect I can control my distaste for the man for another day or so. It certainly is the least I can do for Tía Isabella. She is a dear woman who has formed elaborate plans for my introduction into society at the capital. Although I confess I entertain little interest in such matters at present, it is not my desire to cause her any discomfort or appear ungrateful for her efforts."

Moving her gaze to meet Aggie's concerned expression, she attempted a small smile. "As usual, you're right, Aggie. I yield to your wisdom once again. And now," her smile widening with an obvious attempt to change the subject, Morgana continued lightly, "do you think this gown will do tonight? I am anxious to create a favorable impression."

Obviously satisfied with Morgana's response, Aggie's eyes moved appraisingly the full length of her small frame. The gown in question was styled in a pale blue gauze, shimmering over an embroidered silk foundation of the same color. The close-fitting bodice edged the creamy skin of her shoulders in a narrow row of white lace, dipping slightly to

109

permit a tempting swell of bosom. The large gigot sleeves that ballooned extravagantly to the elbow ended gracefully in a broad ruffle edged with white lace, which swayed lightly with the motions of her slender arms. Nipping tightly at a waist curved to a deep point in the center, the splendid garment flared elegantly to narrow her ankles, where it was edged with the same white lace that adorned the bodice. Pale blue slippers complemented her gown. Her eyes flicking to Morgana's hair, Aggie silently approved the graceful upswept coiffure that made the most of her delicate cheekbones and wide, slanting eyes while still allowing the appealing tumble of glimmering chestnut curls to bob enticingly at her neck. From Morgana's ears dangled the small sapphires she had managed to retain despite the strict liquidation of her family's assets. A glittering matching pendant on a delicate silver chain lay against her breast, completing her attire.

Silently acknowledging with concealed pride that the young woman she had watched grow from child to woman was indeed captivating, her fragile beauty set off to perfection by the simple grace of the marvelous garment adorning her slender proportions, Aggie gave a small, characteristically unrevealing nod before ordering briskly, "Turn around, Morgana."

Turning quickly, Morgana presented her back to Aggie's measuring glance and waited impatiently as she fussed at the waistline of her gown. Realizing Aggie had completed her minute adjustment, she turned back to her thorough appraisal.

"Yes, you will do very nicely in that gown, Morgana. And since it is the hour designated as dinnertime, I suggest you make your appearance downstairs. It also will not do to arrive late for dinner your first evening as a houseguest."

Responding with exaggerated politeness, Morgana exclaimed, "Oh, then I shall have to hurry, shan't I?"

Ignoring the short, unladylike snort that escaped Aggie's lips, Morgana suppressed a smile and turned lightly on her heel toward the door. Her smile stiffening as trepidation began to assume control, Morgana walked into the hallway toward the sala. Despite her agreement with Aggie's observations, she knew it would be exceedingly difficult to acknowledge Devon Howard's presence civilly and maintain a casual conversation with him. She had made such a complete fool of herself with the man that she was mortified at the image of herself reflected in his knowing glance. In addition, her awareness that the deep attraction she felt for the damned Texan had not diminished despite his cruel treatment of her left her feeling extremely vulnerable . . . even more vulnerable when she witnessed how easily he handled the whole episode. Well, she supposed she was not the first woman he had lured to his room with unspoken promises and deeply stirring words that hinted at a deeper emotion than the outright lust that was his true motivation. Suppressing a twinge of something startlingly akin to jealousy at the thought, Morgana raised her head a bit higher and stepped into the hallway. She had been a naive fool, but she had learned her lesson. She would be damned before she would allow Devon Howard to know how deeply he had hurt her . . . how the pain of his betrayal pierced her still. Yes, she would be damned before she would let him know.

His eyes affixed intently on Antonio Santa Anna's face as the latter spoke enthusiastically of his plans for the future of his country, Devon Howard could not overcome his silent skepticism. Damn! How could anyone be taken in so completely by this man? He was a supreme egotist, certain that he and only he knew the best course for his country. Influencing his thinking very strongly, he was certain, was the course that was most beneficial to Antonio Lopez de Santa Anna! It was obvious that the man would discard any and all advice that did not concur with his own thinking, no matter the source. Moving his assessing glance to General Escobar's face, he saw there agreement with the policies espoused, admiration, and complete trust in Santa Anna's motives. The man was a fool, and the most rigidly anti Anglo-Texan he had ever met. It was obvious Escobar tolerated his presence only because it was Santa Anna's wish that he remain. Under any other circumstances, he was certain General Escobar would not hesitate to brand him a troublemaker and a traitor and toss him into the same jail as Stephen Austin, if he had his way. Yes, he was undoubtedly on very uncertain ground here at Manga de Clavo, and he needed to tread lightly, very lightly.

Returning his gaze to the vibrant countenance of Antonio Santa Anna, Devon had to concede he could not fault the man for his superior presence. Even speaking here, in the confines of his sparsely furnished living room as they awaited the arrival of Isabella Escobar and her "niece," he managed to reflect a solid appearance that was uniquely Mexican, a combination of the manners and charm of old Spain and the drive and ruthlessness of the revolutionary. Devon was totally cognizant that the eyes that were now softly lit with idealistic visions of glory for his country, could change unexpectedly to reveal . . .

But Santa Anna had stopped talking and had turned abruptly to the entrance of the room, a revealing emotion flashing in his dark, expressive eyes the moment before he strode toward the two women who stood in the doorway. His fingers tightening dangerously on the fragile stem of his wineglass, Devon watched silently as Santa Anna greeted Isabella Escobar warmly, his eyes, however, only for the breathtaking picture Morgana presented as she stood beside her aunt. Almost overwhelmed by the flood of a strangely heated emotion, Devon followed Santa Anna's actions with tight control as he drew Morgana's hand to his lips.

Damn her! Damn that spoiled little bitch with the face of an angel! Damn that Morgana Pierce! She reveled in Santa Anna's attentions! And for the life of him, he could not understand how it was possible, after the long, grueling journey they had made and the ungodly hour at which they had arisen that very same morning, that she could look so lovely—could sparkle with the selfless, innocent allure that turned him weak inside! Hell, if Santa Anna himself had not taken the initiative to walk forward and take her hand, he might have been stupid enough to have attempted the very same thing . . . just so he might bask again in the glory of her smile. Retaining his implacable facade with distinct difficulty, Devon silently berated his own susceptibility to the little beauty who now smiled and dimpled her response to the attention Santa Anna showered upon her. Yes, the little bitch would do well in this society, which lavishly pampered its women, expecting little more from them in the long run than well-mannered children and complete fidelity. The last thought hitting a jarring note, Devon felt a small tremor move down his spine. Yes, perhaps Morgana Pierce was incapable of that last accomplishment, also. She was doubtless a passionate little witch. He had felt the deep, innate response that shook her body at his lovemaking. Gratingly, he admitted to himself he had never experienced an emotion as deeply soul-shaking as the undefinable feeling Morgana elicited within him. And, damn his own idiocy, he had to admit to the fact that his emotions were still as deeply involved with her as they had been before that last evening on the *Estrellita*.

A burning anger mounting inside him, Devon watched Morgana's immediate and total absorption into the group awaiting her. General Escobar and Doña Isabella smiled at their lovely niece like doting parents, while Santa Anna flattered her in his own unique manner, managing to maintain propriety while still expressing his deep admiration for the beautiful American who would be the new addition to his capital society. Even Doña Ines showed a trace of true warmth in her stiff features. Evidently Morgana had managed to insinuate herself into the woman's affections on the basis of the short time they had spent with her aunt in her quarters earlier that afternoon. Only he possessed the capacity for adding a jarring note to the pleasant scene Morgana had maneuvered so well, and he'd be damned if he wouldn't take advantage of it.

Approaching Morgana with a meaningful smile on his lips, Devon interrupted the buzz of pleasant conversation.

"Good evening, Doña Isabella . . . Morgana. You are both looking very well this evening." Doña Isabella's soft, lilting response was immediate. Acknowledging the woman's graciousness, Devon found his eyes fastening on Morgana

113

with great anticipation of the discomfort that would be reflected in the eyes raising to his.

Intensely aware of Devon's presence from the moment of her entrance into the room, Morgana raised her eyes slowly to the tall Texan who stood at her side awaiting her response. Inwardly wincing at the tight, contemptuous curl to his lips visible to her alone as he faced her squarely, she held his gaze unflinchingly.

"Thank you, Devon. You seem to have weathered the journey very well, also. But I admit to being gratified that the journey is finally over and I am with my family at last. I must also concede I do not envy you your journey back to Texas. After traveling for such an extended period, I'm certain the prospect of another long journey does not seem too appealing."

"Oh, but I won't be leavin' as quickly as I anticipated, Morgana. Doña Ines and Antonio have graciously extended the courtesy of their hospitality until Antonio can send and receive a response to a communication important to the disposition of the matter we have been discussin'. So, you see, we won't be partin' company as soon as expected."

The spontaneous widening of her eyes providing the satisfaction he sought, Devon smiled, maintaining his silence until Morgana could manage a response. Yes, she had expected to be quickly rid of him so she might proceed unhampered by his presence. Shooting a quick glance to Antonio Santa Anna, Devon felt a hot, searing emotion cut his vitals. He would not put it past her to set her sights on Santa Anna himself! Doña Ines's preference for the country was well known, and Morgana had boasted to him that she would carefully choose her next lover from the best the society into which she would be entering had to offer. Knowing Antonio's reputation, he had no doubt that she could succeed famously in that endeavor. Well, he would see about that!

Precluding her effort at a response, Santa Anna reached forward to take Morgana's hand, clearly putting an end to the exchange between them. Smiling into Morgana's eyes, he continued quietly, "If you will honor me, Morgana, I will escort you in to dinner."

His smile broadening at Morgana's small nod of acquiescence, he then tucked the small hand under his arm, leaving Devon to offer Dona Ines his arm as they fell in behind them. Aware of Doña Isabella's bright chatter as she and General Escobar walked behind him, Devon made an attempt to concentrate on Doña Ines's quiet comments, his eyes only for the small beauty who walked so confidently on the arm of the president of Mexico . . . a place where she had obviously ascertained she wanted to be.

"Yes, Morgana, see . . . see how proudly he walks, his head high, strutting his confidence to the world. He is one of my best fighters, and an excellent specimen, don't you agree?"

His hand resting lightly on Morgana's shoulder, Santa Anna motioned toward one particular cage in the row of similar cages that lined the wall of the large house located to the side of the orchard. Having finished a sumptuous breakfast a few hours before, Morgana had accepted Santa Anna's invitation to tour his estate, not realizing her acceptance would subject her to several hours of the discomfort of walking between Santa Anna and Devon, genuinely interested in the explanatory comments of the former while trying desperately to ignore the presence of the latter. But for the most part, she had succeeded, Antonio's soft, melodious voice and compelling enthusiasm at everything that related to his lovely country retreat drawing her mind from her own situation. She had followed him through his richly laden orchard, the warm sun on her shoulders as it filtered through the leafy cover of trees and the supremely delicious scent of all that abounded delighting her senses. They had then progressed through Santa Anna's well-stocked stables, taking time to become acquainted with his favorite warhorse, a white charger that had borne his master through many of the battles that had earned him his fame. Having moved from there to the largest outhouse at the rear of the orchard, Morgana had been startled to see upon entering that the center of the immaculately clean building contained an unusual pit of sorts, around which was

115

constructed a low, wooden wall. Managing to contain her curiosity, she had withheld her questions until Santa Anna had led them to the rear wall, against which were numerous wooden cages, each inhabited by an aggressive-looking rooster. Startled that a man with the obvious refinement of Antonio Santa Anna found the dubious sport of cockfighting to his liking, and indeed seemed strongly committed to it, Morgana hesitated in her response. Her eyes moving assessingly over the brilliant red bird to which he referred, she conceded that he was not like any rooster she had ever seen before. His feathers were clipped in a manner that eliminated the grace in his movements and his comb was docked, affording him a strangely unnatural appearance. He eyed her in return with peculiarly hostile, observant eyes. She had to admit that he did indeed look the part of the gladiator of his species.

Realizing Antonio still awaited her response, she ventured hesitantly, "Yes, he does seem to be an unusual bird, Antonio." And then, with a candor that brought a small smile to the famous Latin's lips, she confessed, "But I must admit to being unfamiliar with the sport of cockfighting. I'm afraid my impressions are that it is a rather brutal sport, and one which I would not expect to enjoy watching."

Moving his hand to touch her chin lightly before dropping it to his side, Santa Anna replied softly, "Yes, it would seem so to one who is not aware of its history and does not possess the knowledge of its challenges." Turning back to Devon, he offered politely, "With your indulgence, Devon, I should like to take a few minutes to acquaint Morgana with some details of the sport."

Fully cognizant that Santa Anna's request was a mere formality, Devon gave a short nod. Managing to maintain a tight smile as the man's attention moved immediately back to the true focal point of all his words since the beginning of his endless tour, Devon groaned inwardly. How much longer would he be forced to endure this farce? The man was obviously extremely intrigued with the latest, if temporary, addition to his household. Had he not been following the two of them around for the better part of the morning, his stomach in tight knots while Santa Anna fawned idiotically over Morgana and she responded with a wide-eyed interest that kept his own temper at a violent edge? Anyone but a blind man could see that the famous Mexican was becoming more enraptured by the moment with Morgana and her diligent attention to his boringly detailed explanations of the workings of the estate. Santa Anna was also visibly impressed with the intelligent, pointed questions with which she responded, which demonstrated a surprising retention of the information he offered so proudly. The scheming little witch was not content to attract Santa Anna on merely one level . . . that of her physical beauty, which seemed to grow more formidable with every hour that passed, but was attempting to impress him with her mental abilities, as well.

His eyes wandering over the slight figure listening intently to Santa Anna's soft ramblings, he had to admit he had never seen her looking more beautiful than she looked at this moment. Despite himself, he felt an undeniable longing to touch the gleaming ringlets swept so casually back from her face and secured behind her ears with delicate combs. The fragile perfection of her features and the flawless, rose-tinted skin seemed more lovely than ever. Her wide, sun-flecked eyes glowed in the light of morning, clear and appealing; and her mouth . . . A deep shudder moving across his body, Devon was abruptly grateful that their conversation had not allowed Morgana and Santa Anna to witness his short lapse. Damn, he had never known a woman who stirred him more deeply. Perhaps it was the pale pink of the simple morning gown she wore that brought the color to her cheek and the fine cut of the garment that lent her the ultimate grace of movement with which she walked. Or perhaps it was just that Morgana was Morgana, naturally lovely and appealing in whatever setting she was displayed, despite the shallowness her beauty concealed. Whatever it was, Devon conceded silently, he needed to be careful, for she was fast gaining dangerous control over his senses. He could not afford this unprecedented vulnerability . . . not now, when so much was at stake.

"You see, *querida*, cockfighting is a sport which dates back to ancient China, India, Persia, and other Eastern countries. Themistocles was said to have exhibited a fight between cocks to his troops in ancient Greece, admonishing them to emulate their bravery. The Romans are credited with bringing the sport to Britain, where its popularity spread rapidly. These birds here, Morgana, are a special strain of game cock evolved from the basic Asian Bakiva strain through the Asil, which is noted for its pugnacity. This characteristic has been developed through the centuries by careful breeding of these roosters.''

"But surely, Antonio," a small frown tightening her brow, Morgana still appeared unconvinced, "these creatures are ill prepared for battle, despite their breeding."

"Ah, but that is where you are wrong, *querida*. These birds are athletes . . . fed special food, exercised, and trained for the sport in which they function. Before they enter the fighting pit they receive special exercises to develop and strengthen their muscles. Their skin is toughened by massage. Their feathers are trimmed and their combs cut to reduce it as a target for opposing birds. Since some roosters have longer spurs than others . . ." At Morgana's quizzical expression, Santa Anna explained patiently, "The spurs are the sharp spines on their legs which they use in fighting. We equalize the contest by slipping metal spurs over the natural spurs, and we are always careful to match the birds as to weight. Their period of training lasts for ten days or a fortnight before the date of the contest. Come see, querida.''

Drawing Morgana away toward the pit in the center of the structure, he continued softly, "The pits vary in size. This one here is about fourteen feet square, surrounded by a barrier so that the birds will not fall off. The cockfight, or 'main,' has very strict rules. Each cock has a handler or pitter. A referee is present to preside over the battle, and all decisions made by him are final. The mains consist of contests between an agreed number or pair of birds. Some last until one or the other cock is killed; some permit the handler to withdraw a badly hurt cock at any time; in others a time limit is fixed. Brave birds live to fight many times, *querida*, before they are retired to the brood yard. These brave birds you see against the walls are the survivors of many battles . . . warriors as well as athletes, and they give me great pleasure with

118

their valor."

Hesitating momentarily as his dark eyes moved slowly over Morgana's upturned face, Santa Anna concluded softly, "And I can also see that I have not convinced you of the value of cockfighting as a sport, Morgana."

Embarrassed that her thoughts could be so easily read in her expression, Morgana flushed a deep crimson, widening the smile on Santa Anna's face as she attempted falteringly, "I . . . I mean . . . well, it is not up to me to judge, Antonio. If a man of your obvious stature finds some merit in the contest and the preparation which goes into it, then . . . well . . . surely . . ."

Raising his hand once again to her cheek, Santa Anna touched the warm surface tenderly, a gleam in the dark, somber depths of his eyes as his voice dropped another notch until it was audible to her alone. "There is no need to explain yourself, *querida*. I should not have expected a woman of your gentle nature to find an interest in a contest such as the ones these brave birds provide. You are made for a much more subtle contest, *querida*, where the conflict may be just as intense, but the reward of victory proves as generous to the loser as to the victor."

Not quite certain as to the meaning of his words, Morgana's small frown of puzzlement was still on her face when Santa Anna turned at the sound of Devon's step behind him. "Ah, Devon! I apologize for abandoning you to your own amusement while I attempted to educate Morgana in the specifics of cockfighting. But it was to no avail, my friend. While Morgana remains unconvinced of its value, I am more convinced than ever that I am in her thrall. And since we are at a stalemate, I suggest that we retire to the hacienda so we may take some refreshment after our long, thirsty walk around . . ."

"Señor . . . ! Señor Santa Anna!"

Turning in midsentence in reaction to the urgency reflected in the high-pitched summons, Santa Anna frowned at the boy of eight or nine years who rushed to his side.

"Señor! Juan instructed me to find you as quickly as possible. There is an emergency in the stable, señor. Jefe Blanco

119

. . . he has been stricken with a breathlessness . . . Juan is uncertain what he should do.''

Concern obvious in his tense expression, Santa Anna turned back to Devon. ''If I may presume upon you to escort Morgana to the household, Devon, I should like to go directly to the stable. Jefe Blanco has been ailing for over a week. Aside from the fact that he is one of my best stud horses, I am extremely fond of him.''

''Of course, Antonio. We both understand, don't we, Morgana.'' Shooting a quick look to Morgana that contained a trace of sarcasm she preferred not to recognize, he continued quickly, ''I shall be happy to take care of Morgana. It has become a kind of second nature to me by now.''

The quiet sarcasm of Devon's tone escaping him in his anxiety, Santa Anna turned quickly to Morgana. ''*Con permiso*, Morgana.''

''*Sí*, Antonio.''

Watching motionlessly as Santa Anna's erect figure cleared the doorway, Morgana was abruptly aware that she and Devon were alone. A sudden rush of anxiety setting her hands to trembling, she attempted to hide her discomfort by clenching them tightly at her sides as she started wordlessly toward the doorway through which Santa Anna had just passed.

''What's your hurry, Morgana?''

A temper held under rigid control for two long hours suddenly erupted to the surface, giving Devon's simple question a harshly accusing tone. It had been madness to accept Santa Anna's invitation in the first place this morning, but the last few minutes . . . Santa Anna's gentle caress of Morgana's cheek . . . his words whispered so intimately into her eager ear . . . had almost pushed him over the edge. If that damned Latin had touched Morgana one more time . . .

Her emotions under tenuous control, Morgana turned with a small frown at the sound of his grating question. Her response was startlingly cool to her own ears. ''I'm not in a particular rush, Devon. It's just that this particular area of Antonio's estate doesn't hold much appeal for me. I would rather . . ."

With a few rapid strides Devon was breathtakingly close. His chest heaving from his suppressed fury that was slowly growing out of control, he interrupted in a low hiss, "Oh, is that so, Morgana? Just a few minutes ago I would've sworn you found this buildin' of incredible interest. Or at least, that's the impression you managed to convey to our friend, Antonio. And I'd bet my last dollar, Morgana, if Antonio was here with us now, you wouldn't be so damned anxious to leave!"

"If you're trying to say that I prefer Antonio's company to yours, Devon, then you're absolutely correct in your assumption!" The rise of her own anger removing the bond of caution from her words, Morgana continued in a heated rush, "Any woman would be a fool not to prefer the company of a distinguished, learned gentleman to that of an unmannered, uncivilized Texan who has no respect for a lady!"

"That's where you're wrong, Morgana. I have boundless respect for ladies. It's just that *you* don't happen to fall in that category, darlin'!"

Catching the small hand that flew in a flash toward his cheek, Devon held it in a crushing grip as he whispered harshly, "You don't have a very long memory, do you, darlin'. The last time you tried that, all it earned you was a slap in return. But if that's what you're wantin', just go ahead and try it again."

Her own breath coming in short, heaving gasps, Morgana fought to free her hand, finally submitting to the superior strength of the man as Devon used her imprisoned hand to pull her a few inches closer. "And while we're at it, darlin', let me tell you, you're wastin' your time with Santa Anna. Oh, he'll be happy to allow you to amuse him for a short time. The man has quite an eye for the ladies, as you must be aware, but this is a strict, Catholic country, Morgana. Antonio Santa Anna was married in church, and in the eyes of the law and the people he represents, he's married for life! His wife is held in high esteem in Mexico. The only name you can possibly hope to earn for yourself if you press with this

121

latest endeavor is that of whore!''

Aware only by the sudden stiffening of the small frame so close to his that Morgana had indeed heard his words, Devon awaited her reply. When it came, Morgana's voice was low, a burning hatred reflected in the gold-flecked eyes staring brightly into his.

"No, Devon. My actions with Antonio are only seen that way through your twisted view of what progressed here. In fact, it is only *you* who came close enough to putting that name to me . . . and I will never . . . never forget it, or forgive you!''

A low, contempt-filled laugh escaping his lips, Devon pulled her closer still. Intensely aware of the long, male length of him lightly pressed against her, Morgana attempted to maintain her rigid posture, her face flaming as Devon sensed her inner struggle.

"So, you'll never forgive me . . . or forget! But that doesn't stop you from wantin' me right now, does it, darlin'? You sure are flexible, aren't you, Morgana? Just a few minutes ago you were sendin' Santa Anna's blood up a notch with every glance you gave him! You knew just exactly what you were doin', didn't you? And now your hero walks out of the buildin' and your poor little weak body decides it'll settle for an ignorant, unmannered Texan in his place!''

Struggling against her rage, Morgana gasped tightly, "You flatter yourself, Devon. Whatever temporary appeal you held for me disappeared that last night on the *Estrellita* when you showed what you truly are!''

"Oh, is that so, sweet?'' His other hand snaking out to take the bright tumble of curls in a brutal grip, he held her face up to his, releasing her hand at last to pull her tight against the lean length of him. Lowering his head, he trailed his lips along the hollow of her cheek, his grip tightening painfully as she attempted to avoid the mouth that moved ever closer to hers. A deep trembling beginning inside her, Morgana felt the rise of panic. The soft caress of his lips against her skin was mesmerizing, sending a warm, fluid heat through her veins that threatened to dissipate the anger which was her only shield. Slowly the soft, caressing lips circled her mouth, pressing light, fleeting kisses on a gradually closing, teasing circle, until she was almost mindless with the conflict raging inside her. Going completely rigid at the first touch of his mouth to hers, she felt the light, exploratory brush of his tongue against her lips. Resisting stiffly for long minutes, she endured the warm, erotic strokes until, with a will of its own, her body submitted to its caress, her lips separating to allow the sweet, warm penetration. A low groan coming from her throat, she was crushed against the full length of him, her mouth surrendered completely to his advances, when Devon abruptly jerked himself away.

Held a full arm's length from him, Morgana felt the full impact of Devon's scathing gaze. The blood draining from her cheeks, she heard the scorn in his voice, felt the derision in his small, tight smile as he whispered, "So you'll never forgive me . . . you want no part of me . . ." His low snicker growing to a full-fledged laugh, Devon released her abruptly with an emphatic thrust that sent her staggering back weakly. "No, witch! It's I who want no part of you and your games!" Taking a few minutes to get his raging emotions under control, he hissed menacingly, "Just remember, darlin'. This time I was the one who walked away, not you! And remember somethin' else, too. You're an American, and everythin' you do in this country reflects on other Anglos. Keep your claws off Santa Anna! And I warn you now, if you cause a public scandal that in any way threatens my negotiations to free Stephen Austin, I won't hesitate to do anythin' I think necessary to get him free. . . ."

Barely able to speak with the humiliation and fury running riot over her senses, Morgana pulled herself stiffly erect, finally managing in return, "You make a mistake to threaten me, Devon. . . ."

His expression hardening at her response, Devon ordered sharply, "Shut up and pull yourself together, because in a few seconds we're goin' to do just exactly what you claim you want . . . get out of here! And I warn you . . . remember what I said or . . ."

* * *

123

". . . remember what I said, or . . ." Devon's words echoing dully in her mind, Morgana lifted her face to Antonio Santa Anna's pleased smile. Always the perfect host, he had apologized profusely for abandoning her the day before to attend to his ailing stallion. He had insisted that in order to compensate for his rudeness, she allow him to escort her for a morning ride over his estate, and, unable to refuse without causing more of a fuss than she wished, she had consented. But the price had been steep, for following at their side the entire morning had been a smiling, polite Devon Howard, whom she truly wished would fall off the face of the earth!

Abruptly realizing Antonio awaited her response, she flushed warmly, grateful for the diversion her restless horse provided as they stopped at the crest of a small hill. Finally getting her thoughts as well as her horse under control, she apologized lightly, "I'm sorry, Antonio. I was so enthralled by the view that I'm afraid my mind was wandering. What was it you asked?"

His pleasure at her response to the beauty of his estate obvious, Antonio repeated, "I said you sit a horse extremely well, Morgana. I admit to being pleasantly surprised at your skill. I was uncertain at first if Bonita would be the right horse for you. She has much spirit, but I can see you are up to her challenge."

"*Grácias,* Antonio." Grateful for his simple compliment in her state of weakened self-esteem, Morgana took a deep breath, determining at that moment to allow Devon Howard's presence to inhibit her no longer. That was exactly what he wanted, wasn't it? In his twisted mind he saw her as some sort of femme fatale out to capture the affections of Antonio Santa Anna. Cutting even more deeply than his poor opinion of her was the fact that his only objection lay in the damage she might cause his political suit! Well, damn him and his superior virtue! Damn him to hell! She would be herself and not allow herself to read his interpretations into Antonio's simple bid to make her feel welcome. Unfortunately, it seemed Devon Howard judged everyone by his own yardstick, and she would not allow his prejudices to affect her.

Taking a deep breath, Morgana allowed her eyes to move slowly over the magnificent scenery that met her eyes, willing away her discomfort. Suddenly she was aware of the reason why there were no formal gardens at Manga de Clavo. The explanation was simple. Antonio's entire estate, the full twelve leagues square of it, was a garden of profuse beauty and abundance. The air was warm and sweet, scented with the fruits of the heavily laden trees that abounded on the estate. Exotic blooms were visible at every step, adding their fragrance to the heady perfume that filled the air. Unusual, brilliantly colored vines wound themselves around the trees in breathtaking patterns of color and scent, flinging their blossoms in casual, dazzling display. The path they had traveled most of the morning was rough, the area vast, but Morgana had delighted in the opportunity to ride again. She had not been on horseback since her father's death, which had necessitated the liquidation of their stables. But she was extremely grateful that she had not disposed of her riding habit. In deference to the heat of the morning, she had abandoned the jacket, which dated the garment as last year's style, and worn only the white, ruched shirtwaist atop the full-cut waterproof skirt of deep forest green. The comfortable tricot drawers held in place by a strap over the instep of her boots were an essential part of the costume, allowing her complete ease while mounted. Leaning forward, she absent-mindedly patted the gleaming neck of her horse. The fine black mare, which she estimated to be approximately three years old, was sensitive to her command, balking only when she attempted to hold her inactive for too long a period of time.

She had not expected Mexico would be such a beautiful country, and she was certain she would have been enjoying the experience far more fully were it not for the presence of the all but silent Texan at her side.

Moving her eyes with determination back to Santa Anna, Morgana felt again the quiet authority the man exuded. Even the manner in which he sat his magnificent white stallion, his high Mexican saddle ornamented liberally with

125

silver, his attire conservative, bespoke a silent sense of command as he moved serene eyes over his vast, impressive holdings. And startling her even more was the appearance of health and vigor he presented, despite the fact that he was indeed at Manga de Clavo and absent from his duties as president of Mexico because of ill health. Well, if she was any judge, he would soon be back at work at the capital, and she would soon be ensconced in her new home there, and away from the nagging presence of the silent man riding at her other side.

Why was it that her thoughts always seemed to return to Devon Howard? He had been all but invisible on the ride this morning. Appearing content to allow Antonio to do most of the talking, his casual smile had stiffened only during the few short instances when Antonio had drawn up beside her to acquaint her more clearly with a particular portion of his estate. Angry that his comments of the day before had cast a pall on the spontaneity of her responses, she had turned to Antonio with a bit more enthusiasm than his comments had warranted, and, while delighting Antonio, she had felt a peculiar satisfaction in Devon's discomfort. Yes, the bastard! Even if the intrigue was in his own mind, she would let him suffer his doubts about her intentions. It was her only vehicle for revenge.

For certainly Antonio was extremely devoted to Doña Ines. It was apparent in his concern and treatment of her . . . his deference to her in almost every area of household preference. He spoke nothing but praise for his wife's conduct of the affairs of their estate during his frequent absences in the capital, and she had no doubt in her mind that Antonio would be utterly delighted if Doña Ines would consent to accompany him back to Mexico City when his period of recuperation was at an end.

But she doubted that Doña Ines would consent. In the short time she had been in the pleasant woman's company, she had sensed the feeling of inadequacy that apparently kept her from capital society. She was too self-effacing . . . unassuming . . . and if capital society was anything like the pretentious society she had left in New York, which she sus-

pected it was, it was a jungle of haughty whispers and condescending criticisms against which a confident expression and
manner were the only shields. No, Doña Ines would not
stand a chance. With a soft, inner sigh, Morgana admitted to
herself that she was reluctant to embark on a trial of that sort
again herself, but she owed Tía Isabella complete compliance
with her requests.

Yes, she would allow Devon Howard to suffer his own suspicions. They were unfounded, but she had already determined she would use them as a weapon against him. Devon
Howard's stay would not be a restful one . . . not if she had
anything to say about it! She would allow him to believe his
precious mission was in jeopardy if that was what he preferred to believe. And, if only in that way, she would make
him pay. . . .

The effort to maintain a casual facade was becoming painful. Certain that the small smile he had pasted on his mouth
at the inception of the ride this morning was now a ragged
grimace, Devon pretended to find considerable interest in
the distant mountains. He was also certain that Santa Anna
had not noticed his discomfort. It was all to obvious that the
only point of continuing concern in Santa Anna's mind was
Morgana. And how was it, he attempted to reason in silent
bemusement, that a man who had been sent on an important
political mission by his native state of Texas had been reduced to playing the role of chaperone?

Darting a quick, silent glance toward Morgana, Devon felt
the sharp prick of the same nameless emotion that continually plagued him in her presence. Ignoring his warnings of
the day before, she continued to pander to Santa Anna's
pride, insinuating herself even more firmly into the famous
Mexican's esteem. And, watching her flaunting her young
beauty in a seemingly innocuous fashion, he was certain she
had also managed to raise the man's physical awareness of
her to the point where it was becoming critical.

It was a matter of wonderment to him that Dona Isabella
and General Escobar had not attempted to restrain their

niece in any way. Was it only he who was aware of the danger of the situation? Was it only he who realized . . . who knew Morgana for the self-seeking, spoiled young woman she really was? Did she really have them all fooled so completely?

But he need be patient for only a short time longer. Each of the two mornings since their arrival at Manga de Clavo, he had seen an early messenger arrive at the estate. Ushered without delay to Santa Anna's office, the messenger had, each time, departed within an hour with the same urgency with which he had come. Devon was well aware that there had not been time for a response to an inquiry about Stephen Austin's case. No, doubtless the urgent messages were related to the growing unrest in the capital. Santa Anna had been absent from his office for a period of four months, during which time Gómez Farías had stringently instituted reforms consistent with the liberal program both he and Santa Anna had openly espoused. It had been a widely accepted fact that the congress wished to abolish conservatism and the army-clerical-landlord system of control. Just the year before, the clergy had been notified not to deal with political matters from their pulpits; government enforcement of the collection of church tithes was suspended; members of monasteries and nunneries were authorized, if not actually encouraged, to forswear their vows and reenter secular life. The missions on the frontier in the Californias had been secularized, the funds confiscated, and the lands distributed to the natives or thrown open to settlement. To complete the liberal reforms, a reduction in the size of the army had been determined, and a policy of moderation adopted in the distribution of military promotions and commissions. The result of the attempted modification of the two powerful elements of the society had been their consolidation in propaganda for "Religion and Rights."

And now, not quite a year later, when the full force of the reform was being felt and opposition was high, Santa Anna was safely "recuperating" at Manga de Clavo, amusing himself with the latest addition to his household.

The sound of rapid hoofbeats pulling him from his

thoughts, Devon turned to see an anxious young man urging his laboring horse to even greater speed as he came across the flat stretch of land immediately below them. His caution assuming control, the young fellow reined his horse to a prudent speed as he negotiated the difficult path that led toward them. His eyes darting toward Santa Anna, Devon saw the dark concentration on the enigmatic Mexican's face as he, also, followed the fellow's advance. His eyes moving to Morgana, Devon felt an angry stab in the pit of his stomach. Her own eyes fixed on Santa Anna revealed an expression of admiration . . . almost reverence. Realizing for the first time that the admiration she professed might actually be real, Devon's anxiety developed a new dimension. No—he was forgetting himself . . . he was forgetting Morgana . . . the self-centered little bitch was interested solely in her own amusement and advancement. No, he must not allow himself to slip into the trap of thinking her sincere. That would be fatal.

Recognizing the young stable hand as he drew closer, Devon could feel his tension building as the fellow urged his horse to Santa Anna's side.

"*Que pasa,* Juan?" Santa Anna's quick question released a stream of rapid Spanish from the young man that was momentarily beyond Devon's comprehension. Quickly tuning his ear to the hurried colloquialisms, he caught the conversation in midstream.

". . . have arrived from the capital, señor! They say their business is urgent! They must not be delayed a moment longer in their mission, and they urged Señora Santa Anna to locate you immediately. *La* Señora makes them welcome as I speak to you now, and urges you to return as quickly as possible."

Startled by the fleeting satisfaction reflected in his dark Latin features the second before Santa Anna turned away from the hard-breathing Juan, Devon watched conciliatory softness replace the revealing emotion as he turned to speak to Morgana.

"Ah, Morgana, once again I must beg your forgiveness for aborting our very pleasant excursion. But you must see that a very urgent matter demands my presence at the hacienda. Therefore," hesitating, Santa Anna turned his attention toward Devon for concurrence, "if Devon will consent to escort you back once again, I will extend my apologies and a promise to atone for my unforgivable behavior in leaving you for a second time in deference to duty."

Anger nudging his senses as Morgana's expression clearly reflected her regret, Devon listened silently to her understanding "Of course, Antonio."

Echoing Morgana's response in answer to Santa Anna's inquiring glance, Devon watched motionlessly as Santa Anna moved his horse immediately to the narrow trail, negotiating it rapidly with the skill of an expert horseman. He had no doubt in his mind that an incident of particular consequence had happened. Unless he missed his guess, the men who inspired such anxiety on the part of Dona Ines and such immediate response from Santa Anna would not have ventured so openly to Santa Anna's country retreat if their mission was not of critical importance. A cautious man like Santa Anna would undoubtedly conduct any such interviews in secrecy if the situation at the capital had not come to a crisis. Suddenly, he was extremely anxious to follow the two figures galloping across the flats below. Stephen Austin's position was extremely vulnerable. . . .

The apprehension in Morgana's glance and the manner in which she shrank back visibly from his quick perusal caused his irritation to exceed rational bounds, and Devon snapped sharply, "Don't flatter yourself, Morgana! You're perfectly safe with me, despite the fact that you seem to feel yourself irresistible! This unmannered, uncivilized Texan has more important things to think about right now than the type of activity you obviously have on your mind!"

The hot color that flooded Morgana's lovely face providing him with a needed, if somewhat perverted satisfaction, he continued, "If you'll exhibit some of the superior horsemanship with which you impressed Santa Anna, I'd like to get back to the hacienda as quickly as possible. I have a feelin' things will be happenin' very rapidly from here on in!"

His only answer was the tight clamping of her lovely lips

into a hard line, and Devon watched with the first prick of trepidation as Morgana wheeled her horse sharply around and onto the steep trail at a pace that was just short of Santa Anna's rapid descent. Managing to stifle the protest that jumped to his lips at her perilous speed, Devon spurred his horse onto the trail behind her, anxiety twisting his stomach into tight knots as he muttered low under his breath, "Damn you, woman! If you hurt yourself with your recklessness, I'll . . ." Impervious to his own danger as he followed behind Morgana's wild, jolting descent, Devon was abruptly aware that the lovely, furious woman in front of him had again managed to take precedence in his mind over matters that should be of more vital concern. Smarting at the knowledge of how well she had manipulated him, he spurred his horse forward at the first stretch of flat ground. Calling over his shoulder as he rode past her, he felt a smug satisfaction at the blaze of anger in Morgana's gold-flecked eyes as he taunted, "Keep up or get left behind, darlin'."

Refusing to look back again, Devon listened intently, despite himself, for the steady hoofbeats immediately to his rear as he raced in the direction of the hacienda. Feeling a perverse sense of pride as they assumed his rapid pace skillfully and without hesitation, he groaned at his own preoccupation with the chestnut-haired beauty galloping tightly at his heels.

"Bitch . . ." he mumbled with reluctant admiration, "You damned feisty little bitch. . . ."

Almost disbelieving her plight, Morgana steadfastly attempted to avoid meeting the glance of the dozing Texan who sat opposite her in the jolting carriage. How was it that fate seemed intent upon torturing her with the forced company of Devon Howard for a seemingly endless period of time? Was this to be her penance for past transgressions, or was it merely some sort of perverse test set by the Almighty to gauge her worthiness? In any case, she was certain she was not up to the challenge!

Shifting her eyes to the quickly passing landscape, Morgana attempted to sort out in her mind the rapid progress of

131

the events of the past ten days. As expected, Santa Anna's important visitors the morning of their excursion across the estate had been emissaries from the capital. Having secreted himself in his study with his visitors, he had emerged three hours later with the solemn announcement that he was returning to the capital to reassume the office of the presidency. He and Tío Manuel had left the following morning with the delegation, but only after he had detailed the arrangements to be made as soon as he reached Mexico City. The arrangements included a contingent of Mexican soldiers to serve as guards for the carriage, which would return to carry Tía Isabella, her servant, Aggie, herself, and—most wretched of all—Devon Howard back to the capital. Apologizing for the unsafe conditions of the roads that allowed safe passage only with adequate protection against the bandits that roamed the area, he had politely charged Devon with the duty of escorting the women safely to the capital, stating his soldiers would be ordered to be sensitive to his requests.

In the time since, Devon Howard had fairly oozed the easy, Texan charm that had so deceived her on the voyage to Veracruz. Tía Isabella, a victim of his slow smile and polite attentions, was graciously and utterly overwhelmed. Even Aggie seemed to lose some of the guarded manner she had formerly exhibited in his presence. Forced to assume the same attitude of acceptance exhibited by the others, Morgana often felt her gracious words sticking in her throat.

But if she were to be honest, she would have to admit that Devon was a consummate actor, the cynical sneer exhibited for her eyes only, changing to a warm, gentlemanly smile in the sight of others. Were it not for the buffer of Tía Isabella's presence, the journey would have been unbearable, and the beauty through which they had been passing for the past five days would have been wasted.

And considerable beauty there was, too. Despite the dust and havoc wreaked by bad roads and the team of ten hard-working mules pulling their carriage, the scenery was an endless kaleidoscope of color and scent, filling the hours with a varied and startling visual experiences. They had stopped briefly at Santa Fe and Zopilote to change mules on the first day. Further on, they had been notified by Tía Isabella that they had finally come to the end of Santa Anna's twelve leagues of property. They had passed the beautiful bridge over the river Antigua, which was surrounded by huge trees flowering with wide, scented white blossoms. The weather had been hot without being oppressive, the road lying in densely wooded mountains with trees of countless variety visible and easily recognizable. Palms, cocoas, oranges, lemons succeeded one another at each turn of the road. The panorama stretched out before them had been intensely arresting when, at one point, they had looked down into a lovely green valley to catch a glimpse of Indian women resting beside a running stream, their long black hair rippling gently in the soft breeze.

Startling Morgana even more than the extreme natural beauty of the mountainous area were the people themselves, seeming as endless in variety as the scenery through which they passed. Indian women with long plaited black hair worked casually with little children slung on their backs. Wearing large, straw hats and short petticoats of two colors, they were almost as brilliant and colorful as the blossoms that surrounded them. It had almost been with alarm that Morgana had viewed a traveling *arriero*. One of a famed group of merchants who drove long strings of mules over the mountain paths carrying wares, mail, and any manner of barter, the fellow had exhibited a wild, swarthy-looking face that seemed to challenge the well-accepted belief that these men were considered one of the most trustworthy groups in the country. Even the simple traveler, with his high, ornamented saddle, his serape of many colors, wide-brimmed Mexican hat, silver stirrups glinting below huge leather boots was splendid material for the artist's pen.

At La Calera they had stopped briefly to absorb a distant view of the sea. Fresh oranges, pineapples, and *granaditas* were available to purchase at the turn of many roads, and had been incredibly sweet to the taste. The first day had slowly yielded to night, leading them to Plano del Rio. After sleeping for a few hours, they had continued their journey past Corral Falso, and been treated to their first view of the peak of Orizaba with its gleaming cap of white snow.

Impressed most favorably in her memory was the town of Jalapa. Little more than a few steep streets, it was very old, with some large and excellent houses, old churches, a very old convent, and a well-supplied marketplace. Marking it in her memory, however, was the fact that there were flowers everywhere . . . creeping over old walls, beneath ancient windows, placed carefully around the statue of the Virgin, and decorating the simplest of shops. But most impressive of all were the magnificent mountain views and the soft music that seemed to issue from every doorway and window.

Even the country surrounding Jalapa was breathtakingly lovely. The Confre de Perote with pine forest of dark green; the white peak of Orizaba towering above all others; the intervening mountains; the stark cliffs and green plains; the thick woods that covered the hills and valleys; the glimpse of the ocean in the distance. The nearby roads were lined with fruit trees; aloes, bananas, chirimoyos, mingled with green liquidambar, flowering myrtle, and hundreds of plants, shrubs, and flowers of every color and fragrance.

Adding the final jewel to the crown that was Jalapa was the steep road they had ascended upon leaving. The view of the mountains had been exquisite, as was the incomparable foliage that banked the road on each side. Large scarlet blossoms and hanging white and purple flowers like lilies, together with huge, double pink roses scented the air as the carriage passed, leaving her with a memory she could never hope to surpass.

Their journey had continued, and gradually the vegetation had begun to change. Sturdy herbage replaced the more exotic brilliant trees and tropical flowers as they climbed. The banana and the chirimoyo gave place to the oak, and, higher still, the dark green of the pine. At San Miguel del Soldado, the country became gradually more bleak, and before they arrived at the village of Las Vigas, nearly all trees but the hardy fir had disappeared. The ground for two leagues from that spot was covered with hardened lava and great masses of calcined rock, as in the crater of a volcano. Tía Isabella had explained that that part of the country was called *mal pais,* and, noting the occasional crosses with their faded garlands that gleamed in the bleak volcanic region, Morgana had shivered her agreement with the title of "evil land."

The road had become more steep and dreary, and after they passed Cruz Blanca, Morgana had begun to notice the chill in the air. Perote, Santa Gertudis, Tepeyahualco, La Ventilla . . . endless villages passed during the days that had begun to blur into one. Ojo de Agua, Nopalucan, Acajete, and Amozoc, small villages all, blending into the landscape, and she could recall only Puebla de Los Angeles on that portion of the journey. Having been told by Tía Isabella that Puebla de Los Angeles was the city second in size to Mexico City, she had been vastly disappointed by the city itself. The streets were clean and regular, the houses large, the cathedral magnificent, but the appearance of discomfort, dreariness and desolation it presented dulled her spirits. Its only asset as far as she could fathom as they left it was its proximity to Mexico City.

Now, realizing they were only hours from the capital and the end of their journey, Morgana felt almost overcome with trepidation. How she wished she could eject the butterflies that kept her stomach in a perpetual turmoil. The state of her future seemed suddenly too vague. Would she function well in Tía Isabella's household? Would she be an asset or a hindrance to her generous aunt? Would she be accepted by capital society, as her new family obviously wished? A sudden rash of questions inundated her mind, bringing to the surface the insecurities she had so carefully managed to avoid. Clenching her hands tightly together to hide their trembling, Morgana swallowed hard against the tears abruptly choking her throat. Despite her most stringent determination, she had handled the entire journey from New York to this strange land extremely badly from the first. The hard-won maturity with which she had handled so well the details of her father's penniless death had proved decidedly inadequate in dealing with her own private life. Shooting a quick look to the Texan, who had aroused himself from his nap and now followed the landscape passing the window thoughtfully with his light eyes, she felt a new tremor shake her already over-whelming instability. What were the contradictory emotions warring within her? Only moments before she had been anxious to see the last of the man . . . and now, faced with the fact that she might never see him again once they reached Mexico City and were swallowed by the routines of their divergent lives, she knew an unusual inner desolation. What was wrong with her? The man had treated her with nothing but contempt from almost the first moment of their meeting. Had she any sense at all, she would pray never to see his face again. Perhaps it was her youth and inexperience that had allowed the sweet touch of his hands to be burned so indelibly into her mind . . . the caress of his mouth against her skin to sear her still, even in memory . . . And how . . . how was it possible that she could despise a man so thoroughly and still allow the subtle male scent of him to disturb her so completely, allow the weight of his glance to set her to trembling? How could she still long to feel his arms around her, holding her close when she knew how well he despised her in return?

No . . . no, she would simply not allow herself to submit to her traitorous feelings! She simply would not allow . . .

Abruptly, as if summoned by her thoughts, the azure eyes scanning the landscape snapped to hers. Catching her breath at the heat in their depths, Morgana swallowed hard. The presence of similar emotions warring in Devon's solemn glance took her by surprise. Realization came slowly, with a growing sense of elation. He despises me, but he wants me still! For all his mocking glances, he is as trapped as I, and perhaps as vulnerable! A small smile growing on her lips, Morgana looked directly into the light eyes holding hers, her glance flicking briefly to his lips. The small, almost indiscernible shudder that moved over his broad frame confirmed her suspicions. Almost drunk with her newfound sense of power, Morgana allowed her glance to move slowly over his face, caressing the hard lines there until a deep flush darkened his natural coloring. Aware that her smile had assumed a faintly mocking quality that did not go unnoticed by Devon's sharp eyes, Morgana inquired with a politeness in direct contrast to her bold perusal, "Will your mission keep

ou long in Mexico City, Devon? Or can we expect we will
oon be deprived of your pleasant company?"

"Oh, I don't expect to be leavin' the capital until my mis-
ion is accomplished, Morgana. With the existin' state of af-
airs, I may be forced to stay for some weeks to come, and
'm fully prepared to do anythin' necessary to bring my mis-
ion to a successful conclusion. The fate of a good man rests
n the outcome of these negotiations."

"And so the fate of a good man is dependent on the actions
f a not-so-good man. . . ."

"Morgana!" Startled by her unexpected remark, Tía Isa-
ella shot her a quick, reprimanding glance.

"No, Doña Isabella, please," Devon interrupted smooth-
y, his smile belying the flash of anger she had caught in his
yes the moment before Tía Isabella had spoken. "I'm not
ffended by Morgana's little joke. We became very good at
radin' words during our long journey together, didn't we,
Morgana? In any case, you musn't be startled by our Anglo
hiding. It means little . . . very little . . ."

Turning to Tía Isabella with true regret for the embarrass-
nent she had caused her, Morgana smiled her apology. "Of
ourse, Devon is right, Tía Isabella." Turning back to
Devon she directed her next words into his eyes, a world of
neaning in her words as she said cryptically, "It all meant
very little . . . very little, indeed."

The flash in Devon's eyes making her acutely thankful for
Tía Isabella's presence even as she smiled boldly into his
arefully controlled expression, Morgana turned her atten-
ion with deliberate slowness to the passing countryside. She
vould allow the conversation to rest on that note. She had
nuch to think about from here on in.

CHAPTER FOUR

Absent-mindedly brushing back a straying chestnut curl from her forehead, Morgana paused, her mind slipping back to the moment just three days before when the traveling party of four had stood on the heights of the mountains, looking down at the superb valley of Mexico. She had truly never seen a more wondrous sight than the framework of magnificent mountains surrounding the capital city. Great, snow-capped volcanos; brilliant lakes, fertile plains; the countless spires of the city barely visible, all seemed a majestic tapestry woven as a gift from the Almighty to man, and Morgana had felt suddenly humbled before it. She had seen the same sense of wonder reflected in Aggie's usually unrevealing expression, and a deep sense of pride on the face of her aunt. Allowing herself a quick, covert glance in Devon's direction, she had been startled by the intensity of his concentration and the coolness with which he seemed able to accept the overwhelming vista.

Unable to resist a whispered jibe at his ultimate insensitivity, she had offered sharply, "You are unimpressed, Devon?" Without allowing him the courtesy of an answer, she had continued with scorn obvious in her glance, "Somehow I can't believe that to be so. I suspect you're a man who's committed to the philosophy that 'he's seen it all,' and whose pride won't allow him appreciation of magnificence, no matter its magnitude!''

Acutely aware by the heat of his gaze that her comment had raised his anger perilously close to the danger point, she had held Devon's gaze with bold determination as he had responded for her ears alone, ''Darlin', I don't really care worth a damn what you think!''

Now, three days after, Devon's words still echoed in her mind, effectively lowering her spirits as the familiar sounds of the street outside her window echoed in her ears.

''Hey sebo-o-o-o . . .'' The prolonged melancholy song of the woman peddler had faded only moments before to be replaced by the song of the *cambista*.

''*Tejocotes por venas de chile?*''

Smiling to herself as the Indian woman's call for exchange of her sweet fruits for hot peppers was drowned out by yet another cry, Morgana watched with much amusement as the barefoot peddler last upon the scene succeeded in driving the old woman further down the street. In a deep, heavy voice, he called for the public to buy his needles, pins, thimbles, shirt buttons, tape, finally drawing a crowd below her window. Young and old they surrounded him, offering him a tenth of the price he asked for his wares in a manner of bargaining that Morgana had come to realize was expected in the city. Her short time in Mexico City had taught her that the man would accept their prices after much haggling, only to set the stage for the Indian standing behind him with tempting baskets of fruit. With careful patience he would begin to recite the names of all his fruits until the cooks or housekeepers among them could resist no longer and called him in.

The sounds of the city were varied and constant, beginning at daybreak with the call of the coal man: ''*Carbón, señor,*'' which to her inexperienced ear had sounded something like ''Carbousiu!''

Next would be the call of the grease man: ''*Mantequilla!* Lard! Lard! At one real and a half.''

The song of the butcher would then follow. ''*Cecina buena!*

Salt beef! Good salt beef!''

And she knew soon after would come, "*Gorditas de horno, calientes?* Little fat cakes from the oven, hot?''

"Who wants mats from Puebla? Mats of five yards?''

At midday the cries of the beggars with their songs and prayers would ring on the warm air. Then the steady succession of "Honey cakes! Cheese and honey? *Requesón* and good honey?'' The dulce men, sellers of sweetmeats, of meringues and candies: "*Caramelos de esperma! Bocadillo de coco!*'' The lottery men: "The last ticket yet unsold, for half a real!''

Toward the evening would ring, "*Tortillas de cuajada?* Curd cakes?'' or "Do you take nuts?'' The last of the night cries would call, "Chestnuts, hot and roasted!'', "Ducks, oh my soul, hot ducks!'' and "Maize cakes . . . maize cakes . . .''

Startling her even more during her short time in the city had been the appearance of those picturesque groups in their slow procession under her window . . . men of a bronze color, wearing nothing much more than a piece of blanket or a serape thrown over them, their skin the precise color of the earthen basins filled with the *mantequilla* or bread they carried so lightly on their heads; women in their *rebozos* and short petticoats of two colors, which were often merely rags bordered with lace, stained white satin shoes on their stockingless legs; the gentlemen on horseback with high Mexican saddles, handsome serapes and gilt stirrups, large, shining black or white beaver hats with silver trim on their proud heads; Indian women with tight petticoats of dark material and tangled hair plaited with red ribbon, their copper-colored half-naked offspring on their backs; and lounging *leperos,* dirty, moving bundles of rags, begging with false-sounding whines.

The contrast between the diverse groups was so great as to create a feeling in her of astonished disbelief at first. But after three days, her disbelief had begun to turn to calm acceptance.

She had found Doña Isabella's home modest, but extremely pretty. Fortunately built in two stories, because of the extreme dampness of the ground floor, it was constructed around a large central courtyard and an adjoining garden full of flowers. Her own room was pleasant, but according to the custom of the country was sparsely furnished and devoid of carpets and window glass to allow the circulation of cooling breezes. The heavy grills on the windows provided the only protection against forced entry of any sort, and, annoyed that her thoughts should run in that vein, Morgana reminded herself that she could not entirely dismiss the stories of thieves and robbers that populated the city and its outskirts. Shaking her head in an attempt to free herself of her unwelcome thoughts, she reached for her dress.

She had far more pleasant things to think of today! After having been almost insolated from all visitors because of the peculiar Mexican custom of announcing new arrivals by the sending of cards before their presence could be acknowledged formally by a visit, as well as the necessity of settling herself thoroughly into her new home, Morgana had received her first invitation! And one of significance it was, indeed! Fluttering her excitement, Tía Isabella had displayed the invitation from Antonio Santa Anna the day before. Smiling to herself, Morgana remembered Tía Isabella's light, bubbling exuberance.

"See, *querida!* The invitation comes from Antonio himself! We are invited to visit him in the palace. He specifically requests your presence, and the opportunity to atone for his leaving so unexpectedly when we were at Manga de Clavo. See! He specifically adds that he should not like a young, lovely newcomer to our country to obtain a poor impression of our hospitality! You have impressed him very favorably, Morgana, and I admit to being very pleased! I will also admit my secret fears that the prejudice some of our people hold against Americans at this point in our history might have made some withhold their acceptance. But now, *querida*, with Antonio's support, you will be accepted without question!" Throwing her slender arms around Morgana's slim shoulders and hugging her soundly, she had repeated warmly, "I am so pleased!"

Now, inordinately grateful for Antonio Santa Anna's gracious invitation, which had given her aunt so much pleasure, she carefully reviewed the gowns hanging in her closet. She wanted to look especially good this evening. She needed the added boost of confidence a good appearance would afford her. And if it was so, as Devon had remarked, that Antonio liked to look at young, good-looking women, she had decided that pleasing him in that way was small payment indeed for the benefits she would reap from his support. She also had to admit to feeling a personal pleasure at the invitation, for certainly Antonio was a charming man whose company she had enjoyed immensely in the short time of their acquaintance. The perfect gentleman, with a wit and intelligence that was stimulating, he was extremely entertaining, as well as mysterious in a way that she found difficult to describe even to herself. Perhaps it was his Mexican heritage, or perhaps it was the fact that he was the president of Mexico, and a warm, attentive human being despite his fame and the adulation of his people. Perhaps . . . well, whatever, she was anxious for this evening, and she hoped, desperately, to do her aunt and uncle proud.

Yes, it was extremely important that her appearance be exactly right. . . .

Adjusting her position on the seat of the carriage once again, Morgana gripped the support in an attempt to hold her position more successfully than she had since beginning the ride to the palace. Frowning slightly, she noticed that Tía Isabella and Tío Manuel, sitting across from her, seemed in no way inconvenienced by the jolting and jarring caused by the excessively poor roads in the city. Suddenly it was no wonder to her that most of the carriages she had seen in the streets, as well as the one in which she now rode, were imported from America and Europe. Surely only the most sturdily constructed carriages would be able to survive an extended period on such poor roads! Catching herself in her silent criticism, she reprimanded herself firmly. She must not fall into the trap of comparison, especially when comparisons found her new home lacking. She was here, after all, because of her aunt and uncle's generosity. Determinedly changing her frown to a smile, she raised a small, tentative hand to finger the blond lace that trimmed the modest décolletage of her dress. After a long hour of uncertainty, she had finally called upon Aggie to help her decide the most appropriate frock to wear for a visit to the palace. The selection had been a simple ivory silk that left her smooth shoulders almost bare to the warm rays of the late afternoon sun. The sleeves tightened at the elbow, ending in a wide ruffle of blond lace. The bodice followed her contours snugly to the waist, which was trimmed with a wide, chestnut-brown ribbon. Bands of the same color ribbon trimmed the hem of the moderately full skirt, and the same soft color was repeated in the soft satin slippers she wore on her feet. The tall crown of her ivory silk bonnet was adorned with small, silk flowers, and the sides of the oval brim were held down by the chestnut-brown ribbon that tied in a bow to the side of her face. She had discarded the ''betsie'' normally worn with the outfit, certain that the small neck ruff was not suitable to the warm climate of the Mexican afternoon.

Viewing Tía Isabella's sober appearance in her black dress and mantilla, the diamonds sparkling at her ears and throat adding the only festive note, Morgana was sensitive to the fact that although her manner of dress was decidedly American, it would not be considered in bad taste because of the subdued color. Had she any doubt, the broad approving smiles on the faces of her aunt and uncle upon her appearance had dispelled them immediately.

Their short journey through the streets of Mexico City had confirmed her previous observation that the city was a study in amazing contrasts. Having left the modest street on which her aunt and uncle lived, they had turned into the Alameda enroute to the palace. The thickly planted, walled enclosure was magnificent, its stately trees, brilliant flowers, and graceful fountains sparkling in the sun. Her eyes following the narrow walks that wove through the grand foliage, she had felt a sudden desire to follow the intricate paths and explore its beauty at close hand. But realizing she must content herself with the view afforded from the carriage drive that wound around the Alameda's edge, she had turned her attention to the sights available to her. Her eyes had followed the occasional gentleman on horseback, her mind marveling at the richness of the men's attire, and the elaborate carriages that traveled the streets beside them, inevitably drawn by teams of fine, matched horses. In strangely jarring contrast to the beauty of the scene had been the presence of the multitude of beggars lounging amidst the splendor, and the aimless, forlorn appearance of those resting on stone benches near the exit of the Alameda.

They had, within the last few minutes, turned onto the Calle de San Francisco, which Tia Isabella had declared the handsomest street in Mexico. Silently agreeing that it surely must be so from the multitude of interesting shops and impressive houses that lined it, Morgana had been intently studying the teeming streets when the carriage had turned into a great square. Her breath catching in her throat, Morgana saw the cathedral for the first time, her eyes darting immediately to the outline of the palace across the square, which was their destination.

Of immense size, it occupied one full side of the square, and Morgana could easily understand how it could house the apartments of the president, his ministers, and all the chief courts of justice, as was its function. Her heart beating rapidly in her chest, she took a deep breath as the carriage pulled to a halt in front of an impressive flight of stairs. Alighting from the carriage with a step that she hoped appeared light and assured, she smiled her gratitude at the thoughtfulness of her uncle as he assisted her from the carriage, and, returning Tía Isabella's smile, followed quietly at their side.

Acutely aware that she was the object of many curious glances, Morgana continued up the staircase, silently remarking to herself at the number of lounging Mexican soldiers in their yellow cloaks, and women in *rebozos* standing idly about on each landing. Following her uncle's rapid step, she kept close to Tía Isabella's side as they turned into a short hall filled with soldiers impressively clad, their shining helmets and flowing cloaks marking them as some sort of special guard. Entering immediately into a small antechamber, she listened politely to the conversation between Tío Manuel and the aides-de-camp who greeted them, her mind reveling in the handsomeness of their uniforms as they turned to lead the way to yet another room. Politely accepting their offer to be seated, Morgana had barely had time to become comfortable when another officer appeared and motioned them to their feet.

Directed through yet another doorway, Morgana stepped over the threshold of the next room, her breath catching in her throat at the size and opulence of its furnishings. Marveling that the room must be at least fifty feet long, Morgana's eyes moved openly over the crimson and gold decor, and the elaborate chandeliers. Her heartbeat accelerated to yet a faster rate, causing a slight breathlessness as a door at the end of the room opened, allowing the entrance of a familiar, smiling figure. Feeling the touch of his dark-eyed glance, Morgana smiled, a true warmth moving through her veins at the spontaneity of the smile that was turned in her direction by Antonio Santa Anna.

Noting his swift, energetic movement as he advanced toward them, Morgana allowed her eyes to move freely over Antonio Santa Anna's impressive figure. Tall, dark, well muscled despite his enforced inactivity while ill at Manga de Clavo, his face extremely expressive, his eyes compelling, Santa Anna was an extremely attractive man. But the magnetism of the man did not lie completely in his physical attributes, of that Morgana was acutely aware. Rather, it lay in the his ability to project a kindly interest that warmed the hearts of those who knew him only slightly, such as she; in the exciting intensity of his interest in subjects dear to his heart, in the gleam in his eye, which signified that interest, and in the warm, heartfelt smile that proclaimed his approval. Yes, the man was surely fated to be marked by history, and she was thrilled to be in his presence.

Hardly aware of the greetings extended and acknowledged by her aunt and uncle, Morgana was only aware of the darkly handsome face turned toward hers, and the deep, melodious voice that addressed her in turn.

"Ah, Morgana, I have thought much of my inhospitable behavior in abandoning you at Manga de Clavo. I am very aware, *querida,* of my unfulfilled promise to conclude the tour of my estate, which we had begun on two occasions, only to be interrupted each time. I should not like you to think that I am not a man of my word, Morgana, and I apologize for my failure in that respect. I admit to being extremely pleased to find you so close by, so that I may atone for my unfortunate behavior.'' Taking her small hand in his as he spoke, Santa Anna held it warmly for a few seconds, finally raising it to his lips as he awaited her response.

A light flush of pleasure rising to her cheeks, Morgana returned his smile. ''There is no need for an apology, Antonio. You are a man of great responsibility, which must take precedence over all social demands. I am well aware of the pressures on your time, and confess to being delighted with your invitation to the palace this evening, when I'm certain you must have many pressing matters that demand your attention.''

''Surely no matters more pressing than entertaining good friends and compatriots. Come.'' His glance moving back to Tío Manuel and Tía Isabella, Santa Anna urged them toward the handsome furniture grouped companionably at the side of the room. ''We will share some wine, and you will tell me all that has happened since I left you at Manga de Clavo.'' Turning his attention to Tía Isabella, he encouraged lightly, ''You must tell me of the arrangements you have made for your niece to be introduced into society, Isabella. We are indeed fortunate to have a young woman of her intelligence and beauty to stimulate a capital society which, I fear, has had little of interest to talk of aside from the devious machinations of the man who took my office with such great promise only four months ago.'' His brow darkening at the conclusion of his statement, Santa Anna was momentarily silent, a new, somber mood obviously having taken possession of his previously gregarious mood. Turning unexpectedly to Tío Manuel, he began somberly, ''I have had a recent communication which I should like you to see, Manuel. If the ladies will excuse us for a few minutes later this evening, I will have them served some tea so that we may discuss the matter without risk of boring them with its details.''

''Sí, Antonio . . . Manuel . . .'' Tía Isabella's light tone

146

precluding Tío Manuel's response, she continued softly, "But Morgana and I will entertain ourselves while you complete your urgent business now. I am certain she and I would both feel much more comfortable if you would take the time to settle your business matters first . . . am I not right, Morgana?" At Morgana's affirmative nod, Isabella encouraged firmly, "Please, Antonio. I know Manuel will not rest with thoughts of an urgent communication on his mind. With your permission, I will show Morgana a few of the public rooms of the palace in the interim. Morgana has not had the opportunity to see much of the city, and I'm certain she would dearly love to explore."

A new light coming into his dark eyes, Santa Anna responded warmly, "*Muchas gracias,* Isabella. And I must admit that your words have provoked an interesting idea. If you will indeed excuse Manuel and me for the next half hour, I would consider it a privilege if you would allow me to introduce Morgana to the history that lies outside the doorway of the palace."

Her eyes sparkling with delight, Dona Isabella's response was a foregone conclusion even before she responded.

"Of course, Antonio." Turning toward Morgana, she awaited only her nod of acquiescence before continuing, "We will be delighted."

The two erect figures had barely cleared the doorway to the room when Doña Isabella turned toward Morgana, her face aflush with excitement.

"Your future is secure, *querida!*" At her niece's startled expression, Isabella's small, doll-like features became suddenly serious and intent. "Surely you saw the many inquisitive glances turned your way when we entered the palace, *querida.*"

"*Sí,* I admit to feeling considerable discomfort in the eyes that followed me, Tía Isabella, but I do not understand . . ."

"And now Antonio has promised to escort us personally on a tour of the square. I myself have lived here much of my life, *querida,* and am well acquainted with the history involved. And so it will be you who will have the honor of his

147

attention for the time it entails. This is an honor that will be well observed by many, and you may rest assured that your presence will be actively sought at every affair at the capital from today forward!''

Well aware of the delight this thought gave to her warm-hearted aunt, Morgana tried diligently to disguise her skepticism. ''Tía Isabella, surely such a small matter will not be given such importance . . .''

Her dark eyes all knowing, Doña Isabella nodded in cheerful insistence as she carefully picked up the decanter and began to pour wine into two small crystal glasses. ''You will see, *querida* . . . you will see. . . .''

''. . . and so, Morgana, this very cathedral was built upon the ruins of the great temple of the Aztecs.''

So distracted had she become by the many curious glances intent on their persons that Morgana had missed a portion of Santa Anna's careful recitation of the history of the plaza on which they now trod. Smiling her interest into his intense dark eyes, she had taken a moment to send a glance of acknowledgment to Tía Isabella, who walked silently on his other side. Yes, Tía Isabella had been entirely correct. From the moment of their emergence from the door of the palace, all eyes had fastened on the figure of the country's president, flanked on each side by a woman. Even without her husband, who had remained in the palace to construct a response to the missive that had caused such concern, Tía Isabella had been immediately recognized by many. Acknowledging polite greetings as they walked, she had managed to maintain strict attention to Santa Anna's steady flow of words. Morgana no longer had any doubt that the identity of the young woman to whom President Santa Anna paid such intense gentlemanly attention would be relentlessly sought the following day. The smile with which Santa Anna accepted the people's curiosity prompted a suspicion in her own mind as well. Surely Antonio knew the nature of his people well, and was fully aware that his acceptance of her would influence those seeking his favor in her behalf. He was openly extending the influence of his position to the niece of General Escobar, and she was intensely grateful for his generosity.

Her eyes moving to the great cathedral before them, Morgana took her mind from the continuing perusal of the curious and allowed her gaze to move slowly over the massive edifice. Baroque in form, with two lofty ornamented towers, it was not overly handsome to her mind, although it was said to be immensely rich in gold and silver.

His eyes taking on a strange intensity, Santa Anna continued, "It is said, Morgana, that the pyramidal temple constructed by Ahuizotl covered the area where the cathedral now stands, as well as part of the plaza and the streets adjoining. Within its enclosure were five hundred dwellings. Its hall was built of stone and lime, and ornamented with stone serpents. There are stories of four great gates, fronting the four cardinal points of the stone-paved court, great stone stairs, and sanctuaries dedicated to the gods of war; of a square for religious dances, and colleges for the priests and seminaries for the priestesses. There was a temple of horror whose door was an enormous serpent's mouth; a temple of mirrors and one of shells. There was a house set apart for the emperor's prayers; consecrated fountains; birds kept for sacrifice; gardens for holy flowers; and a horrendous tower composed of the skulls of victims!" The strange light growing in the dark depths of his eyes, Santa Anna continued into Morgana's awestruck face, "It is here, we are told, that five thousand priests chanted night and day in the great temple to the honor and in the service of the monstrous idols whom they anointed three times a day with precious perfumes. The most austere of these priests were clothed in black, their long hair dyed with ink, and their bodies anointed with the ashes of burnt scorpions and spiders. Their chiefs were the sons of kings."

Stopping only a moment to ascertain that he had her full attention, Santa Anna continued in a low, almost reverent tone, "It is remarkable, also, Morgana, that their god of war was said to have been born of woman, a holy virgin, who was in the service of the temple, and that when the priests, having knowledge of her disgrace, would have stoned her, a voice was heard saying, 'Fear not, mother, for I shall save thy honor and my glory' . . . upon which the god was born, with a shield in his left hand and an arrow in his right, a plume of green feathers on his head, his face painted blue, and his left leg adorned with feathers! But,'' Santa Anna continued solemnly, ''it is believed that the ritual of human sacrifice which the Aztecs practiced was as a result of this myth.'' At her confused expression, Santa Anna explained patiently, ''You see, the mother of the god of war, Coatlicue, was already the mother of the moon and stars and had become a priestess dedicated to a life of retreat and chastity. Her children were enraged at her mysterious pregnancy and planned to kill her. But her child was born just in time to save his mother by decapitating the moon and putting the stars to flight. To maintain the greatest of the gods in his daily cycle of rebirth and triumph, the nourishment of blood had to be maintained . . . and, to obtain blood, war became for the Aztecs a form of worship with the purpose of insuring a constant flow of prisoners for human sacrifice.''

The vividness with which Santa Anna described the ancient rituals sent a chill of terror down her spine, and Morgana protested spontaneously, ''But it is all so frightening, Antonio, so savage. . . .''

A small benevolent smile touching his lips for the first time in many minutes, Santa Anna nodded his head in agreement.

''*Sí*, Morgana, *es verdad*. It does seem, does it not, that our noble ancestors saved the lives of many innocents in the destruction of the temple. There were so many gods . . . gods of water, earth, night, fire, and hell; goddesses of flowers and corn . . . There were oblations of bread, flowers, and jewels, but most dastardly of all were the human sacrifices . . . between twenty to fifty thousand human victims alone!'' Taking her hand, seemingly oblivious to its chill, he urged her toward a huge stone pedestal, set in a place of honor in the courtyard. The center of the stone contained a hollow indentation, toward which Santa Anna gestured dramatically.

''This was the Stone of Sacrifice, Morgana. In here the

victim was placed while six priests, dressed in red, their heads adorned with plumes of green feathers, with gold and green earrings and blue stones in their upper lips, held him down. The chief priest than thrust his knife into the victim's breast, and, cutting it open, threw his heart at the feet of the idol. Afterwards, he put it into his own mouth with a golden spoon! He then cut off the victim's head to make use in the building of the tower of skulls, and, after eating some parts of the victim's body, either burned the rest or threw it to the wild beasts who were maintained in the palace.''

Gasping at the blood-thirsty horror of the tale he had related so vividly, Morgana stared wordlessly into Santa Anna's eyes, almost mesmerized by the strange, indescribable glow of fascination in their depths. The blood drained from her face, leaving her abruptly light-headed as she swallowed tightly against her stomach's violent reaction to the hideous tale.

Appearing to notice her paling for the first time, Santa Anna stated quietly, ''Ah, *querida,* I have been too explicit in my descriptions of the ceremonies which took place here. Instead of allowing you to see the beauty of our capital, I have revealed only its dark history.'' His voice softening, he continued intently, ''But I have told you these tales with a specific purpose in mind, Morgana. There is truly much history here, in this plaza. Our very country is named after the Aztec god of war, Mexitli. I would have you see that we are inevitably tied to our history, Morgana, but we are not inevitably *bound.* There is a difference . . . a difference to which I am dedicated, *querida.* . . .''

Appearing suddenly to snap from his moment of deep inner revelation, Santa Anna turned from Morgana, who still had an intense expression on her face. Seemingly aware of Tía Isabella's presence for the first time in many minutes, he offered politely, ''I hope I have not bored you, Isabella, with the morbid tales of Aztec rule and worship with which you are doubtless well acquainted, but it was my wish to acquaint your niece with the blood that runs through our people's veins . . . the very blood that was spilled so needlessly. In doing so, I hoped to explain the passion with which our people speak and act, and the passion with which we conduct our lives.''

Seeing in Tía Isabella's worshipful gaze the affirmation he sought, Santa Anna barely waited for the conclusion of her soft absolution before turning back to Morgana's sober face.

"We are a people with a tempestuous past, Morgana. The blood of pagans still runs in our veins, as does the blood of great holy men of the Church, the blood of brave warriors and soldiers, as well as great statesmen. . . . We have much to overcome, and much to offer, and we welcome you, Morgana Pierce, to become a part of us.''

Taking her hand with great formality, Santa Anna raised it to his lips in a gracious salute that succeeded in bringing the warmth of tears to the wide, gold-flecked eyes Morgana raised to his. Her voice low in her throat, Morgana began hesitantly, *"Muchas graćias,* Antonio. I will long remember your graciousness and I feel . . .''

"Yes, I'm sure Morgana is feelin' as impressed as I with your generous recitation of the history of this plaza, Antonio.''

A familiar low, rambling voice interrupted Morgana's soft response, snapping her glance to the man who had stood unnoticed to the side of her, as he continued pleasantly, "I apologize for intrudin', but I confess that I've never heard Aztec history described so knowledgeably. You are to be saluted, Antonio. You are an excellent historian as well as a master storyteller.''

Maintaining his smile by a supreme exertion of will, Devon awaited Santa Anna's response. He had taken a chance interrupting the small scene the great man had obviously staged for the many staring curiously in their direction. He was well aware Santa Anna would not have entered the plaza with Morgana and Isabella Escobar if he had not a specific intention in mind. The man was supremely devious. He was obviously still intrigued by Morgana, although he hid his personal interest very well behind the mask of benevolence reflected on his face when he gazed into Morgana's expression of open admiration. Suppressing his disgust, Devon silently marveled that the girl could be such a fool! Or perhaps it was just that she was a superb actress, equally devious as the great Santa Anna. Perhaps it was she who was leading the great man into exactly the position she wanted him. . . . Whatever the case, Santa Anna doubtless had great plans for Morgana . . . plans which would never become public knowledge while he controlled the reins of government. Damn the little witch! She was getting in over her head! She had no idea of the ruthlessness of which that man was capable!

Aware of the hostility in Morgana's glance, Devon allowed his smile to broaden as he turned in the direction of the small woman who stood smiling warmly as she awaited his acknowledgment of her presence.

"Doña Isabella." True warmth in his greeting, Devon took the small hand extended to him, "It is always a pleasure to see you again. I confess I have sorely felt the lack of genteel company in the days since we parted company."

Flushing with pleasure, Doña Isabella responded softly, "Then we shall have to make certain your visit to our capital is not devoted entirely to accomplishment of your mission. You must take some time for entertainment and enjoyment, Devon, so that you may maintain the proper balance and perspective."

"Well, if you say so, ma'am, then I suppose it must be so."

Obviously pleased by his response, Doña Isabella hesitated only a moment before inquiring, "Have you received an invitation to the charity ball, which will be held at the end of the month, Devon? It is a very politic affair that would doubtless bring you much pleasure, as well as allow you to become more familiar with the workings of our country."

"No, Doña Isabella. I haven't." Not quite certain if he would care to participate in such an event, Devon continued hesitantly, "but I'm not wantin' you to go through any extra effort on my part."

"Nonsense! It will be my pleasure! He will be a welcome addition to the affair, will he not, Antonio?"

"Sí, Isabella." His eyes not quite matching the warmth of his agreement, Santa Anna turned to address Devon directly. "I should consider your presence at the ball a great asset to the evening, Devon. It is a rather extravagant affair with fancy dress, but it is outstandingly entertaining."

Feeling distinctly trapped into agreement, Devon murmured indistinctly, "I am in your debt."

Realizing he could allow no more time to pass without a word in greeting to Morgana, Devon turned slowly in her direction. Allowing his eyes to move over her face, he spoke politely, his stomach tightening at the icy coolness that slipped over features filled only moments before with warmth.

"Morgana, it would appear that our paths are fated to cross continually. And it seems that Mexico City agrees with you. You are lookin' very well."

Noting Morgana's frigid smile in return, Devon could not help but remark to himself that his last was a grandiose understatement. Morgana was indeed looking magnificent! In a land where black dresses and mantillas abounded, only occasionally relieved by the same in white, she stood out in the plaza like a small, beautiful flower. It was not as if, he noted unconsciously, she was in need of any artifice to enhance her beauty. Indeed, it seemed that the passage of the few days since he had seen her had only made her more lovely. Was it any wonder that the eyes of every peasant in the square were turned to her? These poor, simple people had probably never before seen hair like hers, that gleamed with burnished highlights in the light of the afternoon sun, nor skin as smooth and fair . . . perfect, unmarked; and it was certain that any one of them who had gotten a glimpse of the large, heavily lashed, sultry eyes flecked with gold would never forget them. Hadn't those same gleaming orbs haunted his own thoughts continually the past few days . . . until he wondered at his own obsession?

"Thank you, Devon." The simple, polite courtesy sticking in her throat, Morgana managed a small smile. Hating herself for the inner trembling that had assailed her the moment she had heard his voice, Morgana suppressed a compelling need to strike out at him, if only with the power of verbal barbs. But Tía Isabella was obviously greatly impressed by him, and she dared not allow room for suspicions with regard to the reasons for her own dislike of the man who had shown her aunt only the greatest courtesy. "I had not realized you expected to be in the capital long enough to attend the charity ball. It was my impression that your business would be concluded within a few days."

"I am afraid Devon awaits official action on my part before he may leave the city, Morgana." Santa Anna's interjection drawing her attention from Devon's faintly contemptuous glance, Morgana felt a deep flash of relief. Gratitude for the opportune interruption warmed her smile, which before had been little more than a grimace, and Morgana turned her gaze fully toward Santa Anna.

Startled by the intensity of the heated emotion that flashed through his body at the admiration so openly reflected in Morgana's gaze, Devon stiffened. The little bitch! She was deliberately taunting him! Well, if that was her game, he would make her pay, and when it came time, he would make certain there was no subtlety involved, just payment . . . long overdue. . . .

". . . but that is a matter that Devon and I must resolve before too many days have passed." Santa Anna's words dimly penetrated the furor of his rioting mind, reawakening Devon to the danger Morgana presented to his mission. "You have left your address with my secretary, have you not, Devon? When I have had the opportunity to investigate Colonel Austin's case more thoroughly, I will be in touch with you."

"But now I am afraid I must return to the palace." Flashing a small smile of regret, Santa Anna continued quietly, "I am afraid I have abandoned Manuel too long to the tedious task that awaits us both. If I may offer my apology once again to my two lovely guests, I am afraid I must forego the pleasure of your company in order that I may attend to this unexpected matter which must be handled with expediency. I will call for your carriage. Lieutenant Morales will escort you home in Manuel's absence."

"That won't be necessary, Antonio." Speaking before he was truly certain what he was going to say, Devon interjected quietly, "I'll be happy to serve as escort for the ladies. As a matter of fact, I will consider it a privilege if you would allow me the honor, Doña Isabella.''

''In that case, Devon, Morgana and I would be happy to allow you to accompany us home, would we not, Morgana?''

Her mind shrieking an unqualified ''NO!'', Morgana managed a small smile, hoping desperately it did not look as sickly as it felt.

''Yes, most happy, Tía Isabella.''

''Well, then, the matter is settled.'' Offering his arm to Doña Isabella, Santa Anna turned toward the palace, leaving Devon to offer Morgana the same courtesy.

Silently, accepting the arm Devon offered, Morgana avoided contact with the dark eyes that mocked her. But she could not ignore the low, soft voice that drawled for her ears alone as her hand moved to rest on the fabric of his sleeve, ''I was enjoyin' that little performance you gave with Santa Anna so well, that I could barely bring myself to interfere with it, darlin'. That wide-eyed fascination with his glory stories must have been really intoxicatin' for a man with an ego the size of Antonio Santa Anna's.''

''You're certainly no one to speak of another's ego, Devon,'' Morgana returned through teeth gritted tightly in a smile. ''But even if it were true, surely Antonio has reason for pride in his accomplishments . . . whereas your ego is based purely on delusions of grandeur!''

Refusing to allow the anger her remark had stimulated to become apparent in his expression, Devon smiled lightly. ''It's strange I didn't get the impression you felt that way about me that mornin' on Santa Anna's estate. Somehow I got the feelin' then that you . . .''

''Damn you, Devon! I don't care what impression you got that morning! I just want you to stay as far away from me as possible, do you understand? That should be clear enough to overcome any mistaken impressions you have about me! I don't want any part of a whoring Texan who can't tell a lady from the usual trash he consorts with!''

''I told you once before, Morgana.'' Devon's eyes flashed danger signals that Morgana was too enraged to see. ''I know a 'lady' when I see one and you, darlin', don't happen to fall into that category."

"You're mistaken once again, Devon." Morgana's barely audible response was disguised with a flirting, under-eyed glance that set Devon's heart to beating erratically despite the poison of her words. "The fallacy in your judgment lies with the fact that, having been raised in a primitive, self-serving society so completely lacking in integrity that it won't live up to an agreement sworn to and by which it was granted its rights to colonize, you are neither *equipped* nor in a *position* to judge *anyone!*"

Feeling a true thrill of victory as Devon's retort was forestalled by their arrival at the steps of the palace, Morgana attempted to disengage her arm from Devon's only to have his free hand clamp over hers in a deceiving gesture that appeared to treat her hand with utmost gentleness while keeping it captive. Allowing her to remove her hand after she realized she could only do so with his permission, Devon turned toward the palace.

Noting the grey-haired military figure descending the steps toward them, he smiled in greeting. The hardening of Manuel Escobar's eyes as they touched on him was only too obvious. Accepting the man's frigid formal greeting, Devon no longer had any doubt as to the origin of Morgana's distorted version of the activities of Austin's Texas colony. It was obvious the general's opinion had changed little in the time since he himself had hotly debated the question of Texan rights with him more than a year before. He was abruptly thankful that Santa Anna was in control of the situation rather than the stubborn, unyielding General Escobar. He knew that despite Santa Anna's deviousness, he could be depended upon to take the position that would yield him the greatest return and advance him the most swiftly toward his goals. It was merely a matter of providing the proper incentive, and determining that incentive was the matter to which he must devote his time or ultimately fail. His eyes moving to Morgana's small figure at his side, he felt again a pang of disgust at his own seemingly hopeless fascination. Damn her! She continually intruded into his thoughts, allowing him hardly an hour of freedom from the picture of her that was constantly before his mind's eye. He needed to purge her from his system, and, considering the obvious depth of his involvement, he could think of only one way to accomplish that.

Waiting politely until the women had bid their temporary farewells, Devon assisted Doña Isabella and Morgana into the carriage in turn. Sitting opposite them as the carriage lurched forward, he was aware of the covert antipathy of the one, and startled by the sudden discomfort of the other.

"Devon . . ." Beginning lamely, in a manner quite uncharacteristic of the spontaneous, well-spoken woman that she was, Dona Isabella continued falteringly. "I find myself in a difficult position . . . that of feeling the need to apologize for my husband's actions." Raising a sincere expression to his startled glance, she continued slowly, "Manuel is a good man, loyal to his country and devoted to its president. He feels strongly about the actions of the colony of Texas and Coahuila since its inception. In his extreme devotion to his country and his dedication to the furtherance of its people, he has little tolerance for those who do not share his opinions." Her expression lightening a small fraction, she continued in a tone that held more warmth than her previous declaration. "But I, Devon, can see the need for equality between all the states of Mexico, and the need for grievance to be heard and considered honestly. Antonio has seen fit to entertain your grievance against Colonel Austin's imprisonment, and I share his desire to see justice done, no matter the way in which the decision falls." An impish spark entering her dark eyes, she added unexpectedly, "I also find you *guapísimo*, Devon, and it is good for an old woman to have a handsome *caballero* in her home again." Her own laughter ringing out as Devon's startled expression turned to one of genuine amusement, she placed her small hands over his. "And so, we are *amigos*, Devon, are we not?"

"*Sí*, Dona Isabella. *Sí, y tu eres una mujer muy agradable, tambien. Estoy contento que quedar en su presencia.*"

Her face flaming at the friendly exchange between her aunt and the man whom she considered her enemy, Morgana ignored the pointed look Devon shot in her direction and resumed her ardent examination of the passing streets.

Barely able to restrain her impatience with the slow movement of the carriage through the streets, Morgana experienced profound relief at the first sight of the Escobar residence. Soon she would be free of the necessity for the stiff smile which she had affixed on her lips, the same smile that threatened at any moment to fall into the sneer that more truly reflected her feelings during the interminable ride. Oh, Devon Howard was clever and amusing with that slow, Texan charm when he wanted to be . . . so generous with his compliments and the warm, sincere manner that had doubtless turned many female heads. Tía Isabella was utterly delighted with him, and Morgana had been forced to laugh at the appropriate times and smile despite the tight knot that had formed in her stomach. Damn him! Was he not the ultimate in hypocrites? He had demonstrated to her, only too clearly, that the success of his mission was of utmost importance to him. And while working closely with Santa Anna, showing him the respect and courtesy due a man of his stature and position, had he not intimated that Antonio was not to be trusted. Hah! That was a joke! If there was anyone who was not to be trusted, it was Devon Howard! Had he not deliberately misled her with his tender ministrations during her temporary illness on the *Estrellita,* with his constant attentions in the days following; and then, had he not turned on her, treating her like a common whore? And in the time since, had he not continued to practice his cruelty, taking the opportunity to demonstrate the fact that although she proclaimed to want no part of him, her protests could not stand up against the power of his magnetism?

Taking a deep, steadying breath as memories threatened to overcome her composure, Morgana took a firmer hold on her emotions. Never again! Never again would she allow Devon Howard close enough to penetrate her defenses. At any rate, he would be leaving the capital soon . . . upon the settlement of Stephen Austin's case, and she would no longer be tortured with his presence. Ignoring the empty feeling that thought evoked, Morgana concentrated instead on devising a plan to avoid Devon's company for the remainder of the evening. She had no doubt her aunt would invite him into the house, and somehow had even less doubt that Devon would refuse. He seemed to take particular delight in her torment . . . or perhaps she was wrong. Perhaps he cared too little to even give her feelings a second thought. Perhaps he was merely interested in ingratiating himself with Tía Isabella, for whatever influence she might have on Tío Manuel. He was obviously aware of her uncle's feelings, and now that Tía Isabella had declared herself neutral, he doubtless felt he could very easily turn her into an ally. Well, whatever the case, she would not be a party to any of these machinations!

Making herself ready as soon as the carriage came to a halt, Morgana waited tensely as Devon alighted and turned to offer Tía Isabella and herself a guiding hand down. Shooting her aunt a quick, apologetic smile, she took the broad hand extended in their direction and quickly stepped out of the carriage. She had determined she would go immediately into the house on the pretext of notifying the servants that they had returned with a guest, and would, from that point on, devise an excuse to spend as little time as possible in the abominable man's company.

Deeply resenting the fact that Devon Howard had been successful in manipulating her until she was behaving in a manner almost as devious as his own, Morgana turned a sweet smile to her aunt's somewhat surprised glance.

Appearing to anticipate her actions, Tía Isabella turned in Devon's direction. "Devon, Morgana and I seem to have been abandoned for the evening and we would greatly enjoy the pleasure of your company at our evening meal. Manuel will doubtless be involved with Antonio for hours, if I am to judge from past experience, and I myself confess an interest in learning more of your home colony in Texas."

"So gracious an invitation would be too difficult to refuse, Doña Isabella." Truly warmed by the small woman's friendly overture, Devon darted a quick glance toward Morgana, in time to catch the momentary flicker of impatience in her eyes before they resumed the opaque quality they had reflected during the course of the ride home. Little witch! Reacting with instinctive anger, Devon turned to instruct the driver of the carriage to return later, his mind railing silently. If it had been Santa Anna who had returned with them instead of himself, Morgana's reaction would have been entirely different, he was sure! He was still uncertain in his mind whether Morgana entertained a sincere interest in Santa Anna . . . was truly infatuated with his charm . . . or whether she was merely more devious than he, and determined to have the president of Mexico dancing attendance at her dainty feet. More resolved than ever to thwart her plans, for a perverse reason he did not quite understand himself, Devon was still talking to the driver when Morgana's soft voice caught his ear.

"*Con permiso,* Tía Isabella, I will go ahead and alert the servants to the presence of our guest."

A bit startled by her niece's unsettled manner, Tía Isabella nodded her concurrence, a small frown creasing her brow as Morgana turned to make a hasty exit.

Too relieved to allow her aunt's thoughtful glance to disturb her further, Morgana moved hastily into the courtyard. Her preoccupation making her momentarily unaware of the uneasy silence that met her arrival, Morgana was about to turn toward the house when her eye caught Aggie's pale face where she stood stiffly a few feet away. The fear reflected there jerked her to an unceremonious stop. Turning her head to survey the scene more thoroughly, she became aware for the first time of the presence of three hard-looking individuals in the corner of the yard, who followed her actions closely with their eyes as they fingered large, evil-looking knives clenched in their hands. The entire household staff was grouped in the far corner of the courtyard, the outright terror on their faces causing her heart to begin a wild thumping in her breast.

Her voice far more bold than she felt, Morgana demanded harshly, "What . . . who are these men, Aggie? What do they . . ."

Her words ending in a sharp gasp, Morgana was abruptly snatched from her feet by the strength of an arm that snaked unexpectedly around her waist from behind, effectively pinning her arms to her sides as she was pulled back roughly

161

against the heat of a perspiring male body. The pressure of a cold blade against her throat thwarted the scream that rose to her lips, forcing her head back as a harsh voice hissed in her ear, "You will be quiet, señorita! You will not make a sound until the rest of your party arrives. We have found little in this house to repay us for our troubles here today, and my men and I will have our payment one way or another . . ."

Breathless with fear, Morgana closed her eyes, gasping as she was dragged from the center of the courtyard to a point indiscernible from the entrance. Panicked by the sound of her aunt's and Devon's footsteps on the tiles, she attempted to call out in warning, only to have the grip tighten, crushing her ribs until her breath came in short, painful gasps. The pressure of the blade increased simultaneously, accompanied by a hot, searing sensation on her neck. A jolt of terror penetrating her dazed state, Morgana realized that the skin of her throat had been pierced . . . that the hot, sticky wetness trickling down her neck and onto her breasts was her own blood!

The voice in her ear was relentless. "Not a sound, señorita! You will not survive the next cut!"

"José! Rosita!" Her aunt's soft tone was tinged with impatience. *"Que pasa? Donde está Morga . . ."*

The sound of Tía Isabella's footsteps and words came to a simultaneous halt just outside Morgana's line of vision. The long, tension-filled moment that followed was broken by Devon's deep voice as he demanded coldly, "What's going on in here?"

His relentless arm crushing the breath from her body, her captor dragged her forward into full view, his knife pressing cruelly against the tender skin of her throat as he grated harshly, "You will move into the center of the courtyard, señor *y* señora!"

Tía Isabella's gasp echoed in the silence that followed, her eyes widening with fear even as Devon demanded in an expressionless tone, "Let the girl go, *hombre.* You will gain nothing by hurting her."

The blade remained at her throat, restricting Morgana's line of vision as she strained away from the sharp edge, not allowing her to see the cold fury reflected in Devon's icy gaze as he demanded again, "I said, let the girl go, *hombre.*"

"*Basta!*" Her captor's rasping hiss was accompanied by a threatening movement of the knife at Morgana's throat. "Now, señora, you will remove your diamonds and give them to my friend. *Sí,* that is correct," he urged slowly as Tía Isabella's hands moved shakily to her earrings. "Now you, señor, you will empty your pockets . . ."

"You play with your own life, *hombre.*" Devon's voice was a harsh whisper. "You are in the home of General Manuel Escobar, a close associate of Presidente Santa Anna himself. The girl is his niece. If you hurt her, you will assure your own death."

A low, evil laugh his only response to Devon's statement, Morgana's captor pulled her even more tightly back against him to whisper gratingly into her ear, "Ah, señorita, the American señor tells me I must not hurt you or Santa Anna will punish me. But I think this American señor would like to take you away from me so that he may console you. Perhaps I will take you with me . . ."

A low growl from Devon's direction brought a harsh laugh from her captor as he jerked Morgana backwards another step. "Keep your distance, señor, or I will slit the señorita's throat!"

"Pedro, Carlos, Diego, *pronto! Vamos!*" Signaling with a sharp movement of his head, Morgana's captor directed his men to the exit. Swiftly following his orders, the men moved momentarily past Morgana's line of vision. Two of them struggled with heavy sacks as the third waved his broad knife threateningly.

Aware of the tensing of her captor's body as his men waited expectantly near the entrance, Morgana felt a wave of sheer terror course through her veins as he mumbled hesitantly, "You are a very efficient shield, señorita. Perhaps I should take you with me . . ."

"No! You must not take her! *Por favor, señor . . .*" Tía Isabella's sharp cry was heard over the gasps of the servants the moment before a large, dark shadow flashed into Morgana's line of vision.

"No! Señor, I warn you!" The voice in her ear was shrill, stopping Devon in his tracks as it continued menacingly, "I will slit her throat! See . . . see how lovely she bleeds, your beautiful señorita . . ."

In a moment of unmitigated horror, Morgana felt the knife move swiftly across her throat! The stinging blade penetrated her skin; a hot stream of wetness cascaded down her throat and onto her breasts! A high, penetrating scream rang in her ears as the courtyard reeled before her eyes! A rapidly encroaching darkness welcomed her . . . blotted out the pain . . . the echo of her own labored breathing . . . the sound of a deep, agonized voice calling her name in the short second before blackness abruptly overwhelmed her.

A deep, soul-shaking fear immobilizing his mind, Devon saw the gleaming blade slip across Morgana's throat. The stream of blood spurting from the cut was startlingly red against the whiteness of her skin, releasing a hoarse cry of rage from his paralyzed throat. Springing forward, Devon caught Morgana's limp body as it was flung brutally to the ground.

Barely conscious of the clatter of horses' hooves sounding a few moments later in the street outside the door, he scooped Morgana up into his arms, and, scaling the steps two at a time, moved rapidly into the house.

Unable to tear his eyes from the streaming wound, Devon laid her on the sitting room chaise.

"Aggie . . . quickly . . . some water and some dry cloths!" Jerking a clean white handkerchief from his pocket, he attempted to cleanse the area of blood so he might view the cut more clearly. He moved the handkerchief across the wound with a trembling hand, a thickness gathering in his own throat as the cloth was immediately soaked with blood. Darting a glance upward to Morgana's face, he noted that it was drained of color . . . that she was still unconscious. Beginning to feel the rise of panic, he called harshly, "Aggie . . . quickly . . ."

Unconscious of the frantic activity that moved around him, Devon was uncertain who had placed the clean cloth in his hands as he attempted to clear the area a little further. His mind registered the encouraging fact that the wound was not gushing the large amounts of blood that would indicate an artery had been severed. Beginning to feel a surge of hope, Devon realized that the bleeding had begun to slow, and, taking care to press gently on the surface of the wound with the cloth, he turned to dip another into the basin of water that had been placed at his elbow. Removing the gentle pressure long enough to run a wet cloth over the cut, he saw clearly for the first time the long, slender slit that ran from one side of Morgana's throat to the other! But it was only a surface wound, he was certain! Rinsing away the new blood that oozed from the cut, he swallowed against the tightness in his own throat. Yes! There was no damage beyond the marring of her flawless skin and a loss of blood, he was sure of it! Already the blood was beginning to coagulate under the gentle pressure of his hand. Morgana's breathing was shallow . . . she was unconscious . . . but she was alive. The thief had obviously cut her just deep enough to cause a diversion that would allow him and his men to escape! Morgana would be all right . . . she *had* to be . . .

Keeping a steady pressure on the wound, Devon turned to moisten another cloth. Carefully running it across her forehead, he then slid the cooling wetness down her cheek and across her still lips. There was a sign of movement around her eyes . . . the dark, incredibly long lashes fluttered against her white cheeks in the few seconds before they lifted slowly to stare with a dazed, disoriented expression into his face. His voice choked with emotion, Devon whispered softly, "Morgana . . . you're goin' to be all right. Don't be frightened. You're goin' to be all right."

A cooling sensation moved across her brow, penetrating the darkness that cradled her. It moved down her cheek and across her lips, the refreshing wetness welcome against the parched surface. But she did not want to awaken . . . Awakening allowed the return of pain . . . the searing heat that burned her neck, making it difficult to swallow . . . the raw ache in her ribs that became more painful with each breath . . . the stark, soul-shattering fear that the darkness had overcome.

But she could hide no longer . . . the sound of a deep voice calling her name dragged her back relentlessly to consciousness despite herself. The voice was low . . . the words indistinct . . . but the tone was gentle, insistent, warmly familiar. Her mind responding instinctively to the emotion present in the deep sound, she struggled to open her eyes. The scene that met her sight was confused, disoriented. Surely it could not be Devon crouched above her. It could not be his broad hand that stroked her brow so gently. But there was a heaviness on her throat . . . a restricting pressure that would not allow the passage of sound, and, knowing a moment of panic, Morgana's eyes flew open wide, tears streaming from their gleaming darkness as her words remained trapped in her throat!

But a gentle hand moved to cup her cheek; a handsome, familiar face moved close to hers to whisper in her ear.

"Morgana . . . darlin' . . . don't be frightened. You have a wound on your throat. The bleedin' has stopped, but I must apply pressure a little longer. I don't want to hurt you, darlin' . . . but I can't take the chance of the bleedin' beginnin' again." Moving back enough so she might be able to focus on his intently serious face, Devon continued softly, "Do you understand what I'm sayin', Morgana? The doctor will be here soon, and he'll bind your wound. You'll be able to speak then, darlin'. Don't be afraid."

Her eyes closing against the pain, Morgana unsuccessfully attempted to swallow. Allowing herself a few moments respite, she attempted the difficult maneuver again. Finally accomplishing the small feat, Morgana opened her eyes to the handsome face that hovered over hers, her mind unconsciously registering the moistness in the dark eyes returning her gaze. But she was tired . . . too tired to understand the soft words whispered encouragingly . . . too tired to do more than allow the warm, gentle sounds to lull her back into a softer, terror-free darkness . . .

* * *

"You must be firm, Antonio! You must stand by your decisions . . . not allow yourself to be deterred from the course necessary to save our country! Gómez abused his office by furthering programs detrimental to Mexico. The damage done during his months in office will be difficult to remedy, but you must . . ."

Nodding silently to Manuel Escobar's ardent words, Santa Anna affixed a thoughtful gaze on his general's serious face. The grey brows were drawn into a frown, the lined face composed into an expression that bespoke the man's sincerity. There was no doubt Manuel spoke from the heart and from his deep conviction that he, Antonio Santa Anna, was the only man who could bring peace and prosperity to his country.

Yes, Manuel was right. He must keep a tight rein on the course of events that threatened his own rule. According to the constitution, the term of the present congress, sympathetic to Gómez Farías, had expired on April 15, while he was still at Manga de Clavo. Taking full advantage of the law, which granted them an additional thirty days if conditions in the country warranted, the deputies had remained the full additional term; and, upon its conclusion, had declared their intention to remain convened for an indefinite period! Incensed by the dilution of his authority, Santa Anna had immediately issued a curt notice stating that if the congress did not disperse, he would turn them out! A vociferous protest had followed, to which he had declared publicly that the vice president and the hoodlum congress had exercised a tyranny over the people, and now that he was once again in control, he would reverse the irresponsible actions of the group and return stability to the country.

His outspoken statement, which had brought him to the very emergency that had necessitated the present conference between Manuel and himself, had caused him to abandon his plans for a pleasant evening including Doña Isabella and her lovely niece, Morgana, just a short hour before. His charges had resulted in Gómez Farías's departure from the capital, his voluntary exile . . . but far more worrisome than that

167

simple action was the advice contained in the missive he had received a short time prior to the arrival of Doña Isabella and Morgana. Suspicion was rife that Gómez Farías was heading for New Orleans, where he was expected to contact the leaders of the rapidly developing Texas discontent. With that news, Devon Howard's presence in the city assumed even greater importance than before. His own dealings with Howard could perhaps turn the sympathies of the Texans in his favor . . . eliminate the threat of a coalition between the two discontented factions. Yes, he had to be careful with Howard . . . he had to keep tight control while he gained the complete support of the people. He already had the support of the Church and the army. During his "recuperation" at Manga de Clavo, he had been in constant contact with the leaders of the conservative faction, and a complete conservative plan had been devised, which he expected to put into action in Puebla, Jalapa, Orizaba, and Oaxaca within a short period of time. Yes, it was time for strong statements and strong policy . . .

Drawn from his thoughts by Manuel's words as he read from the statement they had drafted that evening, Santa Anna listened intently.

"Today the execrable Gómez Farías left the capital, overwhelmed with the just imprecations of the leading city of Columbus's new world on which his terrible acts weighed so heavily. Gómez Farías attracted, like an ill-fated comet, cholera and misery; immorality and tyranny; espionage and treason; ignorance and sacrilege; the promotion of delinquents and the demotion of the honorable; the triumph of the worthless canaille and the debasement of the select people; terror and mourning in families, banishment, sorrow, and death in a thousand and more horrible forms . . ."

The sound of Manuel's voice drifted from his ears as Santa Anna came to a silent conclusion. Yes, it was generally accepted that the liberal legislation enacted by Farías had introduced chaos into the country, and the time was ripe for him to assume full control of the government. He needed to be patient a little longer . . . until the cries of the people were loud and insistent. He would, then, humbly take control of the government in a newer, stronger position than before. He needed only to be patient . . . and firm . . .

A small smile lifting the darkness from his features, Santa Anna's thoughts drifted from the heavy political manipulations that had occupied his mind for the past hour. The presence of Manuel's lovely niece in the capital would allow him to occupy his time with considerable pleasure while he was attempting to be patient. There was no doubt she was much impressed by him. He had seen the same expression of intrigued interest reflected in her eyes many times before. The only difference here lay in the girl's position as the niece of Manuel Escobar. While allowing him to spend much time in her company, it would also impose upon him the need for complete discretion and care. But he had no doubt that an association with the beautiful, exuberant young woman would be well worth any problems he might encounter. He had, in fact, found in the dark hours of the night that her lovely face had returned many times to his mind. He had a driving desire to touch the flawless, white skin that fascinated him so completely . . . to ascertain if it was truly as smooth and soft as it appeared; to satisfy himself that the gentle, womanly curves of her petite figure were truly the delight they appeared to his appreciative glance; to know the comfort her small body would give him; to hear her sigh . . . call his name with sweet passion in her voice. He was certain he would not find it difficult to convince the bright-haired beauty that his need for her was great . . . that his wife, although a fine woman, was not sufficient to fill his needs and that she, dear Morgana, could and would fill the vacuum in his life that Ines saw fit to create with her decision to boycott the capital. He would also convince her that in her position as Manuel's niece, she could, without suspicion, fill the position of hostess on some of the occasions when a hostess was needed for the president of Mexico. She would no doubt be extremely flattered, and bestowing upon her an honor such as that should provide him with many beautiful hours in payment for his generosity. Oh, yes, he had much to look forward too. . . . much to occupy his mind while he waited patiently for the precise moment to take over autocratic control of the government. And he had no doubt he would have a very short wait for both potentialities to crystallize into fact.

He would give Morgana the first taste of his generosity tomorrow. He had already decided to send her a present . . . a mantilla, to replace the horrendous American bonnet she had worn that day. Morgana indeed had the face of a madonna . . . perfect for a mantilla. It would be a welcoming gift to the niece of his friend and compatriot, Manuel Escobar . . . nothing more . . . but it would set the stage perfectly for his plans for the future . . . a future in which he . . .

A heavy, insistent rapping on the door interrupted his pleasant trend of thought, returning his frown in the moment before he responded sharply, *"Entra!"* The brisk command, delivered with a rapidly darkening frown, brought a flush to the anxious servant's face.

"Señor Presidente, there has been an incident at General Escobar's home! A messenger has just arrived with word that General Escobar's home has been robbed and his niece injured by the thieves in their escape. Señora Escobar has requested her husband's immediate return . . ."

"Madre de Dios!" Manuel's short gasp preceded the quick glance he turned in Santa Anna's direction as he silently sought permission to comply with his wife's request.

"Of course, you must return home immediately, Manuel. You need have no worry about the response we have drafted. I will have my secretary take care of it without delay."

"Muchas grácias, Antonio." His face a pale grey in color, Manuel turned immediately in the direction of the doorway. Pausing only a moment at the door to acknowledge Santa Anna's admonition to send him word as to the disposition of the situation that existed at his home, Manuel Escobar made a quick exit.

His eyes focused unseeingly on the door that had closed behind his stalwart associate, Santa Anna frowned even more deeply. Turning back toward the desk, he snatched at the drafted response, his hand unconsciously tightening into a fist as angry thoughts ran chaotically through his mind. It had been his first inclination to go with his friend so he might see for himself . . . assure himself that Morgana Pierce was indeed all right. But such an action, such intimate concern from a man in his position, would be unseemly. Instead, he must wait until Manuel sent word as to the lovely Morgana's condition. A flush of frustration flooding his face, Santa Anna uttered a low epithet. The lovely young American must indeed be all right . . . or he would personally see to it that the thieves were brought to justice . . . that their bodies hung for all to see in the square near the Escobar residence. Yes, he would make them pay if indeed they had thwarted his plans . . . his beautiful plans . . .

Raking a trembling hand through his hair, Devon took a deep, shuddering breath and darted another anxious glance toward the closed door at the end of the hallway. Dr. Zavella had arrived more than a half hour before. Following the short, balding doctor's brisk instructions, he had lifted a semiconscious Morgana carefully into his arms and carried her to her room. After laying her on her bed, he had been curtly dismissed to his own silent fears . . . the same silent fears that had caused him the agony of the last half hour. Refusing to move any farther than a few feet down the corridor from Morgana's room, he had begun a relentless pacing, intensely aware of his own ineffectuality. But he could not seem to get himself in hand . . . to function in any other way than to wait for the door at the end of the corridor to open. The picture of Morgana's white, still face was constant before his mind, as was the panic in her eyes at her temporary inability to speak. The gradual abating of her fear at his gentle reassurances had stirred new violent emotions inside him that shook him to the core. And he was frightened . . . for the first time in his life he faced a fear he could not overcome . . . could not reason away. He was afraid . . . afraid . . .

Turning swiftly at the sound of a light step behind him, Devon saw the short, matronly woman whom Dona Isabella had addressed as Rosita standing behind him.

Her eyes filled with sympathy, she motioned to a glass she held on a small tray. "Señor, it has been a long wait, but *el*

Dr. Zavella is a good man. He will take good care of the señorita. In the meantime, señor . . .''

Grasping the glass with a grateful nod, Devon tossed the contents down his throat in a quick gulp. The stinging liquid burned his throat, sending a resulting warmth through his body. Setting the empty glass back on the tray, he was about to voice his gratitude when the sound of an opening door jerked his attention to the two fingers emerging from Morgana's room. Covering the area between them in a few sweeping strides, he eyed the sober faces of Dr. Zavella and Doña Isabella before grating hoarsely, "Morgana . . . she is all right. . . ?''

Her small features pinched with strain, Doña Isabella replied in a trembling voice, "*Sí* . . . *Sí*, Morgana is all right, Devon. She will recover. The wound is not mortal, *grácias a Díos*.'' Her voice breaking on the last word, Dona Isabella fought to control her tears as Dr. Zavella turned kind, understanding eyes in her direction.

"Do not upset yourself any further, Doña Isabella. Your niece has lost considerable blood and will undoubtedly feel weak for some time, but she is in no danger. She is a strong, healthy young woman. Other than a small scar that she will have for a indefinite period, she will emerge from this incident as healthy and complete a person as she was before.''

The doctor's reassuring words freeing him from the fear that he held him immobile for so long, Devon felt a slow exhilaration sweeping his senses. Unwilling to wait another moment, he turned pruposefully toward Morgana's room, only to be stopped by Doña Isabella's soft admonition, "Devon, Morgana is still shaken and weak. You will please take care not to awaken her if she has slipped off to sleep. I will return in a few moments . . . as soon as I have spoken a little further with Dr. Zavella.''

Nodding automatically to Doña Isabella's warning, Devon reached for the doorknob, his heart beginning a heavy pounding as he opened the door.

Small and incredibly lovely, Morgana lay unmoving against the starkness of the white sheets. Her still face was unnaturally pale, in startling contrast with the tumble of briliant curls stretched across the pillow and the dark fans of ashes resting against her cheeks. The scooped neckline of her delicate night rail revealed a bandage encircling her slender neck, through which a few drops of blood were visible.

Hardly conscious of Aggie's silent presence in the corner of the room, Devon was at Morgana's side in moments. Experiencing a desperate need to hold her close, yet frightened of waking her, he reached out tentatively. The gleaming chestnut curl was silky to the touch . . . warm and alive. His pain so deep it was almost physical; he uttered a low groan. Succumbing at last to his need, he crouched beside her, cupping her pale cheek with his palm.

When had this need for Morgana developed inside him? When had the visual delight of her beauty become indispensable to him . . . the challenge of her indomitable spirit become a necessity . . . the stimulus of her sharp mind and her innate sensuality become an integral part of his existence? The only thing of which he was certain was that the thought of losing her was beyond bearing. He ached . . . ached to hold her close against him, but he dared not. She was too weak. He dared not disturb her.

The skin of her cheek was smooth and cool to his touch, frighteningly white. Caressing it gently, he was not aware of speaking as he mumbled in a low, soothing voice, "Morgana, darlin' . . . sweet darlin' . . ."

The soft, almost indiscernible sound of his voice brought the first sign of movement to Morgana's still features. A small frown moving across her brow, she appeared to resist returning consciousness as her eyelids fluttered slowly open. Her eyes fixed uncertainly on Devon's face for a few long moments before abruptly snapping wide, reflecting the terror with which she greeted the return of memory. Her lips worked desperately to form the words her throat refused to release, causing a wave of panic to sweep Devon's senses in the moments before she managed hoarsely, "Devon . . . I was afraid . . . I was so afraid . . . I could hear your footsteps coming into the yard, but he . . . he cut me when I tried to warn you. I tried to call . . . but I couldn't . . ."

Tears began streaming freely from eyes dark with the re-

newed horror of recollection. Morgana became more agitated, her breathing short and quick. Sharing her distress,
Devon cupped her face in his palms and stroked away
the tears that continued unabated. Lowering his head, he
pressed light kisses against her cool cheeks, the damp eyelids,
the corners of her mouth, mumbling soft words of consolation as she continued to recite the terror still vivid in her
mind.

". . . he jerked me backwards with him. I couldn't see
you, but I could hear you coming, and . . . and he hurt me,
Devon . . . I couldn't breathe, and he laughed when I tried
to struggle free. I could feel the blood running down my
throat . . ." Raising a shaky hand to her throat, Morgana
touched the bandage, a small flicker of confused disbelief
moving across her eyes as her words stumbled to a halt.

Taking the small hand in his, Devon kissed it with a fierce
tenderness. Leaning forward until his lips grazed hers
lightly, he spoke intently, "It's all over now, darlin'. You
don't have to be afraid anymore. The thieves are gone . . .
they won't come back here again. You don't have to be
afraid anymore . . ."

Not seeming to hear his words, Morgana continued in a
low voice that trembled and failed in her anxiety. "Devon
. . . I never . . . I never saw his face . . . I can remember
his arm crushing my ribs . . . his voice in my ear . . . his
breath against my cheek . . . I can remember the way the
knife felt when he . . ." Unable to finish her statement,
Morgana paused a moment to swallow tightly before she uttered in a hushed tone, ". . . but I don't . . . I never saw his
face, Devon . . ."

Feeling helpless against her fear, yet knowing a compelling
need to comfort her, Devon spoke ardently, his tone penetrating the haze of Morgana's disoriented thoughts.

"Morgana, darlin', it's all over now. *I* saw the man's face,
darlin', and I give you my word, I'll never let him or anyone
else hurt you again. Do you hear me, Morgana? Do you
believe what I'm tellin' you? I'll never let him hurt you
again . . ."

Gold sparks glittered brightly in her brimming eyes as

Morgana stared intently into Devon's fierce expression. Holding his breath, Devon waited as Morgana searched his intense face, the wildness in her eyes abating as she attempted to speak again.

Her lips trembling, Morgana nodded, wincing with the pain that ensued as she muttered hoarsely, "Yes . . . yes, I believe you, Devon . . ."

His heart filled to bursting at the trust reflected in her eyes, Devon managed a small smile. Pressing his lips lightly against hers, he whispered in return, "Then rest now, darlin'. I'll take care of you. You don't have to be afraid anymore."

Carefully slipping his arms under and around her, Devon pulled her into the circle of his embrace, a rush of warmth moving through his body as she settled close against him. His throat tight with the myriad of emotions assailing his senses, he mumbled softly, "Go to sleep, darlin' . . . my sweet darlin'."

CHAPTER FIVE

"You needn't get up again, Morgana! I'll do that for you!"

Aggie's rapid step across the sala toward the book that had slipped from Morgana's lap onto the floor was brought to a swift, premature halt by Morgana's spontaneous frown. Standing with slow deliberation, Morgana bent over and snatched the book from the rug. Taking a deep breath in an effort to temper the sharp response that had risen to her lips, she spoke in a slow, emphatic tone directly into the large, owlish eyes fastened on her face.

"Aggie, I do not appreciate being treated like an invalid! Almost a week has passed since . . . since I was injured, and I am all but recuperated now. It is only owing to Dr. Zavella's and Tía Isabella's great caution that I still continue to spend a part of the day resting. I truly feel quite well!"

"You only feel well *because* you spend a good part of the day resting, Morgana! If you were to resume full activity as you wish, you would soon see your limitations. You have lost a lot of blood, and it will take time . . ."

"Nonsense!" Losing patience with Aggie's insistence on a frailty she did not feel, Morgana waved an annoyed, dismissing hand that stopped Aggie's words in midsentence. "You will please desist in this insistence that I have been internally weakened! I am not *weak!* I feel quite strong and *well!* I am . . ."

"Judgin' from the strength of your voice, darlin', I'd say your recuperation is very near complete!"

The low, amused voice coming from the doorway behind snapped Morgana's head in its direction. A spontaneous smile curving her lips, Morgana experienced a flush of pleasure as her eyes touched on Devon Howard. His hard features relaxed in a small, teasing smile, he came to stand directly in front of her before taking her small hands in his and lifting them gently to his lips.

Wishing fervently she could find a way to rid herself of Aggie's relentless supervision, Morgana responded in a voice that did not betray the heavy hammering of her heart. "Aggie and Tía Isabella would have me remain in my bed the entire day if they had their way, Devon. It is only because of my insistence that I'm allowed here, in the sala in the afternoon hours, and only with their severe admonitions to remain seated where I can benefit from the healing rays of the sun and not overdo! I cannot convince them that I am quite well!"

Extremely conscious of the fact that Devon had not released her hands, but continued to hold them warmly in his own, Morgana continued in a tone of pleading insistence, "Look at me, Devon. Do I not look well? Won't you speak to Tía Isabella in my behalf? I should dearly like to walk in the garden for a while, despite . . ." Unwilling to finish her remark as a host of dark memories flashed before her eyes, Morgana repeated doggedly, "Surely the walk down the stairs and across the courtyard is not beyond my strength at this stage of convalescence!"

Fascinated by his broadening smile and the warm light in the light eyes intent on her face, Morgana allowed herself to be drawn nearer the window as Devon replied consideringly, "Well, if I'm to give an accurate reply to that question, I'll have to get a better look, darlin'. Now let me see . . ."

An excited breathlessness slowly consumed reason as Morgana stood silently under Devon's close scrutiny. Conscious of the fact that the glow in his light eyes slowly assumed an intense quality as his gaze moved intimately over her face, Morgana swallowed tightly. Uncertain whether the abrupt weakness in her knees was indeed a sign of waning strength or merely her reaction to Devon's heady perusal, she remained motionless. His gaze held hers for a few silent moments before moving to caress the smoothness of her brow and the delicate planes of her cheeks and coming to rest at her slender, parted lips.

"Morgana." Aggie's inopportune interjection brought a frown to Morgana's face. "You've been standing quite long enough. I do think you should rest now."

"I'm sure Morgana appreciates your concern, Aggie, as I do." Devon's quiet reply precluded the sharp response that had risen to Morgana's lips. "But I'm of a mind that a little exercise will probably benefit her at this stage of recuperation. It won't do her any good to allow her muscles to weaken."

"Dr. Zavella said Morgana is not strong enough to negotiate the stairs." Aggie's reply was adamant, delivered with an unrelenting frown that pushed Morgana over the edge of control.

"Silly nonsense, Aggie! I'm completely recovered! Anyone would think my legs were injured instead of . . ."

"Morgana . . ." Efficiently interrupting her growing tirade, Devon said softly, "Perhaps Dr. Zavella is right. Perhaps you shouldn't attempt the stairs yet. . . ."

"Devon!" Crushed by his sudden betrayal, Morgana stared into Devon's abruptly serious face. A hint of suspicion growing in her mind at the light dancing in the depths of his eyes, she paused to allow him to finish his statement, and was startled when he bent to scoop her up firmly into his arms. Held high against his chest, she was breathtakingly close to the slow smile that so devastated her senses as he continued huskily, ". . . so if you truly want to take a cautious walk in the garden, I'll carry you downstairs."

178

"Madre de Díos!"

Doña Isabella's gasped expletive snapped all heads in the direction of the doorway the second before the small woman rushed worriedly into the room.

"Morgana, you are not well? You are feeling weak? Quickly, Devon, you must take her to her room."

Directing her response into Devon's amused eyes, Morgana replied pointedly, "See? Will you tell them, Devon? They're making an invalid out of me with their concern."

"But . . . but . . ." Doña Isabella's sputtering response demonstrated her confusion, and, turning his most charming smile in the frightened woman's direction, Devon stated agreeably, "I was just agreein' with Aggie, Doña Isabella. Morgana is probably too weak to navigate the stairs safely, but since she had such a strong desire to walk in your beautiful garden, I'll settle the problem by carryin' her down the stairs. She may rest whenever she feels the need when she is there."

Unable to withstand the warm charm of Devon's logic, Doña Isabella hesitated only a moment before replying, *"Sí,* Devon. Perhaps a change in scene will do Morgana good. But you will watch her carefully for the first sign of tiring. . ."

"Tía Isabella, por favor! I am truly quite well!"

Smiling indulgently, Doña Isabella nodded her head. *"Sí.* I am sure you feel well, Morgana, but I am determined to keep you that way. I have come too close to losing a treasured new addition to my family, and I will not risk that happening again."

Attempting to make light of the statement that had touched her deeply, Morgana turned her head to address Devon soberly, "Tía Isabella is right, Devon. You will please watch me carefully. Now, let's go!"

Her aunt's low laughter as Devon carried her easily from the room lightening her mood, Morgana adjusted her arm around Devon's neck, mumbling in a barely audible voice, "Oh, yes, Devon. You must watch me carefully."

Lowering his head to brush her cheek lightly with his lips,

179

Devon's replied softly in return, "I always do, darlin' . . . I always do. . . ."

The heavy thudding of his heart was completely unrelated to the physical exertion of carrying Morgana's light form down the short flight of steps to the courtyard. Devon avoided the intense scrutiny of the dark, doe-shaped eyes closely regarding his face. Hell, he didn't dare look into those eyes a minute longer. If he allowed himself to fall any deeper under Morgana's spell, he would be utterly beyond control. Aware of his own vulnerability, Devon felt a momentary flicker of uncertainty as to which he actually preferred . . . the hostile atmosphere that had formerly existed between Morgana and himself, or the new, openly mutual warmth that now existed between them. Chancing a quick glance into Morgana's glowing countenance, he swallowed hard. One thing was certain . . . the former was much easier for him to handle than the latter. Just where that hostility had disappeared was another thing of which he was uncertain, but he was grateful that it had. While still not quite believing it, he had refused to question the miracle that had transformed the snapping hatred in Morgana's beautiful eyes to a glowing regard that he felt to the core of his soul. As for himself, he had tired of his own subconscious reminders that he was beginning to become too involved with Morgana . . . that there was no future in such an involvement. He was deeply conscious of the fact that he was committed to a cause for which Morgana had not the slightest understanding or regard, and to a life where she would be totally out of place. But that knowledge had not freed him from the sloe-eyed vision that flitted through his dreams . . . the memory of her slender body pressed intimately against his own.

As if he did not have enough to contend with, he was also subjected to Aggie's intense scrutiny on his daily visits since the near disaster. Aggie was distrustful of him . . . an attitude for which he was forced to admit she had due cause . . . but his patience with her interference was beginning to wear thin. After all, perhaps this new relationship that existed between Morgana and himself was

180

transitory . . . a result of the shock of her terrifying experience and the fact that his was the first face she had awakened to see. If so, he was grateful for the twist of fate that allowed him to be there . . . so that he might be holding her in his arms as he was now.

Adjusting his hold as his foot touched down on the courtyard, Devon slid his eyes to the smiling face so close to his.

Deeply stirred as she returned his gaze warmly, he commented softly, "You look like a small, contented kitten, Morgana." Making no attempt to set her on her feet, he continued across the courtyard toward the secluded garden on the far side, ". . . and if I listen closely, I'm almost certain I'll be able to hear you purr."

"And why shouldn't I purr, Devon?" Confirming his observance with a small sigh, Morgana snuggled her head contentedly against his shoulder. "It's a lovely day . . . I'm feeling very well, and I've finally gotten my way after three days of argument and am about to walk in the garden!"

"Somehow, darlin'," his dark brow raised rakishly as he shot her a skeptical glance, "I didn't think it would be this easy to make you purr, but if a walk in the garden is presently the answer to your fondest dream, I'm about to make it come true." Setting her on her feet as soon as he reached the shelter of the flowering shrubs and small trees that lined the cultivated area, he took her hand and urged her deeper into its confines. Finally satisfied that they were at least partially shielded from watchful eyes, Devon drew her into a shaft of sunlight.

"Now, let me take a good look at you so I can make a better judgment about your state of health."

The moment he tilted her face up to his, Devon realized the folly of his action. A slight pallor still clung to the magnificent contours of the lovely face lifted obediently to his. Light circles under brilliant gold-flecked eyes added a touch of fragile appeal that touched his heart, further weakening his badly waning resistance to her almost ethereal beauty. In the unadorned white cotton gown she wore, the wide bandage emphasizing her slender neck, her glowing chestnut curls pulled simply back from her face and fastened behind her ears with ornate combs, she looked like a delicate China doll . . . a beautiful doll he longed to possess completely . . . make his own.

Raising his hand, he touched the gleaming tendrils that had escaped the combs to curl appealingly at her hair-line. In a slow, gentle caress, he ran the tips of his fingers along the contour of her cheek and across her chin, his glance stopping abruptly as it came to rest on the soft, parted lips that trembled lightly under his heady visual assault. He remembered distinctly the taste of their honeyed sweetness; the incredible wonder he had experienced when those lips had parted to allow him full access to her mouth; the velvet softness of her tongue as he had caressed it with his own.

Mesmerized by the full lips slowly descending, Morgana waited in breathless suspense until they touched her own. The low groan coming from deep within Devon's throat as his mouth crushed hers with growing passion sent a flush of warmth across her trembling frame. She leaned fully into his embrace. Yes . . . this was what she had wanted . . . had needed since the moment of awakening from the horror of the nightmare enacted in the courtyard. In the darkness of that ordeal, it had been Devon's face that had shown her the way to light . . . his voice that had guided her back . . . and his touch alone that was capable of dispelling the disquiet that remained inside her. Somehow the heated animosity that had been between them had paled in the face of her need.

With a soft sigh she allowed his mouth to work its magic again on her senses as he took her lips with short, fleeting kisses . . . moved to touch lightly on the line of her cheek . . . brushed across her fluttering lids . . . moved with breathtaking patience to the small shell of her ear to fondle it lightly with his tongue. A giddy light-headedness assailing her, Morgana lifted her hands to cling to his strength, her arms slipping around his neck as Devon crushed her close against him.

Gasping at the pain that shot through her ribs as his embrace tightened, Morgana felt Devon's spontaneous stiffening, heard the concern in his voice as he abruptly slackened his grip and held her supportively by the shoulders.

"What is it! What it is darlin'? Did I hurt you?"

"It's my ribs, Devon. I . . . I hadn't realized how sore they are. That man . . . when he grabbed me from behind he . . ."

"Forget that man, darlin'." Unwilling to allow her to continue an explanation that would necessitate reliving again the horror of the attack, he whispered against her cheek, "You're with me here, now." Drawing himself far enough away so he might look into her eyes, he continued softly, "Doña Isabella said you should rest when you feel the need. There's a bench over there. Come on, darlin' . . ."

Drawing her slowly to the corner of the garden to a carved wooden bench under a small tree, he sat unexpectedly and pulled her full onto his lap. Curving his arm around her back, he supported her gently against his chest, a deep overwhelming tenderness moving through him as Morgana relaxed against him, her head resting on his shoulder, her face pressed against his neck. Closing his eyes momentarily against the tightness in his throat, Devon raised his hand to stroke the warm silk of her hair. Hell, what was wrong with him? He had seen her pallor . . . had known she was still weak, and the moment she was in his arms, all caution disappeared. But not again. He would be careful . . . wait until she was fully recovered, and he would . . .

A flurry of movement at the entrance to the courtyard, accompanied by the rumble of voices, interrupted Devon's thoughts. Experiencing sharp regret as Morgana's head lifted from his shoulder and turned toward the growing sound, Devon felt a tug of annoyance. Realizing from Morgana's sudden stiffening and her immediate attempt to get to her feet that she, too, had recognized the voices of Antonio Santa Anna and her uncle, he contrarily refused to let her rise.

Turning a pleading look into his hardening expression, Morgana said with obvious anxiety, "Devon . . . please

183

. . . my uncle and Antonio have arrived. If they were to come into the garden and find us here like this, they would think . . .'' Morgana's words trailed to a halt, further inciting the anger slowly suffusing Devon's senses.

Coaxing with sharp deliberation, Devon pressed tensely, "Yes, they would think . . ."

Uncertain exactly what she had done to incur the anger surfacing in his eyes, Morgana knew only the need to restore the former softness to their depths. Leaning forward, she pressed her mouth lightly against the firm line of his lips, feeling her tension abate as his mouth slowly relaxed to return her gentle kiss. A small, tentative smile lifting the corners of her mouth, Morgana whispered softly, "Don't be angry, Devon. I must go out and greet Tio Manuel and his guest."

Abruptly ashamed of his behavior, Devon returned her smile, lowering his head to press a final light kiss against her lips before lifting her to her feet and standing beside her. "All right, darlin', we'll both go out. We'll walk another time. . . ."

Nodding her concurrence, Morgana preceded him into the courtyard.

Immediately aware of the disapproval that flicked across the faces of the two men as Morgana emerged from the garden, Devon followed a few steps behind Morgana as she made a surprisingly unsteady advance and greeted them warmly.

His observant eyes assessing her approach and her pallor, Don Manuel took the small hand extended to him in greeting. Lowering his cheek to politely accept Morgana's kiss, he commented quietly, "I think it was unwise of your aunt to allow you downstairs so soon, Morgana. Or perhaps you have been too long on your feet this afternoon. In any case, I think it would be wise if you returned upstairs to the sitting room now. I was just commenting to Antonio how well you were recuperating and he expressed a desire to visit."

"I wanted to walk in the garden, Tío Manuel, and Devon was kind enough to carry me down so I would not overdo." Noting the tightening of her uncle's features at her comment, Morgana continued hurriedly, turning her full attention to the handsome Mexican at her uncle's side, "I am honored that you should take time from your busy schedule to visit me, Antonio. Shall we all go upstairs to the sala? I'm certain Tía Isabella will be as delighted to see you as I."

"Ah, but not as delighted as I am to see you almost well once again, Morgana." His eyes dark with sincerity, Antonio Santa Anna took the small hand that trembled ever so slightly and brought it lightly to his lips. "But I'm afraid I agree with your uncle, *querida*. You are obviously in need of some rest."

"Well, since the opinion seems to be mutually shared . . ." Devon's voice was unexpectedly near her ear the moment before Morgana felt herself scooped up high into the air by a pair of familiar arms. Turning to the face so intimately near, Morgana felt a warm flush rise to her cheeks as Devon continued in a soft, self-possessed voice, "then I expect the best thing to do would be to retire to the sala right now." Turning his broad back on the frowns of the two he left momentarily in his wake, Devon started abruptly in the direction of the steps.

Her glance moving over Devon's shoulder as he started briskly up the staircase, Morgana groaned inwardly at her uncle's obvious disapproval, and the surprisingly dark expression on Antonio Santa Anna's face. A low voice in her ear snapped her attention back to Devon as he whispered, "They don't like it much . . . seein' you in my arms, do they darlin'?" Laughing softly at Morgana's expression, which confirmed only too well his assessment of the situation, Devon continued in the same confidential tone, "Well, that's too bad, isn't it, darlin'? Just too damned bad. . . ."

Barely conscious of the opulence of the reception area into which he was being shown, Devon experienced instead a growing impatience. The long series of rooms through which

185

he had been ushered since entering the palace and the endless protocol restrictions he was forced to endure before he was finally to be allowed to keep his appointment with Santa Anna had caused a knot of irritation to form in his stomach. Barely able to restrain the short, angry snort that rose to his lips, he nodded his acquiescence to the aide's request that he remain in the reception room to await Presidente Santa Anna's appearance.

His eyes followed the short, slight Mexican's retreat back through the doorway through which they had just entered, and Devon raised a broad palm to massage the tightness in the back of his neck. Despite himself, he was feeling extremely apprehensive about his summons to the palace this morning. In the time since his arrival in the city, he had been dutifully shuffled from one aide to another with a long list of excuses that told him only that Santa Anna was not yet ready to discuss Austin's incarceration with him. Now, abruptly, after his unexpected meeting with Santa Anna yesterday in General Escobar's house, he was to be allowed to discuss the business that had brought him to Mexico in the first place! Somehow, he could not make himself believe that this summons had nothing to do with the black looks that had accompanied him as he had carried Morgana up the staircase. Remembering the manner in which Santa Anna's large, hungry eyes had caressed Morgana's face, and sensing, as he had all along, his obvious bewitchment, Devon experienced again the rise of the same raging emotion that had given him little rest that night. It was obvious to him that Santa Anna wanted Morgana, and no amount of denial would be able to convince him to the contrary. Hell, didn't he himself suffer the same malady? Didn't he know only too intimately the power of Morgana's gold-flecked eyes, the sweet persuasion of her smile, and the heady intoxication of her mouth against his . . . her softness pressed intimately close. His agitation becoming more severe, he was again assailed by the suspicion that Santa Anna had indeed experienced a sampling of Morgana's charms and was determined to experience them again. It made no difference to a man of Antonio's many vices that his wife awaited him in Manga de Clavo. Quite the

186

contrary, Doña Ines provided him with the security he desired while allowing him the freedom to indulge his fancies as he saw fit. A nameless feeling so intense that it left him shaken swept Devon's senses. But not with Morgana . . . he would not allow Santa Anna to . . .

The unexpected snap of a door latch, unnaturally loud in the silence of the room, turned Devon to the double doors at the rear of the room just as they began to open. Grateful for the moment's warning, which allowed him the time to disguise the emotions running rampant inside him, Devon returned Santa Anna's smile of greeting. Walking slowly forward, he extended his hand toward the handsome, meticulously groomed president of Mexico, unable to stifle the thought that perhaps Morgana did find him charming, unable to resist, as had countless other women in the past.

"Devon! Welcome to the *palacio!* I'm indeed sorry, my friend, that I have been unable to meet with you sooner, but it took much longer than I thought to have the paperwork on your compatriot's case transferred here so I might study the charges against him."

"Thank you, Antonio. But now that you have had an opportunity to review the case, what are your conclusions?"

Aware from the momentary stiffening of Santa Anna's smile that he must refrain from the direct attack and content himself to allow Santa Anna to set the pace for the meeting, Devon took a deep breath and a firm hand on his emotions. What the hell was the matter with him, anyway? A good man's life hung in the balance of these negotiations, as possibly did the fate of the Anglo-American colony in Texas.

"Ah, if it was as easy a dilemma to solve as that, I would have summoned you much sooner than this, my friend. I'm afraid, Devon, that the evidence I have received from Saltillo puts Colonel Austin in a very precarious light."

"And what evidence is that, Antonio?"

Noting the new harshness in Devon's voice, Santa Anna's voice took on a convincingly warm tone. "Come, let us share a glass of wine before we get down to business, Devon. We

187

are friends, are we not?''

The game of cat and mouse Santa Anna obviously desired to play did not suit Devon's preference, but realizing himself to be at a distinct disadvantage, Devon forced a smile to lips stiff with impatience. Reaching out, he took the glass offered to him, nodding his appreciation, his eyes intent on Santa Anna's cool, self-possessed figure as he turned to pour another glass for himself. An intensely measuring glance belying his casual outward posture, Santa Anna motioned Devon to a chair, taking the other immediately across from his as he began informally.

"You know, Devon, that I, myself, think rather highly of Colonel Austin. I find him to be an extremely intelligent man with great integrity, and for that reason I find the statement taken upon his arrest most disturbing."

"Since I've been unable to find out any particulars about Colonel Austin's arrest, Antonio, I would appreciate it if you would be more explicit."

"All right, Devon." His expression abruptly serious, Antonio stated quietly, "On October first last year, Colonel Austin expressed the opinion to Vice President Farías that if a remedy for the Anglo-American grievances was not quickly applied, the Texans would take the matter into their own hands, and tranquillity would be rudely disturbed. On the following day he wrote a letter to the city government of San Antonio de Béjar in which, after expressing his hopelessness of obtaining any relief in the paralyzed state of public affairs, he recommended that municipality to lose no time in communicating with all the other corporations in Texas and exhorting them to concur in the organization of a local government independent of Coahuila, even if the general government should refuse its consent. That, my friend, constituted treason in Vice President Farías's mind, and in the mind of many others. And I might add, Devon, that this information was forwarded to our attention by prominent Anglo-Americans residing in Texas."

Startled by Santa Anna's frank disclosure of the evidence against Austin, Devon hesitated momentarily before speaking, his mind racing. "Have you spoken to Colonel Austin personally, Antonio, to ascertain his position? As you yourself have stated, Colonel Austin is a man of great integrity. His loyalty to the government prior to this was unquestioned.''

"No, I have not, Devon. I confess that although he is incarcerated in this city, I felt it necessary to examine the evidence against him before taking any steps. But I do understand your concern, and am sympathetic with your desire to have your friend freed. However, because of the wealth of evidence compiled against him, I am powerless to take any steps in Colonel Austin's behalf.''

"But the man is unable to defend himself against those charges! He is imprisoned . . . not allowed communication of any sort! Isn't it the right of every free man to defend himself? Surely you can see the injustice that is being perpetrated here!''

"I see no injustice, Devon!'' A new harshness coming into his tone, Santa Anna paused a moment in an obvious attempt to rein his own flaring emotions under control. "But I do not pretend to be ignorant of your plight, and for that reason I will make a suggestion to you. Also damaging to your friend's case is a statement by the commandant general at Saltillo stating that your friend made severely inflammatory remarks at the time of his incarceration. A number of my personal guards are leaving for Saltillo tomorrow with orders to report to that same commandant general. In an effort to assure you of my cooperation, I will furnish you with a letter to General Nepocino instructing him to give you his fullest cooperation in your investigation of this affair. If you are able to convince him that he was mistaken in his understanding of Colonel Austin's statement at the time of the arrest, it would be very beneficial to Colonel Austin's case. In any event, upon your . . . return . . . I will allow you to visit Colonel Austin so that you may form a defense to be used at his trial.''

No longer any doubt in his mind that Santa Anna would use any circumstances at his disposal to further his own personal cause, Devon struggled to control the heated emotions flaring inside him. "Tomorrow, Antonio? Saltillo is at least two hundred miles from here. I would like to have a bit more time to prepare for a journey of that duration.''

"My men leave at four o'clock tomorrow morning. Their mission is urgent and must not be delayed. Surely, Devon, there is nothing here in Mexico City that takes precedence over the matter of the fate of your friend!''

Santa Anna's gaze challenged him, daring him to mention the fact that he had created a need for haste in a matter that had been left hanging since Austin's arrest four months previous. Devon didn't mention it. Awaiting his response, Santa Anna continued his intense assessment, noting the stiffening of Devon's jaw as he replied in a deceptively calm voice, "No, there is nothin' here in Mexico City important enough to take precedence over the fate of my friend, Antonio. I'll be ready to leave with your men in the mornin'.''

"Bueno!'' Obviously pleased that his objective had been so easily attained, Santa Anna moved quickly to his feet. "In that case, you had best return to your quarters now and prepare for the long journey ahead of you. *Vaya con Dios,* my friend. Be certain to contact me immediately upon your return, and I will arrange for you to speak to Colonel Austin.''

Taking the hand extended to him in a short handshake, Devon replied tightly, "You may be certain that I will do that, Antonio.''

Warmed by the glow of satisfaction sweeping his senses, Santa Anna watched the door close behind the tall, slender Texan. He had turned the situation to his own advantage once again . . . had indeed solved two problems with one solution. And that solution was to get Devon Howard out of Mexico City. His pleased expression falling away, Santa Anna recalled the tender, intimate glances exchanged between Morgana and the arrogant Texan at the time of his visit to the Escobar household the previous day. Yes, it had been a mistake to delay so long in visiting Morgana after the incident, but his need for caution was great. The Texan had seen fit to worm himself into Morgana's affections during her convalescence. Noticing the obvious friction between the two on the occasions he had seen them together previously, he had not recognized the danger. But with Howard out of the way for at least three weeks, he would have time to replace him in Morgana's regard. Yes . . . he had decided long before that he would share Morgana Pierce with no man . . . that the lovely American would belong to him. He would tolerate no interference in his plans. And he cared little that Devon Howard suspected the reason for his abrupt turnabout in the matter of Colonel Austin. It only demonstrated more clearly his own supreme power over everything and everyone in his country. Howard dared not speak out without threatening the reputation of the vulnerable young American woman. Yes, his own position was unbreachable. He was clearly in command.

A warm indolent breeze stirred the heavily laden branches outside the window, carrying the pungent aroma of ripe fruit into the sala. Sunbeams sparkling through swaying branches wove a delicate, lacy pattern on Morgana's chestnut tresses, warming her with their artistic brilliance. Her clear, chestnut-colored eyes sparked with gold trained unseeingly on the man seated opposite her, Morgana's mind wandered momentarily as she unconsciously lifted her hand to her throat. Wincing as her fingertips touched the corner of the healing wound, Morgana frowned. Dr. Zavella had seen fit to allow it to remain uncovered for the past several days and she had not yet become accustomed to the absence of the bandage. She felt little self-consciousness about the uneven scar that ran from one side of her throat to the other, but she had decided she would be far more comfortable when the constant reminder of the ugly incident in the courtyard was no longer visible to her eye each time she looked into the mirror.

"Querida . . . you are far away from me at this time, are you not?"

Flushing at the quiet reminder of her inattention, Morgana looked fully into the dark eyes of Antonio Santa

Anna.

"Oh, Antonio . . . I do apologize . . . I'm afraid the little twinge I felt when I touched . . ." Biting her lips in her anxiety over her ungracious behavior, she hesitated once again. Since her first visit a week before, Antonio had taken to accompanying Tío Manuel when he returned home each day to inquire about her health. His obvious concern touched her deeply, adding more stress to her embarrassment for her straying attention. Her eyes imploring his understanding, she hesitated to continue, at a complete loss for words.

Leaning forward, an expression of abject tenderness suffusing his serious Latin face, Antonio caressed her cheek lightly, startling her with the familiarity of his gesture.

"*No importa, querida.* Do not distress yourself. I have not yet forgiven myself for allowing you to become a victim of a terrible attack in my country. It is for that reason and because of my true affection for you that I come each day to assure myself of your returning health."

Extremely conscious of the smooth palm that continued to caress her cheek, Morgana smiled her reply. "You are too kind and too conscientious, Antonio. You certainly cannot be held accountable for the actions of all the citizens of your beautiful country."

"Ah *querida,* now you are the one who is being kind."

The black eyes moving over her face held an unexpected glow that sent the blood rushing to Morgana's cheeks. Tía Isabella had followed Tío Manuel out of the room on an errand just a few minutes before, temporarily leaving her to entertain her famous guest alone. And she had promptly upheld her aunt's confidence in her by losing herself to her own thoughts in the midst of Presidente Santa Anna's conversation! But she had been so distracted of late . . .

"Come, *querida,* something is bothering you. You have only to tell me and I will attempt to make the matter right for you. You have become very dear to me in these weeks, Morgana. . . ."

Upset by the fact that her thoughts were so easily readable in her expression, Morgana turned away from Antonio's caressing hand. "Oh, it's nothing. I suppose I'm just frustrated by my inactivity. How I long for a good long run on horseback . . . to feel the sun on my head . . . the warm air rushing against my face. . . . But I suppose that is very ungrateful of me, is it not, Antonio? I mean, to feel constrained when Tío Manuel and Tía Isabella have lavished so much affection and care on me."

"On the contrary, Morgana, you are young, and it is only natural that you long for a more active life than you have been leading these past weeks. But you have been recuperating, *querida,* and such was the reason for caution." A small smile moving across his lips, he continued slowly, "but I shall have Doña Isabella speak to the doctor today, and with his approval, I will have a horse delivered from my stable tomorrow morning so that you may ride."

Startled by his generosity, Morgana searched for the proper way to express her gratitude, only to be halted by his next comment.

"But, of course, there is a condition under which I will extend you the use of my stable, *querida.* . . ." His eyes carefully gauging her reaction to his next words, Antonio continued slowly, ". . . and that is that you allow an escort of two of my personal guards to accompany you . . . along with myself. . . ."

"Antonio . . . I am flattered that you should think of taking time from your busy schedule."

His handsome Latin features reflecting his pleasure, Antonio smiled broadly, "Say no more, *querida.* It is a matter of personal discipline that I take some form of exercise each day, and I can think of no more pleasant way than to spend the time riding with a lovely señorita. . . ."

Truly uncertain of why Santa Anna's pleased expression should elicit a vague feeling of disquiet inside her, Morgana forced a polite smile. "Antonio . . . I . . . I shall be happy to accept your offer . . . You are generous, indeed."

"De nada, querida." Taking her small hand in his and raising it to his lips, he concluded unexpectedly, "I look forward to our time together with great anticipation."

* * *

Holding her aching head, Morgana recalled her own words of a few hours before. The darkness outside her bedroom window was oppressive. Yes, she would indeed be happy to escape the house for a few hours . . . to ride tomorrow morning. Perhaps the mountain air would clear her mind of the agony of confusion that overwhelmed her. Yes, Antonio was too kind . . . too generous to a thankless idiot like herself. But that damned Devon! Why hadn't he told her he was going to Saltillo? Why did she have to find out from Tío Manuel that permission for an interview with the commandant general who had arrested Colonel Austin had been granted the week before his last visit? Certainly there was no reason to hide his mission, especially after the closeness they had shared since the incident in the courtyard. But, if she were to be honest, she would have to admit that Devon's actions were typical of his erratic behavior. Why she should be surprised, should allow his absence to affect her so deeply, she could not quite understand, especially in the light of the fact that he had deliberately neglected to inform her that he would be leaving Mexico City for an undetermined length of time.

Moving silently to the high, soft bed in the middle of her pleasant room, she kicked off her slippers and sat dejectedly on the edge for a few moments. Angry at the insistent tears that burned against her lids, she leaned over and blew out the lamp with a quick breath. Lying back against the cool, white sheets, she gave a short sigh before closing her eyes with determination. She would think no longer . . . would will herself to fall immediately to sleep. But a familiar image invaded her mind with an inevitability that left little surprise. Tall, muscular slender, with a slow, casual step, he entered her thoughts, the hard expression on lean, sharp features gradually transformed by the slow wonder of his smile. Damn him . . . damn that Devon Howard! How she wished she had never met him!

The lips against his own were warm and seeking, the soft feminine form pressed tightly against him well practiced in the art of subtle seduction. The heavy, musky scent of her skin was sensually disturbing as she moved in his arms, opened her mouth to his kiss. Surprisingly unaffected by the artful techniques of the woman in his arms, Devon Howard, instead, found his mind working independent of his body. Outwardly responding to his companion's advances, he mentally reckoned the plausibility of such an alluring, accommodating woman accidentally traveling with the same guard as he was to Saltillo. Somehow he could not make himself believe the fates had not had an assist from Antonio Santa Anna.

Freeing his mouth from the clinging lips, he shot a quick glance to the guards who lounged a discreet distance away beside the handsome coach, their backs conveniently turned to afford the maximum privacy available. Only three days into their journey and already the lovely Señora Consuelo Ramerez de Artega had fallen into his arms. Reported to have friends in high places, the young, wealthy wife of one of the oldest members of a socially prominent family had purportedly led a scandalous life at the capital. It had even been whispered that she was for a time the mistress of Antonio Santa Anna himself, and now, seeing the familiarity she displayed with his personal guard, Devon had no doubt that it was true. And how convenient that the lovely Señora had been planning this journey for the past week . . . a journey that coincided so coincidentally with his own, suddenly urgent mission.

Managing to subdue the flash of rage he experienced at Santa Anna's pitifully transparent plan to eliminate him from the race for Morgana's affections, he whispered roughly, "You're a beautiful woman, Consuelo. I can't understand how your husband allows you to travel so far . . . alone . . . with only the company of a maid and a few guards. If I was your husband, I surely wouldn't let you out of my sight for any longer than a few hours at a time." Hell, that was true enough, he thought to himself, barely restraining the sardonic expression that threatened to put a truer meaning to his words than the one he wished to convey.

"Ah, Devon, but my husband is an old man. He is far more concerned with his estates and his wealth than he is concerned with his young wife. And my desire to see my family in Saltillo is so strong . . ."

"And Antonio was so generous in grantin' you the protection of his men for the journey."

"And the comfort of a handsome man to keep me company, Devon . . ."

"Do you always form such quick attachments, Consuelo?"

"Only when they suit my purpose, Devon."

His eyes moved slowly over the unlined, olive-tinted skin, the large black eyes heavy-lidded with passion. The discomfort of three days of travel on poor, dusty roads had left little visible effects on her considerable beauty. "And what is that purpose, Consuelo?"

"To enjoy this interminable journey to the fullest extent possible . . . to allow myself to forget for a few, lighthearted weeks that I shall eventually return to the bed of a man old enough to be my grandfather." A peculiar light gleaming in her eyes, she continued huskily, "And to make this a time we will both remember with great warmth for a long time to come, my handsome Texan."

Shooting a quick glance toward the guards, Devon inquired quietly, "The guards and your maid . . . surely you would not flaunt a temporary liaison so openly . . . a woman in your vulnerable position, Consuelo . . .

"My maid is extremely loyal to me, Devon, and Antonio's guards, especially this contingent, are exceptionally discreet. I have had experience with them before. They may be trusted to maintain a matter in complete confidence."

Realizing that he was probably not the first man Consuelo de Artega had entertained for the president, Devon had considerable difficulty in restraining the urge to fling the clinging woman from him in disgust. So, this pitiful unhappy woman was to be his consolation prize for giving Morgana up to Santa Anna! Surely the fool did not believe this jaded tart could supplant Morgana in his affections!

"You are angry, Devon." Her voice low, Consuelo

purred as she rubbed her willowy body lightly against his. "You are an intelligent man, my handsome Tejicano. It did not take you long to realize Antonio has found another to strike his fancy and it has been politely suggested that I accommodate one who might prove a rival for his new love's affections. But do not waste your time in anger, *mi amór*. Antonio's affections are truly transient. You will have her back again . . . possibly soon . . . and in the meantime, we may both enjoy the delights available to us through Antonio's generosity."

A dark frown creasing his brow, Devon removed the slender arms that slid around his neck with barely concealed distaste. "And you allow yourself to be used so, Consuelo? You are a beautiful woman . . . from a good family . . . you are far too lovely to be squandered so carelessly."

The slender lips so openly available curved in a broad smile. "But I truly go to visit my family, do you not see, Devon? The choice is mine . . . to make the liaison or not, as my preference dictates. And my preference dictates a desire to know you well, Devon. It is, after all, to my advantage, is it not? I am a woman without children. I have considerable wealth at my command, and considerable freedom, due to my unusual circumstances. I lack only the incentive to follow each day through to the finish, and I do believe you will provide that incentive very well for the time we are together."

"And if, unlike you, I am not free to commit myself to an action that might reflect unfavorably on my mission, would you be angry, Consuelo?"

A small frown creasing her high brow, Consuelo fastened the intense gaze of disbelieving black eyes on Devon. "You do not want me, Devon?"

A small snort escaping his lips, Devon replied with a forced smile, "I'm a man, Consuelo. And I do believe any man who says he feels no desire for a woman as lovely as you is not worthy of the name. But anger and resentment stifle desire. I resent bein' manipulated, Consuelo, and I admit to anger at the recklessness with which Antonio uses both of us to achieve his purpose."

The lines of her frown easing from her forehead, Consuelo affixed steady black eyes on Devon's face consideringly. "Ah, you speak so beautifully, Devon, and present your case so convincingly that even I find myself tending to share your reactions. The Texan government has chosen well to send a man of such diplomacy on such a mission."

A true smile turning up the corners of his mouth for the first time, Devon mumbled indistinctly, "I know some who would tend to disagree with you at times, Consuelo, possibly very violently. . . ."

"But not I, Devon." Gracefully sliding her arm through his, she stepped to his side. "I find I have great respect for your convictions, and I intend to spend the time remaining on this journey in examining them far more closely." Urging him back to the area where her maid and the soldiers silently awaited their return, Consuelo continued as she walked, "Yes, I will truly examine your comments more carefully in the days and nights to come, Devon. But you must make certain to remember . . ." lifting her eyes to his, she smiled, a spark glinting in the dark eyes appraising him so intently, ". . . while I am considering what you have said, Devon, you must remember to tell me if you should change your mind . . . ."

It was cooler in the more heavily forested area, the persistent heat of the bright morning sun touching on her shoulders only as it flickered through the leafy cover of trees. Feeling a sudden lift to her spirits, Morgana spurred her horse to a faster pace, her pleasure dulling only slightly with the realization that the two guards riding silently a safe distance behind hastened to match her speed. The damp forest air whipped the loose tendrils of the hair back from her face caressing her cheeks, exhilarating her senses with its keen, fresh scent. For the first time in two weeks, Morgana felt alive, the depression that had seemed to settle over her spirits held at bay by the supreme glory of the morning.

She had to admit to being a bit surprised when she had been informed that a horse had been delivered to her door early that morning. She had only spoken to Antonio yesterday about her desire to ride. She had not expected he would work so fast in obtaining clearance from Dr. Zavella for her outing. And she also had to admit to being silently grateful that she was to be allowed to ride alone, in company with the guards. She somehow had a strong desire to get away from the influence of the household. Tío Manuel had been relentless in the last week in his subtle, unspoken disapproval of Devon Howard. Aggie's attitude clearly showed she considered her suspicions of the enigmatic Texan confirmed, and even Tía Isabella had been less inclined than usual to defend him. But in truth, what excuse could she possibly find for Devon's having left the city without a word when he had pretended such concern for her welfare right up until the day of his departure? But then, she had made the mistake of coming to rely on Devon's presence, his affection, a mistake she had made before with almost drastic results. Whatever had made her think Devon had changed?

Shaking her head in an attempt to free her mind of the very thoughts she had hoped to evade on the ride, Morgana reined her horse to a more reasonable pace. It would not do to wear Antonio's horse out the first morning she was allowed to ride, although she had doubts that the lovely black mare could so easily be overcome by a morning's run. She could still remember the flash of pleasure she'd experienced when she had set eyes on the glistening, well-muscled beauty, and her involuntary gasp of amazement at the magnificently tooled saddle so liberally ornamented with silver. She had never ridden so fine an animal and used so beautiful a saddle, and she had indeed felt a momentary disappointment that Antonio was not present so that she might express her appreciation.

Her mind temporarily leaving her wandering thoughts, Morgana turned her attention to the bridle path on which she rode. It had obviously not been used lately and was a trifle overgrown . . . a fact that surprised her since Antonio's guards had suggested in a manner that had bordered on insistence that she take the road that led out of the city to the very bridle path on which they now rode. But she could not dispute the beauty of the surrounding area. Only a short distance from the crowded streets of Mexico City, she had entered a silent, fragrant world where the beauty of nature had efficiently restored peace to her soul, if only temporarily.

Speaking encouragingly to her mare as she labored up a small incline of loose earth and stones that tested her footing, Morgana smiled her approval as the mare touched down once again on the firm-packed earth. Patting the long, shiny neck moist with sweat, she leaned forward to whisper into the pointed ears that appeared to strain for her words, *"Sí, muchacha! Es una tarea muy bueno! Eres muchacha muy buena!"*

"I am extremely happy to find you so pleased with my choice, Morgana."

Jumping at the unexpected voice, Morgana raised her eyes to the impressive figure a few feet away who sat on the regal white stallion that had become his trademark. Obviously having removed his coat because of the heat of the morning, Antonio was clad informally in dark trousers and waistcoat. His white shirt, in startling contrast to his clear olive complexion, was open at the neck, emphasizing the breadth of his shoulders and the light tufting of dark hair on his chest. The surprising informality of his dress emphasized his maleness, imparting a youthful appearance that was as startling to Morgana as his unexpected appearance.

"Antonio!" Noting in the back of her mind that the guards accompanying him waited a short distance behind, Morgana continued with true warmth, "When your men arrived with Grillo this morning and you were not with them, I expected that you were too busy to ride today. I am so pleased to find you here!"

The momentary flash in his dark eyes gave her a second's unease over her effusive spontaneity. Considerably subdued, Morgana continued quietly, "Yes, she is a lovely horse, Antonio, and I do thank you for your generosity in allowing me to ride her."

"Ah, but certainly Grillo was the only horse for you . . . the only one that could match your beauty and spirit, Morgana. I had no doubt in my mind from the first which horse I

200

would send for you to ride. And now that I have seen you together, you must do me the honor of accepting Grillo as a present, for there is certainly no other I would allow to ride her after you."

Startled by his unexpected statement, Morgana was momentarily at a loss for words. "Antonio . . . I could not accept such a gift! Grillo is a magnificent animal . . . far too valuable to give away!"

"But she is your horse now, Morgana."

Antonio's statement was pronounced with a finality that allowed no further room for discussion, and feeling suddenly trapped by his generosity, Morgana stumbled for a response.

"But . . . but I cannot stable her at Tío Manuel's house. There is no room, and I could not possibly add the cost of her care to Tío Manuel's household expense. It would be asking too much. . . ."

His dark eyes softening with understanding, Santa Anna responded quietly, "*No es importante.* I will continue to care for Grillo along with my other horses. But she will be yours, *querida,* to do with as you wish. You need only to send to my household for someone to deliver her to you whenever you need her. No one else will ride her, so you must remember to keep her well exercised. And I will expect you to visit her from time to time . . . so that we may both enjoy the pleasure of your company. . . ."

"Antonio, you are too generous." Abruptly overwhelmed by the fact that Grillo's beauty and grace now belonged to her alone, Morgana fought to blink back the tears that flooded her eyes. When she had sold the last of her father's horses to pay his debts, she had not expected ever to own so beautiful an animal again.

Obviously pleased with her reaction, Santa Anna waved away her gratitude. "Come, Morgana, I have something to show you not far from here. Follow me." His tone of voice changing in a subtle, inexplicable way, he turned to direct a brief command to his guards. "You will wait here. Señorita Pierce and I will return shortly."

Without awaiting for her assent, Santa Anna urged his

horse forward, his pace steady and rapid as he negotiated the overgrown trail. Concentrating intently on following the path he led, Morgana had no conception of the distance they traveled or the height they climbed until Santa Anna abruptly reined his horse to a halt. Turning in his saddle, he offered confidently, "Had I not known you rode so well, I would not have attempted this climb, Morgana. This trail would be beyond the capabilities of the average horse-woman, but you have negotiated it admirably. You confirm my faith in you." The satisfaction in his smile sent a small chill racing down Morgana's spine, and, unable to explain her strange reaction to his compliment, Morgana turned her head to survey the immediate area. "What is it you wanted to show me, Antonio?"

Moving lithely to the ground, Santa Anna dropped his horse's reins. Obviously there was no need to tether the well-trained animal, and, unable to subdue her admiration, Morgana offered appreciatively, "It is a small wonder that your horse has grown almost as famous as his illustrious master, Antonio. You have good cause to be proud of him."

Coming to stand beside her. Santa Anna raised his hands to her waist. Lifting her lightly, he spoke directly into her eyes, his expressive voice adding a note to his words that sent a flush to her cheek. "In all things, I attempt to surround myself with the best life has to offer, *querida* . . . intelligence, integrity, beauty, devotion. In this way I hope to have these qualities influence and reflect on me . . . on my dealings with people . . . my personal life. It is a method that has served me well."

Acutely aware that Santa Anna's hands remained on her waist after he had set her on the ground, Morgana felt a re-surgence of discomfort. In deference to the heat of the morn-ing, she had worn simply the white shirtwaist and skirt of her riding habit. The bodice material was a delicate batiste that allowed the heat of Santa Anna's hands to penetrate almost as well as if his hands rested against her naked flesh. In an effort to avoid his intense perusal and the flush of color that began to flood her face, Morgana scanned the area with feigned interest. Speaking in a voice that even to her own ears sounded unnatural, she inquired again, "What was it that you wanted to show me, Antonio?"

Unable to see the amused smile that flicked across Santa Anna's darkly handsome features, she breathed a silent sigh of relief when Santa Anna's hands left her waist to enclose her small hand in his. "Come, *querida*, I will satisfy your curiosity at last."

Guiding her carefully through the low underbrush, Santa Anna stopped short as the wooded area came to an abrupt end. From there, a few feet of barren ground ended abruptly in a sharp cliff from which was extended one of the most breathtaking panoramas Morgana had yet seen! Small in scope in comparison with the majesty of the great peaks she had passed on her way to Mexico City, it was nonetheless outstanding in its natural beauty. Below them lay a glittering, winding river that danced in the light of the morning sun. Wildflowers, in all manner of color and hue, lined the edge of the forest and trailed amongst the tall green grass. Not a sign of human habitation was available to the naked eye, while birds, whose grace of flight defied description, soared and glided to the hushed music of the warm morning breeze.

Her misgivings of a few moments before leaving her mind in the face of the exquisite natural beauty exhibited before her eyes, Morgana gasped spontaneously, "Antonio, this is glorious, is it not? A place of true wonder . . ." Her sincere enthusiasm evidenced by the glow of her revealing expression, Morgana turned to Santa Anna's intensely assessing gaze. "Thank you so much for sharing this with me, Antonio. I would never have found this place by myself . . . would never have climbed that trail . . ."

"*De nada,* Morgana. It was a wish I am fortunate to have realized . . . sharing this place of peaceful respite with you. From the moment I saw you ride on Manga de Clavo . . . saw the true appreciation in your eyes for the wealth of beauty given by the grace of God to our beautiful country, I have dreamed of taking you here."

Truly touched by Santa Anna's words, Morgana lifted the warmth of her gaze to his darkly handsome face. "You are indeed fortunate to lead a country in which you can find so much pride.''

"Ah, but it is more than that, *querida*." A strange gleam entering Santa Anna's eyes, he continued intently, "There is a knowledge deep inside me that I was fated to lead my country, and it is to this knowledge that I have dedicated my life. All of Mexico is dear to me . . . its beauty . . . its people . . . and I know, without doubt, that I was born so I might guide my people to their destiny." Raising his hands before him, palms up, fingers spread, Santa Anna declared fervently, "The fate of my people lies in these hands, *querida*, and it is a knowledge that weighs heavily on my soul."

"But you have done so well, Antonio! The people love you . . . you have managed to oust Farías. . . . Tío Manuel says Farías did much to cause chaos in the country during your recuperation in Manga de Clavo."

"*Sí*, I have done all these things, *querida*, because I am a man with a vision."

Entranced by the conviction reflected on the face of the man speaking so eloquently before her, Morgana sat casually on the boulder to the side of the clearing in which they stood, her eyes unmoving from his face as Santa Anna moved to sit beside her.

"The very city of my birth, Morgana, is a haven for my people . . . a haven against the pestilence that makes Veracruz feared for long periods each year. Jalapa . . . 'Water on the Sands,' *querida*, is tucked high into the folds of the mountains, where storms cannot strike her. Her climate is ideal . . . so ideal that corn can be planted every month of the year. Coffee fincas, orange groves and banana fields can be seen from the public square, while chirimoya and mango grow on all sides. Yet only a few miles away on the plateau's edge come successively peaches, and then apples, and cereal in abundance.

"In addition, Jalapa is blessed with a riot of color and grandeur. Red and purple bougainvillea, azaleas, dahlias, geranium, roses, zinnias, carnations, begonias, and the orchid . . . all grow wild. Amidst the best Mexico has to offer, I was born, Morgana. My father was a mortgage broker, and

204

it would have been considered the norm for a boy of my parentage to become a merchant. But I knew from the start that I was not meant to be a 'counter-jumper.' " The small sneer twisting his lips demonstrated his contempt for the mundane career his family would have had him follow. "At fourteen years of age I obtained the position of cadet in the Fijo de Veracruz Regiment of Infantry. A year later I was fighting Indians in the arid frontier provinces, and for many years thereafter I risked my life for my country. Now the people have called on me to become their leader. I am in a position I was born to hold, *querida.* I know that as surely as I know you belong in this place with me at this time in my life. As truly as it is fate that I am here in Mexico City as *Presidente,* I know it is fate that you are here, too, Morgana."

"Antonio . . . I . . . I don't know what to say, except that I appreciate your conviction that I belong here, in your country."

"More than that, *querida.*" His dark eyes solemn, shining with conviction, Santa Anna raised his hands to cup her face with his palms, holding her fast as he lowered his mouth to hers, "More than that, *querida,* you belong here . . . now . . . in my arms. . . ."

"Antonio . . ."

With a strange feeling of numbed disbelief, Morgana felt the touch of Santa Anna's lips on hers. At first light and gentle, the pressure of his mouth slowly increased as his arms slipped around her back to pull her close against his chest. Crushed tightly in his arms as his mouth moved seekingly against hers, Morgana began to feel the rise of panic. Sensing her hesitation, Santa Anna's touch became more gentle, his hands moving with heady persuasion along her back.

Drawing his mouth from hers, he whispered passionately as he pressed light, fleeting kisses against her cheek, "Do you not sense the hand of fate in our meeting, *querida?* Do you not realize the inevitability of being in my arms as you are right now?"

"No, Antonio . . ." Her panic increasing as the soft persuasion of his voice began to work a magic on her senses,

205

she attempted to break free of his embrace. "No, you're wrong . . . this is wrong . . . Doña Ines . . . she would be hurt if she could see us here . . . now. . . ."

"*Querida,* Ines is from another era in my lifetime. She holds no place in my life here at the capital. Here I live as a man of the people, far from the life in which I am bound to her. And it is here, now, that I need you, Morgana, to fill my existence . . . to fill the loneliness . . ."

Shaking her head against the soft, persuasive logic of his voice, Morgana insisted intently, "No . . . you are a married man, Antonio, married to a good woman. I will not be part of a . . ."

"But you are already a part of me, *querida.*" Fathomless black eyes holding hers with unyielding fascination, Santa Anna continued almost hypnotically, "You enter my thoughts through the long day, and invade my dreams through the long, lonely nights. It is then that I long to hold you as I do now. It is then that I dream that I have you so close against me, that you give me the comfort that I need so desperately to make my life here full and complete."

"Antonio, please. . . ." Desperate tears filling her eyes, Morgana began to feel her resistance slip away under the heady persuasion of Santa Anna's words. His appeal was so ardent . . . so sincere . . . his strength so absolute and overwhelming . . . holding her safe . . .

Raising his hand to caress her cheek once again, Antonio whispered hoarsely, "Come, give your mouth to me freely, *querida.* Do not hold back. Let me show you how truly we can blend together as one. . . ."

Not waiting for her assent, Antonio lowered his head to cover her lips once again with his own. This time there was no resistance, merely the meeting of lips and bodies as Santa Anna pulled her to her feet to hold her intimately close in his growing passion. Strangely, almost frighteningly, Morgana allowed Santa Anna's deeply erotic kiss to continue, feeling none of the surging response she felt to the most casual of Devon's caresses, but merely the paralyzing power of his intensely masculine aura. As if in a dream, Morgana allowed Santa Anna to lift her arms to encircle his neck, felt the warm, moist kisses that he rained on her face and neck, listened to his words of love as his hand moved to cup her breast. Lowering his head, Santa Anna allowed his mouth to follow the course his hands had taken so confidently only moments before. It was the touch of seeking lips against the delicate material of her shirtwaist as they sought to cover the appeal of the burgeoning crest that awoke Morgana to the shocking realization of her shame.

Abruptly struggling to be free of their intimate posture, Morgana whispered softly, "No . . . please, Antonio . . . please . . . I cannot do this! It is wrong . . . Doña Ines . . ."

"No, *querida,* do not push me away." The urgent appeal in the voice that commanded armies . . . the plea in the dark eyes that so effectively mesmerized thousands was almost successful in eliminating her tenuous resistance. But the abrupt vision of another pair of eyes, light and penetrating, raking her face, filled with contempt, brought her abruptly back to earth. With a sudden flush she remembered the instantaneous, searing emotions Devon's touch brought to life within her, the wild singing in her veins that so totally overwhelmed her when she was in his arms. No! This was not the embrace for which she longed. She would not put herself in a position where she would warrant contempt in Devon's glance . . . for in truth, his contempt would too closely mirror her own.

"No, Antonio, please . . ." The trembling in her voice matching the quaking of her slender frame, Morgana eased herself firmly from Santa Anna's embrace. Unwittingly raising his level of emotion even higher, she lifted regret-filled eyes to Santa Anna's flushed Latin face. "Under other circumstances, Antonio . . ." Abruptly at a loss for words, Morgana just shook her head with a silent plea for understanding.

The sparks of gold glittering in the moist eyes raised to his struck a fire deep within him, adversely inflaming his emotions to an even higher pitch of desire. But Santa Anna's sharp mind was not overcome by his raging emotions. The brilliant strategist of many successful campaigns, he saw ultimate defeat if he continued to press his suit, attempting to force Morgana to submit to his advances.

With a supreme effort, he quelled his desire, his mind urging patience . . . patience. . . .

"*Sí, querida, mi corazón*. Whatever you wish. You are too dear to me to make you unhappy. Come . . ." Stroking the warm, chestnut-colored strands back from her cheek, he whispered huskily into her lovely, expectant face, "We will continue our ride, now, and in a few minutes we will return to the company of our guards," Guiding her back to the area where their horses waited, he lifted her effortlessly and settled her on her saddle. Mounting in a quick, fluid movement, he eased his horse over to her side. Reaching out, he ran the tips of his fingers in a gentle caress down her cheek.

"*Querida*, to have you near me will have to be enough. . . ."

His eyes still holding hers, his mind finished even more ardently, "Enough for now, Morgana . . . but only for now. . . ."

"Quickly, Morgana, Doña Isabella wishes your presence beside her. The dancing is about to begin!"

Turning in response to Aggie's impatient summons, Morgana adjusted her mantilla with a small frown and began walking toward the staircase to the courtyard. Aware of the open disapproval exhibited on Aggie's severe face, she made an attempt to force a smile onto her stiff lips. She had delayed far too long already in making her appearance at the festivities, but she was unable to shake the sense of apprehension with which she anticipated the evening. The feast of Corpus Christi was a great day in the capital, and an especially important day in the Escobar household and in others where the master of the house was named after the patron saint, Manuel. For that reason a grand party was held annually in the household, where family and friends feasted and danced long into the night. But this year, the party was to serve a dual purpose, and, aware that this was to be her first formal introduction into capital society, Morgana felt the knot in her stomach tighten.

Impatient with her own sense of disquiet, Morgana stood silently at the top of the staircase and surveyed the well-dressed people milling about below her. The courtyard was decorated lavishly, with fragrant flowers in every available niche, and brilliantly colored lanterns flickering in the evening twilight. Subdued music came from the corner of the courtyard where colorfully dressed musicians awaited the cue to begin the light, lively music that would signal the beginning of the dancing. And still she hesitated.

It was not a matter of feeling insecure in her manner of dress. Quite the contrary. Tía Isabella, without her knowledge, had arranged to have a lovely new gown made for her especially for the occasion. In deference to her youth, she had chosen a pale pink cotton, almost transparent in its delicacy of weave. Baring her shoulders in a manner that was deceivingly provocative, the soft bodice swept tightly to her waist, its lack of ornamentation offset by the wide, bouffant sleeves that ballooned to her delicate wrists. Her narrow waist was accented by a wide ribbon in a shade of pink darker than her dress, and by the magnificence of a full skirt that billowed out and down to her pink, satin-clad feet in a series of fragile, lace-trimmed ruffles. Her hair, dutifully dressed by Tía Isabella's favorite hairdresser, was swept to the top of her head in gleaming chestnut swirls and secured by a large Spanish comb in the back. Gracefully draped over the skillfully arranged coiffure was the delicate mantilla that Antonio had formally presented to her on the occasion of his first visit.

And it was this same mantilla which caused her some of her misgivings about the evening to come. Surely, if she appeared on this very important occasion wearing the mantilla Antonio had given her, he would be misled to think that she harbored stronger feelings for him than she had professed over the last two weeks. Things were difficult enough already in that regard, and she did not wish to do anything that could cause the situation to worsen. Not that Antonio had been anything but a gentleman. His manner irreproachable, he had continued to meet her in the same glade as he had the

209

morning of her first ride. Although his gaze spoke volumes, he treated her with ultimate respect, and, admittedly, she had developed a true affection for the enigmatic Mexican who held the fate of his country in his slender, well-shaped hands. But constant, in the back of her mind, holding her back from true enjoyment of her new life, was the memory of a hard, sharply chiseled face, and blue eyes that warmed with a slow smile that melted her heart. Damn that Devon Howard! Where was he? Certainly enough time had passed for him to have returned from his journey to Saltillo. She still had not heard a word from him, and depressing her even more was the thought that she was not truly certain that she would.

Guiltily seeking out her aunt in the groups of people milling below her, Morgana easily spied her petite figure beside the dignified personage of Tío Manuel. Truly impressed with Antonio's acceptance of and apparent affection for her, they had encouraged her to wear the mantilla, and, rather than stir their suspicions, she had consented. She had kept her silence about Antonio's declarations the morning of their first ride, realizing the strain the knowledge would put on her position in the household.

Catching her aunt's eye with a small, quick smile, Morgana descended the staircase. She could hesitate no longer without causing comment, and, realizing she could do nothing that would hurt the two people who had taken her so warmly into their household, she walked quickly toward her aunt's outstretched hand.

"Morgana . . . *querida* . . . your uncle and I had begun to worry about you." The soft brown eyes assessed her critically. "You are not feeling unwell?"

"No, Tía Isabella. *Lo siento, por favor.* Some last minute adjustments to my coiffure took more time than I realized. I'm afraid I am a slave to my mirror!"

Patting her cheek lightly in a manner that demonstrated her true affection for the lovely young woman she had taken under her wing, Tía Isabella said softly, "I know you far better than that, Morgana. That very pretty head is not empty, nor filled with vain thoughts. I am sure your reasons for delay were adequate, and they are, above all, your own private concern. We will speak of it no longer, *mi hermosa sobrina*."

Turning to her husband with a smile that caused a revealing lightness to slip over his heavy, sober features, Doña Isabella offered softly, "You may give the signal now to begin the dancing, Manuel. Our family is now assembled."

At a short nod from his dignified, grey-streaked head, the strains of a light, lively waltz filled the air, raising Morgana's spirits despite her languor of a few minutes before.

"Manuel, you will, of course, begin the dancing with your niece. . . ."

Interrupting Doña Isabella's softly whispered instructions, Morgana responded urgently, "No, I would not miss the sight of my first party in México being begun by the two who have so generously offered me a new life here in their country. Please, Tía Isabella, I will very much enjoy watching you dance."

Tears springing to the warm brown eyes searching hers so carefully, Tía Isabella nodded her consent. "Come, Manuel, we shall dance the first dance together through the graciousness of our lovely niece."

"In that case, I insist you allow *me* the pleasure of the first dance, *querida*."

Turning at the low, familiar voice in her ear, Morgana met Antonio's warm smile. Suddenly extremely grateful that this important man should lend her the support of his presence, Morgana responded in a sincere voice, "I will be delighted, Antonio."

Swept lightly out onto the floor, Morgana realized that she had been allowed a full sweep around the dance floor before other couples joined in the dancing. In answer to her curious glance, Antonio responded softly, "It is a measure of their respect, *querida*, and it is my deep pleasure to share this moment with you."

Finding herself at a loss for a response to his words, Morgana smiled, deciding to allow the music to sweep away the

211

thoughts that had dimmed her appreciation of her first social presentation in Mexico.

Still struggling to regain her breath, Morgana raised her glass and sipped her wine cautiously. It had been a lovely evening so far. All had progressed well, and the smile on Tía Isabella's face indicated she was extremely pleased. Wishing that she could dispel the heaviness that still lingered inside her, Morgana turned her gaze to the young man at her side.

"You are an extremely vigorous dancer, Vincente. My heart has not yet realized my feet have stopped dancing!"

A flush of pleasure moving across his uneven, Latin features, the obviously smitten young man responded quietly, "And I fear it will not be allowed to catch up if I am to judge by your effect on our young men here tonight, Morgana. You are extremely lovely, and you have turned the lot of us into slaves to your beauty and wit."

A flush moving across her own features, Morgana responded with embarrassment, "Vincente, you flatter me. If I have been at all busy with the dancing, it is as a result of the extreme courtesy of your young men in welcoming so warmly a newcomer to your country."

"I fear your recent arrival has little to do with your popularity tonight, Morgana, other than to say each of us rushes to establish a priority in your esteem."

"And it is too late for all of you, my young friend." A new voice entering the conversation turned both their heads to the smile of Antonio Santa Anna. "You see, I have established first priority with the niece of my good friend, and intend to hold it in the manner that serves me best."

Turning his smile to Morgana, to the exclusion of the young man who stood at her side, Antonio said lightly, "You are looking a bit fatigued, Morgana. Perhaps it would be best if we took a short walk in the garden. I fear it is the only way you will be able to escape the young men who even at this moment covet the time I spend speaking with you."

Abruptly grateful for Antonio's suggestion, Morgana nodded her consent. "Yes, I think that would be very pleasant."

Smiling apologetically into Vincente's hurt expression, she offered lightly, "I look forward to another dance with you later this evening, when I am recovered, Vincente."

Taking her elbow in a proprietary manner, Santa Anna moved her efficiently through the crowd, mumbling low in her ear as he did, "Not if I have anything to say about it, Morgana. I find that I am quite jealous of all these young swains that assault you with their amorous glances. I find I prefer to have you to myself, even if it is only for the company of your bright mind and warm presence."

The implication that he would like to develop a relationship that exceeded the present platonic bounds of their friendship was not lost on Morgana. Even in his most innocent conversation, she was intensely aware of his deep sensuality, but choosing to bring their conversation onto safer grounds, she commented casually, "I had not realized the feast of Corpus Christi was such a great holiday in Mexico, Antonio."

"*Si,* I do suppose in your near heathen country the national observance of a religious holiday would seem quite strange."

"Antonio!" Hurt by his reference to the land that she silently still considered her home, Morgana frowned her objection. "Certainly the United States is not a Catholic country, but neither is it heathen! As a matter of fact, many of the first settlers came for religious freedom. Just because . . ."

"*Querida, por favor, lo siento.* It was not my intention to insult you. You are, after all, a loyal follower of the Church. It is not on you that the lack of respect for God reflects so poorly."

Still offended despite his halfhearted apology, Morgana offered coolly, "I'm afraid I don't know what you mean, Antonio."

"Did you not know that one of the conditions of settlement in the Texas colony was that those Anglos choosing to make Texas their home would practice only the true religion of the Catholic Church?"

"Yes, I think I heard that somewhere, but what has that to do . . ."

"Well, rather than practice our holy religion, those settlers who would call themselves loyal *Tejicanos* have chosen to practice no religion at all! I tell you, it is an insult to the Church . . . a reflection of their heathen souls. . . ."

"Antonio . . ." Truly startled by the violence of his objections to the Texans' refusal to accept his religion, Morgana responded slowly, "But had the choice been yours, Antonio, would you so easily accept another's religion?"

"The comparison you offer does not have a sound basis, Morgana, for mine is the true religion. In offering them our land, we also offer them salvation for their souls, and they throw it back in our face!"

Santa Anna was beginning to breathe rapidly as his anger slowly progressed to fury. His face stiffened into harsh, angry lines, and, intimidated by the specter of his rage, Morgana again attempted to change the course of the conversation.

"Well, I expect it was not so much the celebration of the religious holiday that so impressed me, Antonio, as it was the colorful customs that accompany the celebration. This morning Tía Isabella took me through the markets and plazas of the city. Everywhere the little boys of the city were dressed like little native men. On their backs they carried little crates made of sticks, filled with the wares that would normally be taken to market; and the little girls were dressed beautifully in China Poblana and other regional costumes. When we went to mass in the cathedral, it was really quite touching to see the children attending so proudly in their holiday clothes."

"And did not Doña Isabella buy for you one of the tiny mules made of corn husks that are sold in the markets? The flowers and sweets loaded on their backs are a special way we in the capital city have of celebrating this holiday."

Relieved to see that the raging anger exhibited in his eyes only a few moments before had faded as quickly as it had appeared, Morgana responded with grateful enthusiasm, "Yes, she did buy a small corn husk mule for me, Antonio, but she also bought a small mule for each couple attending the celebration here tonight. She intends to present them as the guests depart. Oh!'' Her eyes snapping wide abruptly, Morgana stared with a truly stricken expression into Santa Anna's face. "I had forgotten! Tía Isabella intended the mules to be a surprise, and now I've spoiled it for you! Oh, I am such a chatterbox!"

A smile of true delight erasing the last of the severe lines from his face, Santa Anna took a firmer grip on Morgana's arm and steered her further into the garden. "Well, if you promise to forgive the words I spoke so carelessly in anger a few minutes ago, Morgana, I will promise not to divulge the secret of your unfortunate lapse to Doña Isabella."

"It is a bargain well struck, Antonio."

"Grácias, querida." Raising her hand to his lips, Antonio looked deeply into her eyes.

The sudden realization that, in the lush foliage of the dimly lit garden, they were for all intents and purposes completely alone, returned Morgana's sense of disquiet. She was about to utter some inane remark for the sole purpose of breaking the heavy sensual tension that had suddenly developed between them when the odor of cigar smoke hit her nostrils, accompanied by the low, confidential tones of a man obviously on the other side of the wide hedge that separated them from the patio.

". . .*sí*, Adolfo, but the man is obviously lacking in integrity. For all his pretense and weighty words about the importance of his mission to free Colonel Austin, he has taken time from this matter of some urgency to conduct a romantic liaison with Consuelo Ramerez de Artega!"

"*Sí*, the highest-class whore in Mexico City. . . ."

"Ah, yes, but a whore of such beauty . . . Adolfo, you are not so old that you do not remember the temptations of the flesh . . . were I in his place, I think I might find it difficult to resist a journey to Saltillo that would avail me of three weeks of privacy with that hot-blooded, sultry piece. . . ."

"Especially when her husband is such a rich, doddering fool that he indulges his wife's caprices without a whimper of protest . . ."

"Ha! Perhaps Señor Howard will be grateful if his friend's unfortunate circumstances linger on a bit longer than expected. It will doubtless be difficult for him to tear himself away from the accommodating Señora de Artega while she is still willing to grant him her favors."

"*Sí . . . sí,* you are right, Adolfo." The low, confidential tone suddenly turned to hearty laughter as the voices began to fade into the noise of the party. "*Sí,* we shall have to pray for Colonel Austin's timely incarceration to continue if we are to spare Señor Howard his integrity. . . ."

Hardly conscious of the fact that for the full duration of the personal conversation conducted on the other side of the hedge she had been listening unabashedly, Morgana lifted her eyes to Antonio's inscrutable expression.

"Is it true, Antonio?"

"*Querida,* it is not my concern how Devon Howard conducts his personal affairs."

Unwilling to accept Antonio's obvious hesitation to discuss Devon, Morgana pressed softly, "Please, Antonio. Devon was extremely kind to me after my . . . the incident. I am concerned that he is being maligned. Is it true . . . is it true what those men said?"

Appearing to pause in consideration of his response, Antonio enclosed the small hand he still held within his own. "*Sí* . . . it is true, Morgana. Devon came to me and asked that he might talk to the commandant in Saltillo where Colonel Austin was arrested. I told him that I felt such a journey would not present results that would make the effort worthwhile, and he responded that the journey would be the most enjoyable part of a mission that to date had proved to be a thoroughly fruitless, depressing irritation from its inception."

Clamping her lips tightly together in an effort to still their trembling, Morgana stood silently for long moments as the pain of Devon's treachery washed over her. So, all his tender words were an act . . . a farce. But why? Why did he go to such trouble to cultivate her interest, her aunt's friendship? Of what use could it prove to him if he was not sincere?

Without her realization the words had slipped past her numb lips. "Why? Why did he pretend to care, Antonio?"

"Ah, *querida,* you ask me these questions when the answers

will only hurt you. I do not wish to contribute to the pain of Devon Howard's deception.''

''But, Antonio, I don't understand why . . .''

''Did it not occur to you, *querida*, that Manuel is a dear friend as well as compatriot? It is no secret that his words of advice weigh heavily on my decisions. Does it not seem reasonable that by cultivating the friendship and trust of Manuel's family, Devon Howard hoped to influence Manuel in his favor, and ultimately me in favor of his friend's case. And where, *querida*, was the most vulnerable spot to press his attentions? Who would be the one most easily influenced by a fellow countryman?''

The logic of Antonio's reasoning cut her deeply. Abruptly Morgana was flushed with a deep and burning rage. How dared that boorish Texan attempt to play her for a fool? Despite her strange vulnerability to his touch, she had not been fooled by him from the start. She had realized him to be the undependable, self-seeking hypocrite that he had proved to be, and had it not been for the circumstances of the attack, which had filled her with a deep gratitude for his attentions when she was in need, she would not have been taken in by his well-feigned concern. But he had succeeded . . . had managed to make a fool of her once again, and she would make him pay. Yes, at the first opportunity, she would make him pay. . . .

Lifting her head with a new sense of resolve despite the pain choking her throat, Morgana looked directly into Antonio's assessing expression.

''Antonio, will you take me back to the party now, please? I'm quite rested. I should like to dance.''

His expression reflecting his skepticism, Antonio replied hesitantly, ''You are certain, Morgana? You are certain you feel well enough to dance?''

Forcing a smile to her stiff lips, Morgana slipped her arm through his, urging him back. ''Of course, Antonio. I'm not such a fool that I would allow the deceits of an irresponsible countryman to unsettle me to the extent that I am unable to function.''

''Yes, I expect that would be true if the man was little else

217

to you other than a fellow countryman. . . ."

"I don't know what you mean, Antonio."

His eyes slowly surveying her flushed face, Antonio hesitated, his expression unfathomable. "In that case, no more will be said. Come, we will return to the party. I am certain you have been greatly missed."

Gently covering the small hand that rested on his arm as they walked, Santa Anna barely resisted the urge to turn and shake the young woman who walked beside him to within an inch of her life. So it was true! Morgana harbored a true tendresse for Devon Howard in her heart! And it was undoubtedly those same feelings that stood in the way of his own plans for Morgana and himself. Damned little American fool! Had he not such a strong desire for her that he ached for its consummation, he would cast her aside like the little idiot she was! Perhaps he would do that in the end anyway, but he would have her first! Despite his lack of success in advancing himself into her bed, he was certain he had handled the evening perfectly. Morgana was, in fact, a true challenge to his ability as a strategist. Perhaps that was indeed her major appeal. And then again, perhaps not, he countered, as Morgana lifted her small, intimate smile in his direction, causing a familiar stirring in his groin. Tightening his hand spontaneously on hers, he returned her smile benevolently. No, now was not the time to show his hand. When he held her securely within his control, was finally certain of her, he would make the little bitch pay for the agonies she had put him through. But for now he would continue to play the part of the dedicated lonely patriot who thirsted for her affection. It was a role he played extremely well, and a role, he had no doubts, that would finally win her over.

Taking a tight grip on her emotions, Morgana shot Antonio one last, grateful smile, and stepped back into the courtyard. How much longer would the evening last? The revelation of Devon's betrayal was the last straw in an accumulation of deceits that had destroyed the last remnants of her trust. Consuelo Ramerez de Artega . . . even in her short time in Mexico word of that woman had met her ears. Had she not heard Maria whispering about her the previous

218

morning? Recalling suddenly how the whispers had stopped the moment Maria had become aware of her presence, Morgana felt a hot flush rise to her face. So . . . the whole household was aware of the way in which Devon had played her for a fool. How could she bear to face . . .

Her eyes moving quickly across the crowded floor to assess the glances of those assembled, Morgana stopped abruptly as a familiar figure walked through the entrance to the courtyard. Her heart beginning a wild pounding in her chest, she refused to believe the evidence of her own eyes. No! It couldn't be Devon . . . not yet! She wasn't prepared to face him yet! But it was he! How could she possibly mistake the broad-shouldered, leanly muscled physique, the slow, ambling walk that so deceptively disguised the lightning-quick reflexes that had held her immobile far too often for comfort. She remembered with startling vividness the strength of his arms when he had scooped her up high against his chest and carried her to the very courtyard where she now stood . . . the fresh, manly scent of his skin as she had laid her head against his neck . . . the incredible warmth generated deep inside her by his slow, easy smile as he had looked down into her eyes.

He had not seen her yet, but it was obvious he was looking for someone. Her position at the dark corner of the courtyard would afford her anonymity for a few moments longer, and, struggling to gain control of her badly rioting emotions, Morgana turned away from the sight that was rapidly destroying her composure.

"*Querida* . . ."

Snapping her glance up to Antonio's unfathomable expression, Morgana mumbled stiffly, "I'm sorry, Antonio. For a moment I forgot . . ." She was about to say she had forgotten he was there, but closing her eyes the moment before she uttered the revealing statement, she whispered softly instead, "Perhaps you were right, Antonio, Perhaps I should go upstairs to rest for a while. I find I'm not feeling as well as I thought and . . ."

"No!"

Startled at Antonio's angry vehemence, Morgana snapped

her eyes back to meet his furious glance.

"You will not allow Devon Howard to know how completely he has taken you in! *Caramba!* Have you no pride? The man will laugh at your shaken departure and retell the story to as many as will listen of how the foolish niece of General Manuel Escobar fell to pieces at the very sight of him! If only for your uncle's sake, Morgana, I demand you stay and face the man down!"

Her face flushed with embarrassment, Morgana swallowed hard at the tears that choked her throat. Turning her back deliberately toward the entrance where Devon still stood, she faced Santa Anna squarely.

"Of course, you're right, Antonio. Thank you for reminding me that I do not have only myself to think of now. I should not like to show my appreciation for my aunt and uncle's generosity by making them a laughingstock because of my stupidity." Forcing a bright smile onto her lips, she continued softly, "I would appreciate it very greatly if you would dance with me, Antonio."

Taking her unhesitantly into his arms, Santa Anna replied with a small, triumphant smile, "It is my pleasure, *querida.*"

A dark frown adding a severity to his expression that was formidable, Devon stood uncertainly in the entrance to the Escobar courtyard. Of all the damned luck! His head was pounding as a result of his grueling journey from Saltillo. If he had had more sense, he would have taken more time in returning, instead of sleeping just until before dawn each day and pushing on until it was too dark to see. Hell! the trip to Saltillo had been nothing but a headache from the very start! The time lost pampering the spoiled Consuelo de Artega while she complained about the inconveniences she suffered had been difficult enough to take, but the reception he had received from General Nepocino had been the final straw. Extremely uncooperative from the first moment of their meeting, the argumentative, rapidly balding Mexican had, after two days of waiting and a three-hour tirade against the Anglo-Texans, finally sat back on his skinny haunches and declared that his statement given at the time of Colonel Austin's arrest was a matter of record and could not be changed even if he so desired.

So, he had been sent on a fool's errand! Certain that such a tactic could suit only one purpose, Devon had prepared provisions that same night and started back to Lopez.

Damn! It was hard to believe that the dignified, pompous Antonio Lopez de Santa Anna was so hot for Morgana Pierce that he would risk an incident just to secure her favors. No . . . Shaking his head in silent disagreement with his own conclusions, he attempted to set his thoughts right. No, Santa Anna risked nothing. Devon Howard was less than a speck of sand in this country where Santa Anna was all powerful. Santa Anna held all the cards, and, despite Devon's suspicions as to the reason why he had been sent on a pointless mission, if he wished to win Steve Austin's release, he dared not offend the man with an accusation.

And now he had returned, of all nights, on the feast of Corpus Christi. He had wanted an opportunity to see Morgana alone . . . to attempt to explain the reason for his abrupt departure. And, whether he chose to admit it or not, he had wanted an opportunity to hold Morgana in his arms . . . close against him . . . to touch her skin . . . feel her mouth under his . . . God, he ached to have her. The frustration of not having her was so strong that the pain was almost physical.

Unconsciously adjusting the high collar of his shirt, Devon fidgeted inside his uncomfortable attire. A coat, waistcoat, shirt, and confining trousers on a night as warm as this was the height of stupidity, but fashion demanded that he attend the party properly attired. Three weeks on the trail with little more than a comfortable shirt and well-worn trousers had ill prepared him for the immediate return to formal attire necessary for his political mission. Hell, he was sick of it all! His head was throbbing and his throat was parched, and he wanted to see Morgana . . . he wanted that more than anything. . . .

"Devon!"

The lightly accented pronunciation of his name snapped

Devon's head painfully in the direction from which Doña Isabella emerged through the small social clusters of guests. The sincere delight exhibited in her merry eyes drew a reluctant smile from him in return.

"Devon, you have returned to Mexico City at last! Your presence has been sorely missed in this household. I am so happy you have been able to make it back in time to attend our party."

"Even if I am terribly late, Doña Isabella?"

"Even then, my friend." Smiling as Devon raised her dainty hand to his lips, she continued in a softer tone, "We were all startled to hear that you had left without a word. Manuel explained that you had left on a matter related to your Colonel Austin's incarceration, but I myself admit to being a bit peeved that you had not informed us of your intended journey."

"I'm afraid it was a last-minute arrangement, Doña Isabella, that could not be avoided."

His response seemed to trouble the small, generous woman. "Is that so, Devon?"

"Yes, it is so." More disturbed by the pounding in his head than he chose to admit, Devon felt his patience quickly dissipating. "And Morgana, Doña Isabella." His glance slipping back to the groups of people clustered around the courtyard, ". . . she is well? I haven't seen her yet. She is here at the party?"

"Oh, yes." Turning, Doña Isabella gestured toward the couples dancing to the lilting waltz. "See . . . over there. Morgana dances with Antonio."

Turning in the direction Doña Isabella pointed, Devon felt a sharp, searing pain pierce his vitals. Dancing lightly in the arms of the president of Mexico was Morgana, her beautiful face turned up smilingly to Santa Anna's hypocritically benevolent expression. The pain in his head turning to a deep, steady pounding that threatened to jumble his senses, he mumbled an almost inaudible excuse to Doña Isabella and walked directly to the edge of the floor.

The song was endless, the steady rocking rhythm adding almost unbearable stress to the stress he already suffered.

Unwilling to allow his own sickening jealousy to overcome his better judgment, Devon walked to the refreshment table and picked up a freshly filled glass. Tossing down the contents in a few quick swallows, he cursed his own stupidity as the throbbing in his head resounded even more loudly than before. Abruptly realizing the music had come to a sudden halt, he turned and made his way once again to the edge of the floor. Immediately spotting the small, dainty figure chatting amiably as she walked slowly off the floor, Devon lost no time in approaching her.

"Morgana—" Reaching out unhesitantly, he took the small hand that gestured daintily as she spoke.

"Oh, Devon." Turning toward him with a startling lack of enthusiasm, Devon watched as disinterested gold-flecked eyes raised to his. "So you've returned to Mexico City. It is fortunate you are back in time to attend Tía Isabella's party. She would have been sorely disappointed if you had missed it."

"Yes, welcome back to Mexico City, Devon. You have had a pleasant visit to Saltillo?"

Finding it extremely difficult to be pleasant to Santa Anna's inquiry, Devon responded shortly, "I don't think that 'pleasant' would be the right word to use in describin' my visit to Saltillo, Antonio." Conscious that the music had begun again and extremely anxious to get Morgana away from her zealous guard, he continued rapidly, "But we can speak of that another time, Antonio. Since I'm late for the party, I'd like to try to catch up on some of the dancin' I've missed." Turning again to Morgana, he smiled into her eyes. "May I have this dance, Morgana?"

"I'm sorry, Devon. I'm afraid my dances are taken for the remainder of the evening." Turning to a short, slender young man who appeared at her side, she smiled graciously, "Yes, Vincente. I do remember that this is our dance."

A slow flush of anger suffusing his face as Morgana walked away without another word on the arm of the delighted young man, Devon muttered a soft excuse and walked back to the refreshment table, unaware that Santa Anna's eyes followed him with great satisfaction.

Her heart pounding so loudly in her ears that she was barely able to hear the beat of the music, Morgana stared with a stiff smile into Julio's admiring gaze. It was truly difficult for her to believe that this evening had begun only three hours before. Since Devon had arrived, each minute had stretched into an hour and each hour into an eternity. So far she had been successful in avoiding a direct confrontation with him, but she was truly uncertain just how long her popularity would last. Surely for one of the next dances she would find herself temporarily without a partner, providing Devon the opportunity he obviously sought to get her alone. She had no desire to speak to him and certainly no intention of asking how well he had enjoyed his journey to Saltillo. The answer to that was only too obvious, and she did not intend to provide him with an opportunity to tell her more of his well-fabricated lies.

So caught up in her thoughts had she become that Morgana had not realized the dance was coming to a halt. Startled as the music stopped abruptly, she turned to offer a gracious word to her partner when a strong hand gripped her arm roughly.

"Morgana, darlin', I think this is our dance."

The blue eyes turned down to hers were filled with anger, and, abruptly filled with a matching emotion, she smiled through tightly clenched teeth, "No, I think you're wrong, Devon. I've already promised this dance to someone else."

"Well, that's too bad, isn't it, Morgana, because I feel like dancin', and I feel like dancin' with you."

"Señorita . . . if I may be of service . . ."

Julio's hesitant interruption of their heated exchange alerted Morgana's attention to the fact that they were beginning to draw curious glances, and, determined not to cause a scene, she turned to the concerned young man.

"No, that's quite all right, Julio. I'm afraid Señor Howard is correct. I did promise him this dance. It was my error."

Aware that Devon still held a firm grip on her arm, she

said lightly, "The music has started. Shall we dance, or do you expect to stand here for the duration of the music and glare at me?"

"No, I've changed my mind, too, Morgana. I don't feel like dancin' anymore. I feel like walkin', and since the garden is the only place we can walk without trippin' over someone, I think we'll finish that walk we started a few weeks ago." Flushing at the reminder of that day and the feigned tenderness with which Devon had made such a fool of her, Morgana replied caustically, "No, I think not, Devon. I've had enough walks in the garden tonight. I'm no longer in the mood."

"Well, that's too damned bad!"

Pulling her forward, Devon supported her elbow in a grip that was just short of pain as he steered her relentlessly to the privacy of the garden. Only a few feet within its confines, he jerked her around to face him, his voice a low snarl.

"All right, what's goin' on, Morgana? Had enough of playin' with a no-account Texan and decided to go for better game? Well, I can see you put the time I've been away to good use. You obviously have the great man eatin' out of your hand. But remember, darlin', the great man is married and this is a Catholic country. You're goin' to get yourself nothin' but trouble if you try to play that game."

Uncertain whether she should be angry or glad that her act had worked so well, Morgana replied in a haughty tone, "Really, Devon, I can't see how any of this is your concern. What I do and whom I see is my business. But rather than put Antonio's reputation in a bad light, I will tell you that he is a dear friend of Tía Isabella and Tío Manuel who has taken a kind interest in me. I appreciate his concern . . ."

"You must take me for a damned fool, Morgana!" The vehemence of Devon's abrupt statement sent a jolt of fear through Morgana's senses, causing her to take an involuntary step backward that only resulted in his pulling her closer. She could feel the tension in the tightly muscled body so close to hers and saw the same tensions echoed in his expression as he squinted oddly into her flushed face. "Antonio Santa Anna never did a kind or generous thing in his life

225

without an ulterior motive, and somehow I can't make myself believe you're so stupid as to be taken in by his pretense."

The throbbing in Devon's head was growing considerably stronger. His vision was getting fuzzy, and the extreme heat of the evening added immeasurably to his discomfort. Hardly reacting to his own physical distress, he listened with growing fury as Morgana responded heatedly, "And how is it that you feel you have room to sit in judgment on Antonio? Are you really certain *you* aren't the one guilty of the same despicable deceit that you lay at Antonio's door? Tell me, Devon, why is it you haven't asked me how I'm feeling? You were *so* worried about me after I was injured . . . came faithfully each day to show your concern. Strange, isn't it, how quickly that concern disappeared when Consuelo de Artega crooked her little finger in your direction!"

"Who told you about Consuelo?"

"You don't even bother to deny it's true, Devon? You surprise me."

"Bother to deny what, Morgana? That Consuelo traveled with the same contingent of soldiers as I to Saltillo? That's true. That she is a lovely, desirable woman? That's true, too. What else did you want to know?"

"Nothing! Absolutely nothing! Believe me or not, I care very little what you do in your private moments, Devon. I only resent being played for a fool . . . your attempt to gain my confidence so I might lend support to your cause to have Colonel Austin freed. Just for the record, Devon, I couldn't care less if the man rotted in prison! As far as I'm concerned, he was arrested for treason, and deserved the punishment he's suffering!"

"Selfish, self-centered little fool!" Devon's voice was a low hiss. His flushed face was stiff with anger, his mouth turned down into a contemptuous sneer. There was a strange look in his eyes, and beads of perspiration covered his forehead. His tall frame appeared unsteady, but his heated tirade continued unabated. "You haven't a thought in your head that doesn't concern yourself, have you? You're just like the rest of the indolent rich society friends with whom you were raised . . . vain, lazy, useless for any important work. Just a pretty ornament to adorn a man's arm or fill his bed. And you have the gall to criticize Consuelo de Artega! At least she's honest! She doesn't pretend to be anythin' she isn't and offers only what she's prepared to give!''

"And did you enjoy her offerings, Devon? She should be quite skillful by now, with all the teachers she's had. . . .''

"Oh, is that what you're interested in, Morgana? Knowin' just how well you measure up to Consuelo? Well, let's see how well you compare. . . .''

Jerking her abruptly against his chest, Devon slid his hand beneath her mantilla and tangled his fingers in her hair as he whispered against her lips, "Damn you, you little witch!''

Abruptly his mouth was hard against hers, the pressure cruel and punishing as he forced her lips apart, grinding deeper and deeper into the softness of her mouth. Morgana could feel the sharp pain of her lip cracking against her teeth, the bitter taste of blood even as Devon's tongue savagely plundered the tender warmth of her mouth. His arms strained her close, closer until she was welded to the full length of his body with the force of his passionate assault, which subdued her struggles with an ease that left them almost nonexistent.

Stiffly resisting the rioting emotions assailing her senses, Morgana strained to hold on to her anger, clinging desperately to the hatred that had burned through her at the disclosure of Devon's deception. But slowly, insidiously, the heady languor stimulated by Devon's touch began to assume control. Thoughts of Consuelo de Artega faded, replaced by the searing wonder of Devon's lips against hers. Not truly aware when her arms began to steal around his neck, she heard only his low groan of pleasure as she opened her mouth fully to his, accepted the invasion of his tongue with warmth, licked hungrily at his with her own.

Tearing his mouth from hers, his chest heaving from the torrent of emotions they shared, Devon drew away just far enough that he might look down into her love-drugged expression. Moving his lips hungrily across the heavily fringed lids, he closed her eyes with his kisses, tasted the sweet softness of her cheek, trailed his kisses to the small pink shell of her ear, where he whispered hoarsely, "I dreamed of this all the time I was gone, Morgana. God, I didn't want to leave . . . I ached to hold you, touch you . . ." Sliding his lips down the white column of her throat, he moved his mouth lightly across the fine scar that still remained. Their thundering heartbeats mingled as he whispered jealously, "I didn't want anyone to touch you, care for you but me . . . I wanted to know that you were all right, see the health come back into your face day by day . . . I needed to know you were well, but I had to leave, darlin' . . . I had no choice. Santa Anna told me the only chance Austin had for his trial was to have the commandant general who arrested him repudiate his statement. I had to leave the next mornin'. I had no time to tell you . . . to let you know how much I wanted to stay with you."

With slow relentlessness, Devon's words began to drag Morgana back to reality. Lies! He was still telling her lies! Even now, when he held her in his arms, the lies poured out of his mouth between his kisses! A deep revulsion of her own weakness stealing over her, Morgana abruptly pushed hard at the warmth of his chest, steeling herself against his startled, angry expression as she managed in a cool, even voice, "Well, how *do* I compare, Devon?" To his stunned wordlessness, she continued coldly. "Did Consuelo's kisses stir you more than mine? Did she feel better in your arms than I? Come, Devon, tell me. I've given you enough time to make your comparison."

"Bitch!" A low hiss coming from between clenched teeth, he swallowed tightly. A hard bitterness replacing the tender glow shining only moments before in his eyes, he responded tightly, "The comparison is not quite complete, Morgana. You offer only a samplin' in an area where Consuelo was far more generous. But if you wish a true assessment, darlin', we'll have to find a more private place then this to finish our comparison."

"That day will never come, Devon." Her own pain of disillusionment was so severe that she did not notice the manner in which Devon raised his hand to grip his temple or the sway

228

of his tall frame as he stood rigidly listening to her words. Morgana turned and walked rapidly to the entrance to the courtyard. Filled with disgust at her disappointment when he failed to follow, Morgana fixed a stiff smile on her face, and stepped back into the courtyard.

CHAPTER SIX

She could taste the sweet, gentle persuasion of his mouth against hers again. The intoxicating male scent of him was strong in her nostrils, stirring her senses. In the vague netherworld of her dream, she came alive under the kisses that assailed her relentlessly. Warm lips moved caressingly over her face; touching lightly on the heavily fringed lids that fluttered under their touch; lovingly followed the short, straight bridge of her nose, the splendid countours of her cheekbones; worshipped the velvet softness of her skin until she groaned with desire. The seeking mouth moved to cover her eager lips, drinking deeply of the innate sweetness abandoned so completely to his kiss.

One wide, calloused hand moved gently over her body while the other luxuriated in the unbound silk of her hair. But the touch became more urgent; the hand tightening passionately in the gleaming chestnut-colored spirals spread across the starkness of her pillow. His kisses deepened, the heady invasion of his tongue, as it fondled hers intimately, unleasing a sweeping wave of desire . . . exhilarating . . . impossible to withstand. Abandoning herself completely to the emotion raging through her blood, she returned his kiss without reserve, allowing the searing penetration of his tongue full access to the sweetness he sought.

The broad, seeking hands moved intimately over her flesh; the delicate lace of her night rail fell under their onslaught. The full, rounded globes of her breasts met their caress, a wave of searing ecstasy setting her to trembling as his eager mouth claimed an erect, waiting crest.

Excitement raging unchecked throughout her slender frame, she feared to open her eyes, feared the ultimate result of that betrayal . . . the end of her dream.

Reaching out, she felt the ruffled thickness of his hair under her fingertips, her hands trembling as she clutched him tight against her breasts. But he was not content with the taste of their beauty for long, his mouth following the trail his hands had warmed so efficiently only moments before. The soft white skin of her stomach was devoured by his kiss; the rounded curves of her hips worshipped tenderly; the shapely, slender length of her legs explored patiently by his lips; the gleaming, slender thighs tortured exquisitely; the ravaging heat of his passion culminating in the moist, seeking kisses he pressed so intimately against the tight chestnut curls nestled between.

A low, impatient groan sounded unexpectedly in the silence, the moment before the sensuous weight of the heated male body was lifted from hers. Morgana's spontaneous cry of protest abruptly changed to a sharp gasp at the first, unexpected pain of penetration.

Following through with his initial thrust, pausing only when he was deep inside her, he savored the moment of complete possession, his deep, tremulous whisper throbbing in the stillness of the room.

"Morgana . . . I . . . I've wanted this for so long . . . so very long . . ."

Her eyes snapping wide, Morgana came to the startling realization. She was not dreaming! This was reality . . . reality!

The warm, searing lips moved to cover hers again. The shaft of his passion full and throbbing within her, he commenced a heady, slowly escalating rhythm that raised the fires burning so brilliantly in the core of her being to a raging inferno. Completely overwhelmed by the heat of its blaze, Morgana met and joined each searing penetration, a wild happiness growing with her passion as the rhythm of love brought them closer and closer to the glorious rapture of culmination.

Pausing only briefly at the summit to whisper her name lovingly . . . reverently . . . he brought them abruptly, rapturously, to complete, total reward, the long, spiraling plunge from its breathtaking heights accompanied by Morgana's own spontaneous cry of rejoicing.

The warm, moist heat of his body lifted slowly from hers, and Morgana felt a deep pang of regret. Sliding her arms around his neck, she drew his head down once again to hers. She did not want this to end, this beauty that had begun under the protection of darkness. Feeling again the touch of his lips against hers, Morgana opened her mouth, inviting him in, luxuriating in the sweet music his touch inspired in her heart.

A shaft of moonlight, moving through the windows to the side of her bed, illuminated the hard lines of Devon's face— efficiently negated by the supreme tenderness glowing in the depths of his eyes.

"Morgana, darlin' . . ." The tips of his calloused fingers gently caressing her cheek, he whispered softly, "I didn't intend this to happen . . . I stayed in the garden after you left me. I wasn't feeling well, and I must have fallen asleep. When I awoke, everythin' was quiet. The party was over and I needed to talk to you. I needed to tell you that I missed you while I was gone . . . that Consuelo de Artega . . ."

A slender hand slipping across his lips halted his words.

"No, Devon, please don't say anything else. I don't want to think about anything right now. I just want you to hold me. Will you do that, darling? Will you just hold me?"

His response to her question was a low, muffled groan, and Morgana felt the touch of Devon's mouth as it devoured hers with unspoken passion, and the hard warmth of his body as it moved to cover hers once more.

The bright light of morning streaming through the window intruded into her dreams. Reluctant to open her eyes, Morgana struggled against wakefulness, finally relenting as the sound of morning stirring in the household below reached her ears. She felt warm, strangely relaxed, almost indolent in the new tranquillity that seemed to encompass her being. Slowly opening her eyes, she moved her gaze around the room to find its familiarity unmarred by anything foreign to its makeup. Her attention caught by an object on the floor beside the bed, she leaned over and scooped it up, realization sweeping her senses as the light coverlet slipped away to reveal her nakedness. Holding the light night rail against her breast, she closed her eyes until her breathing returned to normal and the quaking that had come with realization abated. So it hadn't been a dream! Devon had come to her last night . . . had loved her, and she had encouraged him to love her again! But where was he now? She hadn't heard him leave. The abrupt thought that he might have been discovered in her room if he had stayed brought a bright flush to her face. Yes, she had Devon to thank for being spared that embarrassment, for she certainly had not given a thought in that direction all through the long, lovely night. Yes, she had Devon to thank and she would thank him properly . . . oh yes, she would. . . .

The erotic direction of her own thoughts deepened her flush, and, realizing Aggie would soon be appearing at her door, she hopped from the bed with frantic haste. Moving quickly to the washstand, she completed her toilette, the extremely sensitized skin of her more delicate area renewing the memory of the night past to the point where she was more agitated than soothed by the refreshing coolness of the scented water. Swiftly slipping into a fresh chemise, Morgana moved to the wardrobe and took out the first gown that met her hand. A fresh yellow cotton that she had brought from home, it had a pleasant familiarity about it that soothed her rather frazzled nerves. Snatching up her brush as she walked past the dresser, Morgana brushed vigorously at her tangled chestnut locks. But somehow, even that simple task brought back memories . . . of Devon's hands moving through her hair, tightening in his passion, the tender kisses he had showered on its silky length, the way his lips moved against her skin . . .

Oh, Lord! Stopping abruptly in midstroke, Morgana closed her eyes. How would she get through the day . . . get through the time until she saw him again . . . became certain that the tenderness, the loving glow that had shown in his eyes still remained, was not merely a product of a night of passion?

"Morgana! Morgana, are you awake?"

Aggie's voice at the door broke startlingly into her anxious thoughts, and, almost too flustered for a reply, Morgana finally managed in a tone she hoped would pass for the norm, "Yes, I'm awake, Aggie. I'll be down for breakfast in a few moments."

"Señor Santa Anna's men are here with Grillo, Morgana. They said they have been instructed to wait until you were ready to ride, because Señor Santa Anna said that you might be late in rising after last night's festivities."

Damn! She had forgotten that she had promised Antonio she would ride with him this morning. But she dared not change her mind at this late moment. Surely, such an action would raise far too many questions, and, in her disturbed state, she was not certain she would be able to handle either Tío Manuel's or Antonio's assessing glance.

Hastening back to the wardrobe, Morgana reached inside for her riding clothes and boots. Tearing off her dress with frantic haste, she slipped into her riding skirt and shirtwaist and turned to slip her feet into her soft tailored boots. A trifle flushed from her haste, she turned again to the mirror and began brushing her hair, the reflection she saw there bringing her to an abrupt halt.

Hardly able to believe the face reflected in the glass was her own, she stared at the flushed cheeks, was startled by the brilliant sparks of gold that glowed so luminously in her bright eyes, by the soft, lightly parted, inviting lips slightly swollen from the night's vigorous lovemaking. There were slight shadows beneath her eyes, but she had not had very much rest during the night, to be sure, and they did not detract in the least from her altogether radiant countenance! Oh, Devon! Her heart sang in a song that reverberated through her brain until she was almost overcome by the sound. You did this to me, Devon! You made me a woman . . . showed me what it is to love, and now that I know . . . oh, Devon, please come to me soon. I need you, darling.

"Morgana, are you coming?"

Vigorously brushing her hair, she turned toward the doorway as she attempted to secure the heavy length back from her face with a comb.

"Yes, Aggie, I'm coming. Please tell Lieutenant Mirada I'll be down in a minute!"

Taking one last hasty look in the looking glass, Morgana rushed toward the door, halting abruptly with her hand on the knob to take a long, deep breath. Drawing open the door, she stepped sedately out into the hallway. With a short, calm smile flashed in Aggie's direction, she walked serenely toward the staircase.

Spurring Grillo to a faster pace through the almost deserted street, Morgana spied at last the turnoff into the forested area where she truly enjoyed riding. Intensely grateful that she had not been guided to ride in the Alameda where it was more common for the young ladies of the city to ride, she had to admit to certain suspicions as to Antonio's instructions to ride in the particular area he chose. Granted, it was lovely and left almost entirely to its natural state of beauty, but it was also isolated. By providing her with the protection of his private guards, he guaranteed her safety from bandits that frequented the wooded glades, but he also guaranteed that they could ride unseen. Certainly that was his reason for meeting her in the forest instead of openly riding to Tío Manuel's home. Intensely uncomfortable with her thoughts, she searched her mind for a manner in which to discourage Antonio's interest in her. She had no doubt he was an intensely virile man who suffered from the extreme isolation of his position. If only Doña Ines would travel to the capital, surely he would no longer seek her out. But she would not, and in his loneliness, Antonio seemed to sense a kindred spirit in her. If she were to be honest, she would have to admit to the appeal of having the handsome, powerful president of Mexico appeal so tenderly for her affections. And there was no doubt his magnetism, his aura was formidable. Had she not known Devon, experienced the wonder of his touch and finally come to know the depth of beauty they were able to create between them, she was truly uncertain of just how differently the situation between herself and Antonio would progress.

"*Hola!* Morgana!"

Startled by the familiar voice, Morgana turned her head in the direction from which it came. "Antonio! I had not expected to see you so soon in my ride. We normally come upon each other much farther down the path."

"But I have been impatient to see you. I could not wait the few extra minutes it would take for you to reach the usual area in which we meet."

Raising her eyes to Antonio's intense, handsome face, Morgana felt again the draw of his charisma. It was no wonder that this man was able to sway the populace with his oratory, quell disorders by the sharp command of his voice, stimulate the confidence of his army to the point that they followed him almost without question. The fact that this impressive man appealed almost humbly for her affections was a heady compliment indeed.

"I am extremely flattered, Antonio. But what is it that makes you so impatient today?"

"I have decided that today we will have a picnic. Picnics are very popular in your country, are they not?"

Startled by his declaration, Morgana could not suppress a small laugh. "Yes, indeed they are. But it is a bit early in the day for a picnic, Antonio."

A new light coming into his eyes, Antonio reached for her hand as he reined his horse alongside hers. Raising it to his ips, he continued softly, "Yes, but you must trust me that I have planned this all very carefully. You see, I know it is your usual custom to dispense with breakfast until after you ride, is that not true?" Laughing at Morgana's surprised nod of concurrence, he leaned forward to whisper confidentially, "I have heard Aggie harangue you on several occasions for your 'unwise' habit." His smile broadening, he continued, "and since you were so kind as to grant me so much of your time last night at your aunt's splendid party, I felt I should like to show my appreciation in return."

"Antonio, you needn't have . . ."

Finally releasing the hand he had held so warmly in his own for the duration of their conversation, he directed a warm glance into her eyes. "Yes, I know I needn't have, but I have, and so I ask you to follow me so that we may share *desayuno* before it is past a decent hour."

Unable to resist the sheer charm of the man, Morgana smiled her acquiescence. "All right, Antonio, it just happens that I am inordinately hungry this morning, and since I have been unable to break my 'unwise' habit, all the trouble you have gone to will not be wasted, I am sure."

Raising his hand to run it impatiently through the heavy thickness of his hair as he lay abed, Devon closed his eyes for a few seconds in an effort to gain control of his rioting thoughts. Lord, how much longer would he have to wait until he could see her again? Truly, it had not been his intention to hide in the garden until all the guests had left and to steal up to Morgana's room. But the combination of the long journey with little rest, the heat, the wine, and the anxiety at her cool reception had left him with a throbbing pain in his head that had him close to staggering. At the point of Morgana's hasty exit from the garden, he had been truly uncertain if he was capable of following. When he had awakened, he had felt a true panic. He had handled everything poorly. His response to her jibe about Consuelo de Artega could only have confirmed in her mind any stories she might have heard.

And he was tired of misunderstandings between them. He wanted a return of the easy trust and warm closeness that had existed between them the first week after she had been injured. . . .no suspicions, preconceived notions . . . merely the return of that particular light in her eyes that had warmed him down to his soul.

The silence of the night had seemed the perfect opportunity to set everything right between them, but from the moment he had entered her room he had been able to do little else but react to the supreme beauty that lay basking in the silver shafts of moonlight stealing through her window. For long moments he had been capable of nothing more than staring at Morgana. She was exquisite. Truly, he was certain he had never seen anyone more lovely than she. Her hair, unbound from the winding coils that had been hidden under the lacy mantilla, lay in long, gleaming spirals against the starkness of her bed linens. Her perfect profile, etched against the same whiteness, had displayed a high, clear brow and the smooth curve of her cheek, against which the incredibly thick fan of lashes rested so still. Soft, appealing, lightly parted lips had called to him, begged him to cover them with his own. It was a silent plea he had not been able to withstand. Her hair had been warm to the touch, silky, caressing his fingers with its brilliance; her skin smooth; her lips incredibly sweet to the taste. Her body had welcomed him, turned to encourage his caress. Lost in the sweet wonder of her, he had been conscious only of his burning desire, the same desire that had been ever present since the first day of their meeting, to take her . . . to join her body to his . . . to make her his own in the age-old way that could not be disputed. He remembered the silky texture of her skin beneath his lips, the fullness of her breasts as he had fondled them with his tongue, tasted their waiting crests, opened his mouth to accept the sweet flesh, tease it, love it, torture it exquisitely until they were both almost mad with wanting. His hands had wandered the long, sloping curves of her body freely; his fingers had tangled in the bright chestnut-brown ringlets that surrounded the moist heart of her desire, before touching, stroking the aching, anxious bud to life. His kisses had traveled the same path as his touch until he could no longer hold himself back from the moment he was certain they both longed to fulfill. Then he was inside her, the first brief obstacle swept away with a soft gasp from Morgana that still echoed in his mind. And then had come the sweet, searing glory of total possession . . . Morgana . . . his, completely his, at last. . . .

In the radiant aftermath of their fulfillment, she had not wanted his explanations. The sweet sound of her voice still echoed in his mind, ''Devon, hold me, darling, just hold me. . . .''

And he had held her . . . and loved her . . . until she had fallen asleep in his arms . . . until the approaching dawn had forced him to leave.

Sliding a trembling hand across his eyes, Devon took a deep breath in an another attempt to gain some control over his raging emotions. He could feel his taut muscles honed by three weeks of rigorous riding now knotting with desire, the firm shaft of his manhood aching for Morgana's moist warmth to enclose it, welcome him home.

Unable to withstand another moment of the heady torture inflicted so endlessly by the memories assailing his mind, Devon rose from the bed and walked to the dresser. Squinting at his watch in vain, he walked to the window where the bright morning sun illuminated its face. Yes, he would dress and go to the Escobar household now. It was early, but he was certain the household would be awake and busy at work setting the house to rights after the festivities of the night before. Yes, he would take some flowers to Doña Isabella to express his appreciation for her honest, friendly reception when he had arrived. And then he would see Morgana. . . .

His heart pounding like a schoolboy's, Devon hesitated a moment at the courtyard door. Yes, he could hear voices inside and the scurrying of feet. Undoubtedly work was progressing just as he had anticipated, and the household was awake. Breathing a sigh of relief, he pulled the bell cord and waited with limited patience for the door to open.

"*Buenos días,* Señor Howard." Maria's bright face echoed her welcome, and, inordinately glad that he had yet another ally in a household that was not totally friendly toward him, he grinned his reply.

"*Buenos días,* Maria. I am a very early visitor today, but I did want to express my appreciation for Doña Isabella's hospitality. If you will tell her I'm here . . ."

"That will not be necessàry, Devon! *Buenos días!* It is most pleasant to begin the day with a visit from a handsome young man. Do come in."

Placing the brilliant bouquet he carried in her arms, Devon said with a sincerity that was reflected in his eyes, "In appreciation of your kind welcome to your home and your country, Doña Isabella."

"Devon!" True delight was reflected in the older woman's expression. Doña Isabella lowered her head to breathe the sweet fragrance before lifting suspiciously bright eyes to his. "Your gesture is well appreciated, but unnecessary. Your presence in my household is always a pleasure, and Manuel and I will always be grateful for your swift ministrations to our niece at a time when we were all too shocked to react properly. But for you, she may have suffered greater or even permanent damage to her health. You will always be welcome here, Devon." A smile springing back to her lips after her short, sincere statement, she continued rapidly in the manner so indicative of her vibrant personality, "But you have just missed Morgana, Devon. She has already left for her morning ride. She does not usually return before an hour, sometimes two have passed, but you are welcome to come in and share *desayuno* with us."

Startled by the depth of his disappointment, Devon hesitated only a moment. "Does she usually ride in the Alameda? I had intended to ride this morning after coming here, and I might join her there."

"No, I think not, Devon. She has repeatedly told me how she enjoys riding in the forest just outside the city. I believe she takes the old trail . . ."

His brows knotting with concern, Devon interrupted unhesitatingly, "But surely you realize it is unsafe to ride in that area, Doña Isabella, even with a groom. Bandits would not hesitate . . .''

"Calm yourself, Devon." Realizing his concern, Doña Isabella hastened to add her reassurance. "Morgana is quite safe. She rides with an escort of two guards provided by Antonio, and relies on them to show her areas where she may ride in safety. The guards are armed, Devon . . . there is no need for worry."

Abruptly, Devon's concern reached yet in another disturbing direction. Taking the small hand that rested reassuringly on his arm, he raised it to his lips as he responded tightly, "Thank you for your invitation to *desayuno*, Doña Isabella, but I have an appointment I must keep this morning. Many thanks."

"*Adios,* Devon." Watching as the tall, slender Texan turned with a darkening frown and strode purposefully down the street, Doña Isabella felt an inexplicable tremor of apprehension. Turning back toward the courtyard, she pulled the gate closed behind her, mumbling with a shake of her head, "*Quién sabe? Esos extraños Norteamericanos . . .*"

Laughing easily at the dry sense of humor that Morgana had come to recognize as yet another facet of the multifaceted personality that was Antonio Santa Anna, Morgana rested her head back against the ancient tree under which they sat. Completely relaxed, her mellowness undoubtedly aided by Antonio's careful refilling of her wineglass each time it was emptied, Morgana allowed her gaze to move slowly over the enigmatic Mexican as he came to sit beside her.

It had been a lovely morning, and she was truly impressed by the thoughtfulness that had gone into the little "picnic" Antonio had arranged. Leading her up the rugged path to the glade where he had taken her the first time they had ridden together, he had dismounted and lifted her from her horse without explanation. Taking her by the arm, he had led her to a spot where the morning sun made a brilliant, glowing circle in the deep green foliage. Set formally upon a snow-white tablecloth was a banquet that included crisp, delicately fried chicken, bread still warm and fragrant from the oven, golden sweet butter, assorted fruits and sweetmeats, all served on delicate white and gold French porcelain that could easily have been found on a formal dining table rather than in a cool forest glade. To the side stood a delicate crystal decanter of wine and two glasses, and, startled at the unexpected luxury, Morgana had exclaimed spontaneously, "Antonio, this is lovely! You do not mean to make me think you did this all yourself?"

"Of course not, *querida*. Mine was merely the thought. Other hands prepared the setting. I hope you are pleased."

Her eyes scanning the immediate area, she had responded curiously, "But I saw no one but your guards at the foot of the trail. Where . . ."

"Once our picnic had been prepared, I sent the servants away. They will return later to collect the remains. I wanted this day to be special for us, *querida*. I wanted to show my appreciation for the time you have given to fill my lonely hours, and the spark of life you have added to the dreary duties that fill my day."

"Ah, Antonio, you do not fool me with your sober statements. I know you enjoy the challenge of your position as well as the heavy responsibility it entails. You are a man made for such a challenge, and would be lost without it."

A glow appearing in the dark eyes that assessed her so closely, Antonio had nodded his concurrence. "How well you know me, Morgana. Perhaps better than many who feel themselves my intimates in confidence. Yes, my responsibilities have become a part of me, and I look forward to each day spent in the service of my country . . . but, ah . . . the nights are another matter. . . ."

Unthinkingly, Morgana had responded lightly, "Nights are made for sleep, are they not, Antonio? You should not allow thoughts of your duties to interfere with that necessity."

"It is not thoughts of my work that keep me awake at night, *querida*." Shooting her a provocative look that succeeded in bringing a flush of color to her face, he had smiled

242

and let the discussion lapse.

In the time since, he had entertained her regally with stories of his youth, his many campaigns, his dreams for his country, alternating between humor, pathos and glimpses of the supreme dedication and drive that had brought him to the position of president.

Now, as he sat close beside her, his handsome Latin face relaxed, she felt, undeniably, the pure male aura he exuded so effortlessly. But, curiously, she was not apprehensive. A warm light-headedness overrode her caution.

She felt protected by the beauty of the night she had shared with Devon . . . secure . . . womanly . . . equipped to easily handle the emotions flashing in the dark eyes so close to hers.

"Tell me, *querida,* what is it you wish from life? Where would you like your destiny to lead you now that you have come to Mexico?"

Caught completely off guard by the question that rolled so easily off Antonio's tongue, Morgana was silent. What did she want to do with her life, indeed? In the past year she had been so caught up in surviving, she had not had time to pursue the thought past one day at a time. Now faced with the question, she found herself at a loss for a response.

So engrossed in her thoughts had she become that Morgana failed to notice the smouldering warmth in the black eyes looking down into hers, or the hand that moved to fondle an errant chestnut curl on her shoulder.

"I really don't know, Antonio. I think, at the very least, I want Tío Manuel and Tía Isabella to be proud of me. It is the very least I can do after the kindness they have shown me. I should ultimately like to help them, enrich their lives in any way possible." Turning to Antonio's intent perusal, she gave an embarrassed laugh. "I suppose that sounds terribly presumptuous of me, the very same person who came to them as a poor relation only a short time ago."

"No, *querida,* on the contrary. I believe you have already accomplished that objective. I have never seen Doña Isabella so full of life and pleasure. You have filled a place in her heart that was sorely empty with her inability to have a child of her own. Yes, and I can also see the pride in Manuel's eyes when he looks at you. Your place in his heart is doubtless secure.''

''Thank you, Antonio.'' Antonio's kind words brought unexpected tears welling in the great gold-flecked eyes she lifted to his face. ''It means much to me to hear you say those words.''

''And, *querida,* you are dear to my heart as well.'' Raising his hand, he stroked her cheek, his long, slender fingers warm against her skin. ''When first my eyes touched on you, I sensed a *sympatico* spirit. And now that I have come to know you, my affection for you has grown to the point where it can, indeed, no longer be adequately termed as affection. I see in you, *querida,* '' he whispered softly, his face very close to hers, ''the answer to an ideal I have long carried in my mind. A woman of intelligence, beauty, spirit and devotion . . . you are all these things. And all these things,'' he continued in a harsh whisper, his lips moving to close over hers, ''I wish to make my own.''

His lips were warm on hers, gentle at the first touch, eliciting a warmth from Morgana that stemmed from a deep gratitude for his acceptance. His hand slid from her cheek into the softness of her hair at her temple, holding her mouth firm against his as she sought to evade his deepening kiss.

''No, Antonio, please, I don't want this. . . .''

His other arm, moving around her back, caught her in a captive embrace, holding her firmly in his arms as he whispered ardently against her lips, ''But *I* want this, Morgana. All that you are, your intelligence, beauty, spirit and your devotion . . . I want them all for my own.''

His mouth on hers was firm, insistent, moving with an increasing pressure that slowly separated her lips. Panicking as his tongue penetrated the barrier of her teeth, Morgana began to squirm in his embrace, uttering low words of protest that were swallowed by the all-consuming pressure of his kiss. Realizing as his hand moved to cup her breast that she must put a quick end to the madness of the situation, Morgana moaned low in the throat and gave a mighty thrust that

244

availed her nothing but a low triumphant laugh as Antonio shifted his weight, rolling with her until he pinned her underneath him. Smiling as he held her effectively imprisoned beneath his weight, he lifted his hand to stroke her cheek.

"*Querida,* do not be afraid. I will not force you to submit to me. I wish merely to raise our relationship to a different level, one in which I may express my feelings for you in the way I have so longed. I wish merely to kiss you, *querida,* to touch your face, your hair . . . to feel your warmth against me. Just for a little while, *querida,* I need to feel that warmth. Give that to me, and I give you my word, I will not force a submission you do not want. It is not my desire to force you . . . no, never that. But now, willingly, open your mouth to me . . . let me taste you more fully . . ."

Almost beside herself with fear, Morgana snatched at his hoarsely whispered promise. Her lips trembling, she whispered in return, "You give me your word . . . you will not force me?"

"*Sí,* Morgana. I merely need to feel you close to me for a little while . . . to taste your sweet lips . . ."

Her trembling increasing, Morgana pressed hoarsely, "And then I may return home, Antonio?"

"*Sí, querida.* Do this for me today, Morgana. Let me feel your arms around my neck, holding me close. I need this desperately . . . need your warmth, or I fear I cannot go on. . . ."

His dark, passion-filled eyes moving across her face saw her uncertainty. Sensing victory within his grasp, he lulled her with a soft, crooning voice as he took her arms and enclosed them around his neck. "*Sí, querida* . . . see how right it feels, your arms around me. Now . . . *mi pequeña,* open your mouth to mine . . ."

Lowering his mouth over hers, slowly, his eyes intent on hers, Santa Anna saw the gradual dropping of the heavily fringed lids over the frightened gold-flecked orbs, felt the soft, sweet lips separate beneath this, felt the true glory of victory as his mouth pressed deeper and deeper into hers. There was no protest . . . she was his! Child that she was, he would have no difficulty stirring her emotions . . . would gradually raise her level of desire until she craved his body as well as he wanted . . . needed hers. And then he would have her . . . without a broken promise, for she would yield to him without protest . . . she would be his. . . .

A deep trembling besetting her limbs, Morgana allowed Antonio to raise her arms and slip them around his neck. Startled by the foreignness of the feeling, Morgana fought a wave of revulsion. She remembered only too well Devon's body lying similarly upon hers, the warm weight she had welcomed so rapturously. How had she allowed this to happen? How had she allowed the situation to slip so badly out of control? His face was slowly descending toward hers. His soft persuasive voice, low and soothing, did not stifle her distaste. But he wanted only to hold her for a while, to kiss her, and then he had promised to let her go . . . to allow her to return home. Abruptly, the pleasant moments in the glade had turned into a nightmare . . . one which she wished desperately to be over . . . finished.

Closing her eyes so she might hide the revulsion reflected within her, she felt the touch of Antonio's mouth against hers, allowed her lips to separate, almost gagging as his tongue ravaged the inner reaches of her mouth. She must endure . . . endure only a little longer and he would release her. . . . Locking her hands around his neck, she forced herself to remain compliant under the crushing weight of Santa Anna's body as his searching kiss went on and on and on. . . .

"Well, it looks like I'm interruptin' a party . . ."

Her eyes snapping wide at the harsh male voice that reverberated in the silence of the isolated glade, Morgana felt Antonio's mouth jerk away from hers, the immediate freedom of the lifting of the body weight that had held her immobile. Her eyes moved with disbelief to a mounted figure a few yards away, where, his glance filled with contempt, Devon surveyed the scene in its entirety. Unable to tear her gaze from the tight, hard lines of his face, Morgana watched him dismount easily from his horse. Scrambling to her feet, she swayed momentarily, the coldness in Devon's eyes freezing her spontaneous step in his direction. Her words of grateful greeting froze unuttered on her lips.

"How did you find me here, Devon?" Santa Anna's unexpectedly calm response was issued with an unrevealing expression. "I was not expecting visitors."

"I suppose we can say that fact is obvious, Antonio. As for how I found you here, it's well known that you make it a habit to ride in the mornin' whenever you can spare the time. It wasn't difficult to ascertain that you favor this area to ride, where you can be . . . alone. . . ."

"I had not realized my daily habits were a matter of public knowledge. . . ."

"It seems you do manage to keep certain areas of your life private, Antonio, but your daily rides are not among them. And I wouldn't be too hard on your guards. You had them stationed at the bottom of the trail. They were not prepared for anyone comin' over the top of the rise into this area."

"You climbed the steep side . . . from the northern side of the mountain?" Santa Anna's tone was almost disbelieving.

"Yes, it isn't as difficult as it appears. You might keep that in mind the next time you're plannin' a party."

The first hint of anger began to move across Santa Anna's darkening features at Devon's response. Turning abruptly to Morgana's white face, he was unable to subdue the pride that welled within him at her composure under such trying circumstances. His voice was gentle as he took her arm, "Come, Morgana. I think it is time to return to the city."

"Yes, Morgana. Doña Isabella will be worried about you, won't she? Or do you take such lengthy rides every mornin'?"

Her face draining of color under the onslaught of Devon's obvious derision, Morgana stepped back inadvertently into the arm that Santa Anna curved around her waist. A wave of dizziness sweeping over her, she was unable to step free of the support of his arms and leaned heavily against his side.

"I admit to being surprised at findin' you up so early and

247

into such . . . vigorous . . . exercise this mornin', Morgana . . . after such an active night last night. . . . Pausing so she might absorb the full meaning of his words, Devon continued grimly, "but I suppose you're the kind that finds the energy to do everythin' she feels will benefit her in the long run, no matter the cost to herself at the time. I congratulate you for adherin' so strictly to the objectives you've obviously set for yourself."

"I confess," Santa Anna interrupted tightly, "that I have not the faintest notion what you are talking about, Devon! And if I may inquire, I am intensely curious why you should have sought me out in such a devious manner this morning."

A shallow smile spreading across his lips, Devon responded slowly, "We do have some unfinished business to attend to, Antonio, now that I've returned from Saltillo. I thought it might be easier to talk to you when you were relaxed, on your mornin' ride, than in the office with the pressure of your many duties on your mind. But I have obviously interrupted you, and for that I do apologize."

"Your apology is accepted, Devon." His statement issued with a severe expression, Santa Anna added with a heavy thread of warning in his tone, "But such an interruption in my daily schedule will not be tolerated again. I hope I make myself clear."

The fury he had suppressed so tenuously since arriving at the isolated glade almost surging out of control, Devon barely withstood the urge to jerk Morgana from Santa Anna's clutching arm and smash his fist into the arrogant Latin face. Clenching the fists that ached to contact crushingly against the smooth olive skin, Devon fought to regain control of his emotions. Taking refuge in action, he turned to mount his horse in a quick, fluid movement. Turning back, his eyes cold, he responded stiffly, "Yes, you make yourself very clear. I'll be expectin' your summons within the next few days so we may bring the matter to be discussed to a close. That is your wish, Antonio, is it not?"

"*Sí,* it is exactly as I wish. Goodbye, Devon."

Sliding his gaze to Morgana, where she stood still in the circle of Santa Anna's arm, Devon assessed her pale face. A searing desire to cause her pain, to make her pay for the aching disillusionment of finding her in Santa Anna's arms, added a new strength to his sardonic tone.

"Goodbye, Antonio. And goodbye to you, Morgana. I do applaud your fortitude, darlin', and wish you success in your endeavors. But judgin' from everythin' I've seen of you, I don't expect you'll be needin' my good wishes. . . ."

Her color whitening even further, Morgana stood stiffly, humiliation precluding response.

Responding in her stead, Santa Anna's voice was low, the finality in his tone unmistakable. "No, Morgana does not need your good wishes, Devon. She needs nothing from you at all."

His stomach rebelling against the stench pervading the dark corridors, Devon followed the maddeningly slow pace of the short poorly-uniformed guard. He had ridden past the huge stone inquisition building many times since his arrival in Mexico City, aware that Stephen Austin was incarcerated within the forbidding walls, but for all his negative expectations, he had been truly unprepared for the squalor within. Upon entering the building, his senses had been immediately assailed by a peculiar dank odor. With each step he had descended, the odious currents of air had become stronger, until, upon reaching the dungeons in which Stephen Austin was housed, the odor of human excrement, mold, and decay, combined with the smell of unclean human bodies and stale air, had reached a level that was nauseating. With each successive level the dampness had grown more intense until, as he had passed through the last doorway, the putrid moist air had penetrated his clothing, sinking into his bones with a deadening chill, despite the heat of the day on the surface.

Coming to an abrupt halt at a sharp signal from the shuffling soldier who preceded him, Devon waited with growing impatience during the presentation of his pass to the dungeon guard. Noting the startled expression on the man's wrinkled countenance when he spied the signature of Antonio Lopez de Santa Anna affixed at the bottom, Devon stifled a low, ironic snort. Doubtless, it was not often that the soldier actually saw the signature of the "great man," *el Presidente de Mejico,* affixed to a pass to one of these cells. And he would not have seen it this time, either, had the circumstances been different, he was certain.

Maintaining a taut rein on the tightly controlled fury that once again flooded his senses, he was visited with the memory of the tableau that had met his eyes upon entering the forested glade the previous morning. Morgana, only a few hours from the bed in which they had made love, lying unprotestingly under Santa Anna's compact, tightly muscled body, her arms wrapped securely around his neck. . . . The knife of pain stabbing through his vitals was as sharp now as at the moment of confrontation: the agony of despair he suffered was unrelenting. A wave of self-disgust sweeping over him, he realized his agony was of his own making. His endless desire had conjured up a Morgana who simply did not exist, crediting her with a sincere, caring personality completely foreign to her true makeup. Oh, Morgana wanted him, of that he had no doubt. The response of her small, beautiful body was too spontaneous, too untutored to be feigned. But her innocence was purely physical; the penetration of the seal of her womanhood merely the act, which, in thought and inclination, had been accomplished long before. Nagging, eating steadily away at his innards was the realization that with that obstacle out of the way, her virginity no longer a matter of concern, she was free to indulge her passions with the man whose patronage could lead her to the heights of the life to which she doubtless felt she was born.

The memory of the proprietary manner in which Santa Anna's arm had encircled Morgana's waist flashed across his mind, twisting the knife of pain until his eyes snapped closed in an attempt to escape the torturous vision. But the vision remained, only to be replaced by the agony of another . . . Morgana stepping back into the circle of Santa Anna's embrace, leaning against his side for comfort, her great eyes wide, no sound . . . no words coming from between the full, slightly parted lips still swollen from Santa Anna's bruising kisses, Morgana depending on the support of her famous, all-powerful protector . . . her lover . . .

"Señor Howard."

Coming back to reality with a start, Devon snapped his attention to the soldier who had conducted him down to the rank pit where he now waited.

"Señor Howard, you will please follow me to Colonel Austin's cell."

Acknowledging the man's words with a small nod of his head, Devin followed him down the poorly lit corridor past a series of rusted iron doors secured in damp stone until the guard came to a halt in front of one. Inserting the great iron key into the lock, he gestured with a short sweep of his hand.

"Go inside, señor. I will come to get you when your visit is over. If you wish to leave before that time, you may call."

Handing him the lantern he held in his hand, he waited with apparent disinterest as Devon walked slowly through the doorway. Supremely conscious of the door swinging shut behind him, and the grating sound of the key as it turned in the lock, Devon held the lantern high as a tall figure approached him out of the darkness of the corner.

"Devon . . . Devon Howard, is that you?"

Stunned by the sight that met his eyes, Devon was momentarily unable to reply . . . truly uncertain that the startling apparition that approached was indeed the man he had come to see.

Never a man of any great proportions, Austin appeared to have shrunk in stature. In the dim light of the flickering lantern, he saw a pale, unclean face, covered with a beard of at least two months' growth. Scraggly and uneven, it hung in limp, dirty strands, matching the ragged growth that hung unbound at his neck. His clothing, obviously that in which he had originally been arrested, was stained with the marks of his imprisonment and hung limply against his body, silent testimony to his physical deterioration. Behind him in the semidarkness Devon saw a cot covered with straw; the lone stool beside it and an odious bucket in the far corner were the only other furnishings in the vile cubicle. The small sliver of light issuing through a slit high in the wall near the ceiling provided the only illumination and ventilation, other than the small barred window in the door.

"Steve . . . God, man, is it really you?"

"Yes, it's me, all right, Devon." A familiar smile cracking through the beard verified the words, causing Devon to grasp the hand held out to him in spontaneous greeting, the warmth and strength of the handshake confirming the dubious evidence of his eyes. "Three months on short rations and a lack of bathing facilities can make a few changes in a man! And I wouldn't get too close to me either, Devon. I think I have several families of pesty little mites that have made a home on me, and they might be fickle enough to try for better living conditions."

Still stunned at the gross physical deterioration of the man he had admired for the greater part of his adult life, Devon shook his head in disbelief. To the side of him the scurrying of furtive, dark shadows against the wall and the pitapat of small, scratching feet confirmed his suspicions that Steve Austin did indeed share his confinement with life of another species. His flesh crawling at the realization of the conditions under which this good man had been forced to live, he felt a hot rage suffuse his senses.

"How can you joke about this, Steve? Hell, if the committee could see you now, they'd pick up their guns and forget all this damned stupid nonsense about conferrin' with Santa Anna and pin his hide to the nearest wall!"

"That's the last thing I'd want, Devon, and you know it! I want to get out of here, Lord knows, but I haven't been here long enough to make me lose my senses entirely." His expression suddenly intense, Steve shook his head emphatically. "Santa Anna had nothing to do with my arrest. Farías was the one responsible. Santa Anna was not aware . . ."

"Farías! Gómez Farías went into exile almost two months ago! Antonio Santa Anna has assumed control of the country, and you're still in here! So don't tell me that crafty bastard has nothin' to do with your incarceration!"

252

"No, Devon, you're wrong. Antonio is my friend. We spoke in November of last year. I explained the position of the Anglo-American colony in Texas to him, and he's extremely sympathetic to our cause."

"Well, if he's so damned sympathetic, how is it that you're still in here?"

"I've received word from him, Devon. His messenger explained that there's a problem as to where my case should be heard. It seems that there's a dispute between the military and civil tribunals as to which has jurisdiction."

"And in the meantime, you rot in this stinkin' hole! Damn, Steve! Has this place affected your senses? Don't you realize you're bein' held without cause . . . that this charge was prefabricated with some political motive in mind? You're a hostage, Steve! A hostage for our cooperation!"

"No, Devon, you're wrong! I have it from Santa Anna's own messenger that Antonio is looking into my case himself and some movement on my behalf is imminent. Look, I haven't become attached to this fine living! I'm still mighty fond of my comforts . . . as well as I can remember them, that is. But there's a greater issue at stake here."

"What's a greater issue than your life, Steve? Don't you realize that if you stay here much longer, you may suffer permanent damage to your health? Then where will all your stubborn idealism get you?"

"Don't let this dirty beard fool you, Devon. I may have lost a little weight, but I'm just as healthy as I ever was, and more determined than ever to have my say. And I still believe that the only way Texas can go is to keep our allegiance to Mexico. Hell, we signed an agreement, Devon . . . swore an oath! I have to admit that I grew a little impatient myself when I first came to Mexico. I waited three months without anything at all being accomplished, so when I had an interview with Farías, I told him that if some remedy for our problems wasn't quickly applied, the Texans would take matters into their own hands. Then I wrote a letter to the civil government of San Antonio de Bejar telling them that the state here was paralyzed with civil war and they should communicate with all the other corporations in Texas and tell them to agree on the organization of a local government independent of Coahuila even if the government refused its consent.''

"So it's true . . . what Santa Anna said . . .''

"Yes, but I met with Santa Anna after that . . . in November . . . on the question of separation from Coahuila. He told me that he didn't believe the time had yet arrived to erect Texas into an independent state, but he was deeply concerned about the grievances of the colonists. He told me he would urge the state governments to adopt measures of reform that would give the Anglo-Texans just rights in civil and criminal matters. He also said he would show the friendly inclination of his government by abrogating the eleventh article of the law of April 6, 1830. And he did it, Devon. Even though the decree hasn't taken effect yet, Anglo-Americans will no longer be prohibited from settling in Texas! Antonio was true to his word, Devon.''

"You're a dreamer, Steve, do you know that? You always were too damned trustin'. Antonio Santa Anna never did a thing in his life that wouldn't bring him some measure of personal profit or public esteem! The man's a two-faced snake . . .''

"If you feel that way, why in hell did the Commission send you down here to talk with him?''

"Because I know the man, damn it! I know him for what he is, but they know I'll handle him with a smile on my face if it kills me!''

In the brief silence that followed, the sudden burst of laughter from the bearded, scraggly scarecrow and the bellows that came after the laughter were totally unexpected, startling Devon with their intensity. Finally realizing as Steve Austin walked a few steps backwards to sit abruptly on the low stool and wiped the tears from his eyes that the man was not hysterical but had actually found something amusing in his adamant statement, Devon shook his head. "I didn't say anythin' that damned funny, Steve. Maybe you're sicker than you think.''

"No, maybe you didn't, Devon.'' Looking up at him from his seated position, Steve responded with a hint of a smile still on his face, "but the irony of the situation suddenly seemed so ridiculous. I mean, the peacemaker in prison, and the firebrand courting justice from a man he despises, a smile on his face and fire in his eyes. You know, Devon, if you hadn't just told me you're going to handle it, I'd have my doubts right now about my ever getting out of this damned place!"

Staring intently into the abruptly weary expression on Steve Austin's face, Devon shook his head. "You know, you amaze me, Steve. After three months in this pit, I don't think I'd trust anyone or anythin', but there you sit, certain that Santa Anna will come through for you, and that I'll make certain he'll do it."

"Señor Howard, it is time for you to leave now."

The rasp of the key in the lock behind him along with the guard's summons turned both men's heads in the direction of the doorway. Getting immediately to his feet, Steve reached out to grasp Devon's hand, a small smile curving his lips as he said softly, "Yes, I guess you're right, Devon. My mama always did tell me I was an amazin' child." His smile broadening at the responsive smile on Devon's face, he continued quietly, "Go ahead and do what you think best, Devon, but don't alienate Santa Anna. Whether you're right and he's pretending to be on our side because it's politically expedient, or whether he's sincere, he's still our only hope . . . my only hope." His weary smile widening, he continued, "I'll be thinking of you when you face Santa Anna. And remember to keep smiling, friend. Keep smiling . . ."

Grasping Austin's hand firmly in his, Devon shook it warmly. "Don't worry, Steve. I'll stay on good terms with the bastard and get you out of here. At least to some place where you can take a deep breath without wanting to vomit."

"You do that, Devon."

Allowing himself one last look at the inner strength shining from within the thin, bedraggled face, Devon turned on his heel and strode through the doorway. Turning back as the door closed behind him, he frowned as the lock scraped closed once again. Damn that deceitful Mexican bastard,

Santa Anna! Unless he could force some kind of action from the man, he knew with an instinctive certainty that he would continue along in the same manner as he had the past two months . . . investigating Steve's case, perusing all the "details," holding the Texan committee at bay . . . until Steve Austin's incarceration no longer suited his personal purposes. But right now Santa Anna held all the cards . . . all the cards but one. Morgana . . .

Following the uneven pace of the guard as he began his slow climb up the winding corridors and steps to surface level, Devon felt the beginning of a plan forming in his mind. Yes, Morgana . . . if his association with her had proved anything at all, it was that he held a power over her body that she could not deny. While her mind obviously remained true to the purpose of furthering her position with Santa Anna, her body was weak. And he would use her weakness against her. Santa Anna's supreme egotism would not allow him to share Morgana's favors, or even her interest. Yes, he would use Santa Anna's ego against him, and he would get Steve Austin free . . . .

"Yes, you will see that I am right, Morgana. You have been confined in your room far too much lately. If I had realized that the party would have been such a strain on your health, I would have cancelled it this year, or at least would have put it off to a date later in the month."

Seated opposite her in the Escobar carriage, Doña Isabella allowed her eyes to move assessingly over Morgana's sober expression as they jolted along the uneven roads. Realizing her comments had drawn Manuel's attention to Morgana's pale face, as well as Aggie's astute perusal, she momentarily regretted her comments. She had not wanted to put any further pressure on an outing she had hoped would lift Morgana from the confusing mood she had seemed to settle into since the morning after the party. Frowning at her niece's silence, she remembered only too well Morgana's return from her ride the morning after the celebration of Corpus Christi at their home. How grateful she was that Antonio had happened upon her on the wooded trail and had been present to assist when Morgana's weakness had overcome her. She remembered his obvious concern, her own esteem for him growing with the picture of the fond kiss he placed on Morgana's pale cheek the minute before she had been helped by a concerned Aggie to her room. Dear, gracious Antonio! But in the week since the incident, Morgana had remained peculiarly silent and listless, even dispensing with her morning rides, although Grillo had faithfully been delivered to the door each morning since. In her concern, she had hastily organized an outing with an excuse of the feast of San Juan, realizing that Morgana would not refuse to celebrate the religious holiday in the manner customary to her new country. But there was no enthusiasm in the dark eyes that avoided hers, and a peculiar absence of the sparks of gold that usually so significantly personified her bright spirit.

Ah, but even in her somber state, Morgana was so lovely! It was no wonder that she had enchanted the young men who swarmed around her at the fiesta. True, her face was a trifle pale, her perfect features unlit by the brightness of her smile, but her new solemnity revealed yet another side to her beauty. *Sí!* Her hair covered with a fragile mantilla, the delicate white lace outlining the exquisite planes of her cheek; her great eyes large and appealing; her perfect profile etched against the window of the carriage; she looked indeed the perfect madonna. Yes, she had no doubts that before long she would be receiving many requests for permission to court Morgana from the young men of their society. Her personal appeal was great . . . her family impeccable. She would be a marvelous addition to any of the proud families that made up their society . . . especially with Antonio's open acceptance of Morgana . . . his fascination with her youthful exuberance and beauty. But as anxious as Doña Isabella was for her niece's contracting a good marriage, she could not help but anticipate the event with sadness. Morgana had brought her quiet home to life . . . she did not wish to lose her too soon. But a good marriage meant Morgana would be guaranteed to remain in their society, to bear her children in Mexico to a fine Mexican family. She would not only have Morgana, but would have "grandchildren" to love and spoil in her waning years. Ah, yes . . .

Turning her warm gaze to her husband's sober face, Doña Isabella caught and held his glance. A warmth stirred deep within his eyes that she knew from long years of experience glowed for her alone. *Sí,* Manuel, she whispered silently with her gaze, we have been given a gift from God in our Morgana. We must keep her well and happy in our country so she will never leave us.

Turning from Tía Isabella's gaze, Morgana stared silently out the window at the passing landscape as they progressed further into the heavily forested area just outside the city. The sun's sparkling rays moved through the branches above the road, flashing in an ever-changing pattern across her face, its glow welcome. But, peculiarly, the deep heaviness that had settled within her breast remained unwarmed by its heat. Turning back to survey the occupants of the carriage for a short moment, Morgana saw Tía Isabella's and Tío Manuel's glances silently meeting in a look that bespoke the deep devotion that still remained between them despite their many years together. Why could it not be so with all marriages? Perhaps then Antonio would not continue to pursue her so relentlessly, and that terrible morning in the forest would not have happened. And the contempt in Devon's eyes, the derision of his words that still echoed in her mind, would not be haunting her still.

Closing her eyes against the recurring horror of recollection, Morgana recalled that morning in vivid detail, her stomach churning at her ignorance and naivete. How had she believed she could pit herself against a man of Antonio's age and experience? He obviously wanted her . . . he was lonely and in need of womanly comfort in the absence of his wife, and despite her own reluctance to fill that void in his life, she could not help but sympathize with his plight. Had it been that sympathy that had been her undoing? She was uncertain . . . the only conclusion she had reached in the week of self-imposed isolation since that day in the forest was the certainty that she would not allow such a situation to recur. To that end, she had firmly refused to ride each morning when Grillo had been delivered to her door, feigning the same illness that so worried Doña Isabella. So far, she had managed to avoid a private confrontation with Antonio.

But today, on the feast day of San Juan, when the people of Mexico celebrated by bathing in the waters of streams and pools in memory of the original baptism for which the great saint was revered, she would be forced to face Antonio. She knew he had been asked to join their outing. The knot in her stomach that had been ever present since that morning over a week before tightened. But she would settle matters with Antonio today, and then . . . in some way . . . somehow . . . she would see Devon again and explain . . . tell him of her stupidity. And she hoped . . . hoped desperately that he would understand.

Glancing out the window as the carriage drew to a halt, Morgana was startled to see many other carriages in the same area. She cast a surprised glance at Doña Isabella, who answered her unspoken question without hesitation, "Oh, yes, Morgana. Many families come here from the city to celebrate. And it is the perfect Sunday afternoon for such a celebration, is it not? I confess to being quite excited about the prospect of wading in the cool waters of the stream. Of course, many of the youngsters will take the opportunity to submerge themselves and swim in the deeper portions of the stream, but I shall be content to celebrate modestly. Many will throw flowers in the river, and there will be music and possibly dancing, Morgana, along with feasting and pleasant conversation. It will be a thoroughly enjoyable day, you will see."

Her eyes filling unexpectedly at her aunt's obvious effort to raise her spirits, Morgana swallowed hard and responded in a steady voice that she hoped carried at least a spark of enthusiasm, "It sounds lovely, Tía Isabella. I'm quite happy to be able to celebrate with you and Tío Manuel today."

Her eyes shooting in Aggie's direction at the low "humph!" that was meant for her ears alone, Morgana managed to silently convey her disapproval. Aggie was too observant . . . too wise in her ability to read Morgana's feelings. Although she had discussed that morning in the glade with no one, she had no doubt that Aggie knew everything that had happened, for the judgment she had withheld on Antonio had obviously been made to his disfavor, if the manner in which she greeted the famous Mexican was any indication. Aggie's few words with regard to Devon Howard only confirmed that her regard for him did not reach a higher plane. There were truly moments when Morgana began to wonder if Aggie possessed the ability to read her mind, so well did she seem to know her thoughts. Flushing brightly as she descended from the carriage with the aid of Tío Manuel's outstretched hand, she fervently wished that not to be true. She could not bear to think that anyone would know how memories of Devon's arms haunted her through the long day, how well she remembered the touch of his lips against hers and the searing ecstasy she had experienced when their bodies had joined as one. How desperately she wanted to see him again . . . to tell him . . .

Stopping still, the friendly greeting on her lips fading into silence, Morgana watched the approach of a familiar, well-dressed figure, whose black eyes swept her consumingly before moving to Doña Isabella.

"*Doña Isabella, buenos días, y muchas grácias* for your kind invitation to celebrate the feast of San Juan with you here today." Taking her aunt's hand in a courtly, impeccable manner, Antonio Santa Anna raised it lightly to his lips. After a short, warm greeting to Don Manuel, he turned in Morgana's direction, his expressive eyes silently begging her acceptance.

"Morgana, *buenos días* to you, *mi pequeña*. It is a great pleasure to see you again after such a long time. I am sorry to hear that you have been unwell, but a day spent in the sunshine and in good company should be just the medicine you will need. If you will allow me . . ." Taking her hand, his eyes fast on her face to assess her reaction, Santa Anna turned to lead her toward the edge of the stream where a group laughed and chatted informally under a large tree. Her face paling at the reminder of a similar morning in a similar glade, Morgana was startled by the perceptiveness that allowed Santa Anna to remark softly, "Ah, but today we will make new memories, more pleasant for you to bear; and today we will cast aside the mistakes of unfortunate actions and begin again. *Es agradable, querida?*"

Uncertain how completely she could trust the sincerity shining in his dark eyes, Morgana was nonetheless abruptly grateful for Santa Anna's adept handling of an awkward situation. A relieved smile turning up her lips, she answered without commitment, "We shall see, Antonio . . ."

Unable to resist the sharpness of Antonio's wit, Morgana laughed aloud, her intense appreciation of his quip sparking a round of laughter in the group that gathered informally under the large tree. Glancing around at the faces that composed their party, Morgana again reflected at the warmth generated by the auspicious personages assembled.

There were Señor *y* Señora Diaz, dear friends of Tía Isabella and a warm couple who obviously brought along their son, Jorge, for an introduction to Doña Isabella's lovely niece; Señor and Señora Mantalban, distantly related to Tía Isabella and the parents of two lovely daughters, ages four and six, who withstood admirably the chastisements of their parents for their efforts to celebrate the feast day by splashing each other unmercifully; Señora Mantalvo, a new widow, and her lovely daughter, Celeste, who could not disguise her intense admiration for the handsome president of her country; General and Señora Agrado, intimate associates of Tío Manuel and the president and his wife; and, of course, the president himself. In the background, hovering just out of sight and thought were the president's guards and a number of servants who had managed to prepare a tempting table on the ground in the rustic area, and comfortable seating where it would have been otherwise deemed impossible.

In the warm setting and in the safety of numbers, Morgana had begun to relax. The lavish meal of cold meats and chicken, various types of smoked fish, assorted fruits and sweetmeats, and liberal portions of a sweet, local wine had almost succeeded in sweeping from her mind the memory of blue eyes filled with contempt and the cutting sarcasm that pained her still . . . "I do applaud your fortitude, darlin' . . ."

Her face flushed from her consumption of the wine, Morgana rose to her feet. Startled by the unsteadiness of her legs, she made a mental note to be more cautious in the future. Yes, undoubtedly, she needed to take a walk to work off some of the effects of the wine, and, seeing the light in Antonio's eye, she remarked casually, "It seems to me that Linda and Constancia have a good idea in taking advantage of this particular feast day by refreshing themselves. If you will excuse me." Bending down, Morgana whispered softly into Tía Isabella's ear that she intended to find an area of privacy where she would remove her stockings and shoes so that she might wade in the cool waters.

"Sí, Morgana, the area is protected by guards, and you will be quite safe. But do not be too long, querida. We will all miss you."

Grateful for the intuition that allowed Tía Isabella to grant her the privacy she desired, Morgana pulled herself carefully erect, and, stepping cautiously, made her way across the cleared area into the trees. Aware that the dense foliage just a few yards into the wooded area provided an ample shield, Morgana sat on a convenient boulder and took a deep breath. The cool mountain air was refreshing, and, taking a moment to wipe her moist brow with a handkerchief formerly secreted between her breasts, Morgana was startled by the low, drawling voice that sounded from the foliage to her rear.

"Well, good day to you, darlin'. I was wonderin' when you'd give me an opportunity to speak to you today."

Jerking around, Morgana stared wide-eyed at Devon's smiling face.

"Devon!"

Walking forward in the slow, easy manner Morgana remembered so well, he came to stand disturbingly close. His eyes intent on hers, he took the handkerchief from her hand. "Here, let me put that away for you, darlin'."

Her breath catching as Devon carefully tucked the lacy article between her breasts, Morgana watched in stunned silence as a familiar glow warmed in the blue eyes regarding her intently. The hard, sharply chiseled face lowered slowly, the lips she remembered so well coming closer to her own. A low gasp coming from between her lips, Morgana felt a searing heat convulse her body as his mouth touched hers. Not questioning the change in Devon that allowed her the comfort for which she had so longed, Morgana felt an aching sweetness sweep her senses as Devon's arms clasped her roughly close, crushing her against the long length of his body. Her heart pounding loudly in her breast, Morgana felt the first heady penetration of her lips, the glory of Devon's tongue as it searched her mouth hungrily, tasting lovingly the sweetness within; drawing her own into its heady play. Her arms wound tightly around his neck, her fingers tangled in the heavy thickness of his hair, Morgana was uncertain when the searing lips left hers to press moist kisses in a dizzying path down the slender column of her throat, lingering erotically in the hollows at the base of her neck, and moving to the fragrant white swells of her breasts. Almost past reasonable thought, Morgana felt the warm caress of his tongue as it searched the crease between her breasts and the touch of Devon's broad hands as they boldly fondled the fullness beneath through the light material of her gown.

"Devon . . . please . . . someone will come upon us . . ."

"No . . . no darlin', not yet. I watched them as you walked away. They'll wait for your return . . . but you're goin' to be gone a little longer than you thought, aren't you . . ."

His mouth sweeping back to cover hers cut off her reply, allowing Morgana the beauty of a deep, searching kiss as her mouth opened eagerly to his. His mouth was drawing deeply, fully from hers, his hands traveling her back with unrestrained hunger when he pulled his mouth abruptly from hers.

His breath was coming in deep gasps, his chest heaving heavily as he groaned softly against her lips, "Morgana, darlin', come with me now . . . someplace where we can be completely alone . . . where I can make love to you the way I want. I want to feel your flesh against me again . . . I want to kiss . . . to taste all of you . . . I want to slide inside you . . . feel your warmth close around me. Darlin'." Taking her hand, Devon covered the throbbing bulge of his desire, the touch of her hand bringing him to a new level of ecstasy as he whispered hoarsely, "See, darlin' . . . see how much I want you . . ." Her eyes were closed, her lips lightly parted as he worked her hand over the palpitating hardness. "Look at me, Morgana." Devon's sharp command snapped Morgana's eyes into instant contact with his. His breath catching at the passon glowing in their darkness, the golden shafts of desire visible to his eyes, he urged heatedly as he moved her hand caressingly against him, "Feel how ready I am for you darlin'. You want to feel me inside you . . . now. You want to feel me strokin' you . . . moving within you. Remember how it felt . . . to feel me growin' . . . swellin' inside you . . . Tell me, Morgana, tell me that's what you want . . . tell me you want me to make you a part of me again; tell me you want me to . . ."

"No! Morgana wants nothing from you!"

Abruptly Morgana was ripped from the warmth of Devon's body and flung roughly aside. Fighting to retain her balance, Morgana gasped as Santa Anna stepped forward and grasped Devon roughly by the lapels of his coat.

Within seconds, Devon had freed himself, his eyes holding Santa Anna's intently as the flushed Mexican rasped, "You will leave this area immediately, and you will not bother Señorita Pierce again!"

A small smile moving across his lips, Devon replied quietly despite the fact that his chest was heaving with emotion, his fists tightly clenched, "What makes you think I was botherin' Morgana, Antonio? You didn't see her fightin' me, did you? Maybe we should ask her if she wants me to leave."

"Morgana has nothing to say about the matter! You have intruded on a private party. If someone had come upon you, you would have succeeded in ruining Morgana's reputation!"

"What's so different about this and the scene that I came upon in the forest last week, Antonio? Can you tell me that?"

"The difference is that *I* am telling you to go . . . *now!* And I will not tolerate an inquisition from you!"

His eyes a deliberate challenge, Devon pressed softly, "And what gives *you* the right to direct Morgan's affairs? Especially since she doesn't want me to go. You don't want me to go, do you, Morgana?"

"BASTA!"

The fury in Santa Anna's expression sent another jolt of fear down Morgana's spine. Frozen with fright, she had been unable to react to the horror of the moment, but suddenly frightened for Devon's safety in a country where Santa Anna was all powerful, she gasped hoarsely, "Antonio, please, I don't want . . ."

Turning in her direction, Santa Anna commanded, rage contorting his face into a grotesque mask. "*Tonto! Silencio!* Do you not see that this man wishes to use you?" Turning back in Devon's direction, he hissed, "And this I will not allow you to do!"

His jaw tight, his glance intense, Devon responded in a low voice, "And what about you, Antonio? What is it you're wantin' from Morgana?"

Santa Anna's nostrils were flared with rage, his tone low and ominous. "I have told you before, Devon, I will not tolerate your inquisition! You will go . . . *now!* You will leave this area and not bother Morgana again!"

Remaining silent for long moments, Devon held Santa Anna's furious stare. A hard smile slowly moving across his lips, he responded quietly, "All right, Antonio. I'll go now . . . but as for not seein' Morgana again . . . well, I don't know . . ."

"*Bastardo!*" His voice a low hiss, Santa Anna continued menacingly, "You will leave now, before I do something for which I will be sorry in the weeks to come!"

His smile growing, Devon hesitated long moments before raising his hand and touching it to his forehead in a mock salute. "Yes, sir! I guess my presence is no longer wanted."

Shifting his gaze to Morgana, his stomach tightening at the fear reflected on her white face, he said lightly, "Be seein' you, darlin'."

Within moments, Devon's tall, lithe figure had disappeared in the dense foliage. Vastly relieved that the confrontation between Antonio and Devon had not had dire consequences, Morgana watched as Antonio turned to face her. Startled at the rage still reflected in his eyes, Morgana felt a chill of fear move up her spine. Stepping back spontaneously, she was still too slow to avoid the rough hands that reached out to grasp her arms. Shaking her violently, Santa Anna repeated over and over, *"Tonto! Idioto! Tonto!"*

Appearing abruptly to gain control of his emotions, he released her unexpectedly. Staggering backwards as she attempted to retain her balance, Morgana watched as a small grimace of satisfaction moved across Santa Anna's face.

"Now you will compose yourself and we will return to the others! You will tell no one about what has progressed here!"

Santa Anna's autocratic tone causing a spontaneous rise of anger in her despite her fear, Morgana responded sharply, "I will not stand for your calling me names, Antonio, nor submit to your commands. I will not . . ."

"Silencio! Be quiet if you value your safety and your honor! I have done you a great service today, whether, in your stupidity, you realize it or not! When I am so inclined, I will explain the matter to you, but until that time, you will pretend nothing has happened here. Do you understand?"

Realizing she dared not incite his rage any further, Morgana took a deep breath and swallowed hard. "Yes, I understand."

His voice tightly controlled, Santa Anna turned the full force of his burning gaze into her eyes, "And see that you do not forget what I say!"

Her only answer a short, quick nod of her head, Morgana turned abruptly and started back in the direction of the stream, the heavy footsteps following close behind, reverberating in her ears.

His heart still thundering in his chest, Devon spurred his horse forward, forcing him to a dangerous pace on the uneven trail. Rage pumped heatedly through his veins at the memory of Santa Anna's rough grasping of his coat and his obvious attempts to intimidate him. Had it been any man other than Santa Anna . . . did not the fate of a fellow Texan rest on his vacillating moods, Devon knew he would have succumbed to his own spontaneous desire to beat Santa Anna into unconsciousness. The bastard! The simple fact that Santa Anna had reacted exactly as he had planned to his discovery of Morgana and himself . . . that the situation was progressing along exactly according to his plan, left him with little satisfaction. Yes, he knew very well that Santa Anna's guards had seen him enter the grove, and that they would inform Santa Anna immediately that Morgana and he were together. And, as he had known instinctively, it had not been difficult to incite Morgana's emotions. The only thing on which he had not reckoned was the extent of his own emotional involvement in the little scene he had staged for Santa Anna's benefit. Christ! He could feel her in his arms still . . . could still smell the sweet scent of her body. Groaning low in his throat, he recalled the warmth of her hand moving against him.

Making a supreme effort to shake free of the raging memories, Devon forced his mind back to Steve Austin. He had had some limited success in that area in the past week. Only one day after his visit to Steve's cell, Steve had been allowed bathing facilities, a change of clothing, and had been immediately delivered to a military tribunal. Having decided that it had no jurisdiction in his case, the court then referred him to a more commodious prison. Steve's case was next to be submitted to a civil tribunal, but the date had not yet been set. Devon knew instinctively that if he did not force the matter—pressure Santa Anna to follow quickly through with the case—the result would be that Steve would only have changed one limbo for another. And Morgana was that pressure . . .

Santa Anna dared not allow his own intense interest in Morgana to become public knowledge. Calling attention to Devon would do that only too well. His only recourse lay in settling the matter of Steve Austin so that Devon could return to Texas. Today had been the first step in his plan . . . allowing Santa Anna to see how easily he overcame Morgana's token resistance to his lovemaking. The little scene had inflamed Santa Anna far more successfully than he had planned. Annoyed by the touch of anxiety he suffered at the thought, he realized that Santa Anna would doubtless get his revenge on Morgana for the episode once he was safely back in Texas. Well, it would be nothing more than she deserved. As for now, all he had to do was sit back and wait for Santa Anna's next move.

"*Buenos días,* Devon."

Accepting Santa Anna's outstretched hand in greeting, Devon then followed the stern-faced president farther into the palace reception room. He had not expected such immediate action on Santa Anna's part. It had been only yesterday that they had practically come to blows. He had expected Santa Anna to allow some time for a cooling-off period. Evidently he had been wrong. Santa Anna's haste to settle matters was only further evidence of his deep involvement with Morgana. His tension deepening at the thought, Devon began in as casual a tone as he could manage.

"I admit to being a bit surprised by your summons this mornin', Antonio. I thought, after yesterday, I would be the last person you would want to see so soon."

"On the contrary, Devon. I have considered the matter carefully and come to a conclusion. You see, I am not fooled by your machinations. I know you attempt to use Morgana against me. Although I would not admit this to any other, I know you are aware of my deep feeling for Morgana, and my obvious plans for her future. She is, at present, my Achilles' heel, and since you were wise enough to realize that, I will not bother to deny my feelings. I also admit that Morgana feels some tie to you . . . something that allows her to behave in a manner that is far from wise for a young woman with her potential. But, my friend, she is also deeply attracted to me. Had you not come upon us in the glade that morning, the situation would not be as it stands this morning. And I *will* have her, Devon. Make no mistake about that!''

''And your dear friends, Don Manuel and Doña Isabella . . . what do they have to say about your plans?''

''They will never know. I have been discreet before, and for Morgana I am willing to go to even greater lengths to maintain propriety. So, you see, Devon, there remains only the matter between yourself and me to be resolved.''

''And how do you intend to resolve it, Antonio?'' His eyes narrowing with caution, Devon watched Santa Anna's unrevealing expression.

''As you doubtless planned, I will offer you what you want. Steve Austin's freedom.''

His heart beginning a rapid acceleration, Devon was about to respond when Santa Anna continued slowly, ''. . . but not immediately, Devon. I am not fool enough to set Colonel Austin free before you are long gone from the capital. As a matter of fact, that is one of my conditions.'' His eyes abruptly intense, Santa Anna continued in a low tone, ''You will leave the capital, Devon, tomorrow. You need not take time to make your goodbyes. I will inform Don Manuel and Doña Isabella that your mission was completed and that your need for haste to inform your committee was great.''

''And in return?''

''In return I will show you the papers on which Colonel Austin's trial date with the supreme court is set. I also give you my word that I will follow through on his case as expeditiously as possible.''

''Such promises have been made before with little results, Antonio.''

''. . . but not by me!'' His expression reflecting his flaring indignation at Devon's comment, Santa Anna hesitated a moment longer before continuing. ''In any case, you have no recourse. If you remain in the city beyond tomorrow night, I will have you arrested and thrown into the same prison as Colonel Austin. Your committee may then decide the appropriate means by which to have you *both* freed!''

269

Startled by Santa Anna's vehemence, Devon was silent for long moments before he shook his head consideringly. "No, you would not risk the further alienation of the Anglo-American colony, Antonio."

"If you know me at all, Devon, you know I will risk anything I must to achieve my ultimate ends!"

Abruptly realizing that in his last statement Santa Anna had been utterly and completely truthful, Devon hesitated only a moment more before responding. Hardening himself against his distaste for his next statement, he finally offered in a low tone, "All right. Show me the papers on Colonel Austin's case."

Immediately turning to the table at his side, Santa Anna took up a sheaf of papers and placed them into Devon's hands. Reading slowly, in an effort to allow his racing mind time to come up with an alternative, Devon finally turned in Santa Anna's direction.

"All right, Antonio. I'll be out of the city by tomorrow night. You may have me escorted or followed . . . whatever you wish."

"I will require your signature on this letter, acknowledging the resolution of our agreement regarding Colonel Austin, but you may rest assured that I will make certain your departure is a fact before I take any action on Colonel Austin's part. But I know you will not be fool enough to attempt anything irresponsible. Also, I do not feel you have any true feelings for Morgana. A man who truly cares for a woman would not attempt to use her as you have. Morgana is well rid of you."

A surge of anger flushing his face, Devon signed the document in a careless script before retorting heatedly, "And she is better off with you?"

A slow smile spread across Santa Anna's even Latin features. "Oh, yes, far better off. I will treat my beautiful American flower well, and when the time comes that I tire of her, I will provide her with a well-established husband who will keep my confidence."

"Like Consuelo de Artega?"

"Consuelo has been adequately paid for her favors, has

she not? In any case, I do not believe I will tire of Morgana easily. I expect we will do long and well together.''

Allowing Santa Anna only one more contempt-filled glance, Devon turned abruptly toward the door. His stride rapid, he walked through the doorway, the one thought on his mind to exit the palace before he succumbed to the urge to beat Santa Anna's leering face to a bloody pulp. The low laughter that followed him down the empty corridor rang loudly in his ears long after he was out of range of the sound.

CHAPTER SEVEN

The August day dawned clear and warm, with bright promise for the hours ahead. But Morgana had not slept well. She had not slept well for over a month, and if she were to be truthful, she would be able to trace her sleeplessness directly back to the day she had been notified that Devon Howard had returned to Texas. Devon's departure had been abrupt, without a word. It was only after a week of frustrated confusion on her part as to the reason for the unexpected departure that Antonio had taken pity on her. Managing to find a way for them to speak privately, Antonio had reluctantly revealed the proposition Devon had put to him. His face reflecting his embarrassment for her, Antonio had related the arrogance with which Devon had presented his demands. Hinting broadly how well he controlled Morgana's emotions, he had insisted Colonel Austin's case be given propriety over the many others that filled the court calendar, and that the colonel be given preferential treatment until he was released. He had stated boldly that refusal of his proposal would mean embarrassment to General Escobar and personal discomfort to Antonio. To her own self-disgust, she had been so taken in by Devon that she had actually doubted Antonio's words until she had seen the agreement Devon had signed stating the terms of the bargain. There had been no doubt of the paper's authenticity, and there was no longer any doubt in Morgana's mind that she had been a fool.

Still feeling the heat of her intense humiliation, Morgana jumped abruptly from her bed and walked to the washstand. Antonio was right. Devon had used her well. Adding additional fuel to her rage was the realization that through Devon she had proved herself a liability to her uncle in the first situation with which she had been presented. It had been only through Antonio's generosity that Tío Manuel had been spared embarrassment. She would never forgive herself or Devon Howard for that betrayal.

Pouring water impatiently into her washbowl, Morgana lowered her head to splash her face with the cool liquid. Oh, if she could only as easily rinse away the thoughts of Devon Howard that still haunted her. The only time she managed to escape her railing thoughts was during her morning rides. She was supremely grateful that she had allowed Antonio to convince her to resume the practice. True to his word, he had allowed her to retain her solitude during those hours, and she truly appreciated his restraint. But again, if she were to be completely truthful, she would have to admit to a certain uneasiness. To her mind, Antonio's feelings for her were becoming a bit too transparent for comfort.

Moving unconsciously to her wardrobe in a ritual she had stringently maintained for the last month, Morgana pulled out her riding clothes. Quickly stripping away her night rail and donning her chemise, she slipped into the light shirtwaist and skirt and pulled on her boots. Turning to the mirror, she brushed her hair vigorously, almost painfully, until it was entirely free of the snarls resulting from her restless night. Securing her hair carelessly behind her ears with several combs, Morgana stared motionlessly for long moments into the glass. The face reflected back at her was small and solemn, thinner than it had been upon her arrival in the country. There were light circles under her great, sober eyes and a gravity to her expression that conveyed only too well the unhappiness deep inside to which she did not wish to admit.

Damn! Abruptly angry with her own morose thoughts,

Morgana turned toward the doorway. She would not allow Devon Howard to get the best of her! She didn't need him! She didn't need anyone! Hadn't she overcome the countless obstacles of her father's indebtedness and determined to make a new life for herself here in Mexico? And she'd be damned before she'd let a scheming Texan take all she had accomplished away from her! He had already taken enough. . . .

With a rapid step, Morgana was at the door. Pulling it open, she stepped into the hallway, abruptly colliding with the tall, sturdy form that stood at the door.

"Aggie!" Gasping with surprise, she was still unable to suppress a smile at the woman's startled expression. "What on earth are you doing standing here so silently? You gave me a terrible fright!"

"I was listening to hear if you had awakened. Señor Santa Anna's men have been waiting for at least an hour."

Nodding her head in silent acknowledgment, Morgana walked quickly down the staircase, her eyes on the entrance to the courtyard. Smiling as she neared the glistening black mare, she cooed words of greeting as she raised her hand to smooth the soft black nose.

"Ah, Grillo, you have been waiting for me this morning. But we'll soon be on our way."

Turning to the two guards, she smiled apologetically, "*Lo siento,* Enrique . . . Roberto. I'm afraid I slept poorly and missed my usual hour of rising."

"*Es nada, señorita.*" Cupping his hands, Enrique offered her a step up onto her saddle, obviously deciding enough had been said. Concurring with his opinion, Morgana boosted herself onto Grillo's back. Waiting only a moment until her guards were also seated, she turned onto the street, her spirits already lightening with the prospect of the hour ahead.

Trotting gracefully on the trail she had traveled many times, Grillo shook her head, her ears pricking up at a sound she ascertained in the foliage to their right. Frowning at her horse's obvious nervousness, Morgana glanced into the heavy underbrush. She saw nothing, and deciding she would have to make certain not to keep the high-spirited mare waiting again, she spurred Grillo forward. Yes, the ride was working its usual magic. With each yard of ground that slipped under Grillo's hooves, Morgana felt the cares that had so suppressed her spirits slipping farther away. The damp forest air was invigorating, cool . . . the feel of the powerful animal beneath her so responsive to her commands, giving her a sense of freedom she knew in her heart she did not truly possess. But she had determined that she would allow the obvious danger of Santa Anna's affection to have little effect on her spirits. Other than putting the problem on Tía Isabella's doorstep, she had little recourse but to allow the matter to run its course. Only, she worried . . . that there would be talk that would embarrass Tía Isabella and Tío Manuel. Already at some of the functions she had attended, Santa Anna's preference for her company, his obvious devotion, although it was never given without the most extreme courtesy, was beginning to cause a few whispers behind fluttering fans. Increasing her discomfort was the fact that Tía Isabella continued to encourage her to express her preference for one of the flock of young men who gathered around her when Santa Anna chose to vacate his position at her side. Yes, it was generally accepted that she was Santa Anna's favorite, but so far there was no outspoken adverse connotation connected with the designation. But, in the end, she had no recourse but to handle things a day at a time, and she was certain that . . .

Startled as a large brown stallion rode out of the underbrush to her right, Grillo reared suddenly, her eyes frightened and wild as Morgana fought to keep her tenuous seat.

"Grillo! Grillo, *tranquilate! Sí . . . Sí, es mejor, nina . . .*"

Totally absorbed in her strenuous efforts to calm the frightened animal, Morgana could not spare a glance for the rider who sat stiffly a few feet away, his great horse unmoving. Finally having gotten Grillo under control and wondering absent-mindedly why her guards had not rushed forward to aid her in her distress, Morgana lifted her gaze to the mounted figure before her.

"*Tonto!* Anyone less than a fool would have more sense than to ride out in front . . ." Morgana's railing words trailed to a stop as her gaze touched on the figure before her. Her skin beginning to crawl, Morgana felt a peculiar breathlessness assail her. Her hand rose to the small scar on her throat as her eyes became fixed on the masked face of the mounted man who stood in her path.

"Who . . . who are you? What do you want from me? I have no money . . ." Turning abruptly to look behind her, she saw her two guards were surrounded by a group of mounted masked men who had moved noiselessly out of the underbrush. Her eyes jerking back to the man blocking her path, Morgana suddenly regained her voice. "I demand you stand out of my way, señor. You will find yourself in dire circumstances if . . ."

"*Basta!* You have said enough!" The cracking command issued in Spanish halted Morgana's words in midsentence. There was something about the man, a certain terrifying familiarity that seemed to steal her breath . . . encouraging the echoes of the silent screams that raged inside her brain. Despite the size of the horse he rode, the man appeared to be of rather small stature, thin and wiry. His trousers and shirt were cut in the Spanish style so common to the city, his boots well made but badly worn. A black mask made from a bandana was tied over his face, covering all of his forehead and face as far as his mouth. Small holes were crudely cut to allow him ample visibility and an area through which to breathe, but the lower portion of his face, exposed to her eyes, showed a skin of dark color, similar to that of the *mestizos* of the area.

Attempting to control the wild quaking that had beset her limbs, Morgana began haltingly, "What . . . what is it you want from me? I carry nothing of value . . . nothing but the horse I ride is valuable enough to take . . ." When there was no response, Morgana demanded again, her voice quickly escalating to a pitch of hysteria. "What is it you want? Tell me! I dem . . ."

"Señorita . . . *tranquilate!* It will do you little good to lose your composure." The heavy lips displayed below the mask parted to reveal uneven, yellowed teeth. Fighting to overcome the weakness assailing her, Morgana heard him continue, "You do not need to carry anything of value, Señorita Pierce, for you, yourself are of ultimate value . . . valuable to General Escobar . . . valuable to our Presidente Santa Anna himself. Is that not right, señorita?"

Swallowing hard against the thickness in her throat, Morgana clutched the saddle tightly, her strength quickly abating as she attempted to respond. "You . . . what do you intend to do?"

"I will allow your guards to return to our *presidente*. They will carry a note telling his excellency that you will be staying with us for some time . . . until he is willing to give us enough money to send you back to him. But in the meantime, señorita . . ."

In a lightning-quick movement, the masked man spurred his horse forward. A short, well-muscled arm reached out and jerked her swiftly from her saddle, depositing her roughly on his horse in front of him. The grip of the strong, stubby fingers on her arms sent a jolt of horror through her veins. Aided by the strength of pure terror, Morgana fought desperately, squirming and twisting on the saddle, pulling and scratching at the hands that restrained her so securely.

"*Basta!* Enough!"

In a flashing movement, Morgana's arms were pinned to her sides by the arm that slid with breathtaking strength around her waist. She felt the cold sharpness of a blade against her throat. Silent screams echoed over and over inside her brain as Morgana strained backwards to avoid the sharp edge that glinted beneath her chin. In a moment of terrifying recognition, Morgana strained to avoid the blade that had cut her once before, a deep gasp escaping her lips as the voice whispered into her ear with great satisfaction, "*Sí*, Señorita Pierce . . . we meet again!"

The world was rocking crazily beneath her, back and forth, rolling her from side to side like a carelessly stored piece of cargo. She had no strength in her limbs . . . she was unable to move . . . it was dark and she was frightened, but

277

she was unable to scream . . . to utter a sound. What was wrong . . . where was she? Closing her eyes in an attempt to gain control of her confused thoughts, Morgana fought to move her hands. They were numb. She could not move them because her wrists were tied behind her, as were her ankles. She could not speak because a gag was tied securely around her mouth. There was a blindfold around her eyes! Moving her fingers weakly against the rolling floor beneath her, she felt the roughness of wood. She was in some sort of wagon . . . a wagon that moved slowly, almost leisurely.

Where was she? The last thing she remembered was the flash of the glinting blade against her throat. . . . Morgana could feel the heat of tears beneath her lids . . . tears she could not shed because of the blindfold tied so securely around her eyes. She longed to cry out . . . to scream for someone to hear her . . . to rescue her from the madman who had attacked her once before. But he had not cut her this time. She could not raise her hand to her throat, but the stinging, well remembered pain of the blade was absent. He had not cut her . . . he had not cut her.

Memory returned abruptly, bringing with it a terror even deeper than that she had suffered upon awakening. The bandits . . . they were going to hold her for ransom! Probably even now Antonio was reading the note sent with Enrique. Perhaps they were looking for her now. Antonio would lend his soldiers to the search. He would not abandon her to the hands of these bandits!

An abrupt change in the pattern of the wagon's movement snapped Morgana's attention from her rioting thoughts as the wagon drew slowly to a halt. Supreme, soul-shaking terror filled her being. They had arrived at their destination . . . the place she was to be held captive until the ransom was paid. But in truth, would they ever set her free? Especially now that she had identified the man as the same one who had robbed the Escobar household only a few short months before? Was this indeed the place she was to be held—or was it here that they would . . .

Listening intently in an attempt to perceive her location, Morgana heard a sound strangely like a cracking sail . . .

the movement of sheet of canvas over her head. She could feel the warmth of the sun begin to warm her skin. A refreshing breeze blew across her face, moving the stuffiness that enveloped her. The sound of boots scraping against wood sounded close by. The floor beneath her shook with a heavy step. Someone was walking toward her on the wagon.

Her heart pounding so heavily that she was almost unable to breathe, Morgana felt fingers working at the knot of her blindfold. Within moments the rough cloth was removed from her eyes. The brightness of the afternoon flashed into her eyes, temporarily blinding her with its glare. Blinking against the sudden illumination, Morgana fought to focus on the figure that remained crouched beside her. Her vision cleared, her eyes widened with disbelief as she came to full recognition. A wild fury racing through her veins, she fought to shriek her hatred of the man who stared unsmilingly into her face. His name was a curse that remained unuttered on her lips.

The supreme, deadly silence was finally broken by a low, familiar voice.

"Yes, Morgana . . . it's Devon."

Struggling wildly against her bonds, Morgana knew only a fierce desire to be free . . . to scratch the placid composure from the hard, unrelenting face that stared into hers.

A mirthless smile on his lips, Devon caught her face in his hands, his fingers digging into the soft skin of her cheeks as he forced her face back to his. Holding her prisoner in his gaze, he stated coldly, "Don't waste your strength, Morgana. Your bonds are secure. I made sure of that myself before I paid Valesquez and his men."

His bold admission that he had indeed been the one behind her abduction sent a fresh wave of fury washing over Morgana. Trembling with rage, she fought to be free of the hands that gripped her face securely.

"Don't be a damned fool, Morgana!" Beginning to show the first sign of impatience, Devon stated tightly, "Just be quiet and listen to what I have to say. I won't untie you until I'm done, so behave yourself and your discomfort will be over sooner. Do you understand?"

279

His pale eyes held hers intently until she stiffly nodded her head. "That's right, darlin'. I don't intend to waste much more time here. By now the ransom note has been delivered to Santa Anna. Poor Antonio! He's no doubt upset! You were gettin' on so well together, weren't you? So well, in fact, that word of the scandal moved more quickly to Saltillo than I did! 'The American girl who has bewitched el presidente . . . has Santa Anna under her spell. The cold, unfeeling woman who breaks the noble Doña Ines's heart! Typical of her countrymen . . . amoral, with no respect for the sacraments of the church . . . adulteress . . . !' "

A sneering contempt twisting his features, Devon continued harshly, "It didn't take you long to make your move once I was removed from the scene, did it? It made little difference to you that the prejudice you stirred against Americans could hinder Colonel Austin's suit . . . that he could suffer drastically for your indiscretions! You didn't really think I'd allow you to ruin Steve's chances of bein' set free . . . to cast the shadow of your wantonness over all the good Anglo-Americans in Texas! No, darlin'. With you removed from the scene, Santa Anna will settle back into his usual routine. When he finds a new lover, he'll be more discreet. I never thought the man to be such a damned fool . . . to risk his image for the sake of a woman." His glance as it flicked over her in the few moments before he abruptly released her face revealed his scorn only too clearly.

"This is the way things are going to be now, Morgana. As far as Santa Anna knows, you've been abducted by bandits for ransom. He doubtless has his soldiers scouring the hills at this very minute, racing to the south where bandits are known to inhabit the hill country. We, in the meantime, have been movin' north slowly, with caution. Within a few days a new ransom note will be delivered, with more specific instructions. If Valesquez is lucky, he'll collect twice for his work today. But poor Antonio will not get you back, no matter how quickly he pays, for you will have disappeared! You'll have returned to Texas with me, and there you'll stay until Colonel Austin is freed. When he's safely at home, you may return to Mexico . . . do whatever you wish. I really

280

don't care much what you do once Steve is safe.

"And just a little warnin' to you, Morgana. Should you decide to return to Mexico, you might consider telling Antonio and General Escobar that you finally managed to escape the bandits who held you hostage. Your aunt is a lovely woman, but your uncle is extremely old-fashioned. He would doubtless come after me and force a confrontation to vindicate your honor, and you may rest assured that I'll defend myself, Morgana, no matter the cost to your uncle."

His gaze leaving hers for the first time, Devon reached for the ropes that bound her feet. His fingers worked at the knot slowly, adding to Morgana's soaring frustrations. Her eyes dropping closed with momentary relief as her ankles were freed, Morgana waited impatiently as Devon worked at the bonds at her wrists. No sooner had her wrists been freed than Morgana raised her hands stiffly and jerked the gag from her mouth. Her lips were numb, her throat parched. Unable to speak for a few, short moments, Morgana swallowed hard. Her first words were a rasping whisper.

"Bastard!"

"Watch what you say, Morgana!"

The tightening of Devon's jaw had little effect on Morgana as she continued heatedly, "Is this how you repay my aunt's kindness to you? Antonio was right! You used me . . . us . . . all along, hoping to gain favor for your precious Colonel Austin! As far as I'm concerned, he's a traitor, and I'm glad he's in jail where he belongs! I couldn't care less about what happens to him, or you, for that matter!"

"True to yourself right to the end, aren't you, Morgana? Selfish, self-centered, carin' only for yourself . . ."

"Oh, but I do care about some people, Devon! I care about Tía Isabella and Tío Manuel. Do you realize what you're putting them through right now? And Aggie . . ." A new tightness coming into her throat at the thought of the agony they were suffering, not knowing whether she was alive or dead, Morgana swallowed tightly in an effort to retain her control.

"It's too bad they have to suffer, Morgana, but you can lay the blame on your own conscience, not mine!"

"Bastard!"

"I told you to take care what you say! I won't stand for your abuse. You've only gotten what you've earned."

Catching the hand Morgana swung toward his face, Devon twisted it behind her back, his breath hot against her face as he assessed the searing hatred in Morgana's expression.

"Don't try that again, Morgana. I told you I won't stand for your abuse, either verbal or physical. Make no mistake about this, I mean what I'm about to say to you now. If you behave yourself, you'll most likely be free within a few months. But if you have any thoughts of escapin' me . . . or doin' anything that might jeopardize either Colonel Austin or Texas's future, remember, I'm thoroughly committed to my plan." With slow deliberation, he continued slowly, ". . . and I'll see you dead before I'll allow you to forfeit either of them for the sake of your selfish ambitions."

The grimness with which his last statement was uttered started a cold shiver of fear up Morgana's spine, despite the heat of the day. Realization of the true magnitude of her situation touched her for the first time, stimulating a surge of weakness that caused her to drop her eyes closed for brief moments as Devon's final words sounded in her ears.

"So set your mind to it, Morgana. You'll be with me until you no longer serve my purpose. If your lover, Antonio, is true to his word and sets Colonel Austin free, you'll be free. You see, it all depends on him, darlin'."

Releasing her arm abruptly, Devon moved back. Turning, he reached for a small bundle of clothes in the front of the wagon and threw them in her lap. "Now put these clothes on. You're too conspicuous in the outfit you're wearin'. In this Mexican blouse and skirt, with a *rebozo* and a hat on your head, you'll look like any other Mexican woman accompanyin' her man back home. No one will give you a second look."

Raising her eyes slowly to his, Morgana responded softly, her voice hushed, "Do you really expect you'll not be found out . . . be punished for what you're doing?"

"I wouldn't worry about me, Morgana." Raising his

hand, Devon ran a finger lightly across the small scar on her throat, his eyes blue ice. "Worry for yourself. If necessary, I can kill very silently."

Her face blanching, Morgana turned away, jerking herself from his touch. Getting slowly to his feet, Devon walked to the end of the wagon and stepped down. Watching until he turned toward the horses, Morgana closed her eyes for a brief moment. With slow, badly shaking hands, she began to undress.

The wagon had been abandoned in the coolness of the mountains far behind them in favor of the horses on which they rode. The merciless heat of the brilliant sun overhead had long since dulled Morgana's senses. Her mind no longer raced with anger and frustration. Indeed, she seemed no longer capable of coherent thought as her mind settled into the hypnotic rhythm of the interminable journey. How many days had they been traveling? At this moment in time, she could not really recall. She was conscious only of the fire of the incessantly burning rays of Mexican sun consuming her fair skin; the groaning protest of a body forced to endure endless hours on horseback with little or no respite; the growing stiffness of muscles traumatized to the point of pain . . . muscles screaming for relief when none was forthcoming.

She had long since ceased her silent railings against the steady, jolting pace of the horse beneath her. She had, in fact, found some consolation in the mesmerizing quality of the unchanging tread that continued into early afternoon of a day that had begun for them in the dark hours before sunrise. Shining beads of perspiration covered her body, trickling down the hollow between her breasts and along the sagging curve of her spine. She felt again the flick of a stray wisp of gleaming chestnut hair that had escaped the hastily fashioned knot at the nape of her neck, the second before it adhered to the damp skin of her cheek. It was so hot . . . so hot . . . too hot to wear the sombrero that shielded her face from the sun, and certainly too hot for the *rebozo* that guarded her white shoulders and arms from the intense searing rays holding her

283

prisoner.

Abruptly unable to bear even its light weight a moment longer, she jerked the large straw hat from her head. She reveled in the freedom she experienced as a light, hot breeze moved against her perspiring face, touching and ruffling the stray wisps adhering to her temples into tight, gleaming tendrils that bounced thankfully in silent gratitude. Shrugging off the coarse *rebozo,* she gave a small sigh of contentment, the lifting of its weight from her shoulders allowing her the strength to hold herself erect a few moments longer on the grueling, endless journey.

"Put your hat back on your head!" The deep male voice, low with warning, jolted her from her silent lethargy. She had almost forgotten Devon's presence at her side. The sharp interjection of his command raised familiar hackles on her spine as he repeated, obviously irritated by her lack of instant compliance with his order, "Put your hat back on, Morgana! And the *rebozo,* too! NOW! I won't have that tender skin burned to a crisp and holdin' me up. You've slowed me down enough already, and I'll be damned if I'll . . ."

The low, arrogant commands succeeded in jerking Morgana from the almost trancelike state into which she had fallen during the last draining hours on horseback, allowing her to snap back with a spontaneous anger of which, a few moments before, she would not have believed herself capable.

"And wouldn't that be unfortunate!" Pausing to direct a heated glance into his blue eyes that held her fast in their glance, she continued pointedly, "It wasn't my idea to be part of this endless journey. You may believe me when I say I have no desire whatever to see your precious Texas . . . and even less interest, if that's possible, in what may happen to your Colonel Austin!"

"Yes . . . true to yourself right to the end." The small sneer that twisted his lips in a familiar grimace tightened the knot in Morgana's stomach. "You couldn't care less what effect your actions could have on someone deservin' of more consideration than yourself."

"You're the only one who says Colonel Austin is so 'deserving of consideration.' My uncle and Antonio are agreed that he's a traitor!''

"That's not what Antonio told me the last time I spoke with him. He said he realized Steve was an honorable man.''

"I have only *your* word for that, and you know how highly I value *your* word! And I'm sick of hearing about the Texan cause. Texas is a part of Mexico, you know . . . in case that fact has slipped your mind! When your Steve Austin was granted permission to establish your colony, he swore an oath . . . you *all* swore an oath . . . to live under Mexican rule, to respect Mexico's rules and the Catholic faith.''

"And we lived up to our oath! But it's our privilege as free men to protest when our liberty is being threatened.''

"Your liberty . . .'' Morgana's sneer showed her feelings only too clearly.

"Yes, our liberty.'' Devon's low growl snapped Morgana into silence as he continued silently, "No free man could live with pride when his state was divided, with only one section, the *Mexican* section, having any influence on the laws . . . where the judicial system was all but nonexistent for any except the wealthy . . . where people of his own kind were no longer allowed to enter the area to live . . . where he was considered second in all respects to his Mexican counterparts!''

"Tío Manuel said all the Anglo-Texans were treated fairly . . . that there is no basis in fact for your claims!''

"Your uncle is a prejudiced fool, blinded by Santa Anna's great words of promise for his country. He will not allow himself to think freely, but follows Santa Anna, refusin' to believe the signs of his corruption that are everywhere!''

"My uncle and Antonio are honorable men! They're dedicated to the country to which they owe their allegiance! You couldn't hope to understand them!''

"You're a fool!''

"And *you* are a supreme egotist who has set himself up as judge, jury, and *per*secutor!'' Her voice picking up new venom, she hissed meaningfully, "And you're painfully ill equipped to handle any of those positions but the last!''

Pale, fathomless eyes moved over her face in silence, causing the pounding of her heart to escalate to a fearsome intensity while Morgana maintained her frigid glance.

"Well, since we're bein' painfully honest, darlin'," the low, purring drawl was menacing, holding her attention more effectively than the power of a shout, "I don't care much what you think . . . or say, or do, for that matter! The only exception to that bein' when you do somethin' so damned reckless that you endanger the welfare of others!" Pausing as he raked her insolent expression with his eyes, he demanded, "Now put on that hat and *rebozo,* damn it, or I'll put them on for you!"

Jumping at the unexpectedness of his abrupt demand, Morgana gritted her teeth tightly, her face flaming at the reaction he had so efficiently obtained from her shattered nerves. Her fingers tightening crushingly on the wide brim, she lifted the hat in one quick movement and jammed it tightly onto her head. Turning, she raised the *rebozo* that had slipped to the saddle behind her and adjusted it across her shoulders, which were almost bared by the simple Mexican *blusa* she wore. Allowing him a last, deadly glance, she turned her burning, sienna-colored eyes to the trail ahead, effectively dismissing him from her mind.

Her anger faded quickly under the broiling heat of the sun as the afternoon progressed. Strangely, the steady, draining ache in her body began to fade into a numbness that mercifully alleviated her silent torture. She was aware that Devon still sat loosely in the saddle, his glance moving systematically from side to side with an easy alertness she found incredible after their long hours on the trail. But she no longer cared. She could no longer feel the reins in her hands, the gnawing ache of her empty stomach, the screaming stiffness in her legs and back that had caused her almost unbearable pain. She no longer felt the horse beneath her, plodding his way over the uneven trail. She no longer felt anything . . . anything at all. . . .

Slowly, yielding without protest, she slipped into the beckoning darkness that so generously opened to accept her.

* * *

A searing pain in her ribs brought her abruptly back to the light. The discomfort of a strong arm encircling her waist jolted her roughly. A low moan escaped her lips as she attempted to evade the binding arm that crushed her so carelessly.

"Morgana! Damn you, don't fight me! You were fallin' from your horse!"

Startled to find herself seated across Devon's saddle, Morgana accepted the incredible truth murmured angrily against her ear. But, curiously, she could not respond . . . could not make her body react to the commands her mind issued so feebly. Her body limp and unresponsive, she felt herself being adjusted to rest against Devon's chest. Her sombrero no longer a problem, she allowed her head to fall back against the muscled strength that supported her, incapable of vocal protest against the softly muttered accusation.

"Damned stupid little fool . . . too proud to say you needed to stop!"

Her whirling brain would not allow the response that echoed in her mind. "Would it have made a difference?" A flash of anger caused her to struggle momentarily against the arms that gripped her fiercely tight.

"Damned little fool." Was she imagining it, or did the voice carry a softer note in its tone? "Stop fightin' me, Morgana. Just lean back . . . that's it. We'll be at a place where we can rest in a few minutes. Lean back . . . that's it."

The low, caressing drawl was comforting . . . as soothing to her tired mind as the lean strength that supported her. Yielding to the new security, Morgana allowed herself to relax, to slowly submit to the darkness that gradually welcomed her back.

A refreshing coolness moved against her face, dulling the heat that seemed to numb her brain. Her eyelids were heavy, their weight unsupportable, but she struggled to raise them. Her mind was still fuzzy and disoriented as a moistness moved against her lips. Accepting greedily the small trickle of cool water that filled her mouth, she swallowed deeply, her

287

hand rising shakily to guide the flow of precious fluid that trickled unsteadily out of the corner of her lips.

But even that small effort was taxing to her meager strength, and, unable to support her own weight any longer, she collapsed heavily against the arm that supported her. Once again the coolness touched her forehead, moved gently over her closed eyes and cheeks. Gradually awareness returned. She was no longer mounted . . . she was reclining in an area where the sun could not touch her abused flesh. Opening her eyes, she saw that the man beside her had turned to refresh a cloth from water held in his inverted hat. Unconsciously following his movements, she met his glance steadily when it returned to her face.

His heavy brown brows were drawn together in a frown, the light eyes beneath them inscrutable. The strong features were intensely serious. Allowing his eyes to move slowly over her face, he maintained his silence for long moments, finally speaking in a tone that startled her with its gentleness.

"You should have told me you were exhausted, Morgana. I didn't intend to drive you to the point of collapse. It's just . . . just . . ." Stammering uncharacteristically, he took a deep breath and continued in a stronger voice, "It's just that I'm accustomed to long hours on the trail, and I was angry past the point of caution. I apologize for being so unconscious of your difficulty."

Having made his apology with noticeable difficulty, Devon maintained silence again as he continued his gentle ministrations. Her strength returning rapidly, Morgana stayed the hand that moved to run the cool cloth against the slender column of her throat. Amazed at the weakness of her own voice, she managed a weary croak. "I . . . I can do that. You . . . you don't have to trouble yourself about me anymore."

Conscious of the abrupt darkening of his expression, Morgana shakily took the cloth from the broad, calloused hand and attempted to raise herself to a sitting position. Instantly strong arms were around her, assisting her surprisingly feeble effort until she rested with her back against the trunk of the tree under which she had lain. Glancing around, she saw

288

they were in a small wooden grove beside a narrow creek. Shielded from the devastating heat of late afternoon, Morgana felt her mind rapidly clearing. Looking to the man who still crouched beside her, she managed hoarsely, "Have we stopped for the day?"

The voice that responded carried a new gruffness that she was unable to fathom. "Well, I don't think you're in condition to travel any farther, do you?"

Rising to his baiting tone despite her weakness, Morgana struggled to get to her feet. "I'll be able to travel in a few minutes! You needn't lose any more time because of me. As far as I'm concerned, the sooner we get to Texas and I'm away from you, the better!"

"Don't act like a fool, Morgana!" Placing his hands on her shoulders, Devon pressed her back to rest against the tree trunk, holding her there as he instructed tightly, "You'll stay just where you are until I tell you to move! You're exhausted, and you'll end up fallin' again if you try to get up now. We'll camp here for the night. After some rest and a good meal, you'll be all right. But I'm tellin' you now," his hands tightening painfully on her shoulders, he continued in a fierce tone, "I want you to tell me if you feel weak on the trail again, because the next time you collapse, you'll have *me* to reckon with when you come to!" He held her eyes steadily with his. "Do I make myself understood?"

"You make yourself very clear!"

Taking only a moment longer to gauge the worth of her response, Devon abruptly released her shoulders and stood up. Turning swiftly on his heel, he moved toward the horses, and within moments he was involved in preparing their first cooked meal in three days.

"You *will* eat, Morgana!"

"I told you, I'm not hungry!"

Seated only a few feet apart near a small fire he had built to cook the bird that still roasted over it, Devon glared heatedly into Morgana's uncompromising expression.

His low drawl intensifying as he obviously strove to control his patience, Devon said tightly, "All right, you don't have to eat right now, but I expect to see you eat a fair share before you go to sleep tonight."

With unexpected abruptness, Morgana's stubbornness flared into anger. "Whether you realize it or not, I am not a child, and I will not be treated like one!" Morgana's eyes were blazing, her anger almost overcoming the pain of her aching muscles as she struggled to restrain persistent tears. But she would be damned before she would admit to Devon that every movement she made was a true test of will . . . that the short walk to the fire had been enough to aggravate her pain to the point where her raging appetite of a few moments before had disappeared. In fact, her nausea seemed to increase with every aching movement, and she had begun to reach the point where she felt if she did not lie down soon, she would be violently sick. Another wave of nausea swept over her as Morgana struggled to her feet. Her cramping thigh muscles screeched their protest, causing a low, inadvertent moan to escape her lips as she turned to lower herself to the merciful haven of the blanket under the tree a short distance from the fire. Lowering herself with considerable difficulty, she uttered a low sigh of relief the moment before she realized Devon had followed her silently to the blanket and was standing close beside her.

A knowing expression covered his sharply chiseled features.

"So, that's it."

Uncertain whether she had heard the mumbled words correctly, Morgana watched out of the corner of her eye as Devon strode toward his saddle. Within moments he had returned to stand towering over her, a small bottle in his hand.

"All right, Morgana. There's only one thing you can do about muscles in your condition on the trail. Roll onto your stomach!"

"What!" Her face flushing a bright red, Morgana gasped sharply, "I will do no such thing!"

An expression of supreme disgust crossing his hard features, Devon responded with grating clarity. "Just to set things straight, I'll make my intentions very clear. It's obvious that your discomfort is makin' you ill. I do *not* intend to wait until you've overcome your protestin' muscles sufficiently to allow us to continue our journey! Now, roll over! This liniment will help your discomfort." When Morgana still hesitated, he added sharply, "I'd do the same for my horse, Morgana! Now do as I say, damn it, or I'll turn you over myself!"

The threat in the depths of the azure eyes looking down into hers left no doubt that Devon would follow through with his words. Turning onto her stomach, Morgana lay unresisting as Devon slipped the rough cotton blouse from her shoulders. Within minutes she realized he had moved to straddle her narrow hips with his knees. With a surprisingly gentle touch he swept the long chestnut curls that lay unbound against her back to the side. At the same time that the sensation of cool liquid touched her shoulders, a pungent aroma met her nostrils.

"Now, just relax and let me take some of the ache out of you." Reacting stiffly to the sensation of the broad, work-toughened hands moving familiarly along her neck and shoulders, Morgana flinched at the impatience in the low, angry growl. "I said *relax!*"

Gradually, after a few more sharply uttered commands, Morgana felt herself relaxing under the arrogant Texan's experienced hands. But it was impossible to resist the strong, caressing hands that sought out the cause of her pain with infinite patience, and, slowly, with unceasing diligence, stimulated and massaged the screaming protest of her muscles into a soft purr. Marvelous! It was absolute heaven! Again she felt the application of the cool liquid against her skin, not truly conscious that Devon had bared her back to continue his work.

Knowingly, the experienced hands moved to smooth and soothe the tightness from her slender neck, the tautness from her narrow, aching shoulders, the crying ache from between her shoulder blades, the stiff rebellion of her lower back until it was finally almost nonexistent. She made no protest when Devon slipped her skirt easily from her body, and could barely restrain her sigh of contentment as he poured the cool

291

liquid on the backs of her thighs. Again he began his gentle assault, smoothing, kneading, massaging away her pain.

Her protest was instinctive when the broad hands reached up to pull the brief underdrawers from her body, only to be stifled a moment later by the wave of almost pure bliss as the strong, knowing hands continued their heady ministrations on the bruised muscles of her shapely buttocks.

She did not resist when the strong hands turned her over to her back; was almost unconscious of her partial nudity until a low, tortured gasp sounded heavily on the warm evening air.

"Oh, Christ!"

The thick fan of lashes lying against smooth golden cheeks lifted slowly to Devon's face. Still kneeling astride her, his face was flushed with emotion, his teeth clamped tightly together in an apparent attempt at control. His chest heaved with revealing agitation beneath the homespun cloth of his shirt. Turning, he picked up the bottle with shaking hands. Carefully scooping a small amount of liquid into his palm, he turned back, his eyes catching and holding hers in the short moment before he applied it to her shoulders.

Gradually, with infinite thoroughness, he moved the path of his massage from her shoulders to her upper arms, working and stimulating fully the aching flesh before proceeding to the softness of her chest. His hands trembling, he massaged the perfect rounded globes of her breasts, the slender crevice of the valley between, the tired, aching muscles beneath, before moving caressingly to the narrow rib cage.

Stopping still, he frowned as his eyes touched a long, fresh bruise that stretched across her ribs. Touching it lightly with his fingertips, he whispered hoarsely, "Did . . . did I do that to you, Morgana . . . when I pulled you from your horse this afternoon?"

"I . . . I don't know . . ." Her heart was pounding wildly. It was difficult to breathe. The glow deep in the light eyes that moved briefly to her face had started a trembling deep within her . . . unleashed a stab of pleasure that inflamed her to the center of her being. Slowly the dark head lowered to press kisses along the darkening bruise. She was gasping from the wild emotions assaulting her senses when the strong

292

hands returned to their heady tasks seeking the muscles in her slender hips, moving meticulously along her thighs and calves, to conclude by carefully, lovingly, working each slender foot.

He was no longer touching her, but his breath was hot against her lips. Her eyes snapping open, Morgana was unable to tear her gaze from Devon's deeply affected expression. Cupping her cheeks with his hands, he looked deeply into her eyes.

"Morgana, darlin', I want you more than I've ever wanted any woman in my life. You're a self-centered, pampered, schemin' little bitch, and I despise everythin' you stand for. But I want you. Christ, I've wanted you from the first moment I saw you . . . and I want you still. . . ."

The words were heard, their meaning rejected in the deep recesses of her brain as the full, sensuous mouth that had taunted her relentlessly lowered to cover hers. A low groan escaping his lips at the moment of their contact with hers, Morgana felt the sudden weight of Devon's lean, rangy body atop hers. Gasping at the exhilarating pleasure that suffused her, Morgana felt the sensitive play of his tongue against hers, its coaxing sweetness as it fondled and caressed her into a similar play of her own. Gradually, with searing thoroughness, Devon allowed his lips to follow the same course his hands had touched only minutes before.

The unexpected closing of his mouth over the pink, taut crest of her breast sent a jolt of heat through Morgana's veins. Suddenly there was no more clothing between them, the sensation of Devon's virile nakedness stretched full length atop her driving her past conscious thought in the moment before his knee moved to separate her legs. Quickly, unexpectedly, Devon slid deep within her, renewing his claim on the moist, inner reaches of her body. Again and again he thrust, raising her with fluttering veils of ecstasy at each searing penetration. She was beyond conscious thought, her body exulting in the raging beauty of the emotion so brilliantly nurtured to bloom within her. She did not want him to stop. She wanted . . . she wanted . . .

His lips were close to hers again. His voice, low with emotion, coaxed her eyes open to look into his impassioned face.

"Morgana . . . darlin' . . . do you want me? Do you want me now?"

Why was he doing this? Why was he bringing her back to conscious realization of this moment? Why?

"Morgana . . ."

"Why . . . why do you want . . ."

"Tell me, Morgana. Tell me you want me." Her lingering hesitation inflamed him. "Damn you. I know you do! I can feel your body quivering, aching for release. I want to hear you say it . . . I want to hear you say you want me."

"No . . . I can't say . . ."

"Say it, damn it!" Moving subtly inside her, enough to send a fresh wave of ecstasy sweeping her senses, he groaned low in his throat at the passion that moved across her flushed face. "Say it, now, damn you, or I swear I'll leave you . . . walk away from you without even the slightest . . ."

"No . . ." Suddenly unable to bear the thought of separation from the lean, strongly muscled body that created such beauty between them, she whispered urgently, "No, don't leave me Devon. I . . . I want you . . . I do want you. . . ."

There was a moment of silent hesitation as Devon's eyes raked her face. "More than you want Santa Anna?" His eyes boring into hers demanded a response from her startled lips. "Do you want me more than you want Santa Anna, Morgana? Tell me, you little witch. I want to hear you say it now, or I'll never touch you again. Morgana . . ."

"Yes." Her response a faint gasp, she lowered her eyes, unbidden tears sliding from the corners, ". . . yes, I want you more than I ever wanted Santa Anna. . . ."

A low, strangled note sounding deep in his throat, Devon cupped her face roughly in his hands, his mouth closing over hers with a wild urgency that throbbed between them for long, bittersweet moments. Abruptly jerking his mouth from hers, Devon began a rapid, violently driving penetration of her body, his passion wildly unrestrained as he raised them with soul-binding escalation to the blazing summit of their desires. With a deep groan, Devon's explosive, searing climax took Morgana in a shower of soaring glory to the culmination of the ecstasy that was theirs alone to share.

Drifting slowly to earth from the euphoria Devon had created so faultlessly for the two of them, Morgana allowed her eyes to meet and hold the cerulean gaze that remained unmoving on her face.

Barely suppressing a gasp as Morgana's sated, sienna-colored glance met his, the brilliant golden sparks glowing within their depths confirming the words her lips had uttered in passion, Devon slipped his arms around her to hold her close and firm against him. Words rushed to his lips unbidden, only to be stifled by the thought that she was his for just a little while, and would soon be gone. . . .

Silver creases of dawn marked the morning sky. The fading glory of a thousand stars sparkled through the branches over his head as Devon raised himself on his arm to allow a clearer look at the woman who slept in his embrace. A light blanket covered them both, binding them together in a cocoon of warm intimacy that Devon loathed to break. It had been so perfect last night . . . Morgana's arms warm and welcoming, her body opening to his with an eagerness that almost matched his own. Almost, for surely his desire for her, the driving force that had held him near long after he had been told to leave; the same force that had driven him back to the capital from Saltillo after the rumors of Santa Anna's blatant attentions to Morgana had reached his ears; his enslaving desire for her, could not be matched. And even now, after the long, loving night behind them, he wanted her still. His eyes moved slowly over the small, perfect face turned blissfully toward his shoulder, a warm tenderness growing inside him as Morgana moved herself closer against his side in sleep. God, she was beautiful! Would he ever become accustomed to her beauty? Even in the dim light of dawn her hair glowed with a vibrance all its own as it curled against his arm and wound its silkiness against the contours of her slender throat and the creamy whiteness of her shoulders. Raising his hand, he touched the small, curling spirals of hair at her temple tentatively, his hand longing to caress the smooth ivory cheek. The dark fan of lashes resting there fluttered at his touch, causing him to resist his longing. He didn't want to awaken her yet. He needed a little more time . . . time to indulge himself . . . time to sate his overpowering need to consume her with his eyes.

Hell, the first three days on the trail with Morgana had been almost more than he could bear! He had wanted her so badly that he had barely withstood his desire to ravage her—take her with or without her consent. And through it all, Morgana had remained cool, aloof, resolute in her determination to refuse him even the satisfaction of acknowledging his existence. Her aloofness almost more than he could bear, he had extended the long hours on horseback in a desire to bring a quick end to their journey . . . so he might be free of Morgana . . . and free of his consuming desire for her. And he had pushed her too hard . . . almost made her ill. Hell, her small, tender little body wasn't prepared for the grueling punishment of their first days on horseback. He should've realized it would be too much for her. God, he hadn't wanted to hurt her! He had only wanted . . .

His mind refused to finish his thought as it returned to the memory of the night before. He had held her in his arms last night and loved her until they were both so weary that they could not fight off sleep, and it had been beautiful . . . more beautiful than he had dreamed possible. And now, upon awakening after the long night, he only wanted to love her more. Was she a witch . . . had she put him under her spell? What other explanation was there for his helplessness against the desire that was presently the driving force in his life?

Did she have the same effect on Santa Anna? Was that the reason for the president's devotion to Morgana that was opening him to such scandal? How many times had she lain with Santa Anna like this? How many times had Santa Anna awakened to Morgana's beautiful face lying beside him on the pillow? Had he made her cry out in passion . . . felt her small, delicate hands clutching him close? Did she make him mad with wanting her . . . drive Santa Anna past caution as she had driven him? A wild surge of jealousy flushed Devon's senses. Hell, he knew what Morgana was . . . a conniving, self-seeking little witch whose total concern was in advancing her position in life to regain the wealth and luxury that she had lost with the death of her father. She had admitted to him that she hadn't wanted Santa Anna as much as she wanted him . . . and he believed her. He couldn't doubt the passion that had raged in her trembling body last night. But he had found her lying docilely underneath Santa Anna's weight in the forest that morning, her arms wrapped tightly around his neck.

The abrupt return of the revolting memory brought a surge of bile into Devon's throat. A trembling began deep inside him, and, unable to face the jealousy that flushed his being, he slid his arms under and around Morgana's sleeping form and pulled her close.

"What . . . ? Devon . . ."

Thoroughly disoriented, Morgana blinked the sleep from her eyes as Devon buried his face in the softness of her neck. A rapidly encroaching warmth permeated her being as his broad hands moved hungrily against her nakedness. Closing her eyes once more, Morgana gasped as his knowing touch caressed her soft breasts, smoothed the silken thighs, separating her legs to allow him access to the waiting bud of her passion. Moving his hand within the slender crease, he caressed her warmly, his fingers moving knowingly within the moistness, soothing, raising her level of pleasure as his mouth covered hers for a deep, searing kiss.

She could not catch her breath, so great was her heady agitation as Devon's hands moved freely within the tender slit, stimulating, teasing, torturing her. His mouth ravaged her breasts . . . kissing, fondling, lifting her to a wild anticipation that held her trembling under its onslaught. But he was not satisfied with the low groans of ecstasy that shook her slender form. He needed more . . . more. Abruptly slowing his heady assault, he allowed his tongue to draw light, leisurely circles around the swollen crests of her breasts, teasing the aching nipples that longed for the warmth of his mouth. But still he continued, his hand moving erotically in the warm moistness between her thighs, eliciting gasps of pleasure from Morgana's love-swollen lips.

Uncertain what exactly was happening to her, Morgana groaned in the searing pleasure of Devon's attentions and begged for the entry that would afford her relief from the exquisite pain that seared her body. But still Devon persisted, withholding himself from her, caressing, teasing, fondling, until, in a burst of burning ecstasy, Morgana was carried over the edge of passion, tumbling, whirling, thrilling to the rioting emotions exploding inside her until she lay at last, breathless and shaken, in the warm velvet of Devon's arms.

Restraining the searing urgency building inside him, Devon had curbed his growing need to enter Morgana. His eyes moving across her impassioned face, he had gloried in the violent emotions that shook her slender frame. He had wanted this . . . had needed this . . . had needed to know he controlled Morgana . . . held her as deeply within his power as she, unknowingly, held him. Ignoring his own growing physical need, he had brought her gradually, persistently, glowingly to the edge of her passion, his own heartbeat accelerating to heart-stopping proportions as he had sensed her feeling the first edge of panic . . . saw the startled expression in her glowing eyes as she began to lose control . . . watched hungrily, his gratification complete as she surged to climax, the outpouring of her body's sweet homage coming in deep, gasping spasms that shook her small frame, jerking, contorting until she was spent.

He had watched ardently as the black lashes lying against her flushed cheeks slowly rose, her magnificent, gold-flecked eyes searching his face in wonder.

"Devon . . . I never . . . I don't know . . ."

Her stumbling words falling to a halt, Devon waited long moments, bringing his own searing emotions to rein as he whispered hoarsely, "I wanted to watch you come to fulfillment, Morgana. I wanted to see the passion in your eyes, see the growin' ache in your body, watch it move under my caress. I wanted to touch . . . to feel . . . to see your love nectar escapin' you. I wanted it all, darlin', and I wanted it all from you."

Abruptly flipping himself over on top of her, Devon

moved the enlarged shaft of his desire against her, his heartbeat surging to new heights as Morgana's eyelids fluttered in renewing passion.

"And now, darlin'," his voice low and shaken, Devon continued, "And now we'll do it again . . . together." Lifting himself in a swift, fluid movement, Devon slid himself inside her, his own low groan joining hers as he began the rapid, surging quest for ultimate reward. A subconscious glow of satisfaction permeating his being, Devon felt Morgana's emotions rising to join his, swiftly, unhesitatingly, with burning intensity. With a suddenness that stole the breath from his body, Devon reached the peak of his passion, his eyes opening to see that Morgana joined him at the apex of his glory, soared with him in a brilliant burst of radiance that sent them careening . . . delivered them shaken and fulfilled into each other's arms.

There were long, silent moments before Morgana's breathing returned to normal. Still wrapped in the warmth of Devon's arms, she felt safe, secure, the turmoil of her life far from her mind in the aftermath of their lovemaking. Slowly lifting her lids, she allowed her eyes to move over the face that looked silently into hers. A brief flicker of emotion flashed across his sober expression. Her eyes trained on the clear blue gaze that moved slowly across her face, she was startled to see Devon's eyes growing slowly cold. The last flicker of warmth disappeared as he separated himself from her. Getting immediately to his feet, he stood staring down at her.

"Get dressed, Morgana. I want to be on the trail as soon as possible. I'm already late by at least a month in arrivin' in Texas, and I don't want any more delay."

Abruptly embarrassed at her nakedness, Morgana scrambled for the blanket at her feet. Devon's low laugh held a derisive note that brought a flush to her cheek. "Don't you think it's a little late for that now, darlin'? No need to play the modest little virgin. You stepped out of that class a long time ago."

"How . . . how dare you talk to me like that?" Gasping her indignation, Morgana felt a raging anger flush her senses. Dragging the blanket up with her as she stumbled to her feet, she wrapped it clumsily around her nakedness. "Last night you *told* me you had no intention to . . . to . . ." Her words slowing to a halt, Morgana abruptly continued in a rush, ". . . and then you took advantage of my trust! I believed you."

His mouth turning down into a deprecating sneer, Devon retorted coldly, "And I suppose I forced you again, this morning. Yes," he continued with a small nod of his head as he touched the tender spot under his ear where she had bitten his neck in frustrated passion, "I do seem to bear a few scars from your defense of your virtue, darlin'. And you sure did have a strange way of fightin' me, Morgana. I guess I'll have to keep that in mind the next time we get together." His face growing darkly serious, he concluded tightly, "Now do as I said, and get dressed. We have a long way to travel today."

Still unable to believe the events that had transpired in the small grove, Morgana stared disbelievingly into Devon's hard features before abruptly bending down to snatch up her blouse and skirt. Turning in the direction of the stream, she mumbled over her shoulder, "When I'm done bathing . . ."

His voice impatient, Devon interrupted tightly, "And make it fast! I told you I . . ."

"I know!" Turning back, her eyes clashed violently with his. "You're in a hurry to get back to Texas! But you'll have to be delayed a few minutes longer. I feel decidedly unclean this morning. I need to wash . . . to feel clean again."

She had started toward the stream when Devon's low voice came over her shoulder, "Do you really think that's possible?"

The last light of day was beginning to fade as Devon directed the horses into an area where a few trees provided shelter.

"You'll have to use water sparingly tonight." His short sentence was the first he had spoken in many hours, and the greater part of the total number of words they had exchanged the whole day. The realization that she was to go without even the simple necessity of bathing facilities after the long, hot day on horseback abruptly had Morgana close to tears. Unwilling to show Devon even that small sigh of weakness, she turned her horse abruptly toward a small patch of grass and hurried to dismount. Allowing herself to slip to her feet, she groaned at the protest of her aching muscles. She was abruptly glad Devon had taken her riding skirt and shirt-waist, as well as her riding boots, from her the first day on the trail, and had substituted the simple Mexican skirt, blouse, and sandals. The attire had served her well, allowing the maximum of comfort in the burning Mexican heat. But even with the discomfort that thought portended, she seriously considered asking Devon to allow her to resume her former attire, so she might be free of the clothes that had absorbed far too much of the dirt of the trail for her to wear in comfort another day. But she was being a fool! She could not even bathe tonight, much less wash her clothes! She *was* a fool. . . .

Fighting back persistent tears, Morgana turned deliberately toward a clump of bushes at the far end of the area. She was aware that Devon's eyes followed her, and knew he would not challenge her attempt at a few moments' privacy, even if they were the only moments she was allowed on the damned journey.

Returning a few minutes later, Morgana fought to control the tightness in her muscles that appeared to worsen with each step she took. She still was in considerable pain, but she had to concede to an improvement in her condition after Devon's ministrations the night before . . . damn him!

A small fire burned brightly, a small pan heating appealingly over it. His eyes assessing her unsteady gait, Devon responded only to her interest in the warming pan.

"I'm makin' some tea, and that's about the only warm thing you'll put in your stomach tonight." Turning, he removed an unappealing strip of dried beef from his pack. "Not as appealin' as last night, but I can't take the time to hunt two nights in a row."

"We . . ." Her stomach gnawing with hunger, Morgana

301

accepted the stringy strip of beef, her unsatisfied appetite causing her to probe cautiously, "We should be coming upon an inn somewhere soon, shouldn't we? I mean, this area isn't entirely uninhabited! Surely we can then stop long enough for a bath and a good meal."

Turning slowly in her direction, Devon lent the full weight of his contempt to his glance. "You must really think me a fool, Morgana, to think I'd go anywhere near an inn with you."

"What do you mean? You said no one would be looking for me in this area . . . that the search was probably being conducted in the opposite direction. Why should you worry about . . ."

"And what would I do with you? Carry you into the inn gagged and tied? You don't mean to let me believe you wouldn't take the first opportunity to alert someone to your identity?"

Her glance avoiding his, Morgana shrugged unconsciously. They had met few people on the trail so far, but with each encounter, Devon's hand had moved warningly to the knife at his belt, sending a tremor of fear down her spine. Somehow, deep inside, Morgana knew with blood-chilling certainty that, despite their intimacy, Devon would not hesitate to use the thick, sharp blade. She remembered too well the sensation of her flesh's being severed . . . the horror of her own blood's streaming from the wound, flowing over her breasts. The Devon that had shared her pain then had been a different man . . . not the same Devon who was capable of loving her with infinite tenderness one moment, and turning coldly away from her the next. This new Devon was diabolical, impossible to anticipate . . . and, she feared, totally capable of killing her if she endangered his mission. No, she was frightened, too much a coward to go against him now.

"I suppose if I gave you my word I would speak to no one, you wouldn't . . ."

"Save your breath, Morgana." His light eyes raking her face, he gave a low snort. "We'll have to be up early again tomorrow."

Her color flaring, Morgana did not deign to respond.

302

Consuming her dried beef in silence, she drank the remainder of her tea and stood up. A single blanket was stretched near the fire, and, spying another blanket still rolled neatly on Devon's saddle, she walked stiffly toward it and removed it with a jerk. Almost groaning at the strain of the effort on her aching muscles, she turned as easily as she could manage, and, seeing a likely spot under a far tree, started in its direction.

"No, Morgana, I think we'll sleep here, closer to the fire."

Indignation flaring at the implication of his statement, Morgana turned slowly in his direction. "You may sleep near the fire if you wish, but I'm going to sleep over there!"

Not waiting for his reaction to her response, Morgana turned back in the direction of the far tree. She had not gone three steps when she felt a hand close on her shoulder. Turning her firmly toward him, Devon stared silently into her face for long seconds, his expression unrevealing. When he spoke his voice was low, his tone emotionless.

"Let's come to an understandin', Morgana. We'll be travelin' together for at least a month. We don't like each other very much." A small ironic smile twisted his lips. "Hell, that's puttin' it mildly, isn't it? I've had you kidnapped . . . interfered with your plan to be at the top of Mexican society, haven't I. If you didn't hate me before, you sure as hell do now. As for me, I despise everythin' you are. I have no use for you . . ." His eyes lowering to her lips, he continued hoarsely, ". . . no use but one."

The hand firmly gripping her shoulder began to stroke her gently as the other slipped to the back of her neck to draw her closer. His mouth teased her lips as he spoke, sending little tremors down her spine with his hoarse whisper. "But we want each other, Morgana. I couldn't think of much else all day today, other than the time when we'd camp for the night and I could make love to you again. It's the same with you, isn't it, darlin'."

The vehement denial that sprang to her lips was stopped by the light flicking of Devon's tongue against their tortured surface, and the shameless tremor of desire that shook her

303

frame. Her reaction did not go unnoticed by Devon's sharp, assessing gaze. He pulled her tight against him, the bulge of his passion taunting her as he trailed his lips across her cheek, stopping to nibble heatedly at the small lobe of her ear as he mumbled thickly, "We need to exorcise this passion from our systems, darlin'; so we'll both be free again. It's the only way, darlin' . . . you know it's the only way."

Hanging on desperately to her last shred of sanity as Devon's tongue licked hungrily at her ear, increasing the quaking of her small frame until she could hardly speak, Morgana responded hoarsely, "No . . . you . . . you're making a whore of me."

A note of finality in his throbbing voice, Devon's response was filled with sad acceptance. "You are what you are, Morgana. . . ."

Closing her eyes as Devon scooped her easily into his arms, Morgana was unaware of the roughness of the blanket beneath her back as her clothing quickly fell away. Feeling only the ecstasy of his touch, the sweet warmth of Devon's flesh as it closed over hers, she heard the echo of his words in the back of her mind as he slid inside her.

"You are what you are. . . ."

The heat of the long afternoon had been intense and wearying. His eyes returned worriedly to Morgana's swaying form, guilt plaguing him relentlessly. At the time it had seemed the only sensible thing to do . . . remove Morgana from the capital so that the scandal in the offing would not affect Austin's trial, but now . . . now he was unsure. She was exhausted. Long hours in the saddle during the day and his ardent attentions during the short night were beginning to take their toll. Even he was beginning to feel the effects. But damn, despite his most stringent avowals, the moment Morgana was in his arms, all rational thought left his mind. Lifting his hat, he ran an anxious hand through his heavy brown hair in a gesture fraught with frustration. It was too early to stop. There were hours of travel yet ahead of them. The journey was endless. . . . And through it all, Morgana would not allow him the satisfaction of asking him to . . .

"Morgana!"

His heart leaping in his chest, Devon caught Morgana's arm, startling her into wakefulness just before she began to slump from the saddle.

"What . . . ?"

Morgana's gaze was muddled and disoriented as it met his. Realizing she could support herself no longer, Devon lifted her from the saddle, settling her astride his horse in front of him. Jerking her hat from her head, he hung it carelessly over his saddle horn. Slipping the stifling *rebozo* from her shoulders, he then leaned over to take her horse's reins and secure them to the back of his saddle. Pulling her back firmly against his chest, he mumbled gruffly into her ear, "Go to sleep. We have a few more hours' ridin' yet today, but you can sleep for a while."

Attempting to pull free of his arms, Morgana managed a final protest. "No, I can ride. I don't need . . ."

A surge of annoyance brought a sharpness to Devon's voice. "Stop arguin' and lean back against me, damn it! And go to sleep."

Having spent her last ounce of strength, Morgana was capable of doing no more than following Devon's order. Slumping back against his chest, she quickly drifted off to sleep.

Her slender frame still rested against his chest, swaying with the steady movement of the horse. She had been sleeping for over an hour, the sweet, natural perfume of her skin taunting him relentlessly. Her narrow shoulders seemed to burn his chest, increasing his desire as her head rolled beneath his chin. She was so delicate, so small in the circle of his arms . . . so lovely. Nothing, not the scorching heat, the discomfort of their journey, his relentless wearying attentions . . . nothing was able to dim the glory of her beauty. Contrarily, unbelievably, she grew more lovely each day. Her pale white skin had turned a lovely golden color, emphasizing the glorious eyes that melted his heart. A great fiery glow had been added by the sun's brilliant rays to her already glowing halo, and if there were slight shadows under her great eyes, they only added a touch of ethereal beauty. His hand encircling her rib cage, holding her fast, was tortured gloriously by the warm globes of her breasts as they bobbed against his sensitized skin. Moving his hand, he cupped the tempting swells, his thumb massaging one soft nipple until it hardened under his touch to press against his hand erotically.

"Devon . . . ?"

She had begun to stir. An overwhelming wage of desire sweeping his senses, he looked down into her upturned face. Cupping her chin, he covered her mouth with his. The kiss grew deeper, more intense. Tearing his mouth from hers, Devon whispered shakily, "We have a few more hours' traveling yet today, but I want you, Morgana."

Unable to speak past the trembling that had begun deep inside her, Morgana felt the broad, calloused hand slip under her blouse to cup her breast. Her skin was moist to the touch, and warm and Devon groaned at the passion that leaped to life inside him.

"Devon . . . no, I don't want . . ."

"But you *do* want, Morgana. You know you do. . . ."

"No, Devon." Unable to trust herself, Morgana turned away from his eyes. Hating herself for her body's spontaneous protest to her denial of him, Morgana swallowed hard.

Allowing his hand to drop to her waist, Devon felt the echo of her wilding beating heart. His own passion flaming out of control, he slid his hand through the closure to her skirt. The skin of her stomach was warm to his touch. His seeking fingers moved beneath her flimsy underdrawers, a shaft of desire gripping his vitals as they closed on the tight ringlets he sought. Morgana stiffened responsively.

"Let me touch you, Morgana." His voice was gruff; his breathing quick and agitated. "I need to touch you."

Gradually the tension in Morgana's body began to fade under Devon's caressing hands, her body jerking responsively as he found the tender slit he sought. With a low groan, he met the bud of her desire, touched it, fondled it, the responsive wetness that aided his assault driving him to further heights of passion.

Morgana was breathing heavily, her own deep gasps matching his agitated breathing. Abruptly, she attempted to pull his hand from her aching body. "Devon, no, don't do this to me." Raising her eyes, she pleaded softly, "Not here . . . like this . . ."

"Yes, here, Morgana . . . now."

His mouth moving to cover hers with searing passion, Devon renewed his tender assault, tearing his mouth from hers as he gasped tightly, "Lean back against me . . . that's right, darlin' . . . Let me feel you open to me . . . that's right . . ."

Her body unconsciously following his commands, Morgana leaned back against Devon, allowing him further access as she reacted wildly, erotically to his relentless caresses. Abruptly, a strong tremor began to shake Morgana's body, lifting her on brilliant wings to a plane of shuddering ecstasy. Sensing she was at the brink, Devon whispered shakily into her ear, his voice deep and throbbing. "Lean back and give to me, Morgana. I want to feel you give yourself completely . . . now . . ."

In sudden, jerking spasms, Morgana's body surrendered to Devon's heady assault, a low groan escaping her lips as Devon's hand tightened in the fiery ringlets accepting her body's homage for the ecstasy he had brought to life within her.

Holding her tight in his embrace until the final tremor had passed, Devon turned her face to his. Covering her mouth with his, he kissed her searingly . . . deeply. Hours later, Morgana still rode in his embrace. Tears slipping silently down her cheeks, she closed her eyes against her pain, the voice that echoed in her mind taunting her, "You are what you are, Morgana. . . ."

Two weeks on the trail had wrought a great change in Morgana. Gone was the young, immature girl who had been abducted in another lifetime. Instead, a new maturity showed in her eye. Her sore and aching muscles had toughened, strengthened, until she could well match Devon's endurance. She was thinner, the new hollows in her cheeks emphasizing the graceful slope of her cheekbones. Her lightly tanned skin, carefully shielded from the baking sun under Devon's watchful eye, was free of blemish as it stretched over her magnificent facial contours. The sparkling shafts of gold in her great sienna eyes were suppressed, coming to life reluctantly and only under the warmth of Devon's caress. Her expression for the major part of the day was sober, unrevealing, her emotions carefully guarded. Her soft lips, so often in the past curved into a warm smile that called an appealing dimple at the corner of her mouth into play, were set in a serious line. Her former extensive toilette, nurtured by the fortune enjoyed in her youth, had changed from elaborate perfumes and scented water to a much welcomed bath in an occasional stream when available, supplemented by the plain soap Devon carried in his saddlebag. Instead of the extensive wardrobe she had enjoyed since her early youth, her attire for the past grueling weeks had been a simple cotton blouse and skirt, carefully washed in available streams at the conclusion of the day's travel, hung on branches of trees or strung across brush, and assumed in the morning for that day's travel. But strangely, through all the deprivation and hardship she had experienced, Morgana had grown more beautiful.

His eyes flicking to her straight, slender figure as she rode beside him, Devon could not deny the small core of pride he silently nourished in his heart. Damn if she hadn't turned into quite a woman, his Morgana! His Morgana. The words twisted the knife of pain in his stomach that had grown with his knowledge that his homestead was near . . . that their solitary journey would soon be done. Her initial resistance over, Morgana now accepted his attentions openly. When had the change taken place? Was it after that day on horseback, when he had caressed her to fulfillment? He had needed to take her then, needed to show his mastery over her emotions so that he might retaliate in some way for the power she unknowingly wielded over him. Unwilling, but unable to resist him, she had lain back against him, allowing him access to her body. God, he remembered it still . . . the

308

warmth of her back pressed against his chest, her sweet moistness against his hand. He closed his eyes briefly against the vividness of the memory, clenching his teeth tightly shut in an attempt to control. He could feel his body swelling, his desire growing. If he were to take her from her horse now, on this very trail, would she refuse him? He knew she would not.

She had adapted well to their daily routine in every way. Long days on the trail without a whimper of protest. Simple, sometimes meager meals shared in silence, broken only when her curiosity about some aspect of their journey could not be restrained. Their few conversations touching on political matters still ended in anger. That had not changed. No, the long weeks had not softened her attitude in relation to her uncle and the Santa Anna who remained unblemished in her mind. His anger stirring anew, Devon knew in his heart that she would remain true to her convictions, no matter the price.

But the nights . . . they were a different matter. With their only mattress the hard earth covered by a rough blanket, they made beautiful love together. Never the one to instigate their lovemaking, Morgana nevertheless now turned to him without hesitation at his touch, her arms raising to welcome him, her mouth opening to his kiss, her body accepting him warmly and with open passion. His experience with women was extensive, begun at an early age and aided by his slender good looks and the charm he wielded like a weapon. But Morgana was a new experience . . . totally woman. In searching his mind, he could not remember a time when he had touched her that the magic of her aura had not lit a fire inside him; could not remember a time his eyes had rested on her that he had not felt one of any number of violent emotions assail his senses. Desire . . . pride . . . joy . . . jealousy. Yes, the last had grown with each day that passed. His Morgana. His possessiveness was a joke . . . a joke of which he was the victim. Somewhere, at what point he was uncertain, his plans had gone awry in that respect. No, it was not supposed to be this way . . . his desire growing with each night she spent in his arms . . . the persistent dreams he could not suppress where Morgana turned to him with love in her eyes . . . the stubborn ache that accompanied his realization that their idyll would soon be over, that he would be called upon to fulfill his part of the bargain as she had fulfilled hers . . . to release her to return to Mexico and her lover, Santa Anna. He had no doubt Santa Anna would accept any story she saw fit to tell him. Wasn't his obsession with Morgana almost as binding as his own? Yes, Santa Anna would take her back, into his arms and into his bed, and *his* Morgana . . . his *own* Morgana would no longer exist.

The haunting memory returned again to his mind . . . Morgana lying underneath Santa Anna, her arms wrapped around his neck as he ravaged her mouth . . . drank deeply from the depths of the sweet, loving well that was his . . . his alone. Yes, he had warned Morgana that he would see her dead rather than allow her to forfeit Steven Austin's future. The violence in that threat was real, but it was not a product of his political convictions. Instead, it was that some haunting memory that had stirred the wildness within him . . . the wildness that remained with him still. . . .

A peculiar sensation had begun prickling up the back of Morgana's neck, a vague, animal warning that caused her to turn her eyes searchingly to the brush alongside the road. But she saw nothing. Turning to the trail beside her, Morgana's eyes snapped into contact with Devon's chilling glance. Startled at the venom in his stare, Morgana swallowed hard, unable to break contact with his gaze. In the end, it was Devon who turned away, his eyes returning to the trail ahead of them silently, without explanation.

Not realizing she had been holding her breath, Morgana released a shaken sigh. They had been together day and night for over a month, and with each day that passed, Morgana grew less and less certain which was the true Devon Howard. Who was he, really? Was he the intense, well-dressed Texan who had been sent on a diplomatic mission as a representative of his fellow Anglo-Texans? Was he the handsome man who had stirred her hatred on the voyage from New York and then charmed her so completely on the voyage to Veracruz? Was he the caring, compassionate man who had nursed her wound that terrible day in the courtyard, and come each day to assure himself of her returning health? Was he the man Antonio had claimed him to be . . . a man who had used her aunt's goodness against her to insinuate himself into a position suitable to favor his precious Colonel Austin's case? Or was he truly the man he had shown himself to be since the inception of this journey . . . hard, unyielding, violent? Somehow, she had no doubt that his threat against her life made the day of her abduction was sincere. The man whose chilling glance had sent a wave of fear coursing through her senses only a few moments before was capable of using that broad knife strapped to his belt against her. She remembered his light touch against the thin scar on her throat, and the coldness in his eyes.

Even his appearance had changed since the inception of the journey. His dark hair was longer, hanging thickly almost to his shoulders in unruly waves. His face, hard and bereft of the slow smile that wrought such a change on his features, was sober and uncompromising. The slimness she had noted in his formal dress was instead a tightly muscled frame, broad-shouldered but lacking in the fleshiness she had become accustomed to seeing in the men of her acquaintance. She remembered only too well the strength of the well-formed arms that held her, the rippling muscles of the chest against which she had rested her head, kissed warmly as her emotions soared, the narrow hips she had clutched in her passion . . . clutched even closer as he had plunged deep inside her. Dressed in his traveling clothes: a broad-brimmed hat shadowing his alert, assessing eyes; a light cotton shirt clinging to his broad-shouldered, well-toned frame in the heat of the day; worn, snugly fitting trousers that made no secret of the strong thigh muscles that served him so well; and the supreme manliness to which she could attest firsthand, he exuded sheer animal strength and virility. But ever present, more sensed than declared, was the violence that seemed to simmer just below his surface calm. A violence that called out to her in warning . . . a warning she dared not ignore.

But she also remembered the nights they had spent together. A slow flush suffusing her body, Morgana fought the memories that invaded her mind. Her resistance had been futile from the first. Devon had proved his power over her body too many times in the past . . . on the ship, on the feast day of San Juan, and in the silence of the night in her own room. Whatever he was, she knew only one certainty. The touch of his hands was magic against her flesh; his mouth against hers a searing drug; and possession by his body a wonder beyond her wildest dreams.

A sudden thickness choking her throat, Morgana knew a moment of true panic. She had to get away from him! She had to be released soon, or it would be too late . . . too late to break the addiction she felt building inside her. He had sought to exorcise their desires so they would be free of the passion that bound them. If it were only true for her! She was afraid . . . afraid that when he set her free at last, sent her back to Mexico, she would no longer have the desire to go. Oh, there was no love between them. How could there be? He spoke to her only in anger or in command. He had openly declared his contempt for the woman he believed her to be. Was she truly that woman? She was no longer sure. She was only sure she had to be free of Devon, before it was too late.

The scent of the bird they roasted over the small campfire teased her mercilessly. The day had been long and hot, the approaching night threatening more of the same. The humid air hung heavily on her shoulders, damp and oppressive. Unwilling to break the silence that reigned between them, Morgana followed Devon's movement with her eyes as he adjusted the makeshift spit on which the browning bird rested. The sound of the stream close by beckoned her tauntingly. They had camped only a short time before, Devon's pensive mood of the afternoon carrying over as twilight approached. Suddenly angry with herself for the fear his chilling glances had instilled in her that afternoon, she pulled herself to her feet. She didn't need his approval to take a bath, and if the food cooled by the time she returned, it would be she, not he, who would suffer. Walking quickly to Devon's saddle, she removed the waning bar of soap and turned in the direction of the stream.

"Where are you goin'?"

Holding up the soap and a blanket she had snatched from the ground, she replied coldly, "Where would I be going with soap in my hand? I do have permission to bathe, don't I? I wouldn't want to interfere with the well-established routine of your camp."

Holding her motionless in his cold regard, Devon finally responded in a dismissing tone that inflamed her anger even further. "It makes little difference to me."

Clamping her teeth tightly shut against the retort that rose on her lips, Morgana turned toward the stream.

The water was inviting to the eye, clear, with considerable movement for its size. Following its path with her eyes as it curved beyond the small grove of trees in which they camped, she saw that its narrow confines widened a little further down, forming a placid pool. Moving quickly in its direction, Morgana's feet had barely touched the bank when she began shedding her clothes. The lure of the clear water was overpowering to a body tortured with dust and sun from a day that had started at dawn. The water was startlingly cold as it covered her feet, drawing goose bumps to her fair skin, and, suddenly filled with the joy of the moment, Morgana laughed at the tingling sensation. The water caressed her calves boldly, stroked her well-shaped thighs, and, unable to bear the torture of slow submersion, Morgana lowered herself in a sharp, breathtaking movement. The water was exhilarating! Still gasping from the sensation of the frigid water against her perspiring skin, Morgana submerged herself again, making certain to stay under the surface until her hair was completely wet. Walking into the pool a little farther, she was surprised to find that the water deepened to shoulder level, and, abruptly treating herself to a freedom she had not felt for over a month, Morgana slid onto her back and allowed the water to raise her to the surface, to support her in a gentle rocking movement as she closed her eyes at the sheer luxury of the moment.

How long she floated in mindless lethargy, she was not certain. With sudden realization, Morgana saw that night was fast approaching. Forcing herself to relinquish her precious moments of pleasure, she touched her feet down on the bottom of the pool and began to soap her hair. Having succeeded in working up a healthy lather, she scrubbed the grainy specks from her scalp with all-encompassing enjoyment. She had not realized how great had been her discomfort . . . how very lovely it would feel to be completely clean again.

Dipping herself low beneath the surface of the water, Morgana moved her head from side to side, as she held her breath. Certain the last remaining vestige of soap had been removed from the heavy floating coils, she stood up, and, sliding her arms underneath the streaming mass, lifted it from her back.

Taking a moment to brush the water from her eyes, Morgana gave a small sigh of utter contentment and began rubbing soap up the length of her slender arm. An abrupt sound in the water behind her turned Morgana swiftly in the direction of the bank. Her breath catching in her throat, she saw Devon walking toward her, the perfection of his naked muscular frame gleaming in the waning light.

There was a long moment's hesitation before he reached out his hand in a tentative gesture and slowly removed the soap from her hand.

A nagging unrest had begun in the back of Devon's mind as time had stretched on. Morgana had not yet returned from her bath. He was familiar with the area and was certain she had walked downstream to the point where the narrow stream formed a natural pool. Unable to bear his growing concern, he had followed Morgana's course along the stream, a fierce tension gripping his vitals when he had reached the bank. Morgana was nowhere in sight! Abruptly, her slender form burst through the surface of the placid pool, water streaming from the long, curling spirals that hung down her slender back. Sliding her arms under the heavy mass, she lifted it from the flawless skin on which it rested, holding it aloft for long moments, her sheer perfection of form outlined against the approaching darkness. She was a water nymph, graceful, elusive, beckoning to him with a silent allure he could not ignore. Mesmerized by the enchanted scene, Devon slowly slipped off his clothes and walked silently into the cold water. His mind not even registering its coolness, he came closer to the image that drew him relentlessly.

Her heart pounding loudly in her breast, Morgana hesitated for long moments, Devon's strangely intent gaze holding her motionless. She allowed him to take the soap from her hand. His eyes moved across her face as he came to stand intimately close to her. His first gentle touch against her neck sent a wave of warmth sweeping through her veins, the slow, sensuous caress of lather against the slender column of her throat starting a quaking deep inside. Gradually, in ever widening circles, the soothing touch of Devon's hands moved across her shoulders, the slope of her chest, the graceful arms that trembled as he pressed his meticulous attentions. Slowly, leisurely, he circled the globes of her breasts, the erect, waiting crests, moving gradually across the flat stomach to the curve of her slender hips. With persistent attentiveness he soaped the dark triangle of curls between her thighs, his hands moving efficiently, effectively beneath to complete his tender ablutions. Taking her gently by the shoulders, he turned her around. Gathering the dark spirals that gleamed against her back in his hand, he moved the refreshing lather across her shoulder blades, down the length of her spine, massaging the small of her back gently before including the firm, rounded buttocks in his ardent attentions. Turning her back toward him once again, he crouched before her. Encompassing her slender thigh in the width of his palms, he drew the foaming lather down the length of her leg, meticulous in his attentions as he moved to include the other slender length in his single-minded vigilance.

Still crouched before her at the conclusion of his loving service, Devon lifted his eyes to meet Morgana's bemused gaze. Reaching out, he enclosed her rounded buttocks in his palms, drawing her closer. She was trembling, the quaking of her slender body stirring a new wave of tenderness within him. With aching gentleness, he kissed the damp chestnut curls nestled between her thighs; nuzzled the soft nest; moved his lips in a searing path from one crease of her thigh to the other. Urging her body closer with the gentle pressure of his palms, he exposed the tender slit beneath. A soft smile flashing across his mouth, he lowered his head to cover the waiting lips with his own. His tongue slipping between the aching crevice, he caressed the bud of her desire, his mind registering Morgana's low gasp at his first, searing penetration.

Releasing her abruptly, he stood to his full height. Morgana's eyes followed his movement, a new light in their depths as she reached for the remaining soap he held. Her hands were trembling badly as she reached up to smooth the lather across the breadth of his shoulders, the first touch almost destroying her resolve to give him the same sensual luxury he had just given her. The blue eyes regarding her intently were half-lidded, expectant. His heart was throbbing wildly, echoing under the hand she moved up the broad column of his throat. Lowering her mouth to his chest, she touched the small male nipples with her tongue, pausing to press a stirring kiss on each before stepping back to draw an ever widening circle of lather across his chest. Luxuriating in the sensation of running her hands slowly, caressingly, over the lightly furred surface, she did not acknowledge the deep, responsive shuddering that began in Devon's strong frame.

Her meticulous ministrations continued, following the dark hair that trailed in a steady, narrowing path past his navel to the strong, erect shaft of his manhood. Gently, tenderly, she encompassed it in her attentions, abandoning it at last to move on across the line of his trim male hips.

Trembling visibly, Devon abruptly halted her own quaking progress. Taking her small hand in his, he turned, urging her into a deeper portion of the pool where the cool water could lift the last remnants of soap from their bodies. Turning again to face her, he cupped her sober face in his palms. A low, hoarse, unintelligible whisper escaped his lips as he lowered his mouth slowly to cover hers. At the first touch of her lips, the last remaining remnant of his control appeared to slip away. Tearing his mouth from hers, he bent to scoop Morgana into his arms. In a swift movement, he turned and walked rapidly toward the bank.

Floating in a plane of soaring emotions, Morgana was hardly aware of the quick passage of branches above her head in the darkening twilight, her mind registering only vaguely that they had reentered the area of their campsite. She felt the familiar scratch of the rough blanket beneath her back; the heart-stopping sensation of Devon's lean, hard body abruptly stretched full length upon hers. His eyes burned into hers as he cupped her face with his hands; his voice was a throbbing groan that tore at her heart.

"I have an insatiable thirst for you, Morgana. Help me . . . help me to quench my thirst."

The mouth that covered hers was seeking, demanding. Lovingly, ardently, Devon drank from the sweet moistness opened to him, his tongue darting and plunging, tasting and feeling, coaxing Morgana to greater depths of the emotion that already soared within her. Tearing his mouth from hers, Devon trailed his lips along the line of her chin, down the column of her throat, his tongue finding the fine scar that still remained on its smooth surface and caressing it boldly. She was sweet, oh so sweet to the taste, and he kissed the length of her neck deeply, passionately, drawing her flesh into his mouth in his relentless quest. He wanted her . . . he needed her . . . his passion so great that the need to consume her flushed his being. Running his tongue along the line of her shoulder, he licked the beads of water from her skin, the sensation of the velvet softness whetting his desire for more. Gripping her shoulders tightly, he held her fast, his mouth sliding slowly, lovingly over her flesh.

"Morgana, God, Morgana, you taste so good. I can't get enough of you." His trembling unabating, Devon ran his tongue slowly, patiently over the rise of her breast, down the valley between, picking up the drops of moisture that re-

317

mained as he covered each swollen crest with his mouth. But he could not be sated. His need deep, profound, he moved quickly to the shining triangle of curls he had kissed before. He pressed warm, heated kisses against the damp ringlets, his passion escalating to a new high at Morgana's soft protest.

"This is what I need, Morgana. I need to taste you . . . to know you completely. I need to absorb you, consume you. Nothin' else will satisfy me, darlin'. Nothin' else will satisfy either one of us."

A new jubilation filling his being, Devon saw the slender thighs relax to allow his loving advance. Spreading a warm shower of kisses on the soft nest, he pressed more deeply, his tongue moving to touch again the tender bud he had tasted only briefly before. A supreme joy transfusing his senses, he fondled and caressed Morgana's passion to life, dipping and plunging, drawing deeply, hungry for the sweet nectar she still withheld. Slowly, rapturously, he stroked the tender slit, his attentions becoming more intense, his senses more alert, as a deep, spontaneous shudder wracked her frame. With tender relentlessness, he assailed the source of Morgana's soaring ecstasy, a reciprocal emotion gaining control of his own senses as the shudders escalated, became more intense, finally erupting into violent, convulsive spasms that took her wildly, undeniably into the sphere of total reward he had so ardently sought. Deeply, fully, he drew from her loving homage, tasting, luxuriating, indulging until the last tremor had passed her slender frame.

Sliding himself up full length upon her once again, he gazed for long moments into her face. Her eyes closed, her face flushed, her breathing was still ragged, her soft lips parted as she swallowed tightly against the slowly abating emotion that had held her so inexorably within its power. A deep tenderness flushing his being, he gently brushed the damp tendrils from her forehead, stroked the velvet cheek, waiting until he could no longer withstand his own aching desire before moving to possess her fully. Morgana's sweet body closed around him, her sharp intake of breath echoing in his mind as he began a slow, stroking movement deep within her. The rapture building inside him soared wildly at the sound of Morgana's shaken voice.

"Now, Devon . . . I need you now. Take me with you, darling . . . take me with you!"

Pausing only a moment to indulge himself in the passion reflected in Morgana's glowing eyes, Devon whispered in a voice hoarse with emotion, "Sweet Morgana . . . my Morgana . . ."

In one last thrust they were over the edge, falling, spiraling, lost in the whirling vortex of searing, exploding emotions that left them shaken, exhausted, complete in each other's loving arms.

Darkness had fallen when they came out of the pool for the second time. Laughing as Devon wrapped a single blanket around them both, Morgana leaned against his side, reveling in the feeling of his strong arm wound tightly around her waist, holding her close as they returned to camp.

Suddenly coming to a halt, Devon sniffed suspiciously, pulling himself to attention the second before he jerked himself free of the blanket and dashed into their campsite.

Stumbling over the blanket she still held around her, Morgana arrived in time to see Devon crouched beside the fire, a low groan emanating from his throat as he jerked the blackened fowl from the heat. The glance he returned to her was amused. The small curving of his lips worked its usual transformation, lightening the severe planes of his face as he shrugged lightly.

"Well, one side of the bird is eatable, darlin'. I guess we'll just have a smaller share, that's all."

Shaking her head, Morgana said lightly, "It's a good thing we still have some dried beef left. For some reason, I'm very hungry tonight!"

Walking to the grassy spot a few feet away where they had lain before, Morgana sat abruptly, making certain to keep the blanket wrapped loosely around her. Reaching for Devon's brush, she began stroking the snarls from her hair. So intent was she on her purpose that she did not pay an inordinate amount of attention as Devon approached and set a plate nearby. Lowering himself to the ground beside her,

Devon abruptly pushed Morgana backward, cupping her head in his broad palm to absorb the force of contact with the grassy ground beneath her back.

"Devon . . . what . . . ?"

Morgana's heart was thumping wildly as Devon abruptly unwrapped the blanket that shielded her. Sliding the long length of his body atop hers, he whispered lightly against her lips, "You didn't really think you'd get away that easily, did you?"

"Get away?" A spark of laughter lighting her eyes, Morgana responded to his suddenly playful mood. "Did I look like I was trying to get away, Devon?"

A flicker of a frown moved swiftly across Devon's face and he muttered inaudibly. At her responsive frown, he smiled abruptly, "Well, since I did all the work in shooting and cooking this bird, I think you should pay for your share."

Realizing he had led her to the point where he waited for her to ask the obvious, Morgana could not suppress a responsive smile. "And how should I do that, Devon? I have no money."

"Like this, darlin'." Reaching over, he took a piece of the fragrant bird from the metal plate on which it rested and tore off a bite-sized piece. Lowering his head until his lips grazed hers, he said softly, "Now, just how much is this bite worth to you? This much . . . ?" Devon covered her mouth for a short kiss, only to pull away again and continue, "Or this much?" Lowering his mouth to hers again, Devon kissed her longer, more deeply, his tongue stroking hers warmly before he drew away once again.

Her eyes looking into his, Morgana would not admit to the warmth slowly permeating her veins, the slow languor instigated by Devon's hard strength pressed intimately close. With an attempt at playfulness, she responded despite the revealing tremor in her voice, "Well, it's just a small piece, Devon. I don't think it's worth more than this." Turning his face to the side, she kissed him lightly on the cheek.

A low snort escaping his lips, Devon mumbled under his breath, the amused light growing in his eyes negating his words. "You're damned stingy, Morgana . . . but it is a

320

small piece, I agree.'' Popping the meat into her mouth, Devon popped a similar piece into his own, waiting until she had chewed and swallowed before taking another piece and holding it up for her inspection. ''What about this one?''

Her appetite whetted by the delicious morsel she had just eaten, Morgana moaned, ''Devon, am I going to have to 'pay' for every bite I take? I'm starving.'' The low rumble of her stomach in confirmation widened Devon's smile.

''Yes, I think so. Now, how about it? How much will you give for this piece?''

Her brow knitting in frustration, Morgana hesitated a moment before responding with a question of her own. ''Will you take all your payment in one sum, Devon?''

His brow raised in surprise, Devon shook his head. ''I'm not quite certain what you mean, darlin'.''

''I mean this, Devon.''

Slowly drawing his face down to hers, Morgana touched her mouth lightly to Devon's, her arms gradually sliding around his neck in a kiss that deepened erotically. Opening her mouth, she invited the invasion of his tongue, only to steal his play by slipping hers between his teeth for a search of her own. Languidly, lovingly, she tasted him, her tongue teasing him, stroking him, dipping to know the full depth of pleasure awaiting her. Within moments, she was lost in the play of fencing tongues, caressing hands and heated bodies that cried for release. Gasping as Devon's manhood slid abruptly within her, Morgana pulled her mouth from his, her eyes searching his face as he stared down into her eyes. Tears flooded the great glowing orbs.

''What is it, Morgana? Did I hurt you?''

Shaking her head in silence until the thickness in her throat allowed speech, Morgana began falteringly, ''No, it's just . . . I don't understand, Devon. I didn't intend this . . . I just wanted to play your game.''

His concern gone, Devon lowered his head to press light, fleeting kisses against her cheek and eyes, trailing tantalizingly to the corner of her mouth. ''And you play it well, darlin'.''

Shaking her head furiously, she insisted, ''But I only

wanted to kiss you."

Running his tongue lightly over the surface of her lips, Devon felt a need build inside him as he responded, "But it felt so good didn't it, darlin' . . . my hands against your body . . . your tongue deep inside my mouth . . . my hardness growin' against you . . . tauntin' you. You wanted to feel me inside you again, didn't you . . . to feel me stroke away the ache beginnin' to grow there? You wanted me again, and you want me now, don't you darlin'?"

"Devon, I swear, I didn't mean to . . ."

Beginning a slow, sinuous rhythm deep inside her, Devon's voice began to show the marks of his passion.

"You want me, don't you, Morgana . . ." His voice was low, persistent, slowed by the strength of the strokes he plunged deeply again and again.

"Oh, Devon." The searing emotion was coming to life again, its glory blooming, bright and mind-consuming. She could not think past the desire that drove her to clasp him tight against her, to lift her legs to encircle his waist, to hold him tight within as he met each searing penetration, joyfully, willingly. It was beautiful . . . magnificent . . . and in her moment of soaring glory, Morgana wished it would never stop . . . never, never come to an end.

"Devon . . ." Morgana's voice was a low gasp, ". . . I wish . . ."

A sudden, searing explosion deep inside cut off Morgana's words as the kaleidoscope of colors bursting in her brain signaled the climax of the brief, rapturous journey they had unexpectedly shared.

His breathing returned to normal, Devon lifted his head from the silken cloud of Morgana's hair only to see that Morgana avoided his gaze as tears streamed freely from the corners of her eyes.

"What's wrong, darlin'?"

Morgana shook her head. Finally able to speak, she continued in a pained voice, "It's just that . . . I don't know what's wrong with me . . . why I act this way . . ."

Filled with tenderness at her unexpected, stricken words, Devon brushed the tears from her face and swallowed against the thickness in his own throat. This new Morgana . . . this small, helpless girl, was difficult to resist . . . difficult to treat with the harshness that had allowed him to keep his sanity during these long, painful weeks.

"I don't know what's wrong with you, darlin', but whatever it is, I'm stricken by the same malady. Strange, isn't it, darlin'? The only time we can agree . . . the only time we can get along with each other is when we're makin' love. And it doesn't last, does it? The glow fades when the real world comes buttin' in to meet us." Withdrawing himself from her abruptly, Devon flipped over to his back to lie silently for a few long moments, his arm across his eyes. There was a new, harder tone to his voice when he spoke again. "So, let's take this time and accept it, darlin'. We'll be reachin' my pa's and my homestead within a day or so, and you'll be hatin' me again just like you did before."

Lowering her eyes so that Devon could not see the new tears that welled there, Morgana made no response. She knew what he said was true. When the real world intruded, Devon shrugged her aside for his commitments and ambitions for Texas. Tomorrow, in the light of day, the antagonism between them would return, and when they reached his home, he would await his opportunity to be rid of her . . . to send her away. He would return to the "good Texas women," against whom she could not hold her own.

Turning on his side toward her, Devon supported himself on his elbow, to assess her expression. Lowering his head briefly, he pressed a light kiss against her trembling lips. Reaching toward the plate, he picked up the cool fowl that still had an appetizing scent. Moving it back and forth in front of her nose, he could not suppress a smile as Morgana's eyes jerked open and upward toward the luscious morsel.

"Now, what was your original question, darlin'? Let me see . . . yes . . . You wanted to know if I would take all my payment for this meal in one lump sum." Noting the flush that covered Morgana's face, Devon proceeded despite her obvious embarrassment. "Open your mouth, darlin'. You earned this, and you earned the service that goes with it."

Waiting until she had chewed the first portion and swallowed it, Devon took another piece and slid it between her lips. His smile was tender as she chewed obediently, without comment. The true question remained unanswered.

Morgana was feeling supremely unsettled. Two days had passed since that night at the pool. Devon had mentioned that they would be coming to his homestead within a day or so, but since then had said nothing else to relieve her feelings of anxiety. With a small shrug of her shoulders, she conceded that he had said little at all to her since that night. And she had been right. The intimacy they had shared had vanished with the light of day. So startled had she been by his abrupt return to his former attitude that she would truly have considered that it had all been a wild dream, if it were not for the marks of his loving left on her body . . . the bruises made by his passionate kisses as he had traveled her flesh intimately. His eyes flicking toward her as she dressed had touched on the small disturbing circles that marked her skin, the tightening of his expression the only indication that he had noticed their existence.

But he had noted them well, his eyes touching her assessingly when she had undressed that night. And he had not made love to her again. He had lain down beside her and fallen immediately to sleep. For all intents and purposes that lovely night by the pool and all its tenderness had not truly transpired.

But his silence was beginning to fray her nerves. With each bend they turned, she expected to come upon a house or a sign . . . something that would indicate they would soon be at the end of their journey. Sending a nervous glance in Devon's direction, Morgana swore tightly under her breath. Damn him! He had no right to keep her in ignorance this way! Didn't he realize how desperately she needed something to hold on to? Or did he really care . . . ?

Deep-felt anger pushing her beyond the boundaries of restraint, Morgana blurted unexpectedly, "When will we get there, Devon?"

Turning slowly in her direction, his expression unrevealing, Devon remained silent as his horse continued steadily forward.

"I said, when will we get there, Devon? That night at the pool," cursing herself for reminding him of the night when she had displayed her vulnerability so openly, Morgana continued in a rush, "you said then that we'd be at your homestead within a day or so. Well, almost two days have passed, and we're still traveling! Is it too much to ask . . . that you tell me when this damned journey will be over?"

Her face flushed with frustration, Morgana waited as Devon allowed his glance to flick over her dismissively before returning his attention to the road in front of them. She was about to shriek his name, to demand an answer, when he mumbled casually, "We should be there within an hour. As a matter of fact, we're already on Circle H land."

Startled by his response, Morgana felt a slow trembling begin inside her. As difficult as the journey had been, she felt a sudden contrary desire for it to continue so that she might not be forced to meet the uncertainty she feared. What would he say to people at his homestead? What would they think? Would they despise her as Devon did . . . ostracize her . . . keep her prisoner, until she could finally be released? Would they, indeed, release her? The chilling coldness in Devon's gaze returned again to haunt her. He had reverted to that chilling stranger again . . . the man she did not know . . . the man she feared. But her fear of the unknown was far more terrifying than her fear of a confrontation with Devon. Startled at the hoarseness of her own voice, Morgana demanded, "What do you intend to do with me when we get there?" As he turned back toward her, his response was slow and hard. "What do you expect, Morgana? I'll tell them the truth, of course."

"The truth! What truth? The truth as *you* see it?"

His eyes narrowing with an anger he obviously suppressed, Devon clamped his teeth tightly shut and turned his gaze back to the trail in front of them.

"I asked you a question, Devon!" Angered beyond caution, Morgana hissed. "Damn you! It is one thing to face your black accusations in private, but I will not allow you to repeat them in public . . . make everyone believe that Antonio and I . . . to state them as if they are fact!''

His dark stare flicked back to her face, to hold her fast in its glare. "You have no choice, Morgana. We're on Circle H land now . . . my land. I told you at the outset of this journey the exact plan I intended to follow . . . the conditions that would allow you to return to Mexico City, and nothin' . . . nothin' has occurred in the course of this journey to cause me to change my original plan.''

The pain caused by Devon's words was deep. Raising her chin in defense against the tightness that choked her throat, Morgana jerked her eyes back to the trail in front of her. So it was over . . . the closeness they had inadvertently shared, the long nights when he . . . Swallowing tightly, Morgana pulled herself rigidly erect in a desperate attempt to control the pain that swept her. This nightmare would not last much longer. Antonio was a man of his word. He would set Colonel Austin free, and she would return to Mexico City. And she would keep silent about Devon's part in her abduction . . . tell Tío Manuel that she had managed to escape from the bandits and obtain help in returning to the capital. She would never speak of the days she had spent with Devon . . . never mention his name. She would never speak or think of him again. . . .

The humid heat of afternoon was taking its toll. Swaying wearily with the gait of the horse that plodded steadily onward, Morgana glanced carelessly at the cloudless horizon. If it were not for the steady, unabating heat, she would have had to say the weather was ideal for a pleasant afternoon ride. A sudden urge to giggle struck her . . . pleasant afternoon ride . . . Was she going out of her mind? Or was it just that the circumstances were so nerve-racking that she was near hysteria? Lifting the straw sombrero from her head, Morgana pushed back the wisps that had adhered to her forehead with perspiration, noting that Devon had not wasted even a short glance in her direction. She had no doubt that, if she wished, she could abandon the hat as well as the *rebozo* that covered her shoulders. The sun could dry her up to a prune and he wouldn't make even the shortest comment! He was close to home now . . . soon she would be off his hands. Glancing down at herself, Morgana grimaced at the perspiration stain that marked the front of her blouse between her breasts. She had no doubt that the back of blouse under her rebozo also adhered to her skin with a similar stain. She was a thoroughly disreputable sight. She indeed looked the part of the hopeless wanton Devon would describe to his men. But she must make herself look past this day . . . keep her mind on the future, when she would return home . . . to Tía Isabella, Tío Manuel and Aggie. . . . She must keep her mind from the humiliation Devon was soon to cause her.

But what was that? Her heart leaping in her breast, Morgana spotted a structure on the horizon around which several smaller structures were clustered. She strained her eyes, squinting against the glare. Yes, there was activity around the structures. Snapping her head to the side, she waited for some word from Devon, but none was forthcoming. Sitting as erect in the saddle as if the day had just begun, he continued looking steadily forward, ignoring her presence as if she did not exist.

Unable to bear the anxiety building inside her, Morgana demanded with a boldness born of her frustrated anger, "What are those buildings in the distance, Devon?"

Devon did not bother to turn his head in her direction. "It's the Circle H."

Bastard! Nervous tears choking her throat, Morgana fought to still the trembling that had suddenly beset her limbs. Whatever was in store for her, she had determined she would not let Devon have the satisfaction of knowing her true feelings. Glancing down at herself once again, Morgana felt a helplessness overwhelm her. Looking at her now, who would ever believe that only a month before she had worn the best clothes, traveled in the most affluent society in Mexico City? She looked like a common woman of the streets! Abruptly pulling off her sombrero, Morgana hung it on the saddle. How she longed for a few moments to stop and refresh herself . . . to brush the damp hair from her forehead and neck, to wash the dust of the trail from her skin, but she was certain Devon would not agree to any such foolishness. Slipping off her *rebozo,* she allowed it to fall to the saddle behind her. Perhaps the sun would dry the marks from her blouse . . . the hot breeze lift the hair from her perspired head. Her skirt was worn and wrinkled, and the lower part of her legs, exposed as she sat astride the horse, had browned from exposure to the sun. Her feet were bare in the coarse sandals. Yes, she did indeed look like a common woman of the streets, and although Devon had treated her as carelessly, she would not allow him to think he had defeated her. She would go back to the capital and resume her life, and never give him another thought. She had only to get through the time in between, however long that would be.

"Devon! Damn it, boy, I was beginnin' to think you'd never get home!"

The tall, slender, grey-haired man warmly grasped Devon's outstretched hand, pulling him into a tight bear hug that Devon returned just as spontaneously. Sitting erect in the saddle, her expression almost as stiff as her posture, Morgana watched silently. Able only to see the tightly controlled emotion reflected on the face so strikingly similar to Devon's, Morgana felt an odd thickness grow in her throat. She had not seen the look of loving pride in a man's eyes since he had made her debut into New York society. The similarity between Devon's father and her own abruptly grew in her mind. The manner in which he watched the warm welcomes being extended by the other men crowding around his son, his own subconscious chuckles to remarks accompanied by the hearty backslaps of a few of the more boisterous of the group, his pleasure at the worshipful awe in the eyes of the small black children crowding at the feet of their parents as they waited their turn to welcome him—these were the looks of the proud parent for his child, looks that meant love and warmth . . . looks she would never see shining in her direction again. Abruptly her father's image came before her eyes, tightening the lump of emotion wedged so precariously in her throat.

The approach to the homestead had been unhurried. Maintaining his pace, Devon had been silent as they had moved along a narrow trail through wild grassland just beginning to yellow from the sun. The terrain was flat, a small interruption to the left of the horizon the only rise in a landscape stretched out as far as the eye could see. Maintaining her silence, Morgana forced her gaze from the welcome that still continued. Anxious to allow her mind respite from the emotions assailing her, she moved her glance quickly over the house from which the grey-haired man had emerged. A low, sprawling structure, it had obviously been built in sections, with rooms added on as time and resources permitted. It was surprisingly large and graceful, not at all the picture she had formed in her mind of a rough homestead in the Texas colony. The houses set at a small distance from the main house obviously served as living quarters for the few men who had come streaming out of the door at the sound of Devon's voice. Set farther back was a structure that appeared to be the slaves' quarters. And there was no doubt in her mind that these black people were slaves. It showed in their deferential attitude toward Devon, although they obviously adored him. Slavery . . . another point of dispute between the Mexicans and their Anglo counterparts. Slavery had been abolished in Mexico, and although the American colonists had been allowed to bring their slaves with them, all their children born on Texan soil were automatically free. Antonio had spoken to her often of the Anglo-Texans' approval of the slavery he hated. She had agreed with him then, as she did now.

A woman's piercing shriek tore Morgana from her silent thoughts, jerking her eyes toward the sight of a large, grey-haired black woman, her wide skirts flapping against the old legs that moved as quickly as they could carry her. The knot in her stomach tightening, Morgana saw a grin of pure delight stretch across Devon's face as he held out his arms to the approaching woman.

"Come here, Mellie, you old darlin'!" Enclosing her tightly in his embrace, Devon squeezed her fiercely until her

329

loud, merry protest drew him back to face her broad smile.

"You watch you don't break old Mellie's bones! She needs 'em all in workin' condition if she's gonna make her Master Devon his favorite dessert tonight!"

"And what would that be, Mellie?"

"That be peach cobbler!" Winking her eye boldly, Mellie declared loudly, "And Mellie done stored a whole bunch of peaches away for the day Master Devon come home. And this be the day . . . yes sir! This be the day!"

Abruptly, Morgana realized all eyes were no longer riveted on Devon's tall, rangy frame as Mellie rambled on in welcome. Slowly, pair by pair, the eyes drifted in her direction, tightening the knot of anxiety present in her stomach since the homestead had come into view. Devon had not referred to her in any way since their arrival, and the first curiosity had begun.

"Ma'am, it would be my pleasure to help you down from your horse."

So intent had Morgana been in her observance of Devon that she had not noticed the approach of the tall, silver-haired man who could be none other than Devon's father. Her eyes snapping in his direction, Morgana was instantly caught by the kindness in the pale eyes so similar to Devon's. The face was the same, but the hard, sharp features were softened by the years . . . or was it perhaps the warmth of the smile he extended so graciously? His skin was sun-darkened and lined by years. Deep grooves ran from midcheek to the corners of his mouth, almost touching the heavy network of lines that fanned out from the corners of his eyes. A thick grey mustache covered his upper lip, matching the full shock of grey hair that was cut roughly at the back of his neck. Dressed in a homespun cotton shirt and coarse breeches, his attire was similar to Devon's, his body still surprisingly lean and agile. He was the portrait of an older, more mellowed Devon . . . a Devon she would never see.

Startled at the strength in the hands that took her by the waist and lifted her down, Morgana smiled up into the weathered face, a true warmth stirring within her.

"Thank you for your kindness, sir." Certain her simple

330

words of gratitude were decidedly inadequate, Morgana hesitated, noting his puzzled expression. Decidedly at a loss, Morgana sought out Devon's glance, her heart jumping wildly as it came into contact with his angry expression.

Still laughing at Mellie's squeals of laughter, Devon began to feel the first sense of disquiet. Despite Mellie's happy banter, he had become conscious of the gradual drifting of the gazes of the men around him to a point behind his back. There was no doubt in his mind where they stared so silently. Morgana. What man in his right mind would *not* stare at the raw, natural beauty of the woman who waited silently behind him. And she had made certain she would impress the men, even with the minimal resources at her command. But Morgana needed little artifice to draw a man's eye. The simple removal of the awkward sombrero that had shielded her fair skin from the sun, the shedding of the coarse *rebozo* that had spared her smooth shoulders from the same fate, had provided any observer opportunity to view her gleaming chestnut hair flowing in a tumble of rioting curls down her slender back, her smooth, flawless skin tinted a pale gold, her large, sober, eyes fringed with lengths of dark lashes that were startling . . . almost unbelievable, the magnificent contours of her cheeks . . . still a marvel to his eye, the straight, perfect length of her slender nose . . . the perfect cameo, and her mouth . . . God, her mouth. What man could look at her without wanting to taste it . . . own it . . . know it intimately? Not even the worn, faded clothes she wore could detract from her supreme beauty. Gently curving shoulders, slender, graceful arms, perfectly formed breasts, narrow waist, well-turned hips, long, slender legs . . . Even her feet were appealing, their daintiness maximized by comparison with the coarse, awkward sandals she wore. Yes, he had no doubt that the men had assessed it all.

Turning, Devon was startled to see his father standing beside Morgana's horse. But most startling of all was the look on Morgana's face. A startling softness replacing the ice in her glance with which she had looked at him, she smiled softly into his father's lined countenance. There had never been that softness in her eyes for him . . . the quality of com-

331

plete openness and acceptance. Even when he had loved her so completely . . . A slow anger beginning to burn inside him, Devon saw his father reach up to enclose Morgana's small waist in his hands. He lifted her down easily, but Devon had no eyes for his father. Instead, he watched with burning jealousy as Morgana's gaze rose to meet the pale eyes, as she whispered a short smiling phrase, her lovely face flushing warmly. Unaware that his father had turned in his direction, Devon saw only Morgana's glance as it turned to him, catching and holding his fury.

With several strides, Devon was at their side. Directing a heated look into the sienna eyes raised to his, he paused only a moment before turning toward the rotund woman, who eyed them curiously.

"Mellie, this is Miss Morgana Pierce. Take her inside and show her the spare bedroom. Tell Josh to bring the tub so she can clean up."

Ignoring the confusion in the woman's glance as she hastened forward to follow his instructions, he turned back to Morgana, aware of the intense perusal of the group that moved slowly toward them. "Go inside with Mellie, and remember where you are and how foolish it would be to attempt to get away. I'll be in later to . . ."

"Devon, what's going on here?" His father's deep voice reflected his disapproval of the abrupt manner with which his son treated Morgana.

Turning back and regarding his father's disturbed expression, Devon muttered quietly, "It's a long story, Sam. Right now I want to get Morgana into the house. We can discuss it later . . . privately."

"I would like to be present when you talk to your father. I want to tell him the truth about . . ."

"You'll do exactly what I tell you to do, Morgana! Now go inside with Mellie!"

"But I want . . ."

Abruptly, Devon's hand clamped closed on her arm. Muttering an excuse to his father through tight lips, he turned her forcefully toward the house, his step firm as he ushered her up the front steps.

"Devon, you're hurting me!" Stumbling awkwardly as they reached the top step, Morgana looked up into Devon's tight expression.

Allowing her just a moment to regain her step, Devon moved her inside the front door. Refusing to allow her a second to observe the large, sparsely furnished living room through which they moved, Devon dragged her down a broad hallway to the last of a line of several doors. Jerking it open, he pushed her inside, and, following, closed the door with quiet force behind him.

"This is the guest room, Morgana, and this is the room where you'll be sleepin' while you're here. You'll be sleepin' here, and *nowhere* else!"

Not quite certain what she had done to merit such violence from Devon, Morgana shook her head bewilderedly, her lips separating in astonishment as Devon continued heatedly, "And I want you to know that your little games will not work here!"

"Little games? I don't know what . . ."

"Don't play the innocent with me, Morgana. We've come past that point in our relationship. I saw the look you gave Sam, and I saw the way he looked at you in return."

"Sam . . . your father? What are you talking about?"

"My father is an old man. He loved my mother, and he misses her. It didn't take you long to see that vulnerability . . . to capitalize on it, but if you think you can turn the situation to suit your advantage, you're mistaken, darlin'."

A flash of rage inundating her senses, Morgana hissed sharply, "Don't call me darlin', Devon! I'm sick of hearing you make the endearment sound like a curse!"

"You'd rather hear my father call you darlin', is that it, *darlin'*?" Abruptly gripping her shoulders to drag her so close that his lips brushed hers as he spoke, he whispered venomously, "Let me tell you right now, you're wastin' your time, darlin'. Sam's not about to chuck a lifetime of work to please you! While you're here, you'll be treated like a guest, as long as your conduct merits that treatment. You will be confined to the house and the immediate area around it. You will *not* attempt to go riding without someone in attendance.

You can rest assured every man and woman on this homestead will know what you're doin' here, and the rules I've set up for you until you leave. You can believe me when I say you'll not go unwatched, so you can abandon any plans you may have formulated in that devious mind of yours for escape. Even if you should be able to get a few miles away, we'll find you, and you can bet no one will help you get back to your lover. He's not a very popular man around here, and neither is your uncle! So," he growled in a lower tone, "if you know what's good for you, you'll behave yourself and just wait your time out!"

Releasing her abruptly at a step in the corridor, Devon turned toward Mellie's plump figure as it came through the doorway. "Miss Morgana is tired and would like to bathe and rest for a while, Mellie. She has a lot to think about."

Turning toward the black eyes that moved to her face, Morgana avoided their unspoken question. "I find that I'm quite tired, Mellie. I would like to rest for a little while." Moving toward the broad bed that dominated the center of the room, Morgana lay down, her troubled mind barely registering the closing of the door as Mellie and Devon left the room. Yes, she had a lot to think about . . . a lot, indeed. . . .

His eyes flashing with rage, Santa Anna pounded his fist on the desk in front of him. "Fools! I have an army of fools!"

Getting abruptly to his feet, he took a few steps forward, only to begin a steady pacing in front of his desk. Stopping for a moment, he ran an anxious hand through his dark hair and automatically pulled himself erect. His early training unconsciously coming forward, he straightened his back and squared his shoulders. Yes, he had always been proud of his impressive physique and size. In a country of small men, he stood a head over most, his shoulders broad and his chest full. He was careful to keep himself physically fit and trim. He knew he wore his uniform well, that his dark good looks

334

were extremely impressive on the white stallion he rode. It was to that impressive appearance he felt he owed a part of his great success as a statesman in his country, as well as a portion of his success with women. He was well accustomed to the appreciative glances he received from women, but for the last month he had been almost oblivious to those assessing glances. Things had not been going well for him personally . . . not well at all. A barely controlled fury had raged his senses, giving him no respite since the day of Morgana's abduction. Over a month had passed, and she still had not been returned to her home. The ransom had been paid, another point of irritation . . . the bandits had made fools of Manuel and himself by taking the money without returning Morgana. How much longer could he hold off Doña Isabella's tightly controlled inquiries? The woman was at the point of collapse, and he felt true remorse. Manuel's wife was a good woman, true to her husband and unswerving in her loyalty to him. It was a matter of pride that he find Morgana and have her returned to her home, and it was that same pride that caused him the most frustration. Ah, but if he were to be entirely truthful, his frustration was due in part to an entirely different matter. Lovely Morgana . . . he had such plans for her. She was such an excellent companion and so naturally and unconsciously provocative. He could sense the innate sensuality in her, which he longed to taste. He still ached to take her . . . so much so that he had been unable to find an interest in any of the other women available to him in the capital. If the *banditos* had touched her . . . violated her in any way . . . well, he had already decided they would die, but he would make sure they cried out for death many times before they did if they had touched his lovely Morgana. But how had those ignorant, untutored men managed to evade his trained soldiers? How had they managed to get her away? How did they manage to continue to hide her in a country where his supporters were everywhere? Were it not for the gleaming chestnut lock of hair that had accompanied the ransom note, he might indeed consider that it had been a fake. But there was no mistaking Morgana's hair . . . chestnut silk, dark and gleaming with fiery highlights that caught the sun. Experiencing anew the stirring in his groin that accompanied prolonged thoughts of Morgana, Santa Anna groaned in frustration. Yes, he *would* have Morgana Pierce back in his arms again, and this time he would not relent in the face of her feigned objections. He *would* have her, and he would keep her with him as long as he desired. But first . . . first he would have to get her back.

A short knock on the door interrupted his raging thoughts.

"Entra." Frowning as Manuel walked silently through the doorway, Santa Anna questioned curtly, "Well?"

"I have done as you have instructed, Antonio. I have ordered notices to be posted offering a reward for information regarding Morgana's whereabouts. Isabella has insisted that I offer you her earnest appreciation for your efforts, although I know you are very aware of the appreciation we both share."

His dark eyes moving slowly over his friend's lined face, Antonio responded abruptly, "You know it is a matter of personal concern for me also, Manuel. Morgana is a lovely young woman, and I have become quite fond of her. It is also well known that she had become a part of my personal circle of friends, and her abduction is an insult to me as well as a criminal offense. You have my word, Manuel, that for both those reasons, and for other unnamed reasons, I will find the man behind her abduction and see that he is punished."

"Sí, Antonio. *Muchas grácias."* Taking a deep breath in an obvious attempt to shake the deep sadness that had remained with him since his niece's disappearance, Manuel Escobar continued firmly, "There is another matter we must discuss this morning, Antonio . . . one which you no doubt wish to give special attention."

"And that is?"

"The matter of Colonel Austin's trial. His case will come before our supreme court tomorrow. I have spoken to Judge Caliendo about this man, and he awaits your advice as to the disposition of the case."

His brow knitting in a dark frown, Santa Anna turned his back momentarily on Manuel Escobar's military figure. He did not really care to be bothered by this matter at a time when other more personal cares disturbed his tranquillity, but he could not afford to put the matter off any longer. Experiencing another surge of irritation, he realized he would not have had to concede to Devon Howard's pressure had Morgana's abduction occurred a month sooner. But he had given his word, and Howard had returned to Texas with his personal guarantee that Austin would come to trial. For the sake of his credibility, he dared not renege. But he had promised little else than that Colonel Austin would come to trial. He had not promised the outcome of the trial, and Howard, in his certainty that Austin would be found innocent of the charges, had not pressed him for such a promise. Fool! Colonel Austin was too good a hostage for the good conduct of his people. He could not afford to lose him . . . he *would* not lose him to the threats of that arrogant Texan!

"Has Judge Caliendo studied the case, Manuel?"

"*Sí*, he has looked over the statements taken at the time of Colonel Austin's arrest and the conditions under which he was taken."

"And what are his conclusions?"

The small smile flashing across Manuel Escobar's normally sober features brought an unusual gleam to his eye. "He is, at present, undecided as to the disposition he should like to take. He has stated he will await *your* advice, since it is a matter of importance to the future of a potentially troublesome area of our country."

Santa Anna's face creased in a smile for the first time that morning. "Felipe wants to know what I should like to have done with Colonel Austin?"

"*Sí*, Antonio."

"Well, I think we should allow Felipe to maintain his integrity. Since he truly does not feel he can come to a decision in this particular area . . . perhaps he should notify the court that he will take the matter under further consideration until a later time. He may also find it politic to release Colonel Austin on bail, with strict admonitions *not* to leave the capital."

Nodding, instant understanding flashing across his expression, General Escobar smiled. "*Sí*, Antonio. It will do well to keep Colonel Austin as our friend, while still keeping him here to guarantee the conduct of his colony. I will notify his honor immediately. He will need time to prepare an adequate statement."

Watching as Manuel Escobar's erect military figure cleared the doorway, Santa Anna turned back to his desk, his frown returning. Ah, if all his problems were as easy to handle as the trusting Colonel Austin. He had to admit to a certain amount of satisfaction over his handling of affairs since he had returned to control of the country in April. Four short months before, his country had been divided into so many factions fighting to gain control that its future had been truly uncertain. There had been the clerico-army group, strong and in a strategic position, but without a leader; the recently overthrown federalists; the discredited Scottish Rite; the Escocés faction; and then the pure Santanistas, who cried his name with an almost holy fervor. He had always been able to count on the support of Santanistas, and had long since had much in sympathy with the Escocés faction. His problem had been to combine these with the clerico-army group, and he had done that by launching into an undeclared conservative program. The sweeping anti-Church laws had been declared of no effect, and special *fueros* had been returned to the clergy; the university had been reopened on the old basis, and the exiles and fugitives of the preceding year welcomed home once more.

And he had been shrewd enough to keep his own council. Even his good friend and compatriot, Manuel Escobar, did not know the full extent of his plans. Although he had instituted changes, the whole pattern had not yet been revealed. By refraining from sponsoring any one program, he had been able to keep the support of nearly all the doubtful elements while he consolidated his own power. He had even managed to stimulate the United States Minister's interest and respect, and he suspected, if he played his cards right, the future might hold great potential for him in light of the growing desire on the part of the Americans for Texas to be annexed to the United States.

If there was a political dark spot in his future right now, it

338

centered around the persistent problems in the south of his country. There, the stubborn federalist and pure-blooded Indian, Juan Alvarez, appeared to be gaining favor. But the authorities still had matters in control, and there was no immediate danger.

Pulling himself to attention, raising his hand to smooth the dark hair he had ruffled in frustration only a short time before, Santa Anna felt a flash of pride. Four short months, and he all but held the country in the palm of his hand. So why is it, interjected the nagging voice in the back of his mind, that a group of simple *banditos* has been effective in thwarting you at every turn . . . making a fool of you while they keep you from the woman who presently holds your heart?

A deep flush suffusing his face, Santa Anna walked around the side of his desk, his teeth clamped tightly shut in frustration. Yes, he would see that Morgana was returned home. He would find the criminals who had taken her and have them punished severely . . . publicly. And once they were dead, he would allow their bodies to hang in the square until they rotted, as a warning, so that a criminal act that touched him so closely would never be dared again!

"Miss Morgana . . . are you awake yet?"

A hoarsely familiar voice penetrated Morgana's confused dreams, awaking her with a start. Momentarily disoriented, she sprang to a sitting position on the soft bed on which she lay, the light-headedness that followed further confusing her mumbled response.

"Yes . . . I'm . . . I'm awake. Come in."

The slowly opening door gradually revealed the broad, smiling face of Mellie. "Master Sam sent me to find out if you're all right. You been sleepin' for three hours now. Old Mellie makin' a special supper to welcome Master Devon home, and Master Sam wants to know if you goin' to come to the table for supper."

A bit startled by the question, Morgana responded evasively, "I . . . I don't think so, Mellie. I'm afraid I'm not

339

really presentable enough for the supper table. I think it might be best if I ate in my room." It was indeed true that she had slept soundly. But the late afternoon sun beating in the window had heated the room considerably. Touching her blouse, she realized her clothes were drenched with perspiration, her hair adhering to her scalp damply. It was a wonder that she had slept at all, but the day had started early, and the anxiety she had suffered had sorely depleted her energy.

"Supper not goin' to be for another hour yet, Miss Morgana. That boy be right up here with the tub and you be fresh and clean by suppertime!"

Unable to suppress a smile at the woman's perseverance, Morgana shook her head. "I'm not really certain I'd be welcome at the table, Mellie. You must know why I'm here with Devon by now. Anyway, there's no way these clothes can be washed and dried in an hour and . . ."

"Pooh! That no problem to Master Sam! Master Sam got a whole closet full of Miz Betty's dresses. She was a mite taller than you but . . ."

"Who is Miss Betty?"

"Miz Betty was the mistress of this house. She gone to heaven three years ago, but the master keep all her clothes."

"Oh, no! I couldn't possibly use Mrs. Howard's clothes, Mellie! I'll eat something in my room if you don't mind, and when my clothes are dried tomorrow . . ."

"Master Sam not goin' to like that, Miss Morgana."

"Please Mellie." The silent plea in her eyes for an end to the discussion was effective in silencing Mellie. "But I would appreciate a bath. As a matter of fact, that sounds just lovely."

Pausing one moment more as she obviously debated arguing a little further, Mellie turned abruptly, shaking her grey head from side to side as she walked through the doorway mumbling under her breath, "Master Sam not goin' to like it. . . ."

Within minutes a bumping sound in the hallway preceded a knock on the door.

"Yes, who is it?"

"It is Josh, Miss Morgana, with the tub."

Rushing quickly to the door, Morgana pulled it open, her eyes widening in surprise as a massive young black man struggled with a large tub. "Mellie tell me to bring this tub right away. The girls goin' to bring the water." Flashing a quick look behind him, his smile widened. "They comin' already. That Mellie got 'em all hoppin'!"

Walking quickly into the room, the tall young man placed the tub carefully on the floor, stopping for a moment to watch as two young girls hurried into the room and dumped the buckets they carried into it. Pausing only a moment to bob their heads courteously, they ran from the room accompanied by Josh's short hoot of laughter.

Turning toward him with a puzzled expression, Morgana watched him shake his head as he walked toward the door. "That Mellie goin' make a party tonight, and nothin' goin' get in her way!"

Watching with amazement as the process continued, the hard-breathing young women bringing bucket after bucket of water into the room until the tub was more than half full, Morgana finally could stand no more. "Please!" Halting the girls in their steps, she said firmly, "Tell Mellie that's enough water. I'm quite content with that amount, and please tell her how much I appreciate all your work."

Bobbing courteously, the girls nodded their heads.

When the door had closed behind the last of them, Morgana struggled swiftly out of her clothes. The shimmer of the clear water was so inviting, eliminating all thoughts other than those concerning immersing in its coolness.

Stepping into the tub, Morgana was startled to find that the water was pleasantly warm, another thoughtful gesture from the warmhearted Mellie she was sure, and, making a mental note to voice her appreciation personally, she took the bar of scented soap that had been delivered with the fast moving buckets. The tub was deceptively deep, startling Morgana as the water reached to cover her breasts. In her desire to spare the hard-working girls any additional trips, she had not expected the luxury of being so pampered. Sliding down in the tub, Morgana moved herself lower until her head was completely below the surface of the water. Working her hands in her hair, she made certain it was thoroughly wet before surfacing and reaching for the soap. She rubbed it into a full lather, moving the delightful bubbles through the long, heavy mass. It was marvelous! She had not had an opportunity to bathe since that night at the pool. . . . A deep flush accompanied the return of her memory of that night, and, angry with herself for her own weakness, Morgana lowered herself again beneath the surface of the water, holding her breath while she worked the soap from her hair. Fool! Damned fool! The man uses you . . . tells you you're nothing more than a whore to him . . . an available whore . . . and you still thrill with the memory of his lovemaking. You won't be satisfied until you do feel the cut of his knife at your throat! But then it'll be too damned late to admit to yourself that you've been a fool!

Taking the washcloth from the side of the tub, Morgana lathered it heavily and applied the fragrant bubbles to her face. The water was cool against her heated skin, making her even more aware of her revealing flush. Rinsing her face clear of the soap, Morgana opened her eyes and wiped away the last drops of water that blurred her vision, her breath catching in her chest as her eyes made contact with a startling cerulean gaze.

"Devon!" Raising her hand spontaneously to her breast, Morgana felt a flush suffuse her face as Devon mumbled sarcastically, "Don't you think it's a little late for modesty, Morgana?"

"I wasn't pretending modesty!" Angry with her own embarrassment, Morgana continued tightly, "I was just startled, that's all. And I'd appreciate it if you'd leave this room."

Obviously biting back the retort that had sprung to his lips, Devon took a deep breath, his brow darkening. Turning again toward the door, he hesitated only a moment before throwing a garment on the bed.

"What's that?" When he didn't answer, Morgana repeated, "I asked you what you threw on the bed, Devon."

As he turned back slowly toward her, Devon was obviously in tenuous control of his anger. "My father asked me to bring that dress to you. He wanted me to tell you that my mother would want you to use it." Hesitating only a moment more, he continued in a low hiss, "And you'll do as he asks, do you understand? We'll be expectin' you at the supper table in half an hour, and you'll conduct yourself courteously. Everyone knows the circumstances that brought you here, and those that will allow you to leave. Your presence here is accepted as a necessary expediency, and you will be treated with the same courtesy you extend to others. But you *will* come to supper, Morgana, or I'll come here and drag you out myself!"

Blinking at the harsh thrust of his words, Morgana watched silently as Devon turned without waiting for her response and left the room. Swallowing tightly, Morgana sat motionless for long moments. A deep inner hopelessness had begun to take control of her spirits, and she struggled violently for command of the debilitating emotion. She would not allow Devon to know how deeply his coldness cut her. She could not! She would have to face everyone sooner or later. Perhaps it would be better to get it all over with at one time . . . to face them squarely . . . show them she was indeed innocent of the wickedness of which Devon accused her. Picking up the soap, Morgana began to scrub her white skin with a new vigor. She would not allow Devon to defeat her!

Arriving at the doorway as Devon emerged from Morgana's room, Mellie shot a reproachful look in his direction. Ignoring her as if she did not exist, Devon continued on down the hallway in an unbroken stride, his expression that of a man at the edge of control. Through the partially open doorway, Mellie caught Morgana's momentary despair, her esteem for the lovely young woman growing as the emotion was replaced by an expression of angry determination. Despite everything being said about her, she was convinced Miss Morgana Pierce was a lady. There had been a gentleness in her eyes when they had spoken earlier, and a flashing spirit that reminded her much of her mistress. Master Devon would have to talk long and hard to convince her Miss Morgana was indeed the woman he had claimed her to be!

343

Seemed to her that it sounded suspiciously like jealousy, all that talk about Santa Anna and Miss Morgana. But nobody ever listened to Mellie. . . .

Her frown deepening, Mellie took a deep breath and knocked on the door. Her eyes snapping toward the door, Morgana gasped hoarsely, "Who . . . who is it?"

Hearing the concern in her voice, Mellie responded quickly, "It's Mellie, Miss Morgana. I brought you a cloth to dry yourself. It sure be warm enough to let the air dry your skin, but there be a bunch of hungry men downstairs, and they not goin' to want to wait!"

Aware that Mellie had seen Devon leave the room in anger, Morgana looked away from the her assessing glance, extremely conscious of her nudity. There was no doubt that everyone at the homestead would soon be aware of their intimacy now. A deep shame permeating her senses, Morgana could not meet Mellie's eyes.

"You not to worry, Miss Morgana. Mellie's old eyes seed a lot of things since they opened in this life, and she learned long ago that some things be private, and no concern of any but the folks involved. Mellie knows a lady when she sees one, and if Master Devon see the devil where he ain't, Mellie not goin' make it change her mind nohow!"

Startled at Mellie's perceptiveness, Morgana could do no more than nod her head before Mellie urged, "C'mon, now. Hurry up and finish your bath! Old Mellie made a proper feast for the young master's homecomin' . . . his favorite dessert and all!" Hesitating a moment, she added in a mumbled tone, "Not that he deserve it, that ragin' man, but Mellie not goin' let the devil prickin' him spoil the party."

Quickly completing her bathing, Morgana rose from the tub as Mellie held up an oversized cloth and wrapped it around her. Unaware of Mellie's quick assessment of the love bruises that marked her body, she darted a quick smile in her direction as the old woman moved to the bed and took up the bright garment that lay in a crumpled heap on its surface.

"You dry yourself and brush that pretty hair, Miss Morgana, and before you know it, Mellie be back with this dress all pressed and good as new!"

"You needn't bother about that, Mellie! It's late and you've enough to do in the kitchen."

"Pooh! Them girls in the kitchen just sittin' around like they go nothin' to do anyway! Time they put their lazy hands to work!" Turning toward the door, Mellie paused just a moment more. "Besides, this house ain't seed a lady as pretty as you in a long time, and Mellie's right happy to have you here!"

True to her word, Mellie was back before Morgana had had the opportunity to brush the last tangle from her hair. Turning, Morgana saw a fresh chemise lying beside the freshened blue cotton. Flashing Mellie a grateful smile, she was about to offer her thanks when Mellie walked to her side.

"Here, you let Mellie finish that for you, Miss Morgana. My! This hair like real silk . . . shiny and smooth . . . . Any man sure feel it a privilege to touch these shiny curls. I don't reckon I ever seed anythin' like it! There!" Leaning back, her fists resting on her broad hips, Mellie said proudly, "Just perfect! Now you get yourself in that dress and Mellie tell all them hungry men that you be there right quick!"

"They've been waiting for me, Mellie?" A knot of tension tightened in Morgana's stomach.

"Not to worry, Miss Morgana. Them men downstairs, they be happy to wait for a lady as pretty as you, and I swear, they goin' be so struck, they goin' have every thought leave their heads!"

Her quick retort belying the quaking she felt deep inside, Morgana shook her head, "I hope so, Mellie. I get the feeling I'm going to need all the help I can get."

Her legs trembling beneath her, Morgana neared the end of the hallway. The sound of laughing male voices grew stronger with each step, and Morgana felt the quaking in her knees increase. Pausing to smooth a nervous hand against the hair she had swept casually behind her ears and pinned

345

there with the badly worn combs that had served her since the inception of her journey from the capital, she shook her head impatiently. Already the stubborn wisps had broken loose to curl around her hairline, and she could only surmise that the equally stubborn curls she had brushed from her hair only minutes before had begun to return. Why did she not have her mother's straight, easily manageable black hair instead of the stubborn ringlets that refused her the appearance of controlled maturity she sought? Giving her dress a last assessing glance, she smiled as she touched the delicate ice-blue cotton. It was a trifle long and tight in the bosom area, and perhaps a bit loose in the waist, but it was lovely. A modestly scooped neckline edged in narrow white lace allowed the evening breeze to circulate against her slender neck, the elbow-length sleeves edged in the same lace affording her slender arms the same opportunity. The waistline was cut into a moderate point in the center front, from which the skirt flared generously to the floor. She was actually relieved that the skirt of the gown was a trifle long, for it served to hide the coarse sandals she still wore on her feet. The soft chemise that Mellie had also provided was of a fine batiste that fairly caressed her skin, and, except for the same tightness that prevailed in the area of the bosom, forcing the fullness of her breasts to strain at the neckline of the delicate gown a bit more than she would have desired, she was indeed comfortable in the lovely garment, A quick appraisal had shown the gown to be sewn in small, perfect stitches, and since Mellie had mentioned that Mrs. Howard had made the gown herself, she had felt somehow warmed by the loving care with which it had been sewn from the first moment she had put it on.

But now, about to make her appearance, the thought of facing the accusing glances of those assembled and waiting was almost more than she could bear. Smoothing her skirt nervously, Morgana took the last few steps that brought her out of the hallway and into the large living room from which the laughing voices had originated. Fostering an expression of quiet reserve, which belied her welling anxiety, she waited until each man had turned in her direction. A low gasp from

346

somewhere within the group registered in the back of her mind as the room became completely quiet. The veil of silence that greeted her heavy on her mind, Morgana was unaware of the picture she presented as she stood framed in the entrance to the room.

The flicker of the lamp above her head reflected gloriously in the brilliant sheen of her hair. Her smooth, faultless complexion was flushed with anxiety, her heavily lashed sienna-colored eyes luminous and wide. The delicate cut of the gown she wore emphasized the youthful innocence of her extremely lovely face, the full swells of her breasts rising in the modest décolletage adding a sensual appeal that combined with her beauty in an assault on the senses that was breathtaking.

Despising his own susceptibility to Morgana's vulnerable, expectant expression, Devon was abruptly filled with contempt. With a swift glance he surveyed the revealing expressions of the other men, a peculiar tightness constricting his stomach. She had them in the palm of her hand . . . wanting her as much as he . . . Unwilling to speak, to relieve Morgana's obvious tension, Devon coldly watched her discomfort for long moments until Sam stepped forward with a polite smile.

"Morgana, I'm glad to see that you decided to join us tonight." His eyes reflected a quiet reservation not present in their earlier exchange. "Devon has told us the circumstances that prompted him to bring you here. He's assured me that such radical measures were necessary, and I must defer to his judgment. But I admit to bein' uncomfortable with the situation. I hope you will consider yourself a guest here for the duration of your visit. I assure you, you'll be treated as such. I hope we'll be able to allow you to return home soon."

Nodding her head, Morgana fought to retain an air of aloofness as Sam remarked quietly, "You look lovely in the dress, Morgana. Betty would be pleased to see you wearin' it."

His brow furrowing with discomfort, Sam turned to indicate the group of men behind him who eyed Morgana assessingly, "I'd like you to meet my hired hands, Mor-

347

gana.''

The introductions were quick and formal, and Morgana smiled stiffly as each man stepped forward in acknowledgment: Jed Markham, Sam's top hand, a tall, craggy-faced fellow with a shaggy grey mustache, not too many years younger than Sam himself; Bart Tucker, partially bald, and tall, with a florid complexion; Raoul Rafraga, short and dark, with a heavy mustache, obviously Mexican; Jim Warren, a quiet, pale shadow of a man who nodded silently, his animosity most obvious of all in the group. The final man was John Fuller, a young, curly-haired fellow, who colored unexpectedly as he stepped forward. Sandy-haired and lightly freckled, he was broad in the shoulder and chest. Of medium height, he still topped Morgana's small frame by almost a head as he flashed a pleasant, almost boyish smile. His light brown eyes held hers intently, almost searchingly, as he acknowledged the introduction in a voice that was surprisingly deep in tone.

Turning at last toward the table, Sam ushered her to the chair at his left. Shooting a quick glance around her, Morgana noticed that Devon had taken his place silently at the other end of the table opposite his father. As if sensing her glance, he looked up, his eyes holding hers coldly for the briefest second before he turned to speak to Jed Markham, who sat at his side.

Lifting her chin in defiance of his curtness, Morgana turned to find Sam Howard studying her pensively. Unable to think of anything to say, she silently accepted the tray of potatoes passed by Raoul Rafraga, on her left, and began to fill her plate.

The meal seemed to go on interminably. The conversation, after starting stiffly, finally progressed to a fair easiness between the men. Holding herself aloof and silent, Morgana was aware of the friendly glances shot in her direction by John Fuller when their eyes met occasionally across the table. Her plate, sparingly filled, remained barely touched in front of her. The tight lump in her throat and her knowledge that

348

Devon's dark glance turned in her direction each time his father attempted to engage her in conversation, added heavily to her anxiety. Abruptly aware that a broad hand had moved to touch the one she rested on the table near her plate, Morgana raised her eyes to Sam's inquiring glance.

"The chicken's not to your likin'?"

"Oh, no, it's fine." Certainly Mellie had done herself proud with the huge platters of golden fried chicken, potatoes, and a vegetable that tasted suspiciously like mashed turnips, and, watching as her broad figure came again through the doorway with yet another platter of biscuits, Morgana attempted a smile. "Everything is delicious, but I'm not very hungry tonight."

"You don't need to give me any explanations, Morgana. I just wanted to make sure you understood you're to feel comfortable at my table."

"Thank you." Unconsciously darting another quick look in Devon's direction, she saw his scowl had darkened. Hating herself for succumbing to her spontaneous reaction as she removed her hand from under Sam's, she began to pick at her plate. Her eyes lowered, she did not see the glance Sam directed to his son, nor the manner in which Devon's heated gaze rested on her person for a few moments longer before returning to his plate.

A short while later, she was still attempting to consume the cold food when Mellie bustled into the room carrying a large tin from which the delicious aroma of warm peaches wafted temptingly. Walking directly to Devon's chair, Mellie lowered the pan to slide it tantalizingly under his nose.

"How be that, Master Devon? To your likin'?"

His brow unfurrowing enough to shoot Mellie a small smile, Devon took an obligatory sniff. "Looks and smells mouth waterin', Mellie."

"And now you goin' see just how good it tastes!" Taking the serving spoon from the table, Mellie heaped the empty plate in front of him. "This is special for you, Master Devon, just to tell you how glad Mellie be to have her young master home. And especially glad since he brought home such a pretty young lady for Mellie to care for." Noting that her comment had brought a quick return of his frown, Mellie continued purposefully, "Yes sir! Mellie been real lonesome for womenfolk on this place since Miz Betty done passed on to heaven."

His expression tightening, Devon responded in the heavy silence that followed her remark, "Miss Morgana's stay isn't exactly a pleasure visit, Mellie, and I don't expect she'll be here too long."

Staring back daringly into Devon's tight expression, Mellie chipped dismissingly, "Well, we see about that. . . ." Her broad smile flashing again, she turned toward the other men. "Pass your plates down here, boys. Old Mellie's feelin' real generous. I just know she's goin' give everybody extra big heapins' of cobbler tonight!"

Morgana was intensely grateful that in the scramble of moving plates that followed attention had been diverted from her face. Her tension was beginning to have a frightening effect on her stability. A slow churning had begun in her stomach, which was rapidly progressing to the point where the aroma of warm peaches was becoming nauseating. She was beginning to perspire profusely, although she felt a distinct chill starting low in her back and progressing up her spine. She could feel her face draining of color, and, abruptly frightened that she was going to be violently sick, she moved quickly to her feet. Her quick, unwise move had the unfortunate effect of stimulating a wave of weakness that left her swaying for a few seconds before she felt a broad hand on her arm. Brilliant spots of color seemed to block her vision, interspersed with areas of failing light, and, almost unable to focus, she heard John Fuller's voice close to her ear, "May I take you to your room, Miss Morgana? You're lookin' right pale."

Fighting to focus on the worried brown eyes so close to hers as she swayed weakly, Morgana felt the steadying pressure of the broad hand torn from her arm as a familiar hard voice interjected, "Just sit back down and finish your dessert, John. I'll take care of Miss Morgana."

Morgana felt herself being snatched up into Devon's arms. Clinging to the strong shoulder so close to her face, she closed her eyes momentarily, grateful for being relieved of her own weight as the dining and living room moved past her eyes in a blur. Abruptly the softness of the bed was against her back. She could not remember having passed through the hallway, and she was startled to realize that she must indeed have blacked out for a few moments! No sooner had that surprising thought been digested than a pair of intent blue eyes moved into her range of vision.

"So, you've decided to come around, have you, Morgana? That was quite a scene you put on for the spectators back there!"

An indignant gasp echoed in the room at his comment, as Devon's face was efficiently removed from her line of vision and replaced by a broad, nut-brown countenance.

"Lord, almighty! What got into you, Master Devon? You done lost all your good sense? This here young woman not feelin' well at all, and you bother her with that nonsense you speakin'? The devil sure enough is prickin' you tonight! You'd best go back to that table and take . . ."

"Mellie, I'm not goin' anywhere until I talk to Miss Morgana alone!" The sharpness in Devon's voice snapped Mellie's mouth shut as she glared in silent indignation into Devon's flushed countenance. "Now, if you'll wait outside, when I'm done you can come back in and stay with her as long as you want. But now, *move!*"

Turning abruptly, her wide skirt flaring in silent protest, Mellie walked out of Morgana's line of vision, and, within moments, the sound of the closing door echoed in the silent room.

Morgana was trembling. Her nausea had not truly abated, and Devon's black expression only added to her distress. Her presence here at Devon's homestead was difficult . . . more difficult than she ever had imagined it would be . . . a nightmare she wished desperately she could just sleep away. But the rough hands on her arms that shook her back to reality were not those of a phantom.

"Morgana! Damn it, Morgana, open your eyes!"

Snapping her eyes open abruptly in response to his demand, Morgana found she was momentarily unable to focus

351

as the room shivered and quaked into place. But the burning blue eyes boring into hers drew her steadily back to the present.

"Listen to me! You will stop your playactin' immediately! It's not goin' to do you any good here. So if you want to retain a certain amount of freedom and comfort in this house, just mend your ways, darlin'."

Unable to remain silent despite her growing physical discomfort, Morgana rasped softly, "What is there inside you that sees some ulterior motive for everything I say or do? I haven't done anything . . ."

"You're a damned convincin' little liar, you know that? Don't think I didn't see the whispered conversation you and my father were holdin' at the end of the table. And your little innocent glances at John . . . got him figured out real quick, didn't you? You could see what an easy mark he is for you."

"Leave me alone, Devon! Go away! I don't want to talk to you anymore!" Morgana turned away, unable to face his harassment a moment longer, only to feel her arms gripped even more tightly, as Devon growled warningly under his breath, "Lower your voice! If you think I'm goin' to let you appeal to the sympathy of those men out there so you can use it against them, you're mistaken. If you lover's 'honor' is as strong as he claims, Colonel Austin's on his way home now, and you'll be on your way back to Mexico City within another week or two. But until that time, I want to make sure you understand me. While you're here, for however long that will be, you'll conduct yourself carefully! And just so I make myself clear, I'll repeat again, Morgana. Stay away from the men on this homestead! And that includes my father, John Fuller, and every fellow with whom you come into contact on this land! Save your wishes for your lover when you return to Mexico City!" Ignoring the sickening pang in his stomach that his own words evoked, Devon released her shoulders with a thrust that snapped her hard against the pillow. Pulling himself to his full height, Devon took a moment longer to rake her with his gaze. Angry with his inner softening at the stricken expression on her lovely face, he mumbled tightly under his breath, "Face of an angel . . ."

Turning abruptly, Devon strode to the door. Jerking it open without another glance in her direction, he left the room and pulled the door firmly closed behind him.

Turning her face to the pillow, Morgana allowed her tears free rein. Sobbing silently, she was unaware of the presence of anyone in the room until Mellie's voice cooed softly in her ear, "Don't you pay that man any mind, Miss Morgana. Master Devon got the devil drivin' him since he come back. You just rest awhile. Mellie stay right here with you."

Certain she would never be able to rest again, Morgana followed Mellie's concerned instructions and closed her eyes, a voice drumming relentlessly in the back of her mind: When will this nightmare end . . . when . . . ?

Her heart thumping loudly in her breast, Morgana walked down the hallway, her eyes fastened unmovingly on the room at the end. A few discreet questions of Mellie had established that Sam Howard had retired to his study shortly after breakfast, and she had determined that she would speak to him privately in an effort to make him see the sense of allowing her to return to Mexico City immediately. At the very least, she wanted to have an opportunity to tell him the truth. She could not bear to think that fine man thought her to be the person Devon had doubtless described, a devious, scheming woman who would sacrifice her self-respect to function as Santa Anna's mistress.

She had arisen early in the morning, her nausea of the night before only a faint memory. Ashamed of her temporary weakness, she had vowed she would not allow her discomfort to become a physical state again. Dressing once again in the light blue gown of the night before, she had come to the breakfast table only to realize that Sam Howard was already at work in his study. Her resolution firm, she had immediately decided to speak to him alone. Extremely aware that her hand trembled as she raised it to knock on the door, Morgana took a firm hold on her emotions and rapped crisply.

"Who is it?" Sam Howard's response was immediate.

Startled at her sharp reaction to the deep voice, Morgana

responded as briskly in return. "It's Morgana Pierce, Mr. Howard. I'd like to speak to you, if I may."

Within moments Morgana was faced with Sam Howard's sober, expectant expression. "Come in, Morgana." His voice was extremely cordial, but Morgana was aware of the new wariness in his pale eyes. Feeling a moment of anxiety, Morgana sought to hide it in a light perusal of the room. Simply furnished, the room bore the stamp of the man who worked there. A large desk that had seen many years of wear dominated the center, behind which a bookcase with a startling number of well-used books covered the wall. On the colorful Mexican rug that covered the floor almost to the corners of the room rested two large, stuffed leather chairs. A large lamp stood on the desk, and another occupied the entire surface of the small table between the two chairs. Neat stacks of papers were piled high in one corner of the desk, indicating that Sam had spent a good part of the morning in the process of sorting out what appeared to be an accumulation of clerical work. It was a room made to work in comfort, and comfortable it was, the warmth of Sam Howard's personality coming strongly through.

Encouraged by the hospitality of the room, Morgana turned to face Sam Howard's cautious expression.

"I suppose you know why I'm here, Mr. Howard. Devon has no doubt warned you that I would appeal to you and try to sway your judgment of me." The expression on Sam's face confirmed her short statement, and, experiencing a quick dip in confidence, she continued in a rush, "But I could not allow that to stop me. Mr. Howard, I . . ."

"Please call me Sam, Morgana. Everyone does . . . even my son, as you must have noticed."

"Thank you. I want to tell you unequivocally that I am innocent of the guilt Devon charges me with. I . . . I am not Antonio Santa Anna's mistress. I never have been and never expect to be. Antonio is a married man. I have met Doña Ines and I respect her immensely. I also admit to feeling a strong sense of affront that Devon could believe me capable of such deceitful actions."

"Morgana, this explanation isn't necesssary . . ."

"Yes, it is!" Taking a spontaneous step forward, Morgana looked earnestly into his eyes, her own pleading for his understanding as she continued in a low voice, "I have a family in Mexico City, Mr. . . . Sam, an aunt and uncle and a dear friend who has been with me since childhood. They are doubtless frantic with worry. It is cruel to put them through this pain."

"I've thought of that, Morgana, and I truly regret the anxiety they must be feelin', but it's Devon's considered judgment that the step he took was necessary. I don't think I would've attempted such radical action, but I wasn't there to witness the developments as they happened. I have to rely on Devon's assessment."

Fighting to control the anger stimulated by Sam Howard's obstinate support of his son's actions, Morgana felt a slow flush rising to her face. "You are being extremely unfair, Mr. . . . Sam. You are allowing Devon's prejudice against me to influence you. Devon looks at me through very different eyes than any other person I've ever known. We were shipmates from New York to Veracruz and traveled in the same carriage to Manga de Clavo. It was a case of instantaneous friction between us. Tempers flared from the first, and I admit that Devon often saw the harsher side of my personality. But that does not make me the loose woman he has drawn in his mind! I am a respectable woman, sir! I come from a highly respected family of which I am very proud. I deeply resent Devon's harsh judgment of me, and I resent just as deeply your acceptance of that judgment."

Her chin high, her eyes sparking with anger, Morgana stared directly into the pale blue eyes intent on her face.

A slow flush beginning to suffuse his lined countenance, Sam Howard began lamely, "I suppose I should apologize for the hardships you've been made to bear since . . ."

"Your apology is unnecessary, Sam."

The sharp interjection from the doorway behind snapped Morgana around to face Devon's tight expression as he continued in a low tone colored by subdued anger, "She's a damned good actress, isn't she? She even had me fooled for a while and had me dancin' to her tune. She's a damned convincin' little liar, too!''

Her face flooding a deep red as Devon walked forward to stand beside his father, Morgana felt her control beginning to slip in the face of his bald accusations. Her chest beginning to heave with the agitation pervading her senses, Morgana stated adamantly, ''I *do not lie!* Everything I've told your father is true, and you know it!''

A mirthless smile moving across his lips, Devon nodded into her livid face. ''Maybe some of it was true, Morgana. The only objection I have is to the things you deliberately neglected to mention. But you needn't worry. I've filled my father in on the whole picture, not only the portion you would have him see.''

''I don't know what you're talking about!''

''Oh, you know, Morgana. The more colorful parts of the picture . . . like that mornin' I happened to come upon you and Santa Anna in that little wooded glade outside the city . . .'' Morgana's low gasp registered inside him with the pain of a knife, but Devon continued relentlessly, ''and the ease with which Santa Anna fell in with my plan at the feast of San Juan.''

''Your plan?''

''Yes, my plan. The bastard had the audacity to admit he suspected I was using his feelin's for you against him to force the issue on Steve Austin. Darlin', he looked me straight in the face and told me that you were his 'Achilles heel,' and that he had deep feelin's for you, feelin's that you reciprocated!''

''I don't believe you! I don't believe Antonio said those things!''

''What possible reason would I have to lie? He told me he had great plans for you . . . that for you he would go to great lengths for discretion. And he also demanded that I leave the city if I wanted to see Steve Austin freed. He promised to bring Steve before the supreme court to settle his case if I did, and that was exactly what I wanted. Fool that he was, darlin', he was afraid that I would come between you two.''

Morgana's lovely face was stiff, void of expression. ''So it

356

was an act . . . that day at the picnic of San Juan. . . .''

There was a short pause before Devon responded tightly, ''You know exactly what it was, Morgana.''

Devon's low statement hung in the silence of the room as his eyes moved over her face with open contempt.

Lifting her chin a bit higher, Morgana pursued relentlessly, ''So you had what you wanted. Why then did you have me abducted? To punish me . . . to punish Antonio?''

''Don't flatter yourself, Morgana. I don't care enough to punish either one of you. Santa Anna didn't uphold his part of the bargain, that's all. He was goin' to be discreet . . . that was a joke. By the time I reached Saltillo, rumors were rife, and the people were incensed. Consuelo had received a communication that was filled with . / .''

''Consuelo? Consuelo de Artega?'' A new, consuming emotion flushed Morgana with rage. ''You were so anxious to return to report to your committee, but you had to stop to 'pass the time of day' with that . . . that . . .''

''There's an old sayin' about people in glass houses, Morgana.'' Devon's low warning set off a new wave of fury in her.

''Don't you *dare* compare me with Consuelo de Artega! Your perverted tendency to put all women in the same category is insulting, and I will not stand for any more of your insults!''

''I don't think you have much choice, *darlin'*.''

''Oh, yes, she does, Devon.'' Sam's firm contradiction brought an abrupt halt to the heated exchange. ''I have to rely on the reliability of your judgment because Morgana is already here and the deed is done, but I won't stand for any more name callin'!'' Turning to Morgana, Sam continued firmly, ''I don't intend to stand in judgment of you, Morgana. I've already told you that while you're here you'll be treated as a guest. I can't do any more for you than that. And you, Devon,'' turning back to Devon, his grey brows drawing together in a frown, he continued with a shade more heaviness in his tone, ''if there's some bitterness between you two that won't allow you to be civil to Morgana, then

357

stay away from her while she's here!"

Devon's restrained response was slow and even. "It'll be my pleasure."

Turning, Devon strode through the open doorway without another word. Abruptly incapable of speech, Morgana darted a quick look in Sam's direction before turning stiffly and walking slowly out of the room.

His face dark with barely controlled rage, Devon walked rapidly along the hallway and into the living room. Taking a short moment to glance around, he walked silently out the front door and slammed it hard behind him. Damn her! He had been certain she would try to sway Sam in her favor, and she had followed his expectations to the letter. If he hadn't walked in when he had, she probably would have had Sam on his knees. Hell, who could resist her . . . standing straight and proud, looking directly into a man's eyes with a look of innocence on her beautiful face that could melt a stone. Even now he wasn't immune to her. Hell, he wasn't even close to being immune. The very sight of her turned him inside out. He hadn't been able to think of much else but her since that night at the pool, and he knew he would have to stop . . . keep his distance, before she became an addiction he was incapable of breaking. He had tried everything to stop thinking of her, and nothing had worked. With each failure, his rage against her had deepened. Eating insidiously at his insides was the knowledge that she had not hesitated to press her wiles on the men at the homestead, starting with his father and ending with John Fuller. Well, his father was now wary of her, and he himself would make sure John Fuller would spend a lot more time away from the house in the future, at least until Morgana was sent back to the capital. A new tension squeezing at his insides at the thought, Devon scanned the yard. His eyes touching on the curly-haired man striding into the barn, he was seared again by the burning emotion that had given him no rest. John couldn't take his eyes off Morgana, and he had been well aware of Morgana's covert glances in John's direction. He'd put a stop to that

. . . fast!

Not stopping to examine his motives, Devon made straight for the barn. Sam was right . . . there was only one way to handle his weakness for Morgana. Well, he'd stay away from her all right, but he was going to make damned sure everyone else did, too.

CHAPTER EIGHT

His expression dark and forbidding, Santa Anna stood on the outside of the merry groups that formed around the dance floor. His mind far from the gay music filling the air of the graceful Ramerez hacienda and the couples moving lightly around the dance floor, he stood silently, lending his presence to the scene without the slightest participation in the merriment. His mood as dark and forbidding as his expression, he impatiently awaited the time when he would be able to extend his apologies and return to the palace. Had it not been for the necessity of his presence . . . would it not have been a definite slight to refuse the invitation of his deputy minister, he would not have attended this first of the endless frivolities that seemed to precede the year's end. Even the success of his political endeavors could not seem to lift the pall that had descended over his spirits. He was not accustomed to defeat!

He remembered only too well the eager excitement with which he had begun to anticipate the social events of the season when Morgana had arrived in the capital. The simple thought of Morgana made the blood run hot in his veins again. The challenge of her bright mind, the pleasure of her impeccable beauty of face and form, the anticipation of knowing that beauty intimately . . . yes, that had been the source of the enthusiasm with which he had attended the fiestas . . . with which, indeed, he had begun his days! Her abduction had caused an emptiness in his life for which he had not been truly prepared . . . the same emptiness which he had not seen fit to fill in the months since. Truly, he had not had the desire to take another woman since that day in the forest when he had held Morgana's slim body beneath his ever so briefly. He could not remember being so true to an image that lived in his mind since the early days of his marriage. As for tonight, all he wanted was for the present hour to end so he might leave the crowded room for the solitude of his own bedroom and his thoughts. He was beginning to become bored with the capital scene. Politically, he held matters just exactly as he wanted them . . . enough confusion reigning to allow him complete command.

His meeting the week before with regard to the Texas question returned to his mind. He had to congratulate himself on the personages assembled: four secretaries of state, three confidential generals, three representatives to the national congress from Coahuila and Texas, Lorenzo de Zavala and Stephen F. Austin. The deliberation had lasted three hours, with Austin fervently urging the separation of Texas from Coahuila and its formation into an independent state—a suggestion that had been strongly opposed by the state representatives. While still managing to maintain Austin's confidence in him, Santa Anna had made four very important resolutions: that he would mediate maturely the decree repealing the eleventh article of the law of April 6, 1830 that prohibited additional American entrepreneurs and settlers in Texas, and, if no objections were presented, give it his sanction; that a corps, composed of cavalry, infantry and artillery, four thousand strong, should be stationed at Bexar for the protection of the coast and the frontier of the country, to be under command of General Mejía; that proper steps should be taken to have regular mails and to remove all obstacles to the agricultural and other industries of the inhabitants, ''who are viewed with greatest regard''; and, finally, that Texas must necessarily remain united with Coahuila, because it had not the elements warranting a separation. He had added that Texas might be allowed to form a territory if the inhabitants called for it, but the dismembering of a state was unknown to Mexican laws, and he was at a loss how to proceed.

Thus, he had established his desire to negotiate in good faith on the complaints of the Anglo-Texans without alienating those opposed to Texas's separation from Coahuila, and at the same time he had managed to establish the formation of an army, four thousand strong, in the area of greatest concern; an army that would undoubtedly give the Texans cause for consideration should they attempt to adopt more active means of separation. Although he knew the territorial question to be dead, the question was now before congress. He had been asked for his input into the situation by congress, and it was on this personal information he was to supply that many things hinged. He had been able to convince Austin with his earnestness that he would most likely be in favor of Texas and the state, and he was aware that Austin had communicated that information back to Texas. Yes, he was doing very well politically. . . .

Abruptly impatient once again, Santa Anna reached into his pocket for his watch. Just a few minutes more and he would leave to go . . .

A slender hand moved across the face of his watch, to rest lightly in his as a deep, womanly voice cooed seductively, "Ah, Antonio, already you consult your watch for the time? Does the evening move so slowly for you, my dear old friend?"

Allowing his eyes to move slowly upward, Santa Anna noted the smooth skin of the slender forearm, followed it to the gently curved shoulder covered in a pale cream satin, the olive flesh of full breasts revealed far too amply for convention in the bodice of the extravagant garment, up the slender neck to full, familiar lips, before flicking at last to meet the dark, sparkling eyes of Consuelo de Artega.

Always amused by Consuelo's boldness, Santa Anna replied with a small smile, "*Si,* it draws late, Consuelo, and I have had a long day. I will soon make my departure."

362

Slipping her arm through his, Consuelo leaned her slender warmth against his side, her eyes holding his with teasing familiarity, "Ah, but you were not always inclined to such early departures, Antonio. And I remember well that only certain instances made you anxious to retire to your bed. Yes, I do remember those 'certain instances' very fondly."

His dark brow rising, Santa Anna attempted to conceal his amusement with Consuelo's flirtatiousness. He had forgotten how stimulating she could be at times . . . the passion that sparked in her deep, dark eyes. "Many things have happened since those days, Consuelo." Making an obvious attempt to scan the crowded room, he questioned bluntly, "I have not seen your husband recently. Does he accompany you here tonight?"

Refusing to be baited, Consuelo responded by brushing her full breasts against his arm in a manner calculated to gain the exact reaction she obtained as Santa Anna glanced appreciatively down into the soft swells, "*Sí*, he came with me, but he tires easily, Antonio. He has since left for home and left me to enjoy myself as I see fit. He is a dear man for his age . . . much like an indulgent grandfather. In exchange for a few not so grandfatherly pats and touches occasionally when he comes to my bed, he allows me to find what enjoyment I seek. But of course, you know that, Antonio . . . ."

"Yes, your husband was always an accommodating man, Consuelo. He is extremely practical, also. He was only too happy to take himself a beautiful young wife in exchange for a few personal favors regarding his estates. He also assured me he is not a jealous man, but a man only concerned with retaining a certain amount of propriety . . . a minimal amount. I was certain he would be the perfect husband for the young, penniless Consuelo Martinez. . . ."

Pausing only a moment to look deeply into the shrewd eyes as dark as her own, Consuelo allowed her gaze to drop seductively to Santa Anna's lips. Flicking her tongue erotically across her own, she whispered in a confidential tone, "Come, Antonio, let us walk in the garden for a few minutes. It is unbearably stuffy in this room, is it not?"

"*Sí*, I suppose I have a few minutes to talk with you before

I leave, if that is what you wish, Consuelo."

A low laugh escaping her throat, Consuelo responded lightly, "It is a part of what I wish, Antonio, *querido*."

His heartbeat beginning a slow, steady acceleration, Santa Anna returned Consuelo's smile and turned obligingly toward the doors to the patio. He had forgotten how enticing Consuelo could be . . . how very lovely she was . . . but he had not forgotten how very shrewd she was, as well. It would be best he ascertained her motives for her suggestion of a solitary talk before he jumped to conclusions.

The evening air was clear and refreshing after the stuffiness of the crowded room. Walking directly onto the path that wound between the large flowering shrubs and small trees that shielded them from view of the house, Antonio paused to turn to Consuelo.

Taking his hands in hers, Consuelo raised his palms to her lips, holding his eyes as she lowered them to cup her breasts. Her eyes drifting closed for a short moment as his hands encircled the eager flesh, she allowed the warm touch to penetrate the material of her dress before whispering hoarsely as she caught his glance and held it with a sensual, half-lidded gaze, "You have been a long time away from Doña Ines and Manga de Clavo . . . a long time without the comforts of a woman. And I have been a long time without the comforts of a man . . . a real man, Antonio." Her eyelids fluttering closed with her escalating passion as Santa Anna moved his hands caressingly over the warm globes of her breasts, pausing to slide his fingers in the warm crevice between, Consuelo continued purposefully, "I had intended to leave this party shortly, also. I do not find here the stimulation I am seeking." Her breath was coming in short, uneven pants, and, aware of her own arousal, Consuelo moved to press herself against Santa Anna's strong frame. Moving herself sinuously against him even as he continued to caress her breasts erotically, she felt the bulge of his passion, her hand moving spontaneously to stroke it to life as she whispered softly, "Yes, Antonio, I believe I will bid Constancia and Fernando *adiós* within a few minutes, and direct my driver to take me to the lodgings I maintain at the outskirts of the city. You are familiar with the place, are you not, Antonio?''

Realizing from the flush that stained his face and his agitated breathing that her heady stimulation was having the desired effect, Consuelo waited patiently for Santa Anna's response. His unsteady tone sent a wave of exultation through her veins as he responded hoarsely, ''*Sí*, I remember it well, Consuelo.''

''*Bueno*. I will leave you now, and give you some time so you may make a respectable appearance after I make my farewells.'' The bulge of his passion was now full and hard in her hand, and, exhilarated by her power over the impervious Santa Anna, she continued caressingly, ''And I will wait in the great, soft, familiar bed you doubtless remember just as vividly. My flesh will be warm and waiting for you, Antonio . . . my mouth eager to give to you . . . service you. I long to feel your mouth against my flesh, *querido,* to taste you once again . . . Do you remember . . . ?''

''*Basta!*'' His breathing ragged, Santa Anna jerked her hand away from his bulging manhood and stepped back. ''Go make your apologies now, and wait for me in that great white bed. When I am presentable once again, I will do the same.'' Grasping her shoulders unexpectedly, Santa Anna jerked her toward him to cover her lips in a savage, seeking kiss. Releasing her just as unexpectedly, he instructed curtly, ''Now, go! Do as I said, and wait for me. And I tell you, Consuelo, no matter the length of time, it will be worth the wait.''

Taking a moment to adjust her dress with a sinuous movement, Consuelo looked up, her lips parted as she gazed hotly into his eyes. ''*Sí*, Antonio . . . but do not be too long.''

Turning on her heel, Consuleo walked out of the garden toward the entrance to the house, a small, satisfied smile curving her lips.

His posture militarily correct, his expression unfathomable, Santa Anna climbed the familiar back steps. Glancing down momentarily, he noted that the second step from the top was still broken. Making certain to avoid the splintered portion, he stepped onto the second floor. Almost two years had passed since he had last climbed these steps. Almost two years, and Consuelo still maintained the rooms. Doubtless she had brought many men up these steps since he had last been there, but the knowledge did not bother him in the slightest. She had belonged to him alone for as long as he had desired the arrangement to remain that way, and he had provided her with a comfortable lifestyle in payment for her favors. But it was obvious that Consuelo missed him . . . had not found a man that was his match since. It was unfortunate that he could not say the same for himself. Yes, Consuelo had been a devoted and passionate lover, but he had experienced similar passion and devotion in the years since. Unfortunately, it had not been in Doña Ines's bed. He had long since despaired of raising that cold woman to the heights of passion to which Consuelo and her counterparts seemed capable. Well, at least for this night he actively anticipated lying in that large white bed Consuelo referred to so reminiscingly. In her eagerness, he was certain Consuelo would do her utmost to make sure he was totally satisfied. Yes, it would prove to be a fulfilling evening, he was certain; and if the woman he held in his arms did not possess the glorious chestnut locks that haunted his dreams, did not possess the creamy white skin he longed to touch, did not have the face of an angel and incandescent eyes that sparkled with gold, searing him, he would pretend . . . allow himself to believe it was she until his body could be relieved of the tension of the past few months.

The grim expression of a few hours earlier again darkening his features, Santa Anna took a deep breath and approached the familiar door. He did not bother to knock, knowing it would be unlocked. Consuelo used her resources well, to allow her privacy and security in these confidential matters, and he could not suppress a spark of admiration for her thoroughness. Had Consuelo been a man, he would have made certain to have her on his side in all matters. She would have been too worthy an opponent to do otherwise.

Slowly opening the door, Santa Anna allowed himself a

few moments to become accustomed to the dim light that greeted him. The room was much as he remembered it. Dainty furniture imported from France filled the room, one of Consuelo's greatest extravagances. The large four-poster bed was dressed in white satin, matching the drapes that shielded them from the street. Lamps burned low on the night tables on either side of the bed, keeping the silent figure in the bed in the shadows as he moved toward her. The outright seductiveness of the scene was stimulating, and, feeling the resurgence of need building in his groin, Santa Anna drew closer, unable to suppress a short gasp as he viewed Consuelo clearly for the first time. Her eyes half-lidded with obvious passion, she followed his approach closely. The black, shining coils of her unbound hair streamed over her shoulders in gleaming profusion. Her slender, lush proportions were covered in a night rail of the most delicate white lace he had ever seen. The smooth olive skin of her body shone enticingly through the ample folds, beckoning him. Raising herself on her elbows, Consuelo leaned her head back, her full breasts thrust forward, allowing the ebony spirals to sweep her pillow as she eyed him warmly. On closer inspection, it was obvious that she had rouged the enlarged crests of her breasts, and, suddenly finding himself with an urgent need to tear the white lace from her body so he might view the ripe globes unrestricted, he hastened his pace. Without speaking a word, he held Consuelo's silent gaze. He began to undress, his heart thundering in his ears when she licked tensely at her lips as his broad chest was bared to her view.

There was no doubt in his mind that she wanted him desperately, and, aware of the torture he inflicted on her raging passions, he slowed his actions, taking long moments to remove his boots, to slide down the breeches that covered his narrow waist and heavy, muscular thighs. He was extremely conscious of Consuelo's sharp intake of breath when his enlarged manhood was exposed to her view, and the trembling of the hands she lifted to hold out to him.

"Come, Antonio." Her voice a low, pleading groan, she called to him as he stood looking down at her, enjoying the agony of desire in her eyes. "Come to me now, *querido*. I have filled this bed many times with men who bore your face in my mind, and now I long to feel you truly close against me, filling me with your passion."

Still Santa Anna hesitated, the agony reflected on Consuelo's face turning to desperation as she called him again. His enjoyment of the moment was supreme. She desired him . . . longed for him . . . ached to have him touch her . . . just as he desired, longed and ached for Morgana. Somehow the expression of suffering in Consuelo's eyes did much to alleviate his own as he gloried in her pain.

Realizing he was not about to come to her, Consuelo moved to the side of the bed and stood beside him. Winding her arms around his neck, she kissed him passionately, her tongue moving between his lips to savage his mouth as his had done to hers earlier. Long and deep she kissed him, feeling the first abating of fear as Santa Anna's arms came up to clasp her tight against him. But there was no denying the height of his passion, and, sliding her hand down between them as their kiss deepened, she took his manhood tightly in her hand and massaged it expertly, her sense of control growing as Santa Anna's slowly began to slip away. Within moments they were on the soft surface of the bed, their bodies writhing and moving as they strove for deeper intimacy. With the soft groan of rending cloth, the wisp of white lace was torn from Consuelo's body, her own gasp of triumph sounding as Santa Anna entered her swiftly, violently. There was a short pause as Santa Anna strained for control, during which Consuelo tormented him by running the tip of her tongue along his lips and opening her mouth wide to invite the penetration of his tongue. Abruptly beyond the limits of control, Santa Anna began pumping violently into her body, his final driving thrust ending in a groan that signaled the raging climax of his desire. Withdrawing from her body, Santa Anna rolled over to lie limply beside her, his breathing heavy and gasping in the aftermath of his passion.

His breathing returned to normal, Santa Anna remained with his eyes closed for long moments, unwilling to face the reality of the Latin face that lay beside his on the pillow. His fantasy as he had entered Consuelo had been supreme, all encompassing. For long moments he had actually believed it was Morgana whom he had entered, whose body had opened to welcome him so eagerly. He was loath to open his eyes, to see the truth and the end of the dream that had given him such moments of glory.

"Antonio . . ." A low, sultry voice invaded his raging thoughts. "Antonio, open your eyes and look at me, *querido*." When at last he submitted to the low supplication, Santa Anna was startled by the fire glowing in the dark eyes that looked hungrily into his. "And now, my handsome man of Mexico, master of my dreams, now *I* will make love to *you*." Moving to straddle him with her slender knees, she said in a low voice, "We will both remember this night, Antonio, for many years to come. And it will be *my* face you see, Antonio, no other when you recall this night. I have made a vow that it will be so, and I will not be satisfied until you cry out my name in passion as you have just cried out another's."

At his startled expression, she nodded her head, the fire in her eyes glowing with a new heat as she whispered softly, "You will call for Consuelo, not Morgana, and for tonight *I* will be the only woman for you. . . ."

Many hours later, Santa Anna still lay on the broad, satin-covered bed. True to her word, Consuelo had given him a memorable night, in which she had used the many devices of her expertise to extract and prolong the hours of lovemaking they had passed. Physically exhausted, Santa Anna turned to give a short glance into the face of the woman who lay beside him. Her eyes were closed, allowing him a moment of silent perusal. Yes, there was no doubt Consuelo was lovely, and in the time since they had last made love, she had gained in experience that served her well. He had no doubt men still fought to come to her bed, and, once having been there, dreamed of returning. Perhaps he himself would visit her again if the reward he offered was not successful in returning Morgana to him. Yes, Consuelo was lovely and passionate, but she was not Morgana, and it was Morgana who filled his thoughts and dreams.

Aware of his perusal, Consuelo allowed her eyes to remain shut for a few moments longer until the fury that burned inside her was again under control. Yes, she had served him well this night . . . allowed herself the full range of her experience to bring Antonio to fulfillment. Sacrificing her own pride at first, she had submitted to his needs, finally joining in searing climax at the end of long hours for a deeply satisfying reward that had been abruptly stolen from her by the cold look of his untouched heart reflected in his eyes when all was done. The fact was a hard, bitter pill to swallow. While she had never lost her desire and her love for Antonio, his affections had passed on to another. This Morgana . . . the American woman who had been abducted months before, still held his heart. A wild, searing jealousy permeating her senses, Consuelo was suddenly unable to face Santa Anna's silent perusal. She had sacrificed her pride to him tonight, and, in its absence, she felt a burning need for revenge . . . to make him feel the pain he so heartlessly inflicted on her.

It was no secret in her circle of friends that Antonio had been besotted by the American niece of General Escobar . . . that he had indeed been making a fool of himself over her. Jealousy spurring her curiosity, she had learned that Morgana Pierce had arrived in Veracruz on the same ship as the Devon Howard so thoughtfully provided to her for the trip to Saltillo. The realization had filled her with rage that she had been doubly used, and only her secret hope that Antonio would become lonesome enough to take her back, for however short a time, had allowed her to swallow her pride enough to approach him. His use of Morgana Pierce's name in the throes of his passion had been a painful blow, but her own pride refused to accept the coldness with which he regarded her love for him.

Moving from her side of the bed, Consuelo walked slowly to the washstand, pausing to dip the cloth into the bowl and run the freshness across her neck and shoulders before turning back to Santa Anna. Forcing a smile to her face, she said slowly, "It was indeed a fortunate circumstance that allowed you to return to my bed tonight, Antonio."

"Oh, I would not give the full credit to circumstance,

Consuelo. You presented very convincing persuasion in order to bring me here. You are to be congratulated. You are extremely skillful . . . an excellent lover. . . .''

Her fury heightening at the sterile terms in which Santa Anna described the love she had poured out on his uncaring body that night, Consuelo walked slowly to his side of the bed. Her rage concealed by the smile she forced to her face, she sat casually beside him.

"*Grácias,* Antonio. I am happy you appreciate me so completely. In a way, your appreciation makes up for my failure with the Texan that ate so insidiously at my confidence. It was very demoralizing to see myself fail so miserably to incite passion in his miserable Anglo hide.''

Instantly alert, Santa Anna responded tightly, "You are referring, I assume, to Devon Howard, whom I sent to accompany your party to Saltillo a few months ago?''

"*Sí.* He was a very handsome man, and very amusing to be with, but his heart was elsewhere. He confessed to me a passion he had shared on the voyage from America that he could not forget, and, because of his honesty with me, I forgave him.''

Santa Anna's face slowly began to fill with color. "A passion he shared on the voyage from America?'' Intently studying her face for a sign of deceit, Santa Anna probed quietly, "And did he become any more specific than that?''

"No, *querido,* I did not press him any further. I had no desire for him to recite the attributes of a loved one that stirred such fidelity. But I do have my own suspicions. . . .''

"And they are . . . ?''

"They're not important, Antonio. I must be returning home. It would not do to create a scandal by staying out all night. My husband has his limitations of understanding, and I have learned not to push him too far.''

She was about to stand and terminate the conversation when Santa Anna's hand jerked her roughly back to sit on the bed beside him. "*I* will tell you when it is time to terminate our conversation, Consuelo. I fear your husband is spoiling you with his liberal attitude. I should hate to speak to him and tell him I disapprove of your conduct.''

Allowing her anger to surface, Consuelo demanded heatedly, "I should dislike that far worse than you, Antonio. What is it you want to know from me?"

"Your suspicions . . ."

"My suspicions are that your precious Morgana Pierce was *not* abducted by *banditos,* as you believe . . . that she was instead abducted by the besotted Anglo-Texan! No man turns down what I have to offer unless he is certain of something in another quarter. In this case, the only other woman the Texan was interested in was your lovely Señorita Pierce. Did he not travel on the long voyage from New York to Veracruz with your lovely señorita? Did that not give them time to conduct a subtle little affair? Tell me, Antonio, you saw them together on many occasions. Do you not think my idea is very plausible? Does it not answer many questions? The reason you have been unable to find Señorita Pierce and her abductors in the hills is because they are not there!"

Laughing coarsely at the growing fury in Santa Anna's expression, Consuelo was startled as Santa Anna's hand snaked out to slap her powerfully across the face. Pushing her aside, he jumped to his feet and reached for his breeches. Turning back to her once they had been secured, his expression enraged, he stated venomously, "You have gone too far, Consuelo. You, who have played my whore so well tonight, dare to laugh at me! This wild story you have concocted only serves to show me how unworthy you are of my trust!"

Regaining her voice, Consuelo hissed in return, "You *want* to believe it is all a story I have concocted, but you are not sure, are you, Antonio? Right now, at this very moment, your precious Morgana and Devon Howard are most likely sharing a bed . . . making love . . . and you may rest assured that handsome Anglo will make her call out *his* name, not yours!"

His escalating rage reflected in his eyes, Santa Anna grabbed Consuelo roughly by the shoulder. Holding her fast, he slapped her repeatedly across the face, reciting a low, vicious litany.

"Puta! Puerco! Marrano!"

Calling his rage to a halt as a small trickle of blood began to ooze out of the corner of Consuelo's mouth, he pushed her backwards to fall sprawling on the white satin sheets they had warmed so passionately only minutes before. Ignoring the low sobs that tore from between Consuelo's swollen lips, he turned back to his clothes. Minutes later, completely dressed, he faced her once more.

"It is unfortunate that your jealousy has pushed you one step too far to be forgiven, Consuelo. It is only because of the time we shared together in the past that I do not take stronger measures than those I state right now. I warn you. Do not approach me again, Consuelo, under any circumstances. And do not repeat that vile story you have so heinously constructed to vent your jealousy. You know me well enough to believe me when I say there are prisons where a woman may be placed in Mexico where she will wish many times . . . even beg for death before it comes to her. If you do not wish to spend the remainder of your life in the bowels of the earth, you will be silent. I will not warn you again!"

"Antonio." Realizing she had pushed Santa Anna to a point of rage that endangered herself, Consuelo attempted to salve his raging pride, "Antonio, please. You are right. I made the whole story up because I was jealous. I love you. I want you back. I want you never to think of another woman but me."

"*Puta!* From today on you cease to exist for me. And should I be reminded of your existence by the repetition of the vile story you have repeated to me here tonight, I will see to it that you cease to exist at all!"

"Antonio!" Consuelo's last cry of supplication was silenced by Antonio's short command.

"Silencio, puta! Usted es muerte!"

Walking stiffly to the door, Santa Anna opened it, and, stepping through the doorway, slammed it behind him. Taking a moment to gain control of his fury, he unconsciously pulled himself to the erect military posture that was his trademark. Walking forward, he began to descend the staircase in a composed manner that directly contradicted the emotions raging wildly within him. *Puta!* Whore! Everything she said was a lie! His Morgana was not involved with Devon Howard. . . . She was pure and innocent, needing to be awakened by himself. Had she not demonstrated her innocence only too clearly that morning in the forest? His mind, returning to that morning, brought back the picture of Devon Howard's face when he had come upon them . . . seen Morgana's arms wrapped around his neck as she lay beneath him. Morgana had leaned against him for support against Howard's gaze . . . trusted in him to protect her. Yes, he had suspected that Devon Howard had a *tenderness* for Morgana that he hoped to press, but he had stifled any hopes for that with the information about Devon's traveling with Consuelo. No there was no truth in Consuelo's story. There could not be. Santa Anna had conveniently obliterated from his memory his suspicions at the time of the feelings Morgana had for Devon.

Reaching the bottom of the staircase, Santa Anna walked the few steps to the street, the decision made in his mind without conscious resolution. If the story was indeed true, he would see Devon Howard dead!

Pausing a moment to take a deep breath, Morgana lifted her eyes from the soapy water in which her hands rested and allowed them to follow the course of the horizon. She still had not become accustomed to the flatness of the terrain, the lack of even the slightest rise in the earth to interrupt the magnificence of the land. The sky was a brilliant blue, moving to meet the endless stretch of land in the distance. Only the faintest wisp of cloud marred its brilliant azure expanse, allowing the sun to encompass all below it in the full intensity of its golden rays. The air was surprisingly warm for late October. Only minutes before, Morgana had taken her personal laundry out into the yard. Despite Mellie's protests, she had firmly refused to allow the servants to take on an additional burden with her residence. Somehow she could not make herself assume the role of pampered guest.

It was difficult to believe she had been at Devon's homestead for almost two months. If she had entertained the thought of escaping for even the shortest time, it had been thoroughly abandoned after just one week of experiencing the efficient surveillance that surrounded her. Without interfering with her movements in the household and in the immediate area surrounding it, Devon had seemed to work out a system where she was never without someone's careful scrutiny at any time. On each of the few occasions when she had walked to the barn to pass her time, she had only realized belatedly that someone had happened to be going in that direction and had accompanied her, staying until she had returned to the house. Each time she walked into the yard, she noticed the smiling, watchful glances of the female slaves. Even her movements from room to room were monitored ever so casually. In truth, it had taken her a few days to realize how very truly she was imprisoned at the homestead, and a bit longer to admit to herself that escape, even if she should be able to take a horse and get away, would be virtually impossible. Devon had informed her that word of her presence at the homestead had been spread to their neighbors. In a land as vast and unpopulated as this, she knew her chances were nil.

But, after two months, she was still uncertain of when she would be allowed to return to Mexico City. Just a few days before news had been received that Colonel Austin's case had indeed come up before the supreme court as Antonio had promised, but that, instead of dismissing the charges against him as was anticipated, the justice had deferred his decision and released Colonel Austin on bail. Her stomach tightening at just the memory of the rage on Devon's face as he had read the communication, Morgana lowered her head and began carefully scrubbing the delicate blue dress. Her attempt to question Devon . . . to ask him what his plans were for her with the unexpected turn in events, had availed her nothing but a black look.

It had not been an easy two months. Few of the people at the homestead seemed to share Devon's antagonism toward her, but her sense of being in limbo persisted. She certainly could do nothing that met with Devon's approval. The growing affection with which the household staff greeted her was enough to restore his frown; a word exchanged with a hired man was greeted with a stiff reprimand; and even a simple conversation with his father at their evening meal was enough to bring his anger into full play once again. Yes, the nightmare continued, with no end in sight.

In an attempt to clear her mind of her confused thoughts, Morgana bent over the washtub and began to scrub with renewed vigor. She was presently wearing the Mexican blouse and skirt she had worn on her journey from the capital, not wanting to soil her limited wardrobe as she performed her self-imposed chores. Sam had been extremely kind and generous, instructing Mellie to take three more dresses from his wife's wardrobe for her to use. Each was simple, but beautifully sewn and decorated, and Morgana valued them far more than she had the more elaborate dresses she was accustomed to wearing in her former life at the capital. Her former life . . . she was beginning to look back on her residence at the capital as something in the past to which she would never return. The thought was frightening. She had no desire to continue in this limbo in which she had been existing.

"Miss Morgana . . ."

A deep, unexpected voice snapped Morgana from her thoughts, jerking her eyes up to meet John Fuller's warm perusal.

"I didn't mean to frighten you, ma'am."

"Oh, you didn't frighten me, John. I was just involved in my own thoughts and hadn't realized you were there."

"Yes, I know." His smile warm, John allowed his eyes to move slowly over her face. "I've been watchin you for a while. . . ."

"Oh, are you my watchdog today, John?"

His smile widening at her reaction, he shook his head. "No, ma'am. I've been watchin' you purely for my own pleasure. I've been away so much of the time since you came that I reckoned I'd better take in as much of you as I can while I'm here."

Stricken with conscience, Morgana lowered her eyes from his intense scrutiny. She was only too aware of the argument she had overheard only the week before between Devon and his father. Unaccustomed to the routine of the homestead, she had not realized that John was getting an unfair share of the work that would keep him absent from the homestead in the evenings. In his low, sober tone, Sam had stated that he was bringing John back and would not tolerate Devon's allowing his personal feelings to interfere with the running of their homestead. At first refusing to accept his father's statement, Devon had ended the conversation by storming out of the house and not returning until the small hours of the morning.

"It's just a pity there aren't more women in this area of the country so you . . ."

Interrupting her with a small shake of his head, John insisted quietly, "It wouldn't make much difference if there were a dozen women around here, Miss Morgana. I can't make myself believe what Devon claims . . . that you . . ." Unwilling to finish his statement, he continued quietly, "I know I'm not makin' Devon too happy by hanging around here when I get a chance, but it kinda gives a lift to my day just gettin' to see you for a few minutes."

Unable to resist the honest appeal in the warm eyes regarding her so intently, Morgana smiled. There was no doubt John Fuller was an attractive man, in his smiling, open way. And there was a warmth in the broad strength of him that came through his youthful appeal, hinting at the quality of the man beneath his boyish exterior. Feeling the magnetism, the safety of that quiet strength, Morgana stared for long moments into his sober eyes. She realized belatedly that her actions were misleading, as he took a step forward and raised a calloused hand to touch her cheek. The tenderness in his voice was almost more than she could bear as John began to speak.

"I know you're not happy, Miss Morgana. I've got a feelin' deep inside me that makes me want to change the sadness in your eyes."

His eyes moving slowly over her face, he continued in a softer voice, "I'd be real happy if you'd walk with me for a while after supper. You've been here two months and I don't expect there'd be any objection to you walkin' a bit with me.

There's a gnawin' ache inside me that has your name on it, ma'am.'' Trailing his fingertips to the corner of her mouth, he said softly, ''I want to see you happy and smilin' . . . hell, I want to see that little dimple that winks at me from just about here . . .'' Touching the corner of her mouth, he swallowed tightly.

When she still had not responded, but continued to look into his eyes with a stricken expression, he pressed softly, ''Will you walk with me tonight, after sup . . .''

His words stopping abruptly in midsentence, John was jerked from her side. Flung roughly backwards by a powerful hand, he fought to retain his balance at the unexpected assault as Devon placed himself in front of Morgana, his fists clenched tightly at his sides.

''No, she won't walk with you, you stupid bastard! If you know what's good for you, you'll get back to work before I knock all that sweet talk out of your mouth once and for all!''

A bright flush suffused John's face as he steadied himself. His chest heaving with barely controlled anger, he walked slowly back toward Devon. His voice was low and uneven. ''I think it's up to Miss Morgana to answer me, not you, Devon. You may be the boss of this place, but the way I spend my own free time in the evenin's is up to me.''

Her glance moving between Devon's enraged face and the burning anger in John's flushed expression, Morgana began to feel a deep trembling overcome her. She didn't want this! She had only been responding to the gentleness in John's manner . . . the warmth that called out to her. . . .

''Devon, please!'' Turning to John, she said brokenly, ''I . . . I'm sorry, John. I can't walk with you. You . . . you're very kind and I like you very much, but . . . but . . .''

''You heard her, John! Now get out of here and get back to work! And if I ever see you hangin' around . . .''

''There's no way I'm goin' to let you tell me what I'm goin' to do, Devon! Miss Morgana isn't a prisoner here! Sam said she's to be treated as a guest.''

His rage flaring, Devon grabbed John by the shirt in a

378

lightning movement, jerking his face up to his as he grated with the last shreds of his control, "Get out of here now, you bastard, or I'll beat you to a bloody pulp, and when I'm done ... ."

John had just pushed himself free and was coming back at Devon in a blood rage when a booming command echoed in the yard.

"That's enough of that!"

Her eyes jerking to the tall, grey-haired figure who moved swiftly between the two hard-breathing men, Morgana felt a moment of grateful thanksgiving.

"Get back to work, John! We'll settle this another time when everyone's cooled down a little bit." Not waiting for John's response, Sam turned to his son, the anger in his pale eyes flaring anew as they touched on his face. "As for you, Devon, I want to see you in the study!"

"I'm not goin' anywhere until this bastard leaves the yard!'

Sam's eyes flicked back to the spot where John stood unmoving, his breath coming in deep, heaving gulps as he obviously strove to control his anger. "I told you to get back to work, John! Now! I'll be damned if I'll have my men fightin' in the yard like a couple of dogs! Now get!"

Shooting a quick look in Morgana's direction, John turned slowly and within moments was walking in the direction of the bunkhouse.

Following him with his eyes for a few seconds, Sam turned back to Devon, his voice low as he restated warningly, "Now I want to see you in the study, boy!"

Turning abruptly on his heel, Sam walked back toward the house without waiting for Devon's response.

Her eyes darting to Devon's face, Morgana was intensely aware of the heated look of contempt Devon shot in her direction before following silently behind his father.

"What's the matter with you, Devon? You're actin' like a fool! Ever since you brought Morgana back to this house, you haven't been the same man! She hasn't attempted anythin' in the two months she's been here. Hell, she's been a model guest . . . a pleasure to have around! Now I want to know, what's eatin' at you?''

Facing his son across the broad, scarred desk in his study, Sam Howard pinned Devon with his gaze.

''Did it ever occur to you that I might know Morgana better than the rest of you here? You forget, I traveled with her day and night. I *know* her. . . . You don't know how devious she can be.''

''Are you in love with her, Devon? Is that it? Are you jealous of John?''

''In love! That's a joke! Hell, wouldn't that be a fool thing to do! No, when she leaves here to go back to her lover, I'll be a happy man!''

Sam Howard's jaw clenched in anger at his son's response. He didn't like that kind of talk, especially since he had developed a fondness for Morgana. But when it came to her, Devon was completely irrational, and, realizing he could not reason with him, Sam began firmly, ''That doesn't satisfy me, Devon. I want to get one thing straight with you. I won't stand for any quarrelin' between you and any of the men. Whatever it is that's eatin' at your insides, you *settle* it, do you understand? And I won't have you mistreatin' Morgana while she's here in this house! As far as I'm concerned, she's a lady, and she'll be treated as one. Do you understand?''

''Yes, I understand, Sam.'' Devon's voice held a low, ominous tone that Sam could not quite comprehend, but, unable to argue any further in the light of his son's outward compliance, he concluded briefly, ''And I want you to make your peace with her. I'll have no more of this railin' in my house!''

Silent for long moments, Devon directed a long, sober glance into his father's eyes. ''All right, Sam. I'll make my peace with her.''

Waiting only a moment more to allow his sudden change in attitude to be fully absorbed, Devon turned and walked calmly out of the room. Staring silently at the door Devon had closed behind him, Sam frowned uneasily. He did not

380

get a good feeling from Devon's sudden compliance . . . not a good feeling at all.

"The hardest thing for me to understand is how Steve could fall for that sop of Santa Anna's!" His dark expression reflecting his angry incredulity, Devon addressed his remarks in the main to his father. The conversation around the supper table that night had been heated and controversial, with each man present openly expressing his opinion about the communication received from Steve Austin that afternoon. The news had been a blow to Morgana. There still had not been a settlement of the charges against Steve Austin, and it appeared that, despite the optimistic tone of his letter, very little progress had been made with regard to his original mission to the capital. Since having sat down at the supper table, Morgana's despair at the news had slowly turned to a tight knot of tension that had settled in her stomach. Scanning the faces around her with a quick glance, she realized their anger portended ill for the future of relations between the colony and the capital. Jed Markham's lined countenance was unusually flushed; Raoul Rafraga, usually silent in such discussions, had added his disenchantment with Santa Anna's actions; Jim Warren's animosity was more pronounced than before. She was only too aware of John Fuller's anxious glances in her direction as her own anxiety became more apparent.

Of them all, Devon was the most vociferous, his personal antagonism coming through as he continued hotly, "By now Steve should realize that Santa Anna's a wily bastard who knew the outcome of that 'meetin' to discuss the future of Texas' before it started! But he still continues to believe Santa Anna will rule in our favor, even after that 'generous' offer of suggestin' Texas form a territory! He knows damn well that as a territory we would be more subject to the rule of the national government than as a portion of an integral state! And you notice Santa Anna made no reference whatever to our petition on the subject of the tariff!''

"I admit to bein' just as concerned as you are, Devon, but

381

Steve won't allow anything to happen without our knowledge." Continuing in the role of mediator that he had assumed since the inception of the meal, Sam added quietly, "Perhaps it's best that he's unable to leave Mexico City right now. Having someone there to represent our interests seems to be necessary and we . . ."

"I notice you're all quick to attack Santa Anna's motives . . ." Morgana's unexpected interruption caused all heads to snap in her direction, but, unable to hold her silence any longer, she offered tightly, "Has anyone ever thought to consider Colonel Austin's suitability for the job he's being asked to do?"

Aware of the heat in Devon's gaze, Morgana continued tenaciously. "Santa Anna has done so much to pull Mexico together. It's only through him that the factions that were tearing the country apart at the beginning of this year are now being quieted.

Sam's deep voice to her right turned her attention to him as he stated quietly, "You've got things a little mixed up. Santa Anna has a lot to do before he proves himself—"

"How can you say that, Sam?" Morgana was incredulous. "He's a hero! He's led his troops to victory many times, risked his life for his country! He's a man with a vision."

"Hell, yes, he has a vision, all right!" Devon's interruption was harsh and emphatic. "He sees himself as sole dictator of his country's policy! He sees himself revered, exalted, idolized by his people! And he wants great things for them . . . *but only if* he *can accomplish the great things for them!* He sees them with no mind of their own, followin' blindly in the ways he perceives as best for them! And most of all, he sees no progress for his country that does not contribute to his own personal wealth or stature!"

"Devon, you're being unfair! You're describing some sort of monster. Santa Anna isn't like that!"

"It's obvious you're prejudiced in his favor, Morgana." Sam's quiet statement brought a flush to her face as she realized the path everyone's mind was taking. "You just have your facts mixed up a little bit."

382

"I know Santa Anna well, Sam. He's a good friend of my aunt and uncle's. I know what you're thinking . . . what Devon believes, but it isn't true. I just have a healthy respect for everything he's accomplished . . . and hopes to accomplish. . . ."

"Then let me ask you what you know about Colonel Austin, darlin'." Sam's voice was low and patient. "Do you have any idea of who he is?"

Her expression sober, Morgana returned Sam's pensive stare. "No, Sam. I've heard his name mentioned in connection with the mission he had to the capital, but I know nothing about him personally."

"Then let me tell you a little about him, so you'll have a more rounded picture of the situation that has us all up in arms here in Texas. Steve Austin was born in Austinville, Virginia. I suppose the name gives you an idea of the importance of his family to that frontier community. He was brought up in that wild country and his familiarity with the wilderness and fearlessness of its dangers never deserted him. At the age of fifteen he was a student at the Transylvania University in Kentucky. He completed his education there, and when he was twenty years old he was elected to the territorial legislature of Missouri. He was regularly elected for four years until he went to Little Rock, Arkansas, where he was circuit judge of that county. His father, Moses Austin, obtained the original grant from Mexico for this colony we live in, and when he died, Steve carried out the enterprise in obedience to his father's wishes. For a good many years, Morgana, Steve Austin *was* the colony of Anglo-Texans. He supplemented the income of those that were failing with his own, took on the problems of his people, and lived for their advancement. There is no more trusted man in the colony."

"If that's so, why did Farías get a letter from your colony here that caused him to arrest Colonel Austin . . . accused him of inciting rebellion?"

Obviously surprised by Morgana's statement, Sam eyed her flushed face for long moments before responding.

"The problem lay in Colonel's Austin's loyalty to the

Mexican government. He is a man of deep principle, Morgana, and believes firmly that we should work out our differences with the government in Mexico City. Other factions here in Texas considered him too mild on the subject of separation from Coahuila. It was those factions, dissatisfied with Steve's conduct of affairs, who wrote to Farías. If Steve Austin has one fault, Morgana, it is that he seems to bear an almost unshakable respect for Santa Anna, and is too trusting of a man who has shown he works in many ways toward his own personal goals."

"Then you agree with Devon . . . that Santa Anna is untrustworthy." Morgana's voice was low, insistent on an answer.

"I admit I don't have the same personal animosity for Santa Anna that Devon seems to have. I've never met him and know him only by reputation. But I admit to suspicions about his integrity. He has certainly shown a lack of regard for the Anglos in the Texas colony, and his decision to send General Mejía with a force of cavalry, infantry and artillery four thousand strong to be stationed at Bexar, I do *not* believe is for the protection of the coast and the frontier of the country, as he states. I think it is obvious that the president's policy is to occupy Texas with a military force to hold the colonists under control and compel us to accept whatever changes he might choose to make."

"But it's his duty . . . to enforce the laws . . ."

"He has no right to impose his own will on free men."

Staring thoughtfully into Sam's kind eyes for a long moment, Morgana was filled with his quiet strength. Abruptly, she realized that Antonio would do well to pay these men careful attention . . . to listen patiently to their petitions, for the sake of the welfare of his country. In that moment, she determined that if . . . no *when* she returned to the capital, she would speak to him seriously about their petitions . . . attempt to reason with him.

Devon's caustic interjection cut roughly into her thoughts. "Morgana defends her 'friend' well, doesn't she, Sam?"

A low, angry response to Devon's comment turned Morgana's eyes to John's flushed countenance, "It's too bad some men can't appreciate loyalty in a woman instead of allowing their minds to run away with them." His eyes catching and holding hers, John continued in a softer tone, "As for me, I can't think of anythin' better than a woman who speaks her mind, expresses her loyalty, especially when she realizes her position won't be popular. I'd be proud to have a woman like that."

"Yes, it's just too bad there isn't any woman like that available around here for you, John." Devon's cold, heavy response was quick and cutting. "Guess you'll just have to keep lookin'. . . ."

Extremely thankful for Mellie's noisy entrance into the room as she instructed the girls as to the placing of the hot platters, Morgana took refuge from Devon's heated stare in the clatter of dishes and spoons that followed.

Through the long meal, Morgana was aware of the renewed hostility in Devon's intense regard of her face. So conscious of it had she become that she found it difficult to swallow past the lump that had formed in her throat. Extremely grateful when the last plate had been emptied, Morgana rose, and, making her excuses, made a hasty exit from the room. She had not gone more than a few steps when a rough hand closed on her arm, jerking her to a halt.

Flicking her gaze to the brilliant blue eyes burning into hers, she felt a chill move down her spine. Gone was the truce under which they had seemed to function since that day in the yard. The hateful Devon had returned to grate into her ears, "Still Santa Anna's champion, aren't you, darlin'? Can't forget how close you came to sittin' at the head of a country, even if you had to share that position with a malicious bastard intent only on advancin' himself and his absent wife. But don't be too upset. If I have my way, you'll be back where you want to be sooner than you expect. You can console yourself with how happy Santa Anna will be to have you back . . . how tender he'll be . . . until another strikes his fancy! But I forgot . . . he does provide well for the whores who have served him well. And knowin' you as well as I do, darlin', you *will* serve him well. . . ."

Releasing her abruptly, Devon turned and strode out the door before her startled mind could function to allow a response.

Her face absent of color, Morgana watched the door close behind him. She felt drained by the weight of his hatred, unable to move.

"Miss Morgana . . ." The new touch on her arm was firm, but gentle. Turning to John Fuller's sober face, she attempted a smile, but was unable to manage the small effort. His brown eyes were tender, his youthful face belying the wisdom shining in that tenderness. "If you ever need someone, Miss Morgana . . . someone to talk to . . . to help you in any way, just remember, I'm not far away. If Devon gets to be . . . too much for you to handle, I'm your friend. I've made no secret that I'd like to be much more than your friend. Hell, I can't think about much else but you these days, but I'd like you to remember what I'm sayin'."

Nodding tightly, Morgana returned softly through lips stiff with tension, "I'll remember your offer to be my friend, and I thank you, John."

Turning quickly before she lost complete control, Morgana walked rapidly to her room.

Her hands deeply involved in the dough she kneaded, Morgana's mind was intent on that night at the dinner table when she had spoken up so clearly for Santa Anna. How long ago had that been? Three weeks or more? Glancing absentmindedly around the kitchen, she smiled at Darcey and Collin as they moved from the table to the outside oven to place the loaves already readied inside to bake. They were sweet girls and willing workers. Not at all the picture of the suppressed slaves that she had had in her mind with all the literature against slavery she had read when she lived in New York. And Mellie . . . Glancing to the fireplace where Mellie's broad figure filled the usual spot, adding her own personal touch to the basting usually handled by one of the children, she could not resist a small smile. She was certain Mellie no longer considered herself a slave, but a part of the household . . . an integral part. And she was right. The only person who was in excess here, totally expendable, was herself.

The annoying thought came back to haunt her once again. Brushing an annoying wisp of chestnut hair from her cheek with the back of her forearm, Morgana frowned. Unable to stand the tickling sensation that persisted, she wiped her hands on the large white apron that covered her dress, making certain not to dirty it in any way. She was particularly fond of this dress. The color was lovely. A soft yellow that added a lift to her spirits, it was simple in design, high-necked, and form-fitting in the bodice, the narrow sleeves ending at mid-forearm in the same row of white lace that trimmed the neckline. Fine pearl buttons closed the dress down the front, ending at the snug waist, and she wore in her hair two pearl-trimmed combs given to her by John just a week before. Unwilling to accept them at first, she had been persuaded by his earnest expression when he had told her how much pleasure it would give him to see them in her hair. John was a dear man, and there was no doubting his quiet maturity despite his youthful appearance. When he was near she felt warm and safe, but she ached deep inside for the light that grew in his eyes whenever he looked at her. Had it not been for Devon, she was certain she . . .

Once again the nagging thought she had been suppressing all morning returned to bait her. She needed to face it. Had it been three weeks since their discussion of Santa Anna? Yes, and it had been at about that time that Devon had begun to be absent from the homestead for days at a time. There was never a question asked as to his whereabouts, and considering it must be very well-kept secret or a fact that was well known enough not to be discussed, Morgana had been unable to find out the reason for his absences. Her defense of Santa Anna that evening had been instinctive, a product of Tío Manuel's deep loyalty and high esteem for Antonio. Even now, in her heart, she could not truly believe that everything Devon said about Antonio was really true. Certainly Devon's dislike for Antonio had distorted his view of a man who was truly a great patriot. But whatever the case, that night had seemed to be some sort of a turning point in Devon's attitude toward her.

She had not seen Devon today. Out from early morning, he had not yet returned, and it was well past midafternoon. His absence seemed a familiar pattern of late, and she realized that today's absence would probably be extended to encompass a few days, as had happened before.

Devoting her attention once again to the task in front of her, Morgana worked the dough with growing expertise. Yes, this was a chore she could handle well. Mellie had been a good teacher, and she obtained great satisfaction from the crisp, sweet-smelling loaves of bread that were the result of her labors. She had been actually startled by the pleasure she had obtained from Jed Markham's comment about the new lightness he had noticed in the bread he consumed with such enjoyment. Her work in the kitchen had been a secret from the men, and Morgana valued the compliment all the more because she knew it to be sincere.

The sound of footsteps approaching the doorway of the kitchen snapped Morgana's head from her work as Devon burst into the room. His face was reddened from the ride, his clothes still dusty from the trail. His eyes moving directly to Morgana as she regarded him silently in return, he snapped heatedly, "What the hell do you think you're doin'?"

Her face flushing with color as all eyes in the room turned to her, Morgana responded in as haughty a voice as she could manage, "Is it really so difficult to figure out, Devon? I'm making bread."

A low, scoffing laugh escaped his throat. "Just who is this supposed to impress? You never did a day's work in your life."

Her jaw tensing with anger, Morgana responded tightly, "How would you know how much work I've ever done? I happen to *like* making bread, and Mellie said it was all right with her if I . . . ."

"Well, it's not all right with me! Mellie!" Devon snapped toward the fireplace where Mellie stood in silent reproach, "From now on *you* make the bread, like you always did. Miss Morgana's not to be allowed to work in the kitchen."

"But I *want* to work in the kitchen! Sam told me I'm to consider myself at home here, and if I want to . . ."

Jerking her roughly by the arm, Devon glared down into her face. "You are not a slave in this household, Morgana, and I will *not* allow you to give anyone the impression that we force you to labor for your keep!"

"Devon? What's going on in there?" The sound of an inquiring female voice turned Morgana's attention to a young blond woman who walked casually into the kitchen. Tall and slender, with an air of innate confidence, she flicked her sharp glance to Morgana's arm where Devon held her forcefully. "I heard all the growling in here and thought I'd investigate." Waiting a few moments for a response that did not come, she smiled into Devon's eyes. "Why don't you introduce me to your guest, Devon?"

His expression still tense, Devon responded curtly, "You know very well who she is, Helena, and the reason she's here. There's no need to pretend Morgana's here on a social visit."

Shooting a quick grimace in Devon's direction that revealed only too clearly her opinion of his response, the woman turned toward Morgana with a generous smile. "In any case, my name is Helena Trent, Morgana. My father and I have the next homestead. I suppose this is a little awkward, but I'm pleased to meet you. You're not exactly what I expected. . . ." Helena's voice trailed off momentarily, picking up a few seconds later. "I wouldn't have had the opportunity to meet you at all if Devon hadn't had an urgent need for some material he left here so he could complete today's communication for the committee."

"How do you do." Accepting the hand held out to her with an obvious lack of warmth, Morgana was extremely conscious of the unrelenting hand that still gripped her other arm. She made a subtle attempt to shake it off, only to hear Devon's voice grate in her ear, "I want you out of this kitchen, Morgana. You can find some other way to gain sympathy for yourself.''

''There's no need to be nasty, Devon.'' Helena's voice held a note of reproof. ''If Morgana wants to work in the kitchen, I should think you'd be grateful for her help.''

Turning a hard glance toward Helena, Devon responded curtly, ''Morgana is *my* concern, Helena. I brought her here, and I'll be the one to determine her treatment until she's released.''

Obviously miffed at his rebuke, Helena's mouth tightened. ''You're acting like a fool, Devon, but I suppose that's your business, also.'' Her face softening abruptly, she directed her next glance into Devon's eyes, her voice carrying a coaxing note. ''You came here to get some papers, Devon. We're wasting time, you know. If you aren't careful, you and my father will be working late after supper again. As it is, my father sees more of you these days than I do, with all this committee work. You wouldn't want me to start feeling neglected, would you, darling?''

Barely able to conceal the shock that overwhelmed her at Helena's intimate tone, Morgana stood rigidly still. So Helena Trent was the reason for Devon's long absences! What a fool she had been . . . believing that her outburst in defense of Santa Anna had widened the rift between herself and Devon. In reality, it was this outspoken blonde, Helena Trent, who had been filling his absent days and nights. Their common cause was obviously a bond between them, but it was most certainly not the only bond.

His expression unrevealing, Devon reached behind Morgana and jerked the bow of her apron free. Stripping the well-floured shield from her, he instructed curtly, ''Wash the flour off your hands. You're gettin' out of here.''

His eyes following Morgana intently as she stiffly complied with his request, he pulled her alongside him into the living room. Her lips tight with anger, Helena Trent followed silently behind.

Stepping away from him the moment he released her arm, Morgana walked toward the outside door, only to have Devon's voice halt her spontaneously in her tracks.

"Where do you think you're goin'?"

Turning slowly in his direction, Morgana offered with an air of quiet disdain, "Do I need your permission today to take a short walk? I hadn't realized my boundaries were so rigid."

His lips tightening in anger, Devon did not deign to answer. Instead, he turned back to Helena, "The papers are in my father's study, Helena. Why don't you help me find them?" In a lower, more conciliatory tone, he added with a small smile, "I could use your help."

Bastard! Her temper flaring as Devon's slow smile worked its magic on Helena's stiff expression, Morgana turned back toward the doorway and within a few minutes was walking rapidly across the yard. Damn him! Why did she allow him to torment her so? What did he want from her? She could do nothing to please him . . . nothing to bring back even a hint of the man who had traveled with her from Mexico City. She could not take this situation much longer. She was supposed to have been home by now . . . back in Mexico City, where she could actively begin to forget all that had happened to her in the time she had been gone. But the time had stretched on to two months, and now almost three. She wanted to go home . . . get herself away from Devon. The ache inside her tightening as the vision of Devon's small, intimate smile into Helena's eyes returned, she swallowed tightly. She had to get away . . . she had to . . .

Abruptly realizing she was heading in the direction of the barn, Morgana shot a quick glance around her. For the first time that she could remember, no one was ambling slowly after her or watching her covertly. Her heart beginning a rapid beating, Morgana increased her pace. Within minutes, she was inside the barn. Scanning the area quickly, she saw no one was about. Moving to the first stall, she lifted a heavy saddle from the rack. She was about to throw it on the sorrel who eyed her curiously, when its weight was suddenly taken from her hands.

"Plannin' on goin' ridin', ma'am?"

Her glance snapped upward into contact with curious

brown eyes. "Oh, John, it's you!" Taking a deep breath in an attempt to gain control of her racing emotions, Morgana continued tightly, "Please help me saddle this horse, John."

His eyes moving slowly over the bright yellow dress, John's gaze then moved to Morgana's agitated expression. "You sure aren't dressed for ridin'."

"I know . . . I . . . I need to be alone for a while, John. I'd like to ride. . . ." When her explanation had not moved John toward saddling the horse, Morgana pleaded tightly, "Please, John. I need to get away for a little while."

His eyes sober but unrelenting, John looked into Morgana's stricken face. "You know I can't let you ride off alone, Miss Morgana. If it was up to me, I'd take you back home right now . . . today. Hell, I think Devon was crazy for bringin' you here the way he did, but it's done now. Whether he was right or wrong, I can't change what's already happened, and we'll just have to wait until the time is right to let you go home."

Experiencing a moment of panic at the thought of returning to the house while Devon and Helena Trent still remained, Morgana directed an earnest gaze into John's troubled eyes.

"Then will you come with me . . . so I can ride for a little while? You'll be with me all the time . . . I won't have a chance to try to get away . . ."

"I don't know, Miss Morgana."

"John, please . . ."

His eyes moving slowly over Morgana's lovely, agitated face for long moments, John turned abruptly and began to saddle the horse.

The autumn breeze against her skin was surprisingly warm, sweeping her hair back from her face to stream out behind her as Morgana spurred the gelding to a more rapid pace. She was thundering along the flat terrain. The smooth stride of the animal beneath her sent a thrill racing through

392

her veins, the challenge of controlling his power, keeping his path strict to her direction, relieving her tortured mind from the humiliation she had fled. She felt free . . . free of the anger and uncertainty that marked her days. She had all but forgotten that John rode a discreet distance behind her. She was, in fact, uncertain how long she had been riding, or the direction which she had taken. Reining slowly to a halt, Morgana allowed her eyes to run along the horizon, where grassland met a cloudless blue sky, the sweeping expanse balm for her troubled mind.

Suddenly conscious of the rapid breathing of the animal beneath her, Morgana felt a surge of conscience. Patting the long, reddish-brown neck wet with sweat, she whispered apologetically, "Sorry, old boy. I made you work hard this afternoon." Flashing John a quick smile as he pulled up beside her, she pointed toward a small clump of trees in the distance to their left. "I'm going to head for those trees, John. I think this fellow can use a rest." Waiting only a moment for John's nod, Morgana urged her horse forward once again with a light kick to his flanks.

The moderate pace designed to cool the overheated animal beneath her allowed John to ride beside her. Glancing again in his direction, Morgana experienced a sense of warm security, a feeling of peace in his presence. How very different were the emotions set into motion the moment her eyes touched on Devon. The very sight of Devon's tall, muscular frame was an assault on her senses. His startling blue eyes stirred her down to her soul. She could not seem to forget the sensation of his heavy dark hair under her fingers, the glory of being enclosed in his arms, the wonder that came over her body when his mouth closed over hers. But it was obviously a different matter with Devon. He had made no attempt to touch her since they had arrived at the homestead, except in anger. The tenderness of their long nights together was gone, replaced by an anger that seemed to burn hotter each day she remained. Her prolonged presence at the homestead did not follow his plans. He had intended to be rid of her by now so that he might resume his normal routine at the homestead . . . a routine that obviously included Helena Trent. She had to get away. She could not bear to live this way any longer.

Dismounting as they reached the small cluster of trees, Morgana ducked beneath the low-hanging branches, grateful for the shade they afforded as she walked into the sheltered area a little deeper. Finally shielded completely from the afternoon sun, Morgana tied her horse to a low bush and lowered herself to the ground at the base of the closest tree. The glance she turned toward John as he sat beside her inadvertently displayed her inner torment.

Raising his hand to her cheek, John trailed his fingers lightly across its surface, his eyes troubled. "I wish I could take the sadness from your eyes, Miss Morgana. There's nothin' I'd like more than to see you happy the way you were when you were gallopin' across the range. You're so beautiful. . . ." An earnest expression covered his face, causing a tightness in Morgana's throat as he continued softly in his deep, even tone, "I don't rightly think I've ever seen anybody more beautiful than you."

"What about Helena Trent, John?" Morgana's voice was low and pained. "She's a beautiful woman, and much more the type of woman this part of the country needs, from what Devon tells me."

"If that's true, it's to our disadvantage, ma'am. I don't mean to say Miss Helena isn't a nice woman." Hastening to clarify his statement, John continued ardently, "but she couldn't ever hope to compare to you. Hell, who ever saw hair like yours?" Raising his hand, he touched the smooth surface, his voice filled with wonder. "It feels like silk, and glows like fire in the sunlight. And eyes that spark with gold lights . . ." Moving his hand, he touched lightly at the tips of her full brush of lashes, a small smile moving across his mouth as her eyelids fluttered under his touch. "Just like butterfly's wings."

Unable to move her gaze from the soft brown eyes that caressed her so gently, Morgana heard the low throb in his voice as he continued huskily, "I knew Devon was seein' Miss Helena again, and I knew that would make you unhappy when you found out."

394

Morgana's spontaneous protest to his statement was silenced by John's fingers as they touched her lips.

"But I was glad for me that he was seein' her again. It didn't seem to me that you could make each other happy . . . there seemed to be a bitter taste that turned everythin' that happened between you sour. I think I can make you happy again, Miss Morgana. You're relaxed with me, and when you smile, your eyes smile, too. I want to take care of you, make you feel safe and warm." His hand was caressing her cheek, his voice low and soothing, almost mesmerizing as he continued in the same husky tone. "I don't think I ever felt skin as soft and smooth as yours. I've been achin' to touch you like this from the first minute I saw you." His broad hand slid around the back of her neck, drawing her closer to his warm, open face, to the kind mouth that offered her the soft consolation of his words. His mouth moved slowly against her lips, his gentle kiss warm and sweet. He drew away briefly, his eyes searching her expression for a sign of rejection. Unable to speak, Morgana returned his gaze, bemused by the emotions that moved across his face in the moment before he enclosed her tightly in his strong arms, pulling her close against his broad chest as his mouth hungrily covered hers. The moment it happened, Morgana realized the full extent of her foolishness. She had not meant to encourage John . . . to allow him to think she returned his feelings. But his touch had been so warm and comforting . . . had dulled the burning ache inside her. . . .

Not wishing to hurt him any more than the words she knew must follow, Morgana remained passive in his arms as he held her close. John's kiss was pleasant, but she felt none of the emotions that inspired his passion. She felt no response awakening inside her, merely the pleasantness of being held by someone who cared. In a moment of sorrow, she wished she could make herself return the same emotion that . . .

In a sharp, startling movement, Morgana felt herself jerked from the warm embrace and flung backward against the ground. Her mind barely registering in the rapidity of the action that followed, she saw John being jerked to his feet

395

to confront with Devon's enraged face.

"You damned stupid fool! You won't be satisfied until she has you runnin' around in circles, drivin' you crazy, just like . . ." Biting off his words, Devon shot a venomous look in Morgana's direction as she struggled to her feet. "How many times have you been out here with him when I was gone? Hell, I almost rode past this spot, but your yellow dress caught my eye." With a small laugh, Devon shook his head. "But then I should've expected you'd be here, or in some spot like it. You're most convincin' on the ground in the shade of a few trees, aren't you, Morgana?"

His eyes on Morgana's white face, Devon never saw the powerful fist that slammed against his jaw, knocking him sprawling backwards onto the ground. Still stunned by the blow, Devon blinked up at John's furious face as he stood over him, his chest heaving with agitation.

"Don't ever speak to Miss Morgana like that again! If you're too damned blind to see that she's a lady, I'm not goin' to let you take your ignorance out on her!"

"If you don't believe me, then ask her! Ask her if half the country isn't lookin' for her because Santa Anna is so wild to have her back! Lord knows how many bandits he's had executed by now in an effort to find her!"

"It's not true, John!" Fighting to still the trembling that had beset her, Morgana held herself rigidly erect. ". . . the part about my being Santa Anna's mistress. I was never his mistress! I know him well because of my uncle, General Escobar. They may still be searching for me . . . I don't know . . . I think they probably believe I'm dead by now."

"Sure, John." Devon's voice was a sarcastic hiss. "I made it all up . . . had her abducted and took a chance with my life just because I didn't feel like travelin' alone back to Texas. But you were right in what you said: I did make a mistake in bringin' her here. I should've left her where she was. Steve Austin's still not free . . ."

"And you're stuck with me, is that it, Devon?" A shrill laugh escaping her lips, Morgana turned the heat of her gaze on Devon's dark countenance.

"You'll never make me believe Santa Anna would go to

such lengths to keep a woman." John's voice was blatantly disbelieving.

"Then tell me somethin', John." Devon's voice was low, insidious. "How far would *you* go to keep Morgana, if she was your woman?"

His gaze shooting inadvertently toward Morgana, John allowed his eyes to move silently over her face for long moments. His response was low and adamant. "If she belonged to me, nobody would ever get her away from me."

The long moments of silence that followed were finally broken by Devon's harsh command.

"Get mounted! We're goin' back!"

Stepping forward, Devon took the reins of Morgana's horse from the bush and drew the cooled animal to her side. Swinging her up on the saddle without a word, he walked to the spot where he had dropped his own horse's reins and re-mounted.

Waiting until Morgana had preceded him out of the clump of trees, he moved his horse out quickly behind her.

Her limbs leaden, Morgana dressed slowly in the silence of her room. Brushing her hair with lifeless strokes, she walked to the small mirror on the washstand and eyed her image absent-mindedly. The gown was indeed lovely in its simple way, as were all the clothes given to her from Betty Howard's wardrobe. But she had no doubt the woman had considered this gown special . . . to be saved for a festive occasion. The material was a soft, glimmering satin, in a shade she believed she had heard referred to as café au lait. After a few minor adjustments, the garment lay smoothly against her skin. The modest square neckline was trimmed with the inevitable row of lace she seemed to have favored so well, but, except for that minor ornamentation, the bodice lay curved against the graceful contours of her body without adornment. In a moderate version of the gigot style, the sleeves puffed full at the shoulder, tapering to the wrist to emphasize her dainty, long-fingered hands. The skirt of the gown, flaring out fully to a point just below her ankles, allowed a peek of matching bor-

rowed satin slippers. The simplicity of the style and the softness of the color succeeded in drawing attention to the petite
perfection of her form—the ivory silk of her skin displayed so
temptingly above the narrow row of the lace, the graceful
curve of her neck, and the splendid contours of her extremely
lovely face. Gleaming chestnut swirls lay unfettered against
her back. Abruptly, Morgana decided to show her appreciation for Sam's generosity in offering her the lovely garment
to wear for his birthday party that evening by doing the gown
the justice it deserved. Brushing the curling mass to the top
of her head in loose curls, she secured it with combs. Shaking
her head, she tested the security of the hasty coiffure, taking
only a few moments more to secure more firmly the curls that
bobbed so uncertainly.

Her hasty examination of her appearance adjudged it adequate, and, with a considerable lack of enthusiasm, Morgana
turned toward the door of her room. Her absent-minded
state had allowed her to miss the manner in which the soft,
glowing fabric of the gown brought out the glimmering highlights in her hair and sparked the flecks of gold in her heavily
fringed, expressive eyes. She also failed to take into account
that the gown, made for and by a woman who had never seen
her, seemed to be designed for her small, curving perfection
of form, the shade seeming chosen specifically to enhance her
vibrant coloring. Obviously it had never been worn, as if
waiting for her to inhabit it—but even that curiosity had left
her unimpressed. Instead, she opened the door and walked
down the hallway, her mind revolving in the quagmire of her
dispirited state.

Christmas had come and gone; they were almost three
months into the new year and she had not progressed one
step nearer to Mexico City. Somehow she had not been able
to make herself join the merry celebrations of the holiday,
knowing that others suffered the uncertainty of not knowing whether she still lived. As much as she suffered for Tía
Isabella and Tío Manuel's pain, Morgana felt her greatest torment realizing that Aggie was virtually alone in a
strange land, neither fish nor fowl in Tía Isabella's well-
organized household. It was the first Christmas she could

emember in which the reserved but loving Scottish woman ad not played an integral part, and it brought back only too clearly how very alone she herself was in this busy household.

Several months had passed since the day John had ridden with her, but the pain of their encounter with Devon was still strong in her mind. She had seen very little of Devon in the time since, and had learned that the main cause of Devon's absences had been the vigorous activity being conducted by the committee on which he and Matthew Trent served so closely. At least, that was the reason she allowed herself to believe, so she would not be forced to acknowledge daily that Devon preferred Helena Trent's company to her own. How very desperately she wished she could banish from her mind the memories that left her no peace . . . the memory of Devon's touch against her skin, the taste of his mouth as it covered her own, the sensation of his hard, lean body pressed tightly against hers in passion, his arms straining her closer . . . ever closer.

She could hear the sound of merriment from the living room . . . cups clinking, the low buzz of conversation mixed with intermittent laughter. Someone was playing the piano that had belonged to Devon's mother, and a soft, feminine voice was singing softly to the tune. Her step slowed. She had no desire to join the party. It was being held for friends and neighbors, and she fell into neither of those categories. But Sam had insisted she attend and had shyly presented her with the gown she wore so she might join in the merriment as a part of the group. He was a dear man, and, despite her position in the household, Morgana had become extremely fond of the stern but warmhearted old gentleman. Allowing her the only consolation she had found in the time she had spent at the homestead was the thought that Sam Howard had become fond of her in return. Causing her additional anxiety was the realization that Helena Trent would undoubtedly be among the guests, and she had no desire to witness Devon's attentions to his lovely blond neighbor.

With unexpected vehemence a voice inside her mind assailed her troubled thoughts. Fool! You stand here pitifully quaking while Devon is enjoying himself with Helena Trent just a few feet away in the next room! How he would laugh to see how well all your brave speeches have held up. He has cast you aside just as casually as a piece of old clothing of which he had become tired. He wears a new woman on his arm, and if you have any pride at all, you'll show him how little it all means to you!

A light color flooded Morgana's face at the truth of her harsh self-recriminations. The small hands that had been trembling only moments before clenched slowly in determination. Lifting her chin, Morgana took a deep breath. Squaring her shoulders, she began a brisk step forward. She had nothing, no one in this household to depend on but herself, and she would be damned before she would allow herself to be beaten!

Standing momentarily in the doorway to the living room, Morgana allowed her eyes to move slowly around the room. Just as many strange faces as familiar ones met her eye in the small groups clustered in conversation. Her gaze moved to the far corner of the room, immediately touching on the dark-haired figure she subconsciously sought. Listening intently to the short, broad fellow who was speaking to the small group, Devon had not seen her enter. Without conscious realization, she sought to fill her mind with the picture of him as he presently appeared. Dressed in the dark jacket and trousers she had been accustomed to seeing him wear on the voyage from New York, he looked warmly familiar, the Devon who had stirred her emotions so violently from the first moment of their meeting. How very long ago that time seemed, but the memory of her growing awareness of Devon, of the undeniable attraction that had raged between them, was still vivid in her mind. Unlike Devon, she had been unable to prevent that attraction from growing within her, developing into a multifaceted emotion to which she dared not put a name. Her heart plunging to her toes, Morgana saw a slender blond woman move to stand beside Devon. She touched his arm in a small possessive gesture, and, tilting her head up to his, began speaking. Devon's face in profile had been sober, his concentration intense, his eyes unmoving from the man speaking in a low solemn tone, but his attention was diverted instantly and without annoyance by Helena's small, intimate gesture. The warm, genuine smile that spread across his lips as he looked into her face sent a slow coldness moving through her veins.

"Morgana . . ."

Turning toward the sound of Sam Howard's voice, Morgana saw that he had separated himself from the group to the side of the room and was approaching her slowly. Taking her hand, he stood silently before her for long moments, his eyes assessing her openly. Startled by the emotion filling his pale eyes, she listened as his voice took on a low huskiness.

"You look lovely tonight, Morgana." Giving a small, self-conscious laugh, he offered hesitantly, "It gave me a strange feelin' seein' you standin' there in that dress. Betty made it for herself, you know, for the holiday party before she died. But she never wore it. She said when it was done and she had put all that work into it, it just wasn't right for her somehow. She said it was strange, because all the time she was sewin' it, she had been so sure it would be perfect. I can remember how she shook her head and said, 'Maybe it just isn't the right time for this dress, Sam. But I have such a strong feelin' about it that I'm not goin' to take it apart. I'll save it. I'll know when the time's right, and then I'll enjoy it twice as much.' " Shaking his head, Sam continued, obviously in tenuous control of his emotions, "I kinda have the feelin' Betty's enjoyin' it now, seein' it on you. It's like she made it for you, darlin', and she didn't even know it herself, it's that perfect." Pausing to swallow past the lump in his throat, Sam leaned forward and kissed Morgana lightly on the cheek. "Welcome to the party, Morgana, and thank you for bringin' Betty here tonight. I can feel her smilin' now. I can feel it deep inside me."

Too touched for speech, Morgana stared into Sam's sober, lined face, his emotion bringing the warmth of tears to her own eyes. Her response was a soft whisper.

"I think I can feel her smiling, too, Sam."

The full grey mustache quivered lightly for a few seconds

before the mouth beneath broadened into a smile. Taking her arm, Sam tucked it through his and urged her toward the first group of strangers. His voice carried a note of pride. "I'd like you to meet a friend who's stayin' with us for a while. Her name's Morgana Pierce, and we're mighty glad to have her with us tonight."

Morgana's face was stiff from smiling. Finally excusing herself from Sam's protective grasp, she had moved to the buffet table with the excuse of hunger. She wasn't going to allow herself to hang on to Sam's arm like an anchor for the whole evening. He obviously had sensed her apprehension, the dear man, and was attempting to . . .

"Miss Morgana . . ."

Turning at the sound of the familiar deep voice, Morgana smiled with true warmth. Obviously dressed in his best shirt and breeches, his hair slicked down as tightly as the sandy-colored curls would allow, John Fuller stood beside her, his sincere pleasure in seeing her reflected openly in his eyes. She had seen little of John since that day of the ride, and she sensed rather than knew that Devon had something to do with it.

"John, I thought you weren't here! I didn't see you when I came in."

"But I saw you, all right, ma'am. There isn't one man in this room that didn't notice you the first minute you stood in that doorway. You look so beautiful, I can hardly believe you're real."

Her spirits lifting under John's warm regard, Morgana shook her head laughingly. "It's no wonder I like you so much, John. I don't know anybody who pay more beautiful compliments than you do."

Flushing at her response, John shrugged his broad shoulders. "Hell, it's easy to say nice things to somebody like you."

Laughing lightly in return, Morgana leaned back, her hands clasped behind her against the wall as she stared up into John's appreciative face. "Well, I think I'll just lean back and let you go on. You're the right man in the right place, John. You just couldn't suit me any better than you do just now."

His eyes showing a trace of amusement, John took a step forward to whisper jokingly, "I knew you'd come around to my way of thinkin' eventually, Miss Morgana."

Delighted with John's light response, Morgana could not suppress the soft laugh that bubbled up from deep inside her. Stepping forward, she slipped her arm through his. "You are a darling, do you know that, John Fuller? A real darling. And I don't think I'm going to let you get away!"

His eyes following the bright exchange from across the room, Devon felt a stab of jealousy sear his mind. She hadn't changed one bit! Still the same Morgana, taunting and flirting, twisting men around her finger just as easily as she had twisted him. If he were able to manage a semblance of detachment, he knew he would probably be amused with the switch in the situation that existed at the Circle H. Morgana had arrived with him in late summer, his prisoner, being held to guarantee the safe release of Steve Austin. A few short months later, the situation was all but reversed. Thoroughly in command, affection growing for her in all quarters of his household, she had managed to allow him to assume the position of the outsider. His harsh assessment of her was in the minority, his unyielding treatment of her viewed with increasing anger and resentment. His only defense against her had been to alienate himself from her, to attempt to freeze the emotion she stirred so hotly inside him.

Morgana had not allowed her time to go to waste in any quarter. No . . . judging from the familiar manner in which she slipped her arm through John Fuller's . . . The hot stab of jealousy seared him again. Not realizing Helena's eyes had followed his avid gaze across the room and returned to study his face with a small frown, he turned abruptly and walked toward the punchbowl. He filled his glass, and, consuming it, quickly filled it again. His eyes, moving across the room, rested for a few moments longer on Morgana's smiling face. Her delight in John's latest statement was obvious. The sound of her soft laughter cut deeply inside him. There had been so little laughter between them . . . just short periods of familiarity stolen too easily from them by the pressure of events. In the dark hours of the night, he had begun to wish, to dream that they could start over again without the pressures of the colony grievances that had persistently come between them, just Morgana and himself in the fantasy world they had created so beautifully on the journey from Mexico City. His eyes still on Morgana's smiling face, he felt his stomach tighten with pain as she reached up to touch John's cheek lightly. He could almost feel the touch against his own skin, and, thoroughly disgusted with himself, he tossed down the contents of his glass. The sweet, fiery liquid was soothing to his jangled nerves. Mellie was never one to make a punch that could not stand on its own. He filled his glass again, and turned his back deliberately on the picture that caused his discomfort.

The evening was beginning to wear heavily on Morgana's tattered nerves. Shooting a quick smile up into John Fuller's smiling, boyish face, she offered lightly, "John, I do appreciate that you've spent most of the evening with me, but there are any number of young women here and several in particular who've been indicating their interest in you, if I'm to judge by the speculative glances being sent your way. You needn't feel obliged to stay with me."

A small frown moving between his light brown brows, John's response was candid. "I have no interest in any woman here but you, Morgana, but if you'd prefer that I move on for a while . . ."

"You're asking if I would like to find someone else to talk with? John, you forget who I am and what I'm doing here. Sam's courtesy, and the polite treatment from his neighbors can't change that. I'm an outsider, John."

"Only in your mind, Morgana."

Smiling at his response and at the satisfaction she derived

in having succeeded in convincing him to drop the "Miss" each time he addressed her, she touched his forearm lightly, using the physical warmth of the contact to give her the strength to go on.

It was a truly festive party. The house had been readied for the event meticulously by Mellie and her small army of helpers. The food spread out on the lavish buffet table was wholesome and enticing, although it had not succeeded in coaxing Morgana to indulge more heavily than a few polite nibbles. Sam had made sure to introduce her to the many unfamiliar faces that had stimulated her anxiety. In addition to John, Raoul, Jed, and Bart Tucker had stepped up to extend their greetings, but Jim Warren had conspicuously maintained his distance. His dislike for the person Devon had described her to be was more obvious, more intense than any of the other's, and she was distinctly uncomfortable with it. Of all the women, only Helena Trent had approached her in friendliness and remained to exchange a few words. But she had returned immediately to Devon's side as Morgana had tried desperately to ignore the smile with which Devon welcomed her back.

Her earlier mood of determined gaiety had deteriorated with the passage of hours. The growing heat of the room in which so many were gathered, and the deep ache inside that had resulted from the fact that Devon had not even acknowledged her presence, had combined to produce a pounding headache, over which she was beginning to have difficulty in concentrating.

Her thoughts centering more and more around her growing physical distress, she questioned abruptly, "Do you find it particularly hot in here, John?"

The small frown returning, John noted the perspiration on Morgana's brow and the slight squint to her eyes that indicated her discomfort.

"Aren't you feelin' well, Morgana?"

Biting down nervously on her lower lips, Morgana attempted a small smile. "Just a little headache, but I think I'll be saying goodnight, John." Turning to search out Sam's tall form, Morgana's eyes touched advertently on the attractive couple in the corner of the room who spoke quietly into each other's eyes. The pain almost more than she could bear, she watched as Helena raised her hand to touch Devon's lips. Devon's response was immediate. Reaching out, he slid his hands to her waist and drew her closer.

Snapping her eyes back to John's concerned face, she stated hoarsely, "Goodnight, John." Her first step surprisingly unsteady, Morgana had not gone more than a few more before she felt John's hand stay her. "Let me walk with you, Morgana."

Supremely grateful for the steadying arm that slipped around her waist, Morgana lifted her face to his and managed a small smile. Realizing her need to call as little attention to herself as possible, John walked her slowly toward the door, his arm appearing more an affectionate gesture than the steadying tower of strength that it was.

Once into the hallway and out of the crush of the crowded living room, Morgana began to experience immediate relief. By the time she had reached her room, she could actually feel her color returning. Raising her face in a smile, she said lightly, "John, is there no end to the debt I owe you?"

"I consider it more of a privilege than a favor, ma'am."

His small, shy smile was endearing, and, abruptly unwilling to return to the silence of her room, she looked into John's lightly freckled countenance. "John, I have no desire to return to the party, and I seem to have an unreasonable dread of going into my room and having my thoughts overwhelm me again. You won't misunderstand if I invite you in to spend some time . . . so we can talk in comfort without the press of the crowded living room? We can leave the door open so no one will think . . ." Her face beginning to show the first sign of discomfort, she hesitated. "I mean . . ." Her voice slowing to a halt, she continued abruptly, a small apologetic smile moving across her lips. "I think it was a foolish thought, John, and I don't know what made me even think to suggest . . ."

"As I said before, ma'am, I consider it a privilege bein' with you, and I'd be happy to spend some time talkin' with

406

you in your room. It's a bit too cold to go out walkin' tonight, with you all overheated from the party, or I would've
suggested we go outside. I made the offer before, about bein'
there if you ever need a friend, and I meant it. We'll leave
the door open, just like you suggested, and if anyone wants to
make anythin' of my bein' here, they have the right to try.
But I guarantee you, ma'am, no one will ever say anythin'
bad about you while I'm within hearin' distance and get
away with it."

Shaking her head, Morgana hesitated only a moment longer before opening the door to her room. "Please come in,
John. You are my first and most honored guest."

Her eyes shooting to the small china clock on the dressing table, Morgana jumped up with a start. She had been
seated on the side of the bed while John sprawled out comfortably in the only chair in her room. The conversation
had started out awkwardly at first but, after a few faltering
starts, had moved along spontaneously. Looking at the
clock for the first time since their arrival, Morgana had
been startled to see that they had been talking for over an
hour. Her headache had disappeared and she found she
truly loathed to put an end to the conversation, which had
moved from John's hard-working youth and his arrival at
the Circle H, to Morgana's rather strict upbringing and
her emigration to Mexico City.

"Can you believe we've been talking for over an hour,
John? I had almost forgotten what it was like to have a simple, friendly conversation." Taking his hand as he slowly
rose to his feet, Morgana said sincerely, "I want to thank
you for your friendship, John. I hadn't realized how rare and
valuable friendship could be. It's strange, isn't it, that it
takes loss to make appreciation profound? You can rest assured, because of you, I'll treasure Aggie much more than
before. I never realized how very much I took her for
granted."

Taking her hand to hold it warmly, John started toward
the doorway, urging her along with him as he said with a wry

twist to his lips, "Well, I think I would've preferred you had likened me to someone other than Aggie, Morgana, but I suppose if that's the best I can do . . ."

"Oh, John!" Morgana's quick laughter was sincere. "You know exactly what I mean!"

His smile broadening, John's response was still a bit wry. "Unfortunately, I do." Urging her through the doorway with him, he said coaxingly, "After all that talkin', don't you think you'd like to come back to the party for a little while and have some of Mellie's punch? I know I'm mighty dry."

Hesitating only a moment, Morgana slid her arm through John's, surprised to realize how much better she felt. "Yes, I do believe my throat is parched. I've suddenly developed a bit of an appetite, too! I think I'll see if there's any food left . . ."

"You don't have to worry about that, ma'am. Mellie just keeps bringin' it out until the last person leaves the house. There's sure to be a table full of food out there."

They had reached the entrance to the living room, and Morgana's eyes moved to the buffet table in confirmation of John's statement, missing the heat of Devon's dark perusal. Releasing John's arm, she said with a small smile, "Right again, John. And if you'll get the punch, I'll make a dish for you and myself and we can make sure we do Mellie's buffet justice."

Purposely refusing to seek Devon out within the crowd, Morgana allowed only a moment for her eyes to follow John with true warmth as he moved away, before turning to the table.

His eyes intent on John as he approached, Devon stood beside the punchbowl, where he had spent the majority of the time while Morgana and John had been out of the room. The eyes that met John's were filled with silent rage. Momentarily startled by the impact of their gaze, John stopped still. Finally resuming his approach, he offered quietly, "You have the wrong idea, Devon. Morgana and I were . . ."

"Unless you want me to close your lyin' mouth right here and now, John, you won't say another word. Morgana . . ."

A firm, feminine voice interrupted Devon's heated words without hesitation, "Morgana is none of your business, Devon! You've spent most of the night moping around that punchbowl, and I think it's about time you showed me a little of the attention you've been focusing on the door to the hallway for the past hour." Her glance moving momentarily to plead John's indulgence, Helena continued in a more coaxing tone, "Devon, darling, this is supposed to be a party, remember? So far tonight, all I've heard from you is some political nonsense, and a lot of growling, and I have better plans for the remainder of the evening." Urging him quietly alongside her, she frowned at his uneven step. "And I think you should stay away from that punchbowl. You've had more than enough tonight!"

Devon shot one more look into John's tight expression, the heat in his glance unabating. Abruptly, he allowed Helena to pull him away, a look in his eye that sent little jiggles of warning up John's spine. Looking toward Morgana, John saw she had not witnessed the exchange. Instead of relief, he experienced a deepening of his concern. It would really be best if she had seen the expression on Devon's face. Unless he was mistaken, it portended ill for her, and it was best if she was forewarned. But she hadn't been, and, realizing he would not be able to bring himself to mention something that would return the tension to her eyes, John turned back to the table and reached for the cups.

Concerned with filling the plates she balanced precariously in her hand, Morgana turned as a soft voice at her shoulder said quietly, "Well, I have the punch and you have more than enough on that plate for me, Morgana. Do you think Mellie'd mind much if we took her good food into the kitchen? I kinda like the idea of gettin' out of this crowd again."

A bit surprised at the abrupt soberness in his brown eyes, Morgana nodded her head. "That sounds like a good idea, John." Realizing as she turned toward the kitchen that John kept close beside her, she felt a momentary tug of apprehension. Raising her eyes again to his, she saw his small, encouraging smile. Shaking off the last remnants of her anxiety, she continued toward the kitchen.

Morgana was not sleeping easily. The tension of the party had resulted in a multitude of troubled dreams that had invaded her unconscious world to leave her troubled and disturbed even as she slept. Startling blue eyes, glazed with anger, assailed her with their penetrating stare, and she cried out, begged them to leave her alone . . . allow her to rest. But their glare was unabating. What was that she saw in their icy depths . . . a touch of warmth? Lying completely still, she attempted to penetrate the shaded dream, to get a clearer glimpse of the brief warmth that evaded her. Yes, once again the startling eyes came into view, the glow within them growing brighter with each moment. A reciprocal happiness began to blossom inside her. Reaching out, she enclosed a familiar warmth in her arms, felt the pleasure of a familiar touch. There was a touch on her face, a warm mouth caressing hers, and she separated her lips, reveling in the moist invasion that followed. Oh, yes, there was beauty in the glow that pervaded her senses . . . lifting her . . . taking her from her unhappiness of a few moments before to this plane where unconscious thought evaded reason. The light, caressing sensation moved along her throat, shoulders, touched her breasts. Lying completely still, unwilling to make a move that would awaken her from her temporary haven, Morgana felt the delicious sensation moving to encompass her completely. With a thoroughness that set her heart to throbbing, Morgana felt the tingling sensation move over her flesh intimately, past her navel, flutter briefly in the dark nest between her thighs before moving gently, breathtakingly, to the tender slit below. With the first touch, the jarring ecstasy of the moment, Morgana began to stir from her silent world. The second, warm, moist caress stirred her further, forcing her to lift her heavy lids . . . to strain at the darkness of her room, and the third . . . bringing a searing wealth

410

of sensation, awoke her more fully to the reality of the moment.

Reaching down, she touched the heavy mane that brushed against her thighs, felt the warm caress that seemed to go on and on, stroking and fondling the bud of her desire until a wild trembling beset her. Gasping tightly, she wound her fingers in the heavy mane, luxuriating at the familiar feel of its texture under her fingers. Still, not a word was spoken as the beauty increased, drumming through her body with each torturous touch. She was gasping with ecstasy, wild with emotions stimulated within her, unable to withstand the drumming crescendo building inside her as she came to the crashing, shuddering consciousness of climax.

She was still gasping, straining to regain her breath in the aftermath of the emotions that had soared to life within her, when she felt a familiar warmth move to cover her. The voice in her ear was slurred, but heavy with passion.

"Even in your sleep you wanted me, didn't you, Morgana? I didn't need to awaken you to get your response, to feel it come to life. You knew it was I who was tastin' you, darlin'. You opened yourself to me. The taste of you is still sweet in my mouth. I've been longin' for that sweetness, darlin' . . . achin' for it. . . ."

With one swift thrust, Morgana was filled, her heart crying out in ecstasy as the slow rhythm of love began. Joining in the sensuous dance that raised her higher and higher into the world of joy and light, Morgana felt an elation building inside her. Yes, they were one again. . . . There would be no more turmoil, just the beauty they shared, brought to wild, searing ecstatic abandon. The low groan in her ear joined with her own as Morgana tumbled in the final, spiraling plunge from the pinnacle of glory they had ascended together.

Their bodies, moist with the perspiration of their mutual passion, were still joined. Unwilling to see an end to the soaring moment, Morgana clasped the broad frame against her, releasing her hold as the warmth moved away from her at last.

She opened her eyes, straining in the darkness to see Devon's face, but it was too dark. His expression was hidden in a shadow.

"Devon . . ." Her attempt to speak was thwarted by a kiss that drowned her words, by lips that tortured and teased, a tongue that touched and tasted hers until she no longer had a desire to speak.

The warm, drugging mouth lifted from hers at last to move to the soft lobe of her ear, biting and nibbling gently before Devon's low voice sounded quietly, "Go to sleep now, Morgana." His broad hand moved caressingly against her flesh, finally pulling her against his lean, powerful body to be cradled in strong arms. "Go to sleep now . . . that's right. You're where you belong now, in my arms . . . where you always belonged. . . ."

The first light of morning was beginning to rake the night sky in bold, sweeping strokes when Devon awoke. Morgana was lying beside him, curled in the curve of his arm, her face pressed lightly against his chest. He could feel her sweet breath against his skin, a soft, even caress as she slept. Sometime in the middle of the night, he had reached down to pull the coverlet around them against the chill of the room, but she had not awakened. As he looked down at her now, he realized he would never tire of looking at her, never tire of watching the play of emotions across her beautiful face, or even the angelic peacefulness of her beauty in sleep. Straining to see her more clearly in the semilight of the room, he moved his eyes over her face, following the line of her cheek to her lightly parted lips. He fought the desire to cover them with his own . . . to taste again their sweetness. God, he loved her! He could deny the emotion that raged inside him no longer. Where had it all gone wrong between them? When had the animosity started, when had the tension begun to build until he had no longer been able to view Morgana dispassionately? Remembering with pain the happiness on her face when she had returned to the party with John after an hour's absence, he knew, deep in his heart that he had driven her into his arms. But he hadn't truly wanted it that way. He wanted her with him, by his side, the way she was now. Careful not to awaken her, he caressed a strand of her glorious hair. He was not ready to face her yet.

He had taken her last night in her sleep. Her body, taught to respond to his by his long, ardent attentions on their journey to Texas, had reacted automatically. It was only in his semidrunken state that he was able to convince himself that her response was any more than that. Where was there to go for them from here? Morgana wanted to return home. Hadn't she told him that clearly? He had been wrong to take her from Mexico City, but he had been unable to leave her to Santa Anna; had been unable to face the thought of Santa Anna's hands caressing her skin, his mouth covering hers, his body claiming hers night after night. Instead, he had been the one to violate her, to tease her inexperienced body into response, teach her the driving power of the hunger he felt for her. But, somewhere along the line, his feelings had changed, warmed, matured to the point that he was not certain where lust had ended and love had begun. Nothing else, no one else would do for him. He had even begun to despise his use of Helena in his attempt to exorcise Morgana from his heart.

Shooting a quick look to the window, Devon frowned. It was beginning to become light. He didn't want to be seen coming out of Morgana's room. He had damaged her enough already. He could not strike that final blow to her pride.

Gently extricating himself from her, Devon rose from the bed. Dressing quickly, he turned to allow himself one last look before leaving. The desire to awaken her and tell her all he had learned about himself and his feelings for her in the past torturous days and nights was strong. But he could not. Somehow, he could not make himself face her scorn.

Tearing his eyes from her face, he walked quickly to the door. Opening it quietly, he stepped into the hallway and pulled it shut behind him. In the semidarkness of the corridor, he did not see the tall figure that stood a few doors down until he spoke.

413

"Devon!"

His eyes jerked up to see Sam as he stepped out of the shadow. Sam's voice was low, the thread of anger obvious even in a whisper. "I want to speak to you in my room, now!"

Without response, Devon walked toward his father and preceded him into the room. Turning as Sam entered to close the door behind him, he waited as his father turned the fury of his gaze on him.

"How long has this been goin' on in my house, Devon?"

A slow sickness beginning inside him, Devon responded quietly, "This is the first time I've visited Morgana's room, Sam. I haven't touched her before in this house, but it's not the first time I've made love to her."

"How much truth is there in the story you told me about Santa Anna and Morgana? Was that all a lie thought up to provide you with . . ."

"No!" Realizing his father had begun to doubt him for the first time, he continued earnestly, "No, everything I told you about Morgana and Santa Anna is true!"

"Then Morgana has been sharing her favors freely between you . . ."

"No, Sam, that's not exactly true." The pain twisting in his stomach, he confessed softly, "Morgana was inexperienced when I met her. The first time I took her, she was a virgin. She never really wanted me, Sam. It was Santa Anna she wanted from the first, but I couldn't keep my hands off her. Then when Steve's case became so involved, when there was no progress in setting him free, I thought of that plan to force Santa Anna's hand through Morgana. It almost worked, Sam. As a matter of fact, I thought it had. But I hadn't bargained for the way the thought of Santa Anna and Morgana would haunt me after I left the capital. But it seems I had taught her well. By the time I reached Saltillo, it was exactly as I told you, and I started back. Right now, I honestly can't say which motive was the stronger, my desire to assure Steve's freedom, or my desire for Morgana."

Sam's face was stiff and severe. His lips pressed in a tight line, he did not respond for long moments, his disappointment with his son's actions registering openly in his eyes. When he spoke, his voice was harsh. "Then nothing has changed as far as the danger to Steve's case if Morgana's liaison with Santa Anna should resume before he's freed."

"Nothing."

"You are certain Santa Anna would take her back if she were to return now? She's been gone several months. Perhaps he's found someone else."

"I have no doubt he's as wild to have her back now as he was when she was abducted, Sam."

"And you're still certain she won't bring the whole Mexican army down on us if we let her return?"

"Yes, I'm certain. Morgana is ambitious for herself, but she won't allow blood to be shed for revenge."

"Then we have no choice but to keep her here until Steve is exonerated."

"That's right."

A sudden flush of fury rose to Sam's face. He stepped forward, his eyes locking with his son's as his voice quivered with rage. "Then, if you've removed all my choices in this affair, Devon, we'll keep Morgana here! But I'll be damned if I'll stand for this sordid affair to continue in my house! I will not allow you to sate your lust under my roof! It is an insult to your mother's memory!"

"Sam, Morgana is entirely guiltless in this. She didn't expect me to visit her room. She was hardly awake when I took her, and if she had been, I know I wouldn't have taken her that easily. And you're wrong, Sam. This isn't a sordid affair involved in satisfyin' my lust for Morgana. My feelings might have been inspired by lust at the beginnin', but they've long since turned around on me. I love her, Sam. Knowin' everythin' I know about her, I still love her. And she waits for the day when she can get away from me."

His eyes intent on his son's face, Sam waited long moments before replying.

"Then I need say nothin' more to you, Devon. You'll suffer your own penance by stayin' away from Morgana. And you *will* stay away from her while she remains under the protection of this homestead!''

His only response to his father's statement was a short nod of acquiescence. Devon was startled as his father demanded heatedly, ''I will have your spoken word in confirmation of this, Devon!''

''All right, Sam, you have my word. I'll stay away from Morgana for the remainder of the time she spends under this roof.'' His own teeth clenching in anger, Devon added hotly, ''Is that enough for you?''

''It's enough for now!''

Waiting only a moment longer, Devon strode to the doorway and, jerking it open, left the room. He was halfway down the hallway when the pain of his loss struck him for the first time.

''You are certain, Antonio . . .'' Manuel Escobar's voice trailed off uncertainly. He was not accustomed to this side of his friend and president.

''*Sí*, Manuel, I am sure. I have already received the notice that the congress has declined my petition to retire from the presidency. They have granted me a leave of absence instead, and since Gómez Farías is no longer able to assume office in my absence, General Miguel Barragán has been selected to fill the office in the interim.''

Santa Anna eyed Manuel unsmilingly. He was well aware of his friend and compatriot's shock upon learning that he had tendered his resignation as president of Mexico. The only matter of which Manuel was unaware was that he, Antonio Santa Anna, was certain beyond doubt that his resignation would not be accepted. With that certainty in mind, he had made the request, citing the reason that he needed to return to Manga de Clavo to reestablish his health. He had used that excuse successfully before when the monotony of adminstrative routine had become too much to bear. In truth, he had become extremely despondent of late. The new congress that had met on January 4th had contained a majority of delegates of the clerico-army coalition. It was a group that would do his bidding without question, and the spice of

416

opposition had been removed from that portion of his life. He was a man suited to action. He did not have the temperament of a clerk, and it was just that situation he seemed to have slipped into, with all challenge removed from his life.

Sighing inwardly, he diverted his eyes from his friend's assessment and busied his hands in the papers on his desk. The elimination of the lovely Morgana Pierce from his life and his failure to recover her had been a blow to his morale, and had no doubt contributed to his sense of boredom in a capital that had seemed filled with excitement with her lovely face to spark his days. In the time since her disappearance, he had found no one to take her place. Consuelo de Artega . . . that whore . . . she had been petitioning him for forgiveness ever since that night in her flat of rooms, but she had gone too far. Even the memory of the active night she had given him, her considerable skill in pleasing a man's body, could not overcome his anger. And he had no interest in occasional whores. He was a man dedicated to the chase, stimulated by intelligence, impressed by beauty, a man who became bored when women solicited his favors. Ah, with Morgana it would have been different. She was the only woman he had ever met who possessed all of the qualities he admired in women. She also possessed an intense desire to learn about his country so she might appreciate it fully, and she shared one of the ruling passions in his life, his addiction to riding. She was an excellent horsewoman, whom he would be proud to have at his side. And, in addition to all her other attributes, she was a warm and loving young woman who responded to him physically with spontaneous passion. He had sensed the innate sensuality in her from the first, and his one close encounter with her in the forest outside the city had proved to him that she was too inexperienced to feign the response he had stimulated within her. How eagerly he had anticipated teaching her the rites of love. His nights had been filled with the thought, and he had not been able to escape her since.

Perhaps his failure to recover her had been one of the major reasons for his disenchantment with the capital scene . . . he was truly uncertain.

In any case, he needed to get away, to clear his mind and

rest his spirits. He had not seen Doña Ines for a long time, and it was time he returned to establish himself as head of the household at Manga de Clavo. It would not do to allow her to become too firmly entrenched as its head. Not that she would dare to oppose him in any way. Perhaps that was the problem with their lifeless marriage. A woman of good family and considerable wealth, she had little else to recommend her as his wife, aside from her fidelity. He respected her immensely, but had little desire to take her to his bed. But he would return to Manga de Clavo and fulfill his marital duties. Perhaps, in doing so, he would be successful in purging Morgana from his mind . . . but he sincerely doubted it.

He had left one piece of business unfinished that he would have to handle before leaving for Manga de Clavo, and, lifting his head to Manuel once again, he restated quietly, "I have considered the situation in great detail, Manuel, and have reached a firm decision." Picking up an official-looking document, he delivered it into Manuel's waiting hand. "I have instructed the court to pardon Colonel Austin, so he may return to Texas."

"You are certain that is wise, Antonio?"

A smile moving across his lips for the first time, Antonio's eyes gleamed with the secret he was about to share. "*Sí,* I am certain pardoning him will be very wise. Colonel Austin remained my friend and supporter throughout his entire incarceration. If I am to believe what is claimed to have been overheard when Devon Howard visited him, Colonel Austin spoke up heatedly in my defense when Señor Howard sought to criticize me. In any case, Colonel Austin is a sincere man, a bit too sincere and too gullible to be an effective politician, but my actions in his favor will doubtless impress upon him the trustworthiness of my character. In that way, I will have my own personal emissary returning to Texas to carry on the fight for loyalty to the government of Mexico."

Manuel's lined countenance slowly creased into a smile. "You have renewed my confidence in you, Antonio. I should have known better than to doubt you even for a moment."

His expression sober, Santa Anna nodded his head. "Yes,

you should have known better, Manuel. General Barragán has agreed to maintain my cabinet in full during my absence, and to consult with me on all important matters, using a steady run of couriers to Manga de Clavo. And, a few days after I leave the city, you will formally present congress with the portrait of me, showing me as the hero of the battlefield of Tampico. I will not be far away from my office at any time, despite the absence of my physical presence.''

Realizing he had allayed his friend's worries with his statement, Santa Anna allowed instructions on another, more painful matter to pass his lips. ''And now I instruct you, as your friend as well as your *presidente*, Manuel, so listen closely to what I say. Should any word of Morgana's whereabouts be received, no matter how insignificant or tenuous, I wish to be informed immediately. And should she be returned to us by the grace of God while I am gone, you may depend on my immediate return to the capital!'' His voice dropping, Santa Anna continued quietly, ''You will please extend to Doña Isabella my sincere regrets once again for my inability to be successful in returning Morgana to her home, and tell her my failure in that respect is the source of great despair to me.''

Standing abruptly, Santa Anna stared soberly into his friend's face. ''So, I will say goodbye for now and leave the remainder of the unfinished affairs in your capable hands.'' Extending his hand, he grasped the hand Manuel held out in return. ''Goodbye my friend, for a while.''

Devon stood rigidly erect, his eyes on the letter in his hand as he reviewed the contents for the third time. A slow coldness moved down his spine as he read the words again:

    . . . and so, Devon, I am writing to you personally so
    you will know that Presidente Santa Anna has insti-
    tuted proceedings to obtain a full pardon for me. I can
    only say I am relieved to find that my faith in him was
    not unjustified, and I will continue to seek support of
    our grievances through him.

The letter proceeded to thank Devon for his attempt to obtain his release.

A pardon . . . Steve would receive a pardon and would be returning home. Instead of experiencing relief, Devon felt a new tension spring to life inside him. With Steve's release the only valid reason for Morgana to remain would be swept away. He had had little contact with Morgana since the night he had gone to her room. He had confronted her solemnly the following day and apologized for his behavior, stating that his judgment had been impaired by the amount of punch he had consumed. The thread of truth in that statement had allowed him to face her with the lame excuse, but the pain in her eyes had been almost more than he had been able to bear. Had it not been for his promise to his father, he was certain he would have taken her into his arms then and there and poured out his love for her. But he had realized later that day that his actions would have been unwise, when Sam heatedly related that Morgana had come to his study prior to Devon's apology and asked Sam to set a date when she could expect to return home. Burdened by his knowledge of the preceding night, Sam had given her the best assurance he could afford and then poured out his anger on his son for driving Morgana to pleading for release.

He had spent little time at the homestead in the weeks since, and each return was met with a coolness from Morgana, and the realization that an even stronger bond had developed between his father and her. But he now experienced little jealousy over their growing closeness, other than the deep-felt wish that he was able to approach Morgana as easily as his father. He had done his father a grave injustice with his jealousy on the day of their arrival at the homestead, and he had regretted it ever since. His father was an honorable man who was deeply aggrieved by his son's behavior, and Devon had to admit he could not blame him in the least for his feelings.

His fingers tightly clenching the paper he held in his hand, Devon stared unseeingly at its blurred surface. He would soon hold a similar paper in his hand, which would force him to give Morgana the release she waited for so impatiently. His eyes moving from the letter for the first time since it had been put into his hand, he surveyed the bleak countryside. It was late in February, and the land was devoid of the color and scent of summer. In its stead a general greyness had overcome the land. As he ran his eyes over the terrain, the greyness seemed to pervade his soul, and he realized his life would have the same sense of bleakness without Morgana. The knowledge that she had returned to Antonio Santa Anna's arms would make his very existence more than he could bear.

Looking down at the letter once again, Devon took it very carefully between his two hands and rolled it up into a tight ball. Turning slowly, he walked with a measured step into the house and approached the blazing fireplace. He tossed the small white ball into the flames and stood for long moments until the last blackened flakes of its existence had fallen away. Turning, he walked outside and stood for long moments staring at the horizon that had occupied his thoughts only moments before. The letter had been a personal communication to him alone, and he was not obligated to relate its contents to anyone. In his heart he realized he had only a little more time. The committee would doubtless be informed officially of Steve's pardon very shortly, and with the official notification would come the necessity to allow Morgana to return home. But that was in the future, and he could not face that future now. For now he would deal with the present and his need to keep Morgana close, at least close enough that he might see her . . . hear her voice. He would not face her leaving now . . . he could not. . . .

"*Sí*, señores, my duty to the place of my birth has made this decision for me. I will be leaving tomorrow. If God is good to me and I am allowed to survive the encounter which is to come, I will return."

Facing Sam and Devon solemnly, within the limited confines of Sam's study, Raoul Rafraga awaited their response. His eyes moving from Raoul's intense expression, Devon as-

421

sessed his father's worried face. Raoul's declaration had not been completely unexpected. Devon's political activity kept him well informed on the situation developing in Zacatecas. The spirit of democracy had run high for generations in that northwestern province. It was a region where an independence-loving Indian population had defied the conquerors and had forced frontiersmen into settlements described as places where the farmer held his plow with one hand and his gun with the other. When the races had amalgamated, the love of freedom had not abated. Congress had gone too far in ordering the discharge of nearly all the local militia. Zacatecans were exceedingly proud of their local troops and did not wish to be left at the mercy of a regular army controlled by the central government. Devon had been aware that a revolt was imminent, but the realization that Governor Francisco García had actually begun to gather his men in defense of their principles was still chilling. He had no doubt in his mind that this would indeed be only the first in a series of revolts that would alter the map of Mexico radically.

Sam's expression grave, he broke the silence that followed Raoul's declaration. "You have my best wishes for the success of Governor García's endeavor, Raoul. We'll be happy to see you come back when the work in Zacatecas is done, but I admit to strong doubts as to the advisability of an open revolt against the central government."

"We have a very large militia, señor. It is well trained and ready to fight for our liberty."

"I have no doubt your hearts are strong with purpose, but who will lead your men? You do realize that you have no trained generals . . . that your men have never seen military action as a force? You will doubtless be facing Presidente Santa Anna himself. He is a veteran of many conflicts. He has been directing his men in such action since his early manhood. You will be going against a well-trained army that has already functioned as a unit under fire, and a commander who is ruthless."

"We can be ruthless as well, señor."

Realizing the senselessness of arguing a point when it

would accomplish nothing, Sam turned toward his son, his anxiety reflected in his eyes. "Well, I suppose this is the first of it, Devon."

"Yes, Sam." Hesitating only a moment, Devon continued quietly, "When Raoul leaves tomorrow morning, I'll be going with him." The words had slipped from his lips naturally, without conscious thought, but, his decision made, Devon faced his father's startled expression soberly.

"Have you thought this decision through, Devon?" Sam's voice bore a strong note of concern.

"I'm tired of words, Sam. I wasn't comfortable in the position of diplomat in Mexico City. I suppose I'm just not suited for that type of work. I'm much more at home functionin' out in the open, without hidin' behind words and promises. You know how I feel about Santa Anna, and if this is the only way I can fight for what I believe in, well, I'm goin'."

"We will be happy to have you with us, Señor Devon." Raoul's wide smile reflected his pleasure in Devon's decision. Not really feeling the elation that Raoul seemed to be experiencing, Devon returned his smile. "*Grácias,* Raoul."

When Raoul's short, compact form had cleared the doorway, Devon turned back to face Sam's scrutiny.

"Why are you doin' this, Devon? Is it really because you feel so strongly about the Zacatecans' situation, or is it because your own situation here has become too discomfortin' for you?"

"I don't know, Sam." Answering his father's question honestly, Devon shook his head. "Maybe it's a little of both . . . maybe it's my way of payin' back for the mess I made of things when I brought Morgana here. Hell, I realize now I was a fool. There's only one way to stop Santa Anna, and the Zacatecans have the right idea."

"I think you should take some time to think this over, Devon."

"Hell, Sam, I've done enough thinkin'. I don't have to do any more. I'll be leaving with Raoul tomorrow."

"I hope you aren't making a mistake, son."

Shrugging his shoulders, Devon smiled slowly into his father's sober face, "If I am, Sam, it sure won't be my first."

Standing at the window in the grey light of dawn, a coverlet wrapped around her shoulders against the early morning chill, Morgana watched the two men in front of the house as they checked their supplies. Raoul walked to the pack mule and continued his examination while Devon turned to his father's unsmiling countenance. Their expressions were sober, the words that passed between them quiet and restrained.

A deep sadness had remained with Morgana through the long night, the same sadness that had begun at the supper table when Devon had announced his intention to leave for Zacatecas in the morning. She was unaware of the tears streaming down her cheeks as she watched Devon shake his father's hand. After a moment's hesitation, they embraced warmly, and her heart ached to be out there with them . . . to feel Devon's arms around her, hear his whisper of reassurance in her ear. How very much she wanted to tell him that she loved him . . . that this conflict was not his own. But Devon didn't need her concern, and he had no desire for her love. He had not spoken a word to her of his plans. He doubtless considered the general statement at the supper table sufficient for her.

Her heart crying out in silent agony, Morgana watched as Devon turned away from his father at last and mounted his horse. Giving a nod to Raoul at his left, his eyes seemed to flick momentarily in the direction of her window before he spurred his horse forward. His broad shoulders were fading into the greyness of the semilight when Morgana's first sobs began. Still staring into the distance long after their figures had disappeared into the horizon, Morgana whispered hoarsely through her tears, "You never said goodbye, Devon. You never said goodbye. . . ."

Her hand moved to rest on the flat surface of her stomach, her eyes closing against the pain that coursed her senses. She must make certain to be away from the homestead by the time Devon returned. She would not have him know . . . would not keep him bound to her by duty or guilt. She would be away by the time he returned . . . she must.

CHAPTER NINE

A familiar elation moved through his veins. Taking a deep breath, Antonio Lopez de Santa Anna ran his eyes along the green landscape as the strong animal he rode whinnied with excitement. The thunder of hoofbeats behind him was sweet music to his ears. Turning his head momentarily, he allowed himself a glance back at his men. A force three thousand strong followed at his heels, their eyes intent on him, awaiting his command. His spirits high, Santa Anna heard the singing of an exultant voice in his mind. *This is the life to which you were born! This is your destiny!*

A small smile moving across his lips, Santa Anna acknowledged the truth of that inner voice. Yes, he was not born for the mundane chores of this world. He was a man born to action . . . the heat of battle, the thrill of the chase, the glory of victory! His body and soul had been in the doldrums on his estate. Kept in constant touch with the affairs of the capital by frequent messengers, he had returned immediately when movement in Zacatecas had become threatening. He had instantly petitioned the congress for permission to raise a force to proceed to Zacatecas to settle the growing problem, and by the beginning of the month he was already enroute.

Everything was proceeding exactly as he had anticipated. His information on the terrain, the climate, the distances involved, all had been accurate. His early training serving him well, Santa Anna went over in his mind the battles he had studied. Yes, this area was perfect. He would employ the same tactics for which Arredondo had become famous. Even the time of year was conducive to the same sort of attack. Yes, he would be successful against the ill-trained men of Governor García. The man was a fool who deserved to lose his hold on the province! What other man would be so trusting . . . allow information on his defenses to fall into the hands of men not worthy of his confidence? He himself was no such fool! There were few that had his confidence, and, in some matters, he confided in no one. As it was, it had not been difficult to obtain a spy in Garcia's camp, and plans were already under way for the defeat of the idealistic but unrealistic governor!

It had been a long time since he had been at the head of an army, and the old sense of power had returned to intoxicate him once again. Yes, he would be victorious! It was his fate to lead his country to victory! It was the fate to which he was born!

She was walking in a vast, fog-shrouded field. She could hear a voice calling . . . calling her name from somewhere within its murky reaches. It was his voice . . . Devon! It was growing weaker! A mind-searing panic overwhelmed her. She rushed recklessly forward! She stumbled! Her hands shot out in front of her to break her fall, coming into contact with a cold, human form. She strained her eyes to penetrate the ever thickening mist. Dead! The man was dead! She drew back, cringing at the contact, her eyes moving to the area around her. The ground was littered with bodies, twisted and bloodied, lying where they had fallen in battle.

He called her name again, his voice broken, rasping. Torn

427

from her immobility by the heart-wrenching sound, she jumped to her feet. Her eyes searched the ground, silent tears falling freely as she called into the opaque, floating mist.

"Where are you? Tell me where you are, Devon. I can't find you!"

"Morgana . . ." His voice was softer, weaker. Suddenly filled with a sense of raging urgency, Morgana stumbled forward, her eyes moving along the still forms scattered on the ground. She heard his voice again, the direction from which it came clarifying in her mind. She heard his voice once more. Abruptly certain of her direction, she began to move more hastily. But the voice had stopped. She could hear him no longer.

"Devon! Tell me where you are! Devon!"

Her own voice reverberated in the mist, confusing her with its desperate sound. Where was he? Where? There was a still form only a few feet away. Surely it could not be Devon . . . the man was dead! Rushing to the lifeless body, Morgana dropped to her knees, a sense of relief sweeping her senses even as she stared into the stranger's frozen grimace of pain. She crawled to the next body . . . and the next . . . her hands touching the cold flesh, searching the still, anguished faces of death. He was not there!

"Morgana . . ."

Her eyes snapped up at the voice and moved to another form only a few feet away on the fog-covered ground. Jumping to her feet, she rushed toward him, her heart pounding wildly in her breast as the dark head lifted weakly. He called her name once again.

"Morgana . . ."

Dropping to her knees with a low sob, Morgana leaned over him, her hands reaching out to touch his cheek as she muttered hoarsely, "Devon . . . I was afraid I would be too late." Dropping her cheek to his, she allowed herself the small comfort only to hear Devon's low voice in her ear. "You *are* too late, Morgana. It's too late for us . . . too late for me. . . ."

She jerked back only far enough to stare into the light,

428

familiar eyes, her hands roaming caressingly across his shoulders as she rasped in return, "It's not too late, Devon."

Her hands touched on a sticky wetness even as she spoke. Lowering her eyes to his chest, Morgana saw it was covered with blood.

A deep shudder shook his frame . . . a sound rattled in his throat . . . her eyes wide with fear, Morgana looked back into his face in time to see his eyes close . . . his lips still.

"Devon! Devon!" Her voice an anguished cry, Morgana touched his face. There was no response. Her voice was pleading and low. "Devon, please answer me. Don't die, Devon . . . don't die. . . ."

There was no response. Deep, shattering sobs wracked her body, tore at her heart. It could not be too late. It could not be!

"Devon, please don't die . . . don't die. . . ."

The light of morning was harsh against her eyelids. Emerging slowly from the hazy world of night, Morgana fought to attain reality. Tears stained her cheeks; her throat was hoarse from crying. It had been a long, painful night, but she had awakened! It had been a dream . . . just a dream. . . .

Abruptly Morgana was struck with true realization. It had not been a dream. It had been a warning! Filled with a compelling sense of urgency, Morgana jumped from the bed. Within moments she was at her washstand. Quickly pouring water into the basin, she lowered her head and splashed her face with its cool freshness. Stripping off her night rail, she reached for her clothes. She had no time to lose.

The acrid smell of gunsmoke was heavy on the air. The steady barrage of gunfire they had been subjected to for almost two hours was getting closer, more accurate. Defending their position from a small cluster of woods, the company of volunteers, commanded by the swarthy Zacatecan militiaman, had already fallen back twice and was experiencing heavy casualties. Shooting a quick glance around him, Devon could hardly believe the confusion that dominated the scene. Dead men littered the ground almost as far as he could see, the sounds of wounded and dying blending with the rapid exchange of fire between the Zacatecans and the Mexican forces who were so successfully routing them. Militiamen who, only a short hour before, had been shouting slogans of expectant victory were now deserting the ranks, fleeing in the face of Santa Anna's advancing forces.

His mind racing as he returned the rapid fire, Devon acknowledged to himself that doubts about the preparedness of the Zacatecan forces had been strong in his mind since the day of his arrival in their camp. Men of high spirits and courage, the Zacatecans had been supremely optimistic, but a sense of disorder and frivolity had dominated the camp. A man of strong personal principles, Governor García had been nevertheless completely ignorant of the principles of warfare. His inadequacies had been apparent from the first. Insufficient planning, inadequate defenses, a lack of organization in the handling of munitions had resulted in the chaos that now dominated the scene. But Santa Anna's mastery of the battle had been too quick, too complete to be a result solely of his superiority as a tactician. His anticipation of the exact strategy Governor García had employed had been too exact to be the result of a guess.

Devon had little doubt in his mind that Santa Anna had made full use of his loyal followers within the Zacatecan ranks. But whatever the means he had employed, Devon had already accepted the fact that defeat was not an unavoidable reality. The end was near. Incongruous as it seemed, Santa Anna's force of thirty-five hundred men had been successful from the first in routing the five thousand men who had stood ready to defend Zacatecas.

His eyes darting back in the direction in which Raoul had disappeared over a half hour before, Devon felt again a nudge of anxiety. Because of his familiarity with the area, Raoul had been sent with a message to the governor's position. But

430

he had not returned.

A bullet cracked against the rock that shielded him, the splinters of stone cutting his face as Devon's mind jerked from his wandering thoughts. The bullets hit again and again, snapping at the ground around him, sparking the rocks, forcing him to keep his head down without returning fire. There was a sharp cry from the man beside him as he fell to the ground. There was another cry and another. Running his eyes along the ridge of their defenses, he saw that the other men, like himself, were unable to return the fire that was picking them off one by one. A low, hoarse shout came from the burly Zacatecan who had been given command of their group. His bloodied arm hung lifelessly at his side. His face pale under his dark *mestizo* coloring, he called the men to yet another retreat. More fell in the rapid rain of gunfire as they moved to meet his command. It was a senseless slaughter . . . a massacre . . . for which Santa Anna would undoubtedly be hailed a great hero.

His head low, Devon moved slowly along the ground. The gunfire had become so intense, the bullets so exacting, that it was the only manner of retreat left to them. A bugle sounded in command, followed by a roar of voices, a thundering death that advanced upon them with the power of trampling hooves. They were being overrun! Jumping to his feet, Devon began to run, his mind registering that his only safety lay in reaching the band of trees to the rear, where he might find shelter from the advancing forces. His mind registered in the frantic moments as the fleeing men scrambled for cover that there was no glory in this victory, and no honor in this defeat. Massacre . . . bloody death. A low grunt came from the man running beside him. His eyes snapping toward the man, Devon was hardly past the moment of realization that the man had fallen dead when a hot, searing pain slammed into his own back, knocking him to the ground.

He was barely conscious, aware only of the sound of footsteps running beside him . . . fleeing. The pain in his back was shattering, stealing his breath as he strained to get gulps of air into his laboring lungs. His mouth was dry. He licked

431

his lips only to find the gritty taste of sand on his tongue. The footsteps raced by him. He had no voice to call them back, to ask for help. But there was no help for them . . . no honor in defeat . . . no glory in this death. . . .

The May sun was hot on her head, the breeze warm against her face as Morgana's horse flew over the ground. Turning back momentarily, she searched the distance for a sign of someone in pursuit, but there was no one. Her eyes moving forward once again, she kept her gaze steady on the broad back in front of her, her mind drumming, "They won't catch us . . . they won't . . ."

Their flight had started in midmorning of that day. Somehow she was still disbelieving that John had actually consented to take her to Zacatecas without Sam's knowledge . . . to help her get away. But she had been unaware of the desperation reflected in her eyes when she had pleaded for his help. Abruptly, John was signaling her to stop. She reined up beside him as he directed a level glance into her eyes.

"We'll walk the horses for a while, Morgana. We've run them long enough." Nodding her head, Morgana fell in beside him, her eyes darting to his unsmiling face.

This was a John she had never seen before, a new, determined man whose eyes reflected his strength of purpose. Gone was the warm, friendly light she had come to associate with his smile. Instead, a hard, defensive barrier had sprung up between them.

"John, you're angry with me, aren't you?"

Taking long moments before he returned her gaze, John spoke slowly in reply. "I'm not angry with you in particular, Morgana. And you aren't makin' me do anythin' I haven't wanted to do many times in helpin' you get away. Hell, Devon had no right to take you to Texas in the first place. His idea was crazy." His eyes lingering on her face for long moments, he continued in a softer voice, "Although, I can almost see how he fell into the trap of his crazy reasonin'. He was jealous . . ."

432

Morgana shook her head in spontaneous denial. "No, John. Devon doesn't care about me that way."

John's sober expression was adamant. "You have a blind spot where Devon's concerned, Morgana, and the trouble is, he's got the same blind spot for you. You've both been workin' at cross purposes since the time you arrived at the Circle H. Hell, for a while it sort of gave me hope. I figured you'd never get together at that rate and I'd stand a chance with you. But I know now that's never goin' to happen."

"John, I'm sorry . . ."

"That's why I'm helpin' you, Morgana. I figure that there's only one way you're goin' to straighten up your life, and that's to get back to Mexico City. I agree with what you said. With all that's goin' on in Zacatecas, now's the best time to put in an appearance." His eyes moving over her worn peasant clothes and *rebozo,* the same in which she had traveled to Texas, he nodded tightly, "When Santa Anna sees you all wrapped up like a Mexican Indian, he'll believe for sure you escaped from the bandits in the excitement, and that you talked me into takin' you to him. As a matter of fact, Morgana, I suppose Santa Anna will believe just about anythin' you want to tell him if what Devon says is true."

"It's not true, John." Her expression tight, Morgana pleaded his understanding. "But Antonio is a friend on whom I can depend. That's the only reason I want to go to him. He'll take me home."

"If he's victorious."

"Even if his forces aren't victorious, John, they won't dare hold the president of Mexico prisoner. He'll be released, and when he returns to Mexico, I'll go with him."

"I could take you back myself, Morgana."

"No!" Unwilling to admit that she needed to be sure of Devon's safety before she could leave with Santa Anna, she continued rapidly, "In the crush and excitement of the returning hero, I'll be all but forgotten. And that's the way I want it to be, John."

433

Nodding his head in silence, John turned his attention back to the trail in front of him. Whatever her reasoning, Morgana deserved the right to make her own way . . . to live her life as she saw fit, and he was going to make sure she did.

The supreme commander and his entourage walked proudly among the exultant troops. Eyes gleaming, Antonio López de Santa Anna graciously received the homage of the cheering men, his chest swelling with the glory of the moment. Victory! Governor García's troops had been crushed after only two hours' combat! He had already faced the humbled governor, given orders for the officers of the rebellion to be placed under arrest, and, if the first count was correct, managed to hold in his power twenty-seven hundred prisoners from the defeated army! And now his men hailed him!

Again and again the cheers sounded around him, at last bringing a smile to Santa Anna's sober features. The men's spirits were high, soaring . . . and they deserved a reward . . . the ultimate of rewards for their loyalty. His decision made, Santa Anna turned back in the direction of his temporary headquarters, a small house close enough to the area where the prisoners were confined and where the inevitable tasks involved in the resolution of matters were to be carried out. He knew from experience that it was best that he keep his camp in tight control at this time of wild celebration. He would have nothing go amiss now.

His shoulders squared, his posture proudly and militarily correct, Santa Anna entered the house and proceeded directly to the dining room, where the table served as his desk during his occupation. He had no idea where the owners of the house had been sent, and he cared little. His thoughts centered around the spoils of victory, he took a piece of paper from the table and scribbled his orders. Signing his name with a flourish, he handed the paper to his second in command.

"Inform the men of the contents of this order immediately! Tell them that their commander is deeply moved by their loyal service, and as a reward gives them the city of Zacatecas for their own until we return to the capital!"

The hesitation on the part of the silent general was obvious. Irritated by the man's sober acceptance of his announcement, Santa Anna frowned, his eyes snapping with annoyance as he questioned sharply, "What is wrong, Arturo? You take exception to my command?"

"You do understand what you are doing, Antonio? The men are in a state of excitement. The thrill of victory is pumping through their veins and restraint will be long forgotten in acceptance of this announcement."

"*Sí*, I understand very well what I have given them!" Santa Anna's voice was harsh, impatient. "I have given them the city and all within it to do as they see fit until we leave. I will reward loyalty and punish the traitorous conduct of the Zacatecans with this one sheet of paper, and when all is done, I will have men who will follow me to the ends of the earth in battle when they are needed!"

"But the innocent, Antonio! There will be no distinction made between those who supported the rebellion and those who did not!"

"Those who did not support the rebellion in action did so in spirit! I will crush that spirit . . . wipe it from the face of the country! I have no sympathy for those weak fools! To the victor belongs the spoils, and I will see that my men have their just reward!"

His eyes blazing, Santa Anna kept his gaze on the flushed face of his subordinate until the man lowered his eyes and began to turn away.

"Arturo, you will not leave yet. There is something I would have you do first." Waiting only until the silent general had turned his stiff face back toward him, he continued unhesitatingly, "Before that order is issued you will make sure that a more than adequate guard is maintained in the camp; that the prisoners are heavily guarded; and that an adequate number remains so that our guard will be fresh at all times! I will not have a misstep now." Hesitating a mo-

435

ment, he continued slowly, "I should also like to walk through the ranks of the prisoners so they may view me at close hand. I wish to impress upon them, burn into their minds, that Antonio Lopez de Santa Anna is the man whom they have opposed, and that he is the very same man who brought them to a crushing defeat! I would have them face that fact . . . deal with it squarely . . . so that they will not dare oppose me again!"

Nodding in response to his commander's words, the weary general turned in the direction of the doorway, his back stiffening as Santa Anna's words reached his ear.

"You follow my orders with obvious reluctance, Arturo." There was a new softness to Santa Anna's tone, and amicability that turned the man back toward him warily as he continued speaking. "It is not that I am a man without feelings, my friend. It is merely that I feel very deeply the pain of the traitorous actions that have taken place here today. I do not wish to have it happen again."

"And you feel this is the manner in which to guarantee loyalty, and achieve the love of your people?"

"When I have their fidelity, I do not necessarily need their love. I will accept their submission in its stead. And, Arturo," beginning again as the greying general was about to turn away, "you will summon a guard to escort me among the prisoners. I would see them now, while defeat is still strong in their minds."

"*Sí*, Antonio. I will summon a guard immediately."

"And you will accompany me, Arturo, among the prisoners." His smile broadening, Santa Anna continued softly, "I will have them remember that you were at my side as strongly supporting me as you do our government."

There was a lapse of a brief moment in which General Arturo Ayala studied Santa Anna's intense expression. His response was clear, without reservation. "It will be my honor to accompany you . . . to walk at your side, Antonio."

Nodding his head, his eyes burning into the lined face, Santa Anna responded slowly, "*Gracías,* Arturo. I will review the prisoners as soon as the guard is assembled."

The slumped, dirty groups of men parted as he advanced through their midst. His eyes moving from side to side in appraisal, Santa Anna saw the dark eyes drop from his. A new elation beginning to soar through his veins, Santa Anna lifted his chin proudly. They were humble in defeat! He would have no further trouble from the Zacatecans!

Low moans met his ears, turning Santa Anna toward an area where wounded men lay on the ground, roughly covered with the jackets of a few of the more sympathetic. Walking toward them, he suppressed the smile that moved to his lips. These fellows would soon be released from their prison by a grant from the Almighty. It might do his image well to show compassion.

Walking among the uneven rows, Santa Anna tensed at the odor of blood and death that permeated the general area, and his flesh crawled. It was one thing to die gloriously in battle, but this slow, lingering death was foreign to his thinking. His eyes moved slowly among the men. He had no desire to prolong his stay in this area of the . . .

Jerking to a halt as his eyes touched on a still form lying at his feet, Santa Anna felt the shock of recognition move across his senses. Devon Howard! His eyes moved over the still face, his gaze moving to the bloodied chest that moved so shallowly. He still lived, the arrogant Texan who had dared to bargain so boldly with the president of *Méjico!* Consuelo de Artega's words came to his mind, renewing his rage. No, the insidious whore had made that whole tale up . . . there was no possibility that Devon Howard knew where Morgana was being held. No, there was no possibility of that. . . .

The pale lips moved slowly in reaction to some anguished dream. He was obviously becoming more agitated. Unable to tear his eyes from the stiff lips that muttered indistinctly, Santa Anna strained to hear his words, a flush suffusing his face as he heard the low voice rasp painfully, "Morgana . . ."

437

Jerking his head around to face his guard, he ordered sharply, "Take this man to my headquarters and have some-one attend his wounds. When he is conscious I wish to speak to him."

Turning to face General Ayala, he said stiffly, "I've seen as much as I care to see of this area of the camp." Signaling his men, he turned and retreated through the ranks of prison-ers, his expression hard and unrelenting. His former mood of jubilation was gone.

Morgana's face swam before him, darting in and out of the dark passageways that filled his mind. He was warm, unbearably warm. He attempted to rake at the collar of his shirt, but the simple movement of his arm made him cry out in pain. It was difficult to breathe in the slow heat that was consuming him. He was thirsty, and Morgana stood before him, her eyes sober. She held a cup of water in her hand. He attempted to raise himself toward it, but she snatched it back with a frown. He couldn't really blame her for wanting to hurt him. He wasn't angry with her. Instead he wanted to tell her . . . let her know how he really felt.

"Morgana . . ."

The harsh rasp was painful, difficult to get past his stiff lips, but she stared at him still, her eyes hard and unrelent-ing.

"Morgana, I want to tell you . . ."

The words were in his mind, crying to be spoken, but Devon could not manage the small task. Supreme impa-tience with his impotent state gained control of his emotions, and he fought desperately the weight that seemed to crush his lungs, restrict his voice.

His world was abruptly shaking around him. A loud voice was calling in his ear. He struggled to escape from the dark netherworld where he was helpless against himself. His eyes were heavy weights that he fought to lift, the effort exhaust-ing him as he felt someone shake him again, shout even louder into his ear, calling him back to consciousness. The light of waning afternoon began to move between his parting lids. He was lying down. Tall, still forms stood around his bed. Someone shook him again, and he turned toward the hovering shadow with a frown. He did not want to be awakened, not yet. . . .

A heavy, strangely familiar voice called him. The voice raised the hackles on the back of his neck, and he felt an unknown anger assail his senses. He blinked against the blurring shadows that encompassed the faces of the men, his eyes slowly clearing . . . slowly clearing to realization.

"Devon Howard . . . I can see that you recognize me, Devon. I had begun to think that I had instituted all this care to no avail."

His vision was clear, allowing him to read the enjoyment on Santa Anna's face as he continued slowly, "Circumstances are quite changed since the last time we spoke, are they not, Devon? You faced me boldly on that morning, and I told you I would allow you your minor victory because of my desire for Morgana. We made a bargain that day, do you remember?"

Santa Anna's face was beginning to fade away when Devon felt the rough hands shaking him again back to consciousness. Santa Anna still stood beside his bed, his eyes filled with annoyance as he instructed a man beside him to shake Devon once again. An anger at his helplessness snapped Devon's eyes open wide to meet Santa Anna's tense stare. Santa Anna signaled the blurred forms around him to leave, turning back to Devon once they were alone in the room. Bending low over the bed, he hissed sharply, "You will remain conscious, Devon. You will remain conscious until I am finished speaking with you. I have waited long enough to find out . . ." Stopping abruptly to take a deep breath, Santa Anna turned to search the immediate area with his eyes. Taking a few steps away, he returned in a few seconds with a chair. Obviously in better control of his emotions, he sat down and spoke slowly, his dark eyes trained on Devon's face.

"You have been wounded, Devon, and you are in a house

439

under my care. Many others like you have not been so fortunate . . . they lie in a long line within the prisoners' compound, waiting to die. Unfortunately, we do not have adequate men to help them in their distress, and I regret it deeply. But I *am* in a position to help you, Devon *if* you will agree to help me in return.''

The pain in Devon's shoulder was increasing. A low throbbing had begun that seemed to echo in his brain. He was warm . . . so warm . . .

''Pay attention to me, Devon! I will have my answer now!''

Devon moved his gaze back to Santa Anna's dark face. Santa Anna was not so much in control of the situation as he would have him think.

''We made a bargain, Devon. You would leave Mexico City, and I would see to it that Colonel Austin came before the supreme court. You would leave Mexico City, Devon, and Morgana would be mine. . . . She would no longer be bothered by your unwanted attentions. Do you hear me, Devon?'' Santa Anna's voice rose with impatience as Devon's eyes dropped closed against the pain that seared him.

Devon's eyes snapped open again in response to Santa Anna's impatient inquiry. Realizing that Devon looked at him clearly once again, he continued in a softer tone. ''Shortly after you left the city Morgana was abducted while riding in the hills. Her abductor was masked, but he was clearly a *mestizo*. I have my men's word on that. Morgana has been gone for many months, Devon. Despite the fact that we paid the ransom demanded for her, she was never returned to us. My men searched the hills, raided the camps of known *banditos,* but she was not recovered.'' Abruptly, Santa Anna's hands were on his shoulders, his strong hands inflicting excruciating pain on Devon's already pain-wracked body. The deep voice was relentless in his ear.

''Tell me, Devon! Tell me! Were you party to her abduction? Do you know where Morgana is? Tell me, damn you, or by all that is holy . . .''

The small smile that moved across Devon's lips brought a

jerking halt to Santa Anna's words. *"Bastardo!"* Santa Anna's voice was a low, venomous hiss. "You dare to laugh at me now . . . when I could so easily arrange your death by just walking away . . . ?"

Devon's lips moved in response, and, desperate for his answer, Santa Anna leaned down to hear his words. "Tell me now, Devon. If you wish to live, you will tell me now. Where is Morgana?"

Santa Anna's face was fading away, the rage reflected on his dark features allowing him a moment of mindless satisfaction. He whispered in response, but the words would not come past his lips. He tried again, finally emitting a soft, unintelligible reply.

"I don't understand you, Devon. Speak again! What did you say?"

". . . Sh . . . she's mine . . ."

Jerking back as if he had been stung, Santa Anna hesitated for long moments, his face flushed with the emotion sweeping through him. Taking a deep breath, he quizzed relentlessly, "You are telling me that you know where Morgana is . . . that she . . ."

The pain was intense, sweeping great, undulating swells of darkness across his mind. Devon heard Santa Anna's heated question. The sound reverberated in his mind, and he strained to answer again, to give him the only answer that he would or could.

His lips were stiff; his breath short. The weight of his heavy eyelids was becoming too much to bear. With the last of his energy, Devon forced his lips to part, compelled his voice to respond.

". . . Sh . . . she's mine . . . Morgana is mine. . . ."

Santa Anna sat impatiently at his makeshift desk. The joy had all but disappeared from his glorious victory. And it was all because of the damned Anglo who fought for his life in the room at the end of the small hallway only a few yards away! Damn that Devon Howard! But he would not allow the man to die until he found out exactly where Morgana was

. . . how he could get her back.

He had spent a horrendous morning in the completion of the endless details that accompanied a victory of this magnitude. He had been visited with a legion of complaints about the conduct of his men, charging them with plunder and rape, stating that the injustices practiced against Americans and English were particularly harsh. He cared little about the complaints of the defeated. As far as he was concerned, they had forfeited their rights when they had risen up in arms against him. The victory was now two days old, and he would soon have things well enough in hand to begin his triumphant march back to Mexico City. But he had sworn to himself that he would not make a move from this house until he had received an intelligible response from Devon Howard. He would find out where Morgana was, and then he would give Howard to his men to return to the rest of the prisoners. Howard would not last long under the harsh conditions under which they were being housed. And then he would be rid of Howard for good.

Looking at the clock on the mantel, Santa Anna shook his head. He had a few more people to see this morning, and then he would be done for the day. Arturo had arranged for two more interviews this morning, and he was anxious for them to be done. He ran an impatient hand through his dark hair and pulled himself erect in the chair. He would then go to the room at the end of the hallway and get an answer from Devon Howard. He would get it today, one way or another. His patience was almost at an end.

Morgana's knees were quaking badly. Sending a quick look to the two men who walked at her side, she felt again a rush of fear. The tension in her glance was met by John's steady brown eyes, the strength in their depths filling her with a fresh wave of courage. Her eyes moved to Raoul Rafraga's tense face, and she gave a silent prayer of thanksgiving. Had it not been for their chance meeting with Raoul and the miracle that had allowed him to remain uncaptured at the end of the battle, she would not be taking the steps she was taking now.

The pillage and plunder that had met their eyes when Morgana and John had reached Zacatecas had been overwhelming. Black clouds of smoke filled the sky, casting a choking screen over a ghastly tableau of death and violence. Bodies lay strewn across the countryside as grieving families attempted to retrieve their dead, their mournful cries blending with those of outraged, violated women who openly sobbed their despair. Bands of drunken soldiers roamed the city to take their pleasures where they chose, completing a scene of willful destruction that would be burned into her mind forever.

They had come upon Raoul at the entrance to the temporary headquarters set up by the victors of the short uprising. Her heart had leaped at the sight of Raoul's familiar figure, only to have him explain that he had been separated from Devon during the battle, but had found out that Devon had been taken prisoner and that he was wounded. Realizing there was no way in which to tie him to the revolt that had just transpired, Raoul had boldly decided to approach Santa Anna's officers for information on Devon, explaining that he had hoped Devon's position in the Texas colony would allow him special consideration. But Morgana's arrival had changed his plans.

Morgana's eyes moved to the doorway in front of her, her gaze flicking back to the men who stood expectantly at her side. So much depended on her . . . she dared not fail . . . she dared not. . . .

Her eyes moving levelly to the guard who stood at the doorway, she stated quietly, "We have permission to speak to the *presidente*, General Santa Anna, on a matter of importance.

The guard's dark eyes flicked over them briefly as he nodded his concurrence, realizing they would not have gotten into the house without clearance. Turning away from them, he knocked on the door, opening it on Santa Anna's short response.

"Three more people to see you, general."

Not bothering to lift his head, Santa Anna snapped a short

"*Entra.*" Raising his gaze as footsteps sounded within the room, Santa Anna's dark frown fell away, his jaw dropping with incredulity as he rose spontaneously to his feet.

"Morgana!"

His expression of disbelief turning to incredible joy, Santa Anna moved quickly around the table. Sweeping Morgana into his arms without hesitation, he held her tightly against him for long moments in an effort to convince himself she was indeed real. Still holding her tightly, he allowed Morgana to separate herself from him slightly, his eyes only for her as he murmured in a low, intimate tone, "*Querida, querida* Morgana. I had begun to think I would never see your beautiful face again, but you have returned and we . . ."

His eyes abruptly jerking to the men who stood behind her, Santa Anna was acutely conscious of the suppressed anger of the broad, blond fellow and the inscrutable *mestizo* countenance of the shorter man at his side. He had little patience for their assessing eyes in his desire to welcome Morgana more intimately.

His attention returned to Morgana, his annoyance falling away as his gaze touched on her incredibly lovely face.

"*Querida,* there is much I must learn about your disappearance . . . your absence as well as your return, but for now I must allow myself to look at you, to fill my eyes with your beauty." His hands moving to her cheeks, he cupped her face with his hands. His voice filled with emotion, he whispered softly, "I have missed you greatly, *querida.* It is in answer to my many prayers that you are returned to me." Lowering his head, he pressed his mouth against hers for a short, warm kiss. Summoning all his will, he drew himself away, his arm slipping around her waist as he raised his gaze to the two men.

"But first you must introduce me to your companions. Since I have no doubt it is to them I owe your return, I would like to thank them personally."

Turning toward John's tight face, Morgana smiled, hiding her nervousness in an expression of smiling gratitude. "This gentleman is John Fuller, Antonio, the man to whom I owe my successful escape from the men who held me captive, and this man is Raoul Rafraga, whom we met by chance on the way to your headquarters. He is an employee of Devon Howard." Turning to Santa Anna's suddenly dark expression, she questioned tensely, "Is something wrong, Antonio?"

"I find it strange that Devon Howard's name was closely associated with your disappearance by a particular friend of mine, and now that you have returned unexpectedly he has once again come onto the scene after an absence of months. I find it too strange to be coincidental. . . ."

Morgana could feel the arm curved around her waist stiffen. Realizing she had no choice, she turned into Santa Anna's arms and pressed herself against his chest. "Antonio, please. It has been extremely difficult for me these past few days. It is only through an almost unbelievable set of coincidences that I was able to escape the men who held me. I only knew their first names, Antonio, but they were *mestizos* who decided to throw their lot in with Governor García in hopes of personal profit from the battle. But you were victorious, as I knew you would be." Managing to feign a light of admiration in her upswept eyes, Morgana continued in a tone she hoped would be convincing, "I knew this would be my only chance, Antonio, with you so near." True tears filling her eyes as she contemplated the outcome if Santa Anna did not believe her story, she reached up to touch his cheek tenderly. "I was fortunate enough to meet Mr. Fuller, and it was through him that I managed to find you without suffering at the hands of the madness that is progressing in the city."

His heart melting at the sight of her tears, Santa Anna lowered his head to kiss her lips once again. Shrugging aside Devon Howard's cryptic response to his questions as the ramblings of fever, he pulled Morgana tight into the circle of his arm and turned back to John Fuller. The young man's expression was sober and unrevealing, and, abruptly reasoning that his suspicions had allowed him to read more into the young man's gaze than was true, he extended his hand warmly.

"Señor Fuller, I will be forever in your debt. You will not go away unrewarded." His expression stiffening, he turned

445

toward Raoul Rafraga. "Unfortunately, señor, I am not sure I will be able to help you. . . ."

"Oh please try, Antonio!" Morgana interrupted Santa Anna's sentence with a torrent of words. Deciding to stick as close to the truth as possible so she would not catch herself in an untruth, she continued convincingly, "Raoul told me that Devon was fool enough to join in the uprising against you . . . that he is presently a prisoner and is wounded. At one time I was very fond of Devon, Antonio. I will admit to you that prior to arriving in Mexico, for a few weeks at sea, I actually fancied myself in love with him." Her face flushing at the statement, Morgana continued quietly, "It was only after I arrived in Mexico . . . after I came to meet her people," Morgana's eyes insinuating a hidden meaning to her words, she continued, "that I came to realize the error in my thinking. But as you know, Antonio, it was exceedingly difficult to discourage Devon's attentions once they had been stimulated. He seemed to have a proprietary feeling for me." Almost choking on her words, Morgana swallowed hard. "As a result, I feel obligated to him. He was exceedingly jealous of you, Antonio, and it is my thought that that may be the reason for his turning against you so foolishly. The thought haunts me, Antonio. Since I have met Señor Rafraga, I have known no relief from the thought. After so many months as a prisoner, I could not bear to think that another suffered the same way because of me. . . ."

"If he suffers as a prisoner, it is because of his own traitorous acts, not because of you, *querida*." Santa Anna's tone was consoling.

"My mind knows that, Antonio, but my heart is heavy. I've asked Señor Rafraga to come with me here today because I wanted to have total peace in returning home . . . so I might forget those months spent in the *mestizo* compound."

"There is no relation between the two, Morgana."

"In my mind there is a relationship, Antonio." Pressing herself a fraction closer against him, Morgana could feel his body's response to her warmth. Turning the full power of her gold-flecked gaze to his, she said softly, "Please, Antonio."

Lost in her eyes, Antonio felt only the raging pull of his desire. Yes, he could understand why Devon Howard would mumble that Morgana was his. Had not he, himself, considered Morgana his own? Had he not known that when she was returned it would be into his arms, as his lover? No doubt Devon Howard felt the same, but he was wrong. No, he wanted to do nothing that would turn Morgana against him for even the slightest moment. Devon Howard was no threat to him now, and if he allowed the *mestizo* to take him home, surely it would be a sign of his generosity, and his desire for peace. He would gain much by such a magnanimous gesture, but, most of all, he would gain Morgana's gratitude.

His hand moving to the silk of her hair, Santa Anna said softly, "All right, if it is what you wish, Morgana, I will allow Devon Howard to return to his home with this man. As a matter of fact, I have already taken steps to have his health assured. He is in this very house, in a bedroom down the hallway, under the care of a doctor who will visit him again tonight."

A trembling started deep inside Morgana. Devon was in this house, in a room down the hallway! She longed to run to him. Instead, with the sheerest power of will, she kept her expression consistent, her voice even. "He is badly wounded, Antonio?"

"*Sí*, it is a serious wound. It is the doctor's opinion that the bullet that entered his shoulder from behind passed through him, damaging him internally as it did. He feels that the bullet missed the lung, but his condition is serious, nonetheless. He has a fever and has been delirious much of the time." Santa Anna did not mention that his only concern for Devon's health prior to this had been that he might die before he could be questioned further. His eyes moved instead to Raoul, missing the revealing momentary drop of Morgana's eyelids as she fought to regain control over her anxiety. "We will be returning to Mexico City soon. I had thought a certain matter would necessitate that I remain in Zacatecas a bit longer, but the situation has changed, and we will be returning as soon as possible. You may take Señor Howard with you as soon as you feel it is safe to do so. I will issue instructions that the matter is in your hands. As far as I am concerned, Devon Howard was never here." His eyes moving back to Morgana's pale face, he said softly, "I have matters of more intimate concern to fill my mind at present."

Abruptly unable to withstand her anxiety a moment longer, Morgana stated quietly, "I would like to see Devon, Antonio. Despite the angry words that have often passed between us, I would feel more at rest if I saw him alive and recuperating. I have seen enough death the past few hours to last a lifetime."

His expression suspicious, Santa Anna studied her expression for long moments before replying. "*Sí*, if that is your wish, Morgana. We will go now, down the hall. Your friends may accompany us. It is perhaps better that we settle this matter and dismiss it completely from our minds."

The smile that moved across Morgana's lips was warm and appreciative. "You are a very understanding man, Antonio."

Within moments, they stood before the room at the end of the hallway. Her heart pounding, Morgana waited as Antonio slowly opened the door and urged her inside. Carefully guarding her expression, she allowed her eyes to move to the bed that dominated the center of the small room. Her gaze intent on the man that lay in a restless sleep in the silence of the room, she walked slowly forward, aware that the three men followed behind her. Stopping at the foot of the bed, Morgana hardened herself against the pain reflected in Devon's expression. His face was flushed with fever. Beads of perspiration covered his forehead and upper lip, and he shivered unexpectedly. A large blood-stained bandage covered his one shoulder and part of his bare chest, and he began to mumble unintelligibly in his unconscious state. The surging response to his need was strong inside her, the ache of suppressing her own driving desire to rush to his side almost more than she could bear. Almost beyond her endurance, she was immensely grateful for Raoul's quiet interjection.

"There would be no objection if I remained with Señor Devon? He is obviously in need of attention, and his father would be exceedingly grateful to me if I aided in the saving of his son's life."

448

"No, I have no objection." Turning away from Raoul, Santa Anna was about to address Morgana when Devon's eyes slowly opened. His glance moved unsteadily around the room, jerking to a stop the moment it touched on Morgana's still face. Staring, as if he was uncertain whether to believe his eyes, he attempted unsuccessfully to speak. Licking dryly at his lips, he managed a low, rasping word.

"Morgana . . ."

"It seems he recognizes you, *querida.*" Urging her forward to stand beside the bed, Santa Anna slid his arm around her waist, pulling her close against his side as he spoke. "Yes, it is Morgana, Devon. It is fortunate, is it not, that she was able to escape her confinement and return to me? I feel a deep gratitude that this unfortunate uprising provided her the opportunity she awaited so long." Turning to look into Morgana's still face, Santa Anna raised his hand to cup her cheek. Gradually, deliberately, he lowered his mouth to hers, his kiss slow and deep.

Trembling so hard she could barely stand, Morgana allowed Santa Anna's mouth to cover hers, his lips to move caressingly as she fought the desire to push him away and rush to Devon's side. Frightened that Santa Anna's suspicions were stronger than she feared, she raised her mouth more fully to his and separated her lips invitingly. Withdrawing his mouth, a new spark in the dark eyes that devoured her face, Santa Anna turned back to Devon, his face flushed with triumph.

"Yes, mine is a double victory, Devon. Zacatecas is crushed under my heel, and Morgana is in my arms."

Devon frowned. He struggled to speak, but could not. Impatient with Devon's weakness, Santa Anna turned toward Raoul. "He is in your care now, señor. You may do as you wish with him." His glance moving toward John, he said lightly, "You will please come with us, Señor Fuller. I should like to show my appreciation to you before you leave."

Holding Morgana close, Santa Anna moved to the doorway. He opened the door and allowed her to precede him into the hallway before sliding his arm around her waist once again. When they reached the dining room, he walked around the table and reached into a box on his desk. He withdrew a small bag and counted out some gold coins. He walked toward John Fuller and offered them soberly.

"I don't want money for bringin' this lady where she wanted to go." John's protest was low, spoken through gritted teeth. He was obviously in tenuous control of his anger.

Interrupting softly, Morgana drew his cold gaze to her face "Please take the money, John. You may be in need of it before you return to your home. I should not like to think that you wanted for anything you needed because you shared your rations with me the past several days."

The soft plea in her voice was effective in softening John's hard expression. Hesitating only a few moments longer, he raised his hand and allowed Santa Anna to drop the coins into his palm.

Santa Anna's voice was low as he spoke, his expression unreadable. "You have my deep appreciation for returning Morgana to me, Señor Fuller, no matter the reason for your deed."

Nodding his head, John turned for one last glance in Morgana's direction before walking silently out of the room.

Waiting until his broad-shouldered figure had cleared the doorway, Santa Anna turned to Morgana. "The young man did not expect you to receive so warm a reception from me, *querida*. He obviously has deep feelings for you. I suppose I shall have to become accustomed to having men's eyes follow you with desire. It is difficult for me to tolerate at present. I admit to being very jealous of you. It would be very unsafe for you to inflame my jealousy, *querida*. I am not a very temperate man."

Her eyes raised to his, Morgana whispered shakily, "These past months have taught me much, Antonio . . . the value of friends and loved ones and the extreme vulnerability of all I hold dear. I would do nothing to jeopardize their safety, and will do anything I can to protect them. You need not worry about me any longer, Antonio. I am here with you now. We will return to Mexico City together, and I will resume my life as before.''

His lips lowering to hers, Santa Anna whispered softly, the portent of his words sending a chill down Morgana's spine.

"Not exactly as before, *querida*. There will be one small difference. You will belong to me, Morgana. Only to me. We have made our bargain today, have we not?''

Her brow gathering in a frown, Morgana was long minutes in coming to full realization of the meaning of Santa Anna's statement. His eyes narrowing, Santa Anna pressed again, the thread of iron in his voice clearly revealing the menace of his words. "*Sí*, Morgana, I accept all you say without question, because I want you. I give you what you want because your gratitude will bind you to me. We have struck a bargain, you and I, and I will have you honor it as you honor your life. We are agreed, are we not, *querida*?''

Swallowing against the tightness in her throat, Morgana held Santa Anna's gaze unflinchingly. When she spoke, her voice was steady and sure. "Yes, we are agreed, Antonio. We have a bargain.''

His lips moved lightly against hers as he pressed relentlessly, "And you will honor it, Morgana." Lifting her arms from her sides, Santa Anna slid them around his neck, a smile flicking across lips that touched hers lightly as she allowed him to pull her intimately close. "I want to hear you say it, *querida*.''

His hands were moving warmly against her back, his body was hard with passion. Her eyes flicked closed for the briefest second before returning to meet his ardent gaze. "Yes, I will honor our bargain, Antonio. I will honor it as I honor my life . . . my life and the lives of those I love.''

"Then we are agreed, Morgana . . . *mi amor* . . . *mi vida*. We are agreed at last. . . .''

The lamp at the bedside burned dimly, its flickering glow illuminating the small, austere room. Standing stiffly beside the smooth surface of the bed, Morgana trembled, her eyes intent on Santa Anna's impassioned face as he approached her with slow, measured steps.

His voice was low, alive with passion. "I have waited a long time for this, *querida*." Reaching up to caress her cheek, he whispered into her eyes, "For no other woman have I ever longed so intensely or waited so long. You are the ideal I have carried in my mind for all of my life. You are so beautiful." His dark eyes moved to the unbound silk of her hair as his hand slid to touch its gleaming surface. "I have never seen hair like yours, Morgana. It appears to live and breathe as it glows in the light. At my first sight of you I was impressed with the perfection of your features, but it was only after I had become familiar with them that I realized the rarity of your beauty . . . fine porcelain skin molded over the magnificent slope of your cheek, expressive eyes that offer a wealth of gold in their depths, and a soft, generous mouth to welcome me . . . give me consolation. I knew then that I must have you . . . possess you for my own."

Santa Anna's mouth moved to cover hers with a searing hunger, his body hard and strong against her as he pulled her into his arms. Closing her eyes against the repulsion gripping her senses, Morgana allowed his mouth to sink deeply into hers, parted her lips at the urging of his tongue, endured the deep, probing penetration of her mouth. She was trembling with revulsion, her mind reacting wildly as she struggled against the urge to jerk her mouth from his, push the eager body that sought to consume her far away, and to run . . . run and escape the horror that was slowly descending upon her.

Pulling his mouth from hers, Santa Anna whispered passionately, "Your body trembles with need for me, Morgana, as mine trembles with my need for you. But first, I wish to see all of you, *querida*. I have seen you naked before me many times in fantasy during the long hours of the night, and I wish to realize my dream . . . this portion first, so I may enjoy you fully. Come, let me see you."

His hands moving tremblingly to the tie of her blouse, Santa Anna undid the closure, and, stretching the neckline wide across her shoulders, pulled it down to her waist. The flimsy chemise beneath was next to fall under his quest, his sharp intake of breath sounding in the room as her full, white breasts were exposed to his avid gaze. Reaching out, he slid his hands down the slope of her shoulders, the length of her arms. Her flesh crawling, she allowed his hands to caress her breasts.

"Perfect . . . beautiful . . ." Lowering his head, Santa Anna covered a pink crest with his mouth, groaning as he suckled her roughly. Holding her tightly, he strained her backward in his eagerness, moving greedily to the other breast to suckle it just as hungrily in turn. Abruptly pulling himself away, he mumbled a low curse under his breath, his eyes shooting up to hers as he hesitated momentarily. "I am almost beside myself with excitement, *querida,* but I do not wish to pass this moment too quickly. I have waited too long."

Slowly undoing the closure to her skirt, Santa Anna allowed it to fall to the floor, pushing the blouse and chemise along with it as he struggled to bare her naked flesh at last to his eye. The small underdrawers were the last to go, the delicate fabric ripping in his impatient hands.

Trembling with shame, Morgana flushed deeply as Santa Anna took a few steps backward to allow himself a more complete view of her naked form. She stood still, her eyes straight ahead, her clothes in a pool around her feet as he walked slowly around her, his hand reaching out to touch and caress her intimately in his wonder. Once again facing her, his eyes were heavy with the passion that held him in its power.

"I have never seen a woman with your beauty, Morgana." His voice was low, his eyes strained with sincerity. "Had I not foolishly agreed to my arranged marriage to Doña Ines, I would take you as my wife, to keep with me the remainder of my life. I have a strong desire to declare you as my woman, *querida,* to feel the pride of knowing all acknowledge that you belong to me. With you I do not wish to resort to the clandestine meetings to which we will be forced. Your position as Manuel's niece will make frequent meetings difficult. Manuel is an honorable man who would not allow a love affair to progress between us, no matter his loyalty to me, and, because I respect him, I shall have to be doubly cautious. Our meetings will be less frequent than I would wish . . . and I chafe at the thought even now, before I have taken you for the first time. You have a body of a goddess, *querida,* white and perfect, and I would wish to enshrine you in my heart and life. But I must content myself with the time which we will be allowed to share between us. And that time begins with tonight, *querida.* . . . this night . . . now.''

Scooping her up into his arms, Santa Anna walked a few quick steps to the bed and laid her gently on its surface. He was breathing heavily, his eyes moving slowly over her nakedness as he began to pull the clothes from his body. His shirt fell roughly away, tossed to the floor as he began working at the closure on his breeches. Within moments, the sight of his naked desire was exposed to Morgana's gaze. She glanced away involuntarily as he stood still beside the bed.

"Look at me, *querida.*" His voice was hoarse with emotion. "I want you to look at me. I wish to feel your eyes touch my body the same as mine touched yours only moments ago." When still she hesitated, he urged impatiently, "Do not be shy, *mi amor.* We shall each come to know the other's body intimately and to take great pleasure in the sharing of our flesh."

Slowly raising her eyes to his, Morgana allowed her gaze to move from his face, to the broad shoulders, the expansive chest, the narrow rib cage and waist. Santa Anna seemed to preen before her, his enjoyment intense as she swallowed tightly and dropped her gaze farther. His manhood stood strong and stiff between the thickly muscled thighs of his rather short legs. Raising her eyes again to his face, Morgana saw the flood of emotion that engulfed him the moment before he moved to the bed beside her, his flesh hot against hers as he kissed her deeply. The kiss went on and on, breaking at last to move to the column of her throat as she gasped from the nausea slowly enveloping her. His lips moved to her shoulders, a low, guttural sound rasping in his throat as he jerked to seize her breast with his teeth, biting painfully before opening his mouth to suckle her once again. He was consuming her, profaning her with his lust, and Morgana felt the rise of bile to her throat. No! She must control herself . . . contain the disgust searing her mind, the loathing for the base, animal act that she was allowing to be enacted upon her body. She must . . . Devon's life hung in the balance of her control. Devon . . . her love . . .

Gritting her teeth against her own self-loathing, she moved her hands to hold his head against her as he snatched at her other breast with his teeth. He groaned under her caress as she moved her fingers in his hair. Biting her lips as his groaning ministrations continued, she had just tasted the bitterness of her own blood in her mouth as a loud banging on the door jerked Santa Anna from her breast.

Muttering a low oath under his breath, he raised himself on one arm. *"Quien está?"*

"It is Lieutenant Arroyes, general!" The excited voice hesitated briefly, only to continue in a rush a moment later, "There is trouble in the prisoners' compound! There is a fire and an attack has been mounted in an attempt to rescue the officers. General Ayala has been wounded and is unconscious. The men are unable to hold out against the attack. We need . . ."

"Basta!" Jumping to his feet, Santa Anna grabbed for his clothes, his movements quick and precise as he dressed with abruptly steady hands. Turning toward Morgana with a short look as she drew the coverlet across her nakedness, he said tightly, "Go to your room. It will not do to have you found here. I will come to you when all is settled in the camp."

Turning toward the door, his teeth clenched tightly shut in angry frustration, Santa Anna opened it only wide enough to allow himself to slide through, as he growled into the young lieutenant's nervous face, "They will pay for this and pay heavily . . . and then they will die!"

Morgana listened intently as the heavy footsteps moved up the hallway and faded from her hearing, finally releasing a low, sobbing breath as the front door slammed heavily. For the first time she heard the sound of gunfire in the distance as the sound of racing hoofbeats moved steadily away from the house. Jumping immediately to her feet, she ran to the window in time to see Santa Anna's white stallion fade into the darkness.

Snatching at her clothes, she pulled them on with trembling hands, gulping against the tears that scalded her cheeks. The horror of Santa Anna's lovemaking still upon her, she slid her feet into her sandals and raced to the door of the room. Opening the door slowly, she glanced into the hallway to find it deserted. She stepped out, pulled the door closed behind her, and started toward her room. Hesitating momentarily at the doorway to the room in which Devon lay, she took a deep breath. No, she could not go to him now. She felt unclean . . . defiled.

Turning away, she continued on down the hallway and turned into her room. Her stomach was churning violently . . . the taste of bile was strong in her throat. She could still smell Santa Anna's strong, musky scent against her skin, and she felt a sharp, jerking spasm in her stomach. The memory of Santa Anna's mouth against her flesh, his teeth snatching at her intimately, returned, and she rushed to the washstand to retch violently. And when she was done, she retched again.

The light of morning moved against her scratchy lids, alerting Morgana immediately to the new day. Her eyes jerked open and her glance moved to the bed beside her. It was empty! Santa Anna still had not returned. Jumping quickly from the bed, Morgana pulled on her clothes, and running a hand through her hair as she approached the door, she jerked it open. She did not wish to be found so conveniently in her room. Stepping into the hallway, she shot a quick glance in the direction of Devon's room. No, she dared not enter to see how he fared. If Santa Anna should return . . .

The aroma of food assailed her senses, increasing her light nausea, but considering the safety offered by the presence of others when Santa Anna returned, she headed quickly in the direction of the kitchen. She did not want to be alone with Santa Anna . . . not so soon.

* * *

She had long before finished the cup of chocolate that sat in front of her. Managing to consume the thick, sweet liquid between intermittent bites of a small piece of bread given to her by a haggard *mestizo* woman forcibly inducted into the service of the general, she listened intently for the sound of returning horses.

A quick, light step turned her in the direction of the doorway as Raoul moved into the kitchen. Her eyes reflecting the anxiety that had raged within her from the moment of her awakening, she raised her questioning expression to his. Raoul's glance moved to the guard at the door as if in warning before he addressed the woman who moved so heavily around the small room.

"*Por favor, señora.* I would like to have some food for myself and the prisoner who is recuperating from his wounds. The General Santa Anna has indicated he is to have what is needed to make him well." As the woman raised her weary eyes, Raoul continued quietly, "Señor Howard is much the same as yesterday, although the doctor feels his wound is clean and will heal. He feels it is just a matter of time until Señor Howard regains his strength."

"I care little about the health of your patient, señor." Her voice low and grumbling, the old woman poured a pitcher of chocolate and put some bread on a plate before turning back in his direction. The glances Raoul and Morgana had exchanged had gone unnoticed, as did the relief in Morgana's eyes as the woman continued impatiently, "You may take this to your patient, and I pray he is soon well and off my hands. I have enough to cook for in this house."

Raoul took the plate and pitcher with a small nod. "*Grácias, señora.*" Shooting Morgana a small, encouraging smile as the woman turned back to her work, Raoul left the room.

A thickness filled Morgana's throat. Devon would get well . . . he had to. And she would return to the capital. Her stomach wrenching again at the thought of the future to which she had sentenced herself, Morgana quickly dismissed the thought. She could not bear to think of the long nights to come, the . . .

The sound of pounding hooves came to her ears. A large troop was returning. Swallowing tightly against the tenseness in her throat, Morgana rose on unsteady legs and walked toward the entrance of the house. She would meet Antonio at the door to show her anxiety for his return. It would not do to make him suspicious of her intentions while Devon was still so vulnerable.

She had just stepped into the living room when the door snapped open to reveal a flushed and angry Santa Anna. He was walking stiffly, his usual military posture sacrificed to the pain that obviously gripped his chest as he entered the room.

"Antonio? What's wrong?"

His eyes moving to her face, Santa Anna gritted his teeth tightly in obvious pain as he responded in a low voice, "We have put an end to the attempted rescue of the prisoners. Those who sought to rescue, now also are in the prisoners' compound, and there they will remain! *Bastardos!*" Gasping at the pain caused by his short explanation, Santa Anna continued in a low hiss, "They sought to capture me, the *idiotos,* and set a trap. My horse was thrown from his feet and I fell to the ground. I feel I have injured my ribs . . . perhaps broken a few, but I have made the *bastardos* pay!" His face whitening as the pain became intense, Santa Anna took a staggering step toward her, only to be caught by the supportive hands of his aide as he began to falter.

. Her eyes darting to the man at his side, she instructed spontaneously, "Call the doctor. The *presidente* is injured." Stepping to Santa Anna's other side, she said softly, "Lean on me, Antonio. I will help you to your room. You need some rest."

His pain-filled eyes moving to hers, Santa Anna nodded his head. "*Sí, querida.* You are right. I will rest for a while and then I will be better." A light gleam coming into his eyes despite his pain, he whispered into her ear as he leaned on her shoulder. "and then we will continue where we left off, *mi vida . . . mi amor . . .*"

* * *

The humid air was choked with the dust of four thousand men on the march toward the capital. A fine layer of the staining deposit lay on her skin as Morgana lifted her head to the warm, May breeze. Once again she wore the large sombrero and *rebozo* that had been her attire on her journey from Mexico, but she felt none of the foolish resentment against their protection that she had experienced before. The large gelding beneath her snorted momentarily, drawing her attention from her troubled thoughts to the landscape through which they passed. Endless and unchanging, it stretched out hypnotically before her eyes, affording her a brief sense of peace. But her respite was short-lived. A short, gruff command snapped her eyes to the man riding at her side. They had been on the trail for over a week and Santa Anna still sat uncomfortably stiff, his ribs giving him far more pain than he would admit. He had been tightly bound by the doctor before he left Zacatecas and had been warned against the danger of traveling in his condition, but the doctor's warnings had fallen on deaf ears. His discomfort acute, he still managed to ride for the greater portion of each day in an effort to reach Mexico City with the least delay possible. He was anxious to report his success to a congress set to be dismissed shortly. There was no doubt he wanted his day of glory in the capital, and would suffer any manner of pain to achieve it.

The last week spent in his company had removed the last vestige of the distorted image of Santa Anna that had clung to her mind. She now viewed him clearly for the first time, and recognized him as the clever, charismatic opportunist that he was. She also realized that the integrity with which she had credited him was truly only in her mind. The first rude awakening had come when she had entered Zacatecas and had seen the carnage he had allowed to go unchecked. It had been monstrous, but all protests had been met with Santa Anna's reply that he had no jurisdiction over their claims, and another official would have to consider them. The second had been the manner in which the wounded prisoners had been left to suffer and die with little or no medical treatment. She had no doubt in her mind that Devon Howard had been afforded differential treatment only temporarily, and, had it not been expedient for him to continue with Devon's care, Devon would have suffered a similar or perhaps worse fate.

Yes, Devon had been right from the beginning, and she, in her foolish stubbornness, had been unable to see Antonio Santa Anna for the man he was until it was too late. And it *was* too late for her now. Only Antonio's injury had spared her the violation of her body that was yet to come. He had assured her most passionately that only a pain of the magnitude he experienced could keep him from proving his love for her over and over again each night.

Devon. Her mind had returned to him countless times in the long days on horseback. How very different this journey had been from the journey she had shared with Devon on the way to Texas. In looking back, she was incredulous that she had not recognized the emotion that had raged through her body at Devon's touch. Even now the memory of his sharply angled face sent a rush of warmth through her veins. She had been able to visit his room covertly once before leaving Zacatecas. Devon had been asleep, but she had been able to see that the flush of fever had left his face, that he rested comfortably. The bandage on his shoulder had been freshly changed at the time the doctor had come to attend to Antonio, and there appeared to be no further seepage of blood. Yes, he was healing, and was doubtless on his way back to Texas by now.

Giving her head a small shake, Morgana attempted to clear her mind of Devon's image. It would do her no good to think of him now. She had made her bargain. Through her own stubbornness in refusing to admit that she had judged Antonio poorly, she had put herself in a position where the bargain she had made had been the only way to save the lives of those she had come to love. In a few weeks, she would indeed be the woman Devon had always believed her to be . . . Santa Anna's mistress. She would prove him right again.

Shrugging away the mist of tears, Morgana slid her hand to rest on the flat expanse of her stomach. She knew she would need to bear Antonio's attentions for only a short while. She would soon be in a position to make his attentions to her far too much of an embarrassment. He would send her away and be forced to find another woman to fill her place. She needed to set her mind on that day in the future when she would be free of him. It was only in that way that she would be able to go on.

CHAPTER TEN

Morgana sat quietly in the familiar Escobar sala and remembered. How long ago was that time when she had spent long days recuperating in this very room? Devon had come to see her every day during that time. He had been loving and attentive. She could remember well the time he had called her to the window so he might look into her face to assess the return of color to her cheek. She had lifted her face to his, and seen the warmth growing in the blue of his eyes. She had been pouting that she was not allowed to walk downstairs . . . that she was really quite well; and he had carried her down. She remembered his arms around her, lifting her easily. She remembered him holding her close in the garden before they had been interrupted by her uncle . . . and Antonio.

A familiar pang twisting inside her, Morgana sought to eliminate the unwanted dark-eyed image from her mind. When she saw Antonio now, she saw him only with the light of lust in his eyes. How had she not realized that that spark had been there from the first? She was truly uncertain, but whatever it had been, she had suffered her penance for her ignorance. No, perhaps she had not suffered it in full, not yet.

A small smile moved across Morgana's lips. She had never considered herself a person who enjoyed another's pain, but if ever there had been a heaven-sent punishment, it had been Antonio's wound in Zacatecas. By the time they had reached Mexico City, Antonio's pain had been intense. His entry into Mexico City had been triumphant! Congress had remained in session long enough to welcome him before adjourning. His posture erect despite his pain, he had accepted the public acclaim and the declaration of the congress that he was "well-deserving in heroic grade." Congress had likewise neglected to withdraw the office of general-in-chief conferred upon him, so he retained those unusual powers as well. In a master stroke, he had pardoned the officers of the rebellion as a gracious act, stamping himself a gracious and generous foe. The masses and the man had gloried in the smashing victory, and his gluttonous nature had been sated.

Her small smile widened. Well, he had been sated in that way, at least. The pain in his ribs and the complications created by his long journey back from Zacatecas had forced Santa Anna to retire to Manga de Clavo only a few short days after his arrival in Mexico City. He had bid her an emotional farewell, his eyes promising much for the time when he returned physically recuperated. Her stomach churning with distaste, Morgana recalled the heat of the kiss he had pressed on her lips prior to his departure. Yes, he would come back to claim her, she had no doubt.

The unpleasantness in her stomach becoming more than she could bear, Morgana arose from the couch and walked slowly to her room. She was beginning to perspire from the persistent nausea with which she had awakened. Nausea had become a familiar state of late, but she had accepted it as a natural part of her condition. Her hand rising to her mouth, she pressed her fingers tight against her lips as she began to run faster. She burst into her room and raced for the basin. And then she was retching, and retching again.

Lifting her head at last, she reached into the pitcher with the small cloth that lay beside it and rinsed her face. She was weak and trembling, and, deciding she needed to lie down for a few moments, she pulled off her gown and was standing silhouetted by the afternoon sun as it shone through the window when Aggie entered the room. Unable to manage a smile, she walked shakily to her bed and lay down. Moving quietly to her side, Aggie looked silently into her eyes for a few long moments. Aware of her obvious tension and her unwillingness to discuss the months she had spent away from them, neither her aunt and uncle, nor Aggie, had pressed Morgana with questions upon her return. Instead, they had showered her with love and attention, and, under their care, she had begun to regain her sense of belonging in the household. But Aggie's wide, owlish eyes were intent on her face, her glance knowing.

"Who is the father of the child, Morgana?"

Morgana's gaze did not falter, but she remained silent. When she did not respond, Aggie's expression became uncharacteristically pained. "Ah, my poor child, is it that you do not know who is the father of your child, is that it?"

Morgana's eyes snapped wide with shock. It had not occurred to her that Aggie would think . . . would assume . . . Unwilling to allow her dear, loving friend to suffer the pain of that assumption, Morgana hastened to assure her.

"Oh, no, Aggie. I know the father of my child very well. I do not wish to divulge his name. He is not aware of my condition, and I do not wish to tie him to me. But, please believe me, Aggie, I'm not unhappy about carrying his child. I am proud and happy to know that I carry a part of him with me, a part that no one can take from me."

Speaking her feelings for the first time, Morgana realized the truth in her words, and a new elation moved through her senses. She carried Devon's child. She would never have Devon for her own, only this part of him. . . .

Aggie's face stiff, her expression unchanging, she stated solemnly, "It is Presidente Santa Anna's child. He is the father of your child."

"No!" Morgana's denial was loud and vehement, startling Aggie with the tone of outrage it carried. "No, that man is not the father of my child." Closing her eyes for a brief moment, she mumbled low, under her breath, "No, I could not stand that . . . to bear his child."

"Then who?"

"It is Devon's child, Aggie. It is Devon Howard's child, and I look forward to seeing him born, to hold that part of his father that we have created together."

"Your child was conceived in love, then?" Aggie's voice was low, her tone carrying unexpected understanding.

"For me, yes, Aggie. I loved Devon when he made love to me, and I love him now, even though his feelings for me did not include love." Taking a deep breath, Morgana continued quietly, the warm gold in her eyes tearing at Aggie's heart, "He has found someone else, a woman he knew before he met me, and I know he has returned to her." Shaking her head as Aggie attempted to question her further, she whispered hoarsely, "I can't say any more, Aggie, except to tell you not to feel sorry for me. I'm very happy . . . or almost happy." A small frown moved briefly across her face as she began her next sentence, "After all my debts are paid, and my pregnancy begins to show, I shall ask Tía Isabella to send me away . . . perhaps back to Veracruz, where I may stay until I have the child. I'll go back to New York or perhaps Philadelphia. Tía Isabella will finance me until I find a job . . . as a widowed nanny with a small child. It should not be difficult to find such work. I am well schooled, and have had the very best of companions since I was a small child."

Her old heart breaking as Morgana continued, Aggie watched Morgana's smile fade uncertainly. "I had intended to ask Tía Isabella to provide for transportation for you, also, Aggie. I should not like to leave you here. We may reimburse Tía Isabella when we find a position. Perhaps we will even be close enough to see each other occasionally."

Shaking off the tears that had flooded her eyes, Morgana said abruptly, "I'm tired now, Aggie. I should like to rest."

Reaching down to pull the light coverlet across her, Aggie nodded her head, and, after a few moments, silently left the room.

The palace was ablaze with lights to celebrate the return of the *presidente*. Seated in the Escobar carriage as it moved through the large central courtyard and pulled up before the impressive structure, Morgana felt the nervous flutters in her stomach increase. She had not seen Antonio since the day of his arrival at the capital almost a week before when the sound of a commotion in the courtyard of the house had drawn her to the railing. She had been momentarily stunned by his unexpected appearance, almost unable to respond as he had followed a happily chattering Tía Isabella up the staircase and come to stand before her. His posture erect, his eyes bright, the glow of health was on his face once again. He had allowed his gaze to move over her slowly from head to toe, the warmth in his eyes increasing as he had stepped forward to place a kiss on her cheek.

"Morgana . . . *querida* . . ." His dark eyes had continued on with silent endearments as he had stared silently at her for a few moments longer. "How is it possible that you have become even more lovely than when I left?" Turning to smile at Tía Isabella's indulgent face, he had stated softly, "I admit to passing much time thinking of our dear Morgana while at Manga de Clavo. It occurred to me that she should have an opportunity to get away from the capital scene for a little while, to recuperate from the hardships she must have endured while alienated from us for so long."

A small frown had moved between Tía Isabella's narrow brows. "Morgana is quite well, Antonio. Had Manuel and I thought the capital too hard on her, we would have taken steps to . . ."

"Ah, Isabella, I handle these things poorly. I did not mean to infer that Morgana suffered by her return to the capital. No . . . no . . . I am certain she was only too happy to return to the bosom of her family. It was for another reason, however, that I made mention of my thoughts. Doña Ines has begun to feel an isolation from the capital scene. I sensed her disquiet, and she admitted to me that she would like to become more involved in my political life. But, alas, she is shy and ill at ease in the capital. It is for that reason that I suggested having Morgana visit us for a few months, just until I am slated to return to the capital and resume my duties in September. In that time Ines might be persuaded to return with us."

Tía Isabella's frown had not lessened. Her hesitation to allow Morgana out of her sight for so long a period was obvious. "I am not sure it would be in Morgana's best interests, Antonio. Perhaps she may visit Doña Ines another time. She has been away from us for so long . . . we have just begun to realize our good fortune in having her returned to us. We should not like to lose her so soon again."

A flicker of annoyance had moved across Santa Anna's face. Turning to Morgana, he had said quietly, "It is a thought we may consider, is it not? I will leave again for Manga de Clavo at the end of the week. My business here is almost complete, and I am not yet fully recuperated." His eyes closing with a covert, unexpected wink sent a flush rising to Morgana's face, and, abruptly amused by her reaction, he had slipped her arm through his as he had urged her with him toward the sala. Taking Tía Isabella's arm also, he walked comfortably between the two women, his unexpected familiarity returning the smile to Tía Isabella's face.

"But we will discuss it at a later time, shall we not, ladies? For now, I should like to reacquaint myself with two of the loveliest Mexico City has to offer. . . ."

The matter had been dropped, but it had not been forgotten. Tío Manuel had returned just the day before from a consultation with Santa Anna, and hinted heavily that Antonio would be very grateful if Morgana would be allowed to return to Manga de Clavo with him for the sake of his lonely wife. Antonio had generously offered to have Aggie travel with Morgana, but Morgana had not been deceived by the ruse. With a deep certainty, she realized Antonio would find a way to come to her at night, even while his wife slept in a room a few doors down the hall. The thought filled her with deep revulsion. Now, on this evening of the lavish, belated victory celebration two days before Santa Anna was slated to return to Manga de Clavo, she was certain the decision would be made with or without her approval. And she dared not refuse . . . she dared not. . . .

The carriage drew to a full stop before the palace staircase. Biting her lip nervously as the footman opened the door, Morgana moved her hand absent-mindedly against her up-swept coiffure. It was a warm night, well suited for the hair style on which Tía Isabella had insisted when she had presented her with the lovely new gown she wore. She had arranged to have it made as a surprise, and a true surprise it had been indeed.

Touching the skirt of the gown lightly, Morgana marveled again at the delicate white batiste. The neckline of the garment exposed the creamy skin of her shoulders, cupping them gently in a narrow ruffle of self material; the exaggerated bouffant sleeves, so very much in style, ballooned out from the shoulder to fit tightly at the cuffs. The bodice of the gown hugged her bosom tightly, pinching in at her waist to a point almost of discomfort, to flare out full and wide to just above her ankles, where a wide band of embroidered satin edged the bottom of the gown. A similar band of embroidered satin was tied around her waist, and similar embroidery appeared on the toes of the fine white satin slippers that peeked out from the hem of the gown. Insisting she wear her hair piled in loose curls atop her head in the style in which she had become so fond of seeing Morgana wear her hair in recent weeks, Tía Isabella had also insisted Aggie pin her diamond clips in a graceful half circle from the back of one ear to the other. In her ears Morgana wore Tía Isabella's diamond stud earrings, and at her neck a single teardrop diamond of which Tía Isabella was very fond. Had it not been for the occasion she was attending, Morgana would have felt a true pleasure in the supreme luxury of her apparel, but anxiety had moved to chase all other thoughts from her mind.

Taking the hand offered to her, Morgana stepped down from the carriage, the long climb up the palace steps accelerating the already rapid beating of her heart to an even wilder rhythm. Unable to absorb the splendor of the ballroom into which they were led, or the magnificent dress of those attending, she saw only, instead, the dark gleaming eyes of the *presidente* as he spotted them at the entrance and walked immediately toward them. Her heart beating at a rate that left her breathless, Morgana nodded at Antonio's warm reception.

"Ah, Isabella, Manuel, and dear Morgana. But you are late, my dear friends. I had begun to believe you would not be attending this dreary function, or so it seemed without the company of my favorite guests. The musicians have been playing for at least an hour." Taking Morgana's hand as the orchestra struck up anew, Antonio made a slight formal bow. "If you would do me the honor, *querida*."

Giving a small nod, Morgana followed Antonio to the dance floor, extremely aware of the pressure of his grip as he held her hand. Turning toward her, Santa Anna swept her into his arms, swirling her to the gay, lilting tune of the waltz as he moved faultlessly across the floor. He did not speak, his lips moving into a tight, tense line as they circled the floor for the second time. Unable to bear the tension a moment longer, Morgana questioned quietly, "Is something wrong, Antonio?"

His eyes moved to her face for the fraction of a second before he guided her slowly to the edge of the floor. A conciliatory smile slipping across his lips, he questioned in a slightly raised voice, "Was the dance too much for you, my dear?" When she did not answer, but stood staring at him with a questioning expression, he took her lightly by the arm. "Come, I will take you outside for a little air. It is indeed close in here." Walking to a small balcony that led to the garden, he escorted her outside graciously. Once out of sight of prying eyes, he pulled her hungrily into his arms, his mouth closing over hers roughly, hurtingly, until she cried out.

Santa Anna was breathing heavily as he drew away, his voice shaky as he responded tightly, "Did I hurt you, *querida?* I do not pretend to be sorry!"

Too startled for an immediate response, Morgana managed at last, "But . . . w . . . why? What have I done?"

"You are over an hour late in arriving here, Morgana! And for the past hour I have watched the door, expecting each face that appeared to be your own! I do not enjoy being kept waiting, *querida.* Patience is not one of my virtues, and I have waited long enough for you already!"

"But . . . but the delay was unavoidable, Antonio. There was a problem with the carriage."

The black eyes looking into hers were hot with passion. "I care very little about the carriage, *querida.*" Dismissing her words carelessly, Santa Anna cupped her face with his hands and drew her mouth to his once again. The invasion of her mouth was deep and consuming, and she had no desire to be consumed. Again a deep revulsion swept her senses. She wanted no hands to touch her skin but Devon's . . . no mouth on hers but his. She wanted to get away from Santa Anna's clutching hands and his heated body, the soft words of love he whispered into her ear in breathless passion. But she had made a bargain . . . a bargain she dared not break. She knew the depths to which Santa Anna would go to avenge his jealousy, and she dared not offend him.

"*Querida . . . querida . . .* I have wanted you for so long." Santa Anna's lips moved across her cheek to her ear as his hands caressed her back. "I have convinced your uncle that you should come back with me to Manga de Clavo. You will bring Aggie, of course, but you needn't fear that I will allow either Aggie or Ines to interfere with the progress of our love. My people at Manga de Clavo are extremely loyal to me. I need not worry that a single word will be said as to where I spend my nights. Ines and I have had separate rooms from the inception of our marriage. That pale stick of a woman has never dared to seek me out

470

in the darkness of the night. We need not worry that there will be any interference from that quarter." His hand was on her shoulder, caressing her skin boldly. Allowing his hand to drop, he ran it over the rise of her breasts, his chest beginning to heave with agitation as he whispered softly into her ear, "I have dreamed of this so often, *querida*. It was a cruel twist of fate that took you from me at the very moment our love was to be consummated. But it will be all the better for the anticipation we have shared, you will see, *querida*. You will see. . . ."

In his impassioned state, Santa Anna had not noticed that Morgana had hardly spoken a word, that her face was stiff, her expression frozen. Instead, he pulled her close again, his mouth ravenous with desire. When he pulled away at last, Morgana was weak with the repulsion sweeping her. His expression amused as she swayed lightly in his arms, Santa Anna whispered warmly, "You must pull yourself together now, *querida*. In a few more days we will be at Manga de Clavo, and I will take you riding as I did before. We will make love under the sun, *querida*, with only the birds and the sky as our witnesses, and you will tell me how much you love me." His eyes abruptly darkening, Santa Anna said softly, "You have never said you love me, *querida*, and I wait to hear you cry out your love for me. I wait for the days and the nights when I will hear those words. . . ."

Abruptly stepping away from her, Santa Anna took a deep breath in an attempt to draw himself under control. His eyes moving assessingly over her, he nodded his head. "All right, we must return now before there is talk. You are ready, *querida*?"

Nodding her head, grateful for the opportunity to escape his attentions, Morgana walked stiffly beside him as they returned to the ballroom. They had just stepped into the room when a voice spoke quietly to the left of her, the familiar sound jerking her head spontaneously to its source.

"So, here you are at last. I had begun to wonder where you had gone." Brilliant blue eyes acutely assessed her

471

incredulous expression, the shock leaving her breathless, capable of uttering only one word.

"Devon!"

Santa Anna's hand on her arm tightened painfully, snapping her eyes to his livid face as he stared silently into Devon's sardonic expression. His voice was a low hiss. "Either you are a fool, or you place little value on your life, Señor Howard. It is only because I do not wish to spoil the nature of the victory party in progress that I do not call to have you arrested on the spot!"

"Which is exactly why I thought this the best place to confront you, Antonio. I arrived at the capital yesterday and decided to wait until this evenin' to make you aware of my presence. I also had a few other important details to settle before I announced myself."

"Important details! What details are so important that they are worth your life, Señor Howard? For surely that is what you forfeit by coming here."

An expression of feigned surprise moved across Devon's face. "I had not realized you felt animosity toward me, Antonio. When I left the capital last, it was under amicable conditions. We had made a bargain."

"A bargain which you break by appearing here tonight! But if it were not for that matter alone, there would still be the fact that you are a traitor to my country . . . participated in a uprising against the central government. . . ."

"Oh, did I? I know I was injured somehow in Zacatecas, and an employee of my father's managed to get me home to recuperate. But Raoul did tell me you said that as far as you were concerned, I had never been in Zacatecas at all . . . that all memory of my participation in the uprising was wiped from your mind. I have no doubt Morgana's appearance did much to encourage your loss of memory." His eyes beginning to show a spark of anger, Devon glanced again in her direction. "No man could keep his mind on business very long with Morgana close by." His eyes moving back to Santa Anna, he continued quietly, "So, I have come here as an official representative of the Texas colony to confer with Colonel Austin. It

472

is indeed unfortunate that you seem to hold some sort of personal grudge against me, Antonio, but I do know you do not wish to have personal feelin's interfere with the official workin's of your government. You have had considerable problems with Zacatecas. You would not wish to risk a similar problem in Texas.''

"Bastardo!" The low response slipped softly from between Santa Anna's clenched teeth.

''As for our personal agreement which you claim I break by returning, Colonel Austin's charges have still not been dropped, and the simple fact that he is still confined to the city, unable to go home, negates our bargain, as far as I'm concerned.''

''And so you come here . . . to flaunt your presence before me! It will do you little good, Señor Howard! I leave for Manga de Clavo within two days, and you shall have to conduct your official business with General Barragán.'' His eyes quickly scanning the crowded room, Santa Anna located the figure he sought. ''He stands over there, in the far corner.'' Returning his gaze stiffly to Devon, he took an even firmer grip on Morgana's arm. ''Since we have nothing more to discuss, I shall leave you to enjoy the party as you like. Come, Morgana . . .'

His face stiffening abruptly, Devon reached out to take Morgana's other arm. ''You are entirely correct when you say there is nothing further for us to discuss, Antonio, but there is much Morgana and I have to discuss between us, since I have only a few hours ago completed arrangements for our weddin'.''

''Your wedding!'' Santa Anna's enraged expression shot to Morgana's startled face. The blood draining from her cheeks, Morgana shook her head. Devon's appearance . . . the conversation that had been taking place between Santa Anna and him—it had all seemed like a dream! His unexpected announcement had confirmed in her mind the fact that this was not reality at all, leaving her startled . . . confused.

''You are insane!'' Extremely aware of the curious glances that had begun to turn in their direction, Santa Anna lowered his voice, turning his back to the crowded floor as he continued, "Manuel has said nothing of this to me! Just this afternoon he gave his sanction for Morgana to return to Manga de Clavo with me."

Devon's quick glance at Morgana's face reflected his contempt. "Well, she won't be goin', Antonio. She'll be marryin' me tomorrow. All arrangements have been completed."

His brief, contempt-filled glance lit the fire of a familiar anger inside Morgana, snapping her to the reality of the moment with the force of a blow. "You *are* insane! You have completed all arrangements with the exception of informing the bride-to-be! It is unfortunate that you have wasted your time if you have indeed done what you say! Myself, I cannot comprehend how such a notion entered your mind!"

An obvious relief passed over Santa Anna's face at Morgana's words. He was once again under control as he faced Devon squarely. "Perhaps you are not truly as recuperated as you thought, Señor Howard. It seems you still suffer from the delusions stimulated by your fever. It is obvious Morgana has no intention of going anywhere but to Manga de Clavo within the next two days and I . . ."

"Morgana will not be goin' to Manga de Clavo, Antonio." An open fury beginning to move aross his face, Devon said slowly, ". . . and she will marry me! I will not allow the mother of my child to live as any man's mistress!"

"Your child!" Santa Anna's glance snapped to Morgana, his eyes reflecting her shock as she took an involuntary step backwards. Had it not been for the hands that continued to hold her arms tenaciously, Morgana would have run— escaped from the scene being played out so incredibly before her!

Her voice was a low gasp. "How . . . how did you know?"

"It is true?" Santa Anna's voice trembled with emotion. "It is true what he says? You carry his child?"

Her eyes still on Devon's face, Morgana nodded stiffly to the low, hissed question, the response causing her eyelids to drop momentarily closed with shame.

"*Puta!*" Proceeding after a short pause, Santa Anna said stiffly, "She is yours, Señor Howard, and you are welcome to her. It was obviously her intention to declare the child mine after enough time had elapsed to make the fact plausible . . . to foist another man's child on me as my own! *Puta! Bribón!*"

Turning on his heel, Santa Anna walked stiffly into the surrounding crowd and disappeared.

Devon's face began to swim before her, contributing to the harsh unreality of the rapid progress of events. What was it she saw in Devon's eyes? The hatred and anger were changing . . . Was it anxiety . . . concern? He was pulling her toward the exit to the ballroom, his arm around her waist, supporting her. They were passing through the arched entranceway as the room began to spin around her, when the weakness in her legs began to assume control. Was this indeed reality, this spinning room . . . quickly ebbing light . . . this darkness . . . ?

The sala was ablaze with light. His lined face tight with anger, Tío Manuel stood stiffly. Tears heavy in her eyes, Tía Isabella stood beside him, absent-mindedly wringing her hands, her expression distraught. Facing them squarely from his position a short distance away, Devon was adamant. Only Morgana sat on the couch, a necessity unanimously insisted upon after her collapse and removal from the palace.

Her uncle's voice was heavy with anger. "You come here not to request my niece's hand in marriage, but to demand it! You tell us you have already made the arrangements for the marriage tomorrow! *Increíble!* You are a madman . . . insane . . . just as I have always maintained! You do not truly expect that my wife and I will agree to such madness! My niece has indicated no inclination for such a contract. The proposal was doubtless as shocking to her as it is to us and probably accounts for her unfortunate collapse! No! I will not honor such an incredible proposal with an answer! Señor Howard, you will leave my house, now!''

Devon's expression was firm, uncompromising. Still dressed formally in a dark jacket and trousers, his shirt white against the sun-darkened color of his skin, he maintained his position opposite her uncle's darkening face. ''You will agree to my proposal, general. The choice is no longer yours to make. Morgana will bear my child in December!''

His expression controlled, Tío Manuel bore the shock of Devon's statement well as his wife ran to sit at Morgana's side. Turning to his niece, his tone was flat and lifeless. ''Is this true, Morgana? You carry this man's child?''

An abrupt perversity assuming control of her mind, Morgana moved to her feet. Standing stiff and erect despite the quaking in her knees, she declared quietly, ''I carry a child, but it is not Señor Howard's!''

A sense of triumph filling her, she heard the low gasps that sounded in the room. No, she would not marry Devon under these conditions! He had obviously come to her out of a sense of duty . . . perhaps he was not even certain in his mind that the child was his own! She could not go through her life feeling the love that overwhelmed her at the sight of him . . . having it stagnate inside her, knowing he had no love for her in return. She could not go through the nights when he did not come home, picturing Helena Trent or some other woman in his arms . . . someone he respected and loved! No, she could not marry Devon . . . she could not!

The silent tableau was tense with angry shock when a low voice from behind Morgana broke the expectant silence.

''Morgana carries Mr. Howard's child. I have it from her own lips, and it was I who sent him word of her pregnancy.''

Turning in the direction of the voice, Morgana fixed her incredulous gaze on Aggie's familiar emotionless expression. ''He is the father of your child, Morgana. It is his duty to support the child and you, as well as it is his privilege to come to know his own offspring. You have no

476

other choice, Morgana, but to accept Mr. Howard's proposal."

"I have no choice? I do not wish to marry him!"

Tío Manuel's low voice broke sharply into the emotional scene, turning Morgana's head back in his direction as he questioned quietly, "It is true, Morgana? I ask you again, and expect you to respond truthfully. The child is Señor Howard's?"

Realizing she could no longer deny the truth, Morgana lifted her chin as she replied clearly. "Yes, the child is his."

Inwardly flinching at the pain reflected in her uncle's eyes, Morgana waited for his hesitant reply. "Then it is true that you have no choice but to marry him, *querida.*"

"No, I will not . . . I won't marry him!"

"*Sí*, you will marry him, Morgana." His voice reflecting the strength of his decision, he directed his glance into Morgana's eyes. "Tía Isabella and I asked you no questions when you were returned to us. We did not wish to stir the pain you obviously suffered, but it is obvious to me now that the time spent away from us was spent with Señor Howard, until you either effected your escape or became disenchanted with him."

"No, Tío Manuel, I did not go willingly."

"It does not matter now, Morgana. You admit to carrying his child. A man has a right to his child and a responsibility to the woman who bears it. I will not see your child born a bastard. . . . I would not have you pass that legacy on to him." Hesitating only a moment longer, Tío Manuel continued in a new, softer tone. "You will marry this man tomorrow, Morgana. If you do not, this house will no longer be your own after that time. I will neither shelter nor clothe you or your child. The decision is yours."

Tío Manuel's words hung heavily in a room that was silent except for the sound of Tía Isabella's tears. The pain of Tío Manuel's words was intense, not lessened by the fact that he had spoken without anger. Slowly turning toward Devon, Morgana met his stiff, unrelenting gaze.

"And so, my decision is forced from me, Devon."

477

A small, sardonic smile flicked across her lips. "Yes, I have searched the options open to me, and I have decided."

Holding his gaze tightly, a fire burning in the gold-flecked depths of her eyes, she said without emotion, "I will become your wife."

His only reaction the jerking of a small muscle in his cheek, Devon nodded, his eyes moving to follow her intently as she turned away and left the room.

The sound of the horses' hooves echoed in the early morning street as the carriage moved steadily forward. The cathedral was on the next street. Her stomach tensing with anxiety, Morgana pulled herself stiffly erect, her quick, jerking movement drawing the eyes of those within the carriage to her pale face. Unable to manage a smile, Morgana returned their assessing stares unblinkingly.

"Morgana, you are all right? You are feeling well?" Her aunt's small, anxious voice chipped at the veneer of icy calm Morgana had assumed to control her racing emotions.

"I'm fine, Tía Isabella."

Realizing her uncle's eyes remained on her face for a few moments longer, Morgana turned her glance to the city that moved past the coach window. She would not allow the open concern on the three faces surrounding her to affect her calm. She was doing what was necessary to guarantee the future of the life that grew inside her. Ironically, she had felt that life for the first time the previous night, and she could remember still the thrill that had flashed across her senses, the mindless elation that had momentarily removed the weight of her cares. Yes, she would function for the sake of the child, would allow the joy to compensate for the agony of knowing that the man she loved despised her, despite the fact that he was to become her husband that morning.

A memory of the fleeting joy she had experienced on seeing Devon in the ballroom the night before, his body

478

tall and strong, completely recuperated from his wounds, returned to haunt her mind. But there had been anger, not love in his expression when he had looked at her. She had wanted . . . needed only a touch, a smile to make her despair turn to joy when he had announced that they would be married this morning. But there was no joy inside Devon, no happy anticipation of the life they were about to begin together, just the knowledge that the marriage was necessary to guarantee the future of the child. She could not feel anger toward Aggie for her decision to inform Devon of her circumstances. In Aggie's strict mind, logic ruled. There was no room for consideration of the fact that love had not been considered when the decision had been made for them to marry.

But she had been prepared like a proper bride for the ceremony that was about to take place. Her eyes filled with tears, Tía Isabella had walked hesitantly into her room that morning, an elaborate lace gown held gingerly in her hands.

"It is my wedding gown, *querida*. I have saved it for many years, even though I do not have a child to pass it to. I believe in my mind that Providence allowed me to have it ready for you, so you might wear it on this day."

Somehow she had been unwilling to accept the garment associated with the strong love that existed between her aunt and uncle. To accept it would be to profane the garment with the mockery of the ceremony in which she was to participate.

Her excuse had been weak. "You are so much smaller than I, Tía Isabella. It will not fit. . . ."

"It has been altered, Morgana, to meet your size. See, this large ruffle on the bottom is new, added for your additional height. And the buttons were adjusted to conform to the size of the dress you wore yesterday. It will be perfect."

"And . . . and Tío Manuel . . . he will not object?"

Taking a moment to swallow past her tears, Tía Isabella had stated hoarsely, "Tío Manuel sends it with his love."

Now, glancing down momentarily at the magnificent

lace garment she wore, Morgana remembered the picture that had stared back from her bedroom mirror. Fitting smoothly to her shoulders and neck, the bodice edged with a fine white lace high on her throat, it had long, full sleeves that gathered to a tight cuff at her wrists. Simple, without adornment, it lay smoothly against the curving contours of her breast before tying at her waist in a wide, satin sash. The skirt flared out in a simple bell shape in endless, graduated tiers that fell to her feet. Her brilliant chestnut curls had been swept to the top of her head and secured with a large Spanish comb, over which hung a mantilla of an incredibly delicate lace. The tears on Tía Isabella's face and the surprising brightness in Aggie's eyes had confirmed the fact that she looked the part she was about to play, that of the exquisite, expectant bride.

A deep shudder passed over Morgana's stiff frame as the cathedral came into view. Abruptly unable to bear the sight of the imposing structure, Morgana jerked her eyes forward and clenched her hands tightly in her lap as the carriage began to draw slowly to a halt. With silent efficiency, she was helped down from the carriage and led carefully up the steps. The morning sun was warm on her head, the early hour accounting for the absence of spectators in the usually crowded street. The interior of the church was dark, lit only by the candles on the altar and large sconces on either side of the long aisle. Blinded by the light of the bright morning sun, Morgana was momentarily unable to make out the shadows that awaited her at the altar. The sound of an organ sounded from the choir loft above her, startling her with its loud, resounding tones. A broad hand took hers and enclosed it warmly. Looking up, she saw the shine of emotion in Tío Manuel's dark eyes as he tucked her arm through his, and, turning, began walking toward the altar.

Her eyes touched on the tall, slender man standing beside the priest at the end of the long aisle. The eyes that met hers were sober, unrevealing, and Morgana felt a flush of color wash over her face. Devon . . . Her heart cried out to him as her face maintained its solemn expression. Devon, if only it

480

could have been different . . . if only you could have told me that you love me.

She was standing at his side as the priest spoke in low, earnest tones. She heard Devon speak in response, his voice clear and firm. She heard her own low-muttered response. And then it was over. The words had been pronounced. They were man and wife.

Devon did not take her into his arms, but instead turned to her aunt and uncle as they surged forward to kiss her cheek. Out of the corner of her eye, she saw Devon solemnly accept the hand Tío Manuel held out to him, as well as Tía Isabella's light kiss on his cheek. The only flicker of emotion had come when Aggie had taken his hand in hers.

They were walking back down the aisle, Devon's hand firm on her arm, as they came out onto the top step outside the cathedral, blinking against the glare of the brilliant sun. The abrupt, jerking movement of Devon's head moved her eyes into the direction in which he stared, in time to see the familiar figure seated erectly on a white stallion slowly turn his horse around and proceed back in the direction from which he had come. His expression grim, Devon looked into Morgana's face. Taking a firmer grip on her arm, he escorted her to the waiting carriage.

The sun was warm on her back. They had been traveling for hours in silence. The scene was a familiar one as they rode side by side along the trail, stirring old memories, old passions. But this time they traveled more conservatively than before. Two pack mules, loaded meticulously by her uncle's men, carried her belongings, as well as ample supplies for the journey back to Texas. It would be a long journey, but she had not been consulted about the manner in which she wanted to travel, although, in reality, there had been little choice. Devon had seemed anxious to get away, back on the trail. She had no doubt in her mind that he was just as anxious to shed his responsibility for her, but it was too late for that . . . too late for both of them.

481

Conscious of the weight of an intense perusal, Morgana moved her eyes toward Devon and was startled to see that he stared at her solemnly. Self-conscious under his gaze, she moved her hand against the light white blouse in which she had elected to travel, and ran her eyes regretfully over the heavy baize skirt. Instead of the large sombrero she had worn on their last journey together, she now wore a smart, flat-brimmed hat provided by Tía Isabella to shield her light skin against the sun. But, strangely, she longed for the light Mexican blouse and skirt that had formerly been her traveling attire. She had many beautiful memories associated with the clothes she had first assumed so unwillingly.

"It's getting too warm to travel. We're going to stop for an hour in that grove of trees ahead." Devon's statement carried no expectation of response, and Morgana did not bother to reply.

They moved slowly under the cover of trees, Morgana emitting a soft sigh of relief as the refreshing coolness hit her perspired skin.

Quickly dismounting, Devon moved to Morgana's side and lifted her from her horse. The touch of his hands seemed to burn through the light material of her blouse, searing her skin. Extremely conscious of her sensitivity to his touch, Morgana averted her eyes and spontaneously moved out of his reach. As Devon secured the animals, she walked toward the small stream that trickled between the trees, and, stooping, scooped some water into her mouth. The cool liquid trickled down her chin, and, grateful for its coolness, Morgana raised her hand to spread the moisture against her perspiring neck. Abruptly, the temptation was too much for her. Sitting down on the bank, she pulled off her boots and stockings and sank her feet into the stream.

She heard sounds of Devon busying himself in their temporary camp behind her. There had been no celebration of their wedding that morning. After the ceremony they had returned to Tío Manuel's house and eaten a quiet meal. Immediately afterwards, she had gone upstairs to change her clothes, and when she had emerged, the animals had been ready to leave. Her goodbyes had been quiet and restrained because of her extreme consciousness of Devon's intense perusal of her. They had spoken only a few words from the inception of the journey, and, strangely, Morgana found she had little to say. Somehow, everything appeared to have already been said.

"Morgana." Devon's voice filtered from within the trees as he walked slowly toward her. A small smile moving over his lips, he allowed his eyes to remain for long moments on the small feet that moved in the cool water. "It's hot this afternoon. That must be refreshing."

Morgana nodded her head, looking up at the hesitation in Devon's voice. "Morgana, there are some things I have to say to you . . . some things I would like to straighten out between us."

A small frown moving between her brows, Morgana said tightly, "There's nothing to say, Devon. It's all been said."

"No, not everythin'. Come with me, please."

The new, softer tone to his voice drew Morgana's eyes to his. Slowly, as if mesmerized by their intensity, she drew herself slowly to her feet, accepting the hand Devon held out to her as she did. They were walking back to the area where the horses were tied, when Devon turned and gripped her shoulders unexpectedly. Frowning as she flinched under his touch, he began tightly, "I'm sorry, Morgana. I'm sorry it has to be like this between us. This tension . . . it seemed to be there right from the start, waitin' to spring up and set us at each other's throats. But I want you to know, I never wanted it this way . . . never wanted you to hate or mistrust me. . . . And I didn't want to be worthy of your mistrust as I have been . . ."

"Please, Devon." Unwilling to face the memories his words were stirring, Morgana turned away from his gaze. "It's all over now. What's done is done. . . ."

"Morgana, please listen to me." The new note in Devon's voice brought her attention back to his face to see the pain reflected in his bright azure eyes. "You're my wife now, Morgana, and I want there to be honesty between us, even if there's nothin' else." Inwardly flinching at his words, Morgana forced her eyes to remain steady.

"After I was wounded . . . when I was well enough to think clearly at last, I was back in Texas. Raoul and John had gotten me back there somehow, although I can't remember much of the journey at all. There was only one thing that I could remember that happened after I was wounded. I remembered you, standin' by my bed, with Santa Anna's arm around you. He was kissin' you, sayin' how glad he was to have you back. I could remember so clearly that you never came near me . . . never touched me, even though I called you again and again. . . ."

"Please, Devon, there's no point to this. I don't . . ."

"Let me finish, please, Morgana." Devon's face was intensely sober, his expression resolute. "I remembered how you opened your mouth under his, lettin' him kiss you more deeply, and I ached, Morgana. I ached with hatred for you. In my mind, all I could think was that you had finally found your opportunity to return to Santa Anna, and had talked John into takin' you to him. All the times we had made love . . . all the times I had held you in my arms, meant nothin' . . . nothin'. . . ."

"They meant nothing to you, Devon. You made sure I knew that."

His frown darkening momentarily at her comment, Devon paused before he continued. "John and Raoul tried to talk to me, but nothin' they said made a difference. Then I received Aggie's letter sayin' you were carryin' my child. . . . But you loved Santa Anna. I had no doubt you were his mistress again, but Aggie had written to me sayin' you had told her the child was mine. I tried to stop myself from comin' down here, Morgana. I tried to be strong enough to let you go. I had given you enough unhappiness, and I didn't want to interfere with whatever happiness you had found with Santa Anna, but the letter kept gnawin' at me. You were carryin' my child . . . and I had a right to see you again . . . to claim you, to take you back with me, even if you didn't love me.''

A slow sense of wonder began to move across Morgana's mind as Devon spoke, a sense of disbelief as his words continued in a rush.

''The following mornin' I found myself gettin' ready to come here. I hadn't come to any conscious decision, Morgana. It had just been a slow realization that I'd do anythin', use any excuse I could, to get you back and keep you with me. When I reached Mexico City and found out you were in town, I went immediately to the church and made arrangements for the weddin', even though I still hadn't formed a plan in my mind as to how I was goin' to get you away from Santa Anna. I knew he hated me, and was jealous, and I wasn't even certain I wouldn't end up in a cell somewhere. Then I saw you with him last night at the ball, Morgana, comin' back with him from the garden. Your lips were still swollen from his kisses, did you know that?'' His hands tightened spontaneously on her shoulders, but Morgana bore the pain without flinching as his low voice continued. ''I lost it all, then, Morgana, and I blurted out the truth . . . that you were carryin' my child . . . that I was goin' to marry you and take you back with me to Texas. I was glad when he turned on you . . . glad that he was through with you, until I saw the look on your face. You loved him and I had done it to you again . . . taken you from the man you loved, and I hated myself for my selfishness.''

''Devon, but I don't . . .'' Placing his fingers over her lips, Devon stifled her response. ''I want to finish, Morgana. Please let me finish what I have to say.''

Nodding her head, her throat too filled with tears to respond, Morgana listened silently as Devon continued, with obvious pain.

''When you came down the aisle this mornin', Morgana . . . you were so beautiful . . . the most beautiful woman I've ever seen, and I knew that this was what I had always wanted . . . you with me, always. I wanted to tell you how I felt, beg you to give me a chance to prove my love, but when we came out, there he was again . . . Santa Anna

. . . He was wantin' you again, Morgana. After everythin' he had said, he wanted you. And I knew he'd take you back if you went to him. That was when I decided . . . when I knew what I'm goin' to tell you now.'' Pausing, Devon took a deep breath. His eyes never leaving her face, he began slowly, ''You're carryin' my child, and I want to see him born, Morgana. You're my wife, and as far as I'm concerned, those vows we took last forever. Santa Anna's no good for you. He's married, and you could never live a full life with him. You weren't meant to be with him, darlin'. If it was meant to be, you'd have met him a long time ago, before he married Doña Ines. You were meant to be with me . . . only me.

''How else could it happen that we could meet on a ship goin' to Mexico, you to begin a life there, and me to accomplish a quick political mission and go home? How else could it have happened that I could've fallen so deeply in love with you that I wasn't able to leave you in Mexico City without feelin' like I'd left a part of me behind? For a while I hated you for that, Morgana . . . makin' me feel like only half a person without you, and then preferrin' Santa Anna to me on all counts.'' The hard lines of Devon's face slowly softened, his eyes warming as they looked into hers. His hand slid up to cup her cheek as he continued more softly than before. ''But I can make myself admit it now, darlin'. I can make myself admit I love you even though I know you won't say it to me in return.''

''But Devon, I . . .''

Shaking his head to still her spontaneous response, he continued softly, ''So I want to tell you now, darlin', tell you that I'm goin' to make you a good husband. I'm goin' to take you back home with me and we'll raise our child together, and I'm goin' to do everythin' I can to make it up to you . . . all the pain I've caused you and all the heartbreak you're goin' to suffer away from the man you love. . . .''

Swallowing tightly, he continued in a hoarse voice, ''I love you, Morgana. I love you so much it's a hard, burnin' ache inside me that just won't quit. And I'm goin' to make you

486

happy, darlin' . . . that's my promise to you today. I'm goin' to make you happy.''

Devon's hands were trembling as he held her firmly in his grasp, his eyes searching hers for a sign of acceptance. A soaring joy coming to life inside her, Morgana could not speak for the emotions that flooded her mind.

''Morgana, darlin', say somethin' . . . Tell me you don't hate me. . . .''

''Devon . . . I don't hate you. I love you, Devon, I love you, and that's all I ever wanted to hear you say to me . . . just those words.''

His expression incredulous, Devon said disbelievingly, ''Santa Anna . . . you don't love him?''

''I never loved him, Devon! That was all something you seemed to manufacutre in your mind! I admired him for a long time, but after Zacatecas . . . well, I faced reality about him after that. He's everything you ever said he was . . . ambitious, vain, arrogant, greedy for power, self-ish—''

''And me . . . what am I, Morgana?'' His eyes were still faintly disbelieving as Devon's mouth slowly moved toward hers. ''Tell me what I am.''

''You're the man I love, Devon. The only man I'll ever love.''

''Morgana, darlin'.'' His voice a low groan, Devon whispered as his lips touched hers, ''That's all I ever want to be.''

His kiss was deep, intense, stirring to life all the wild, soaring passions Morgana had suppressed within her. Her arms slipped around his neck, her body moving closer, closer still as Devon's embrace tightened breathlessly. Abruptly she was scooped high against his chest, her face only a few inches from his as he whispered softly into her eyes. ''I've loved you for so long, darlin' . . . first without realizin' it and then without bein' able to acknowledge it, even to myself. But I never stopped wantin' you, Morgana, never for a minute.''

''And I never stopped wanting you, Devon. Even when I was hating you, I was wanting you.''

487

Still holding her tight within his arms, Devon walked to a spot where a soft green cover cushioned the ground. Lowering her gently, he lay beside her and took her into his arms. His voice was hoarse against her lips, his arms possessive. "You're mine forever now, darlin', you know that?"

"That's right, Devon, for the rest of our lives."

"For the rest of our lives."

Their lips touched, and the communion was complete. No more words were needed. . . .

EPILOGUE

His lips were warm against her skin, trailing a blurred line of kisses across her naked breasts. Gasping as his tongue flicked out to touch a swollen crest in a quick caress, Morgana held his head tight against her, running her fingers lovingly through his heavy, sun-streaked hair.

Staying to caress the aching globes for only a moment longer, Devon slid his mouth down the white skin gleaming in the darkness of their room, seeking the tender nest that awaited him. He longed to taste her intimately once again. It was a glory that never ceased for him, the wonder of knowing that Morgana was his, alone, for all of his life. The desire to assure himself, to renew his possession of her again and again had not left him, and in his heart he knew that it never would.

His Morgana . . . his own Morgana.

A small, hesitant wail at their bedside interrupted his loving quest, snapping his head upward as Morgana began to move beneath him. The cry grew louder, and Morgana whispered softly, "Little Sam needs to be fed, Devon. I'm going to have to pick him up or Aggie's going to be in here in a few minutes to see what's wrong."

Watching as Devon slowly lifted himself from the bed,

Morgana allowed her eyes to follow his broad, tightly muscled form as he walked the few steps to the cradle. A deep love welled up inside her at the expression of loving pride on Devon's face as he reached down and lifted the squirming four-month-old into his arms. She was supremely happy. Little Sam had been born on the day before Christmas, the ultimate gift for them to share on their first Christmas as man and wife. Aggie had arrived a few weeks before to complete the happy circle of love that surrounded her. Were it not for the political unrest that continued in Texas, that even Stephen Austin's pardon could not subdue, and her certainty that the edicts from the central government in Mexico City were pushing the colony slowly and surely into a conflict, Morgana was certain she would be able to say her life was now perfect and complete. Yes, a conflict was coming, but she did not allow it to affect her happiness or her love.

A small smile moving across her lips, Morgana adjusted her position as the hungry wail turned into short, responsive whimpers. Yes, her life was complete and loving. . . .

Turning back to the bed, Devon saw Morgana had turned up the lamp and propped herself against the pillows as she watched them approach. Standing motionless for a moment, he looked at the beautiful naked length of her, long chestnut curls the only spot of color against white velvet skin. Walking forward, he placed little Sam in her arms, warmed to the heart at the sight of his son at Morgana's breast, sucking noisily. Climbing onto the bed beside her, Devon pulled the light coverlet up to their waists and whispered into her ear, "Just in case Aggie or Sam should decide to come in and check the baby. I never know which one of them is goin' to make it to the cradle first when he cries!"

Laughing lightly at his words, Morgana turned her face up to his and raised her mouth for his kiss. Her mouth was sweet and warm, and, cupping her cheek with his hand, Devon held it against his as he drank deeply of the nectar of her kiss, exulting in the beauty they shared between them. Drawing his mouth from hers at last, he turned to whisper into his son's tiny ear, "Hurry up and drink your fill, my little son, so your father can sate himself, also."

490

In response, the small brows drew together in a frown. The sucking stopped momentarily as bright blue eyes so like his father's glared up into his. The low laugh that broke from Morgana's lips was spontaneous, stimulated by the meeting of two strong wills as they opposed each other for her attention.

Raising her eyes to Devon's, the sparking gold in their depths dancing, Morgana said lightly, "Your son doesn't like having to share his mother when it's time for his feeding."

"And his father doesn't like havin' to share his wife when it's time for his lovin'." Devon's reply was soft and low as his eyes moved slowly over Morgana's face. Lowering his head, he kissed her lips once again, and, lowering his head farther, kissed the small bald head of his hungry son. Raising his eyes to Morgana's, Devon said softly into her eyes, "But that's all right, darlin', I don't mind waitin' a little bit. We have the rest of our lives, darlin' . . . the rest of our lives. . . ."

MORE TEMPESTUOUS ROMANCES!

EXCITING BESTSELLERS FROM ZEBRA

STORM TIDE (1230, $3.75)
by Patricia Rae
In a time when it was unladylike to desire one man, defiant,
flamehaired Elizabeth desired two! And while she longed to be
held in the strong arms of a handsome sea captain, she yearned
for the status and wealth that only the genteel doctor could provide—leaving her hopelessly torn amidst passion's raging
STORM TIDE . . . .

PASSION'S REIGN (1177, $3.95)
by Karen Harper
Golden-haired Mary Bullen was wealthy, lovely and refined—and
lusty King Henry VIII's prize gem! But her passion for the handsome Lord William Stafford put her at odds with the Royal
Court. Mary and Stafford lived by a lovers' vow: one day they
would be ruled by only the crown of PASSION'S REIGN.

HEIRLOOM (1200, $3.95)
by Eleanora Brownleigh
The surge of desire Thea felt for Charles was powerful enough to
convince her that, even though they were strangers and their marriage was a fake, fate was playing a most subtle trick on them
both: Were they on a mission for President Teddy Roosevelt—or
on a crusade to realize their own passionate desire?

LOVESTONE (1202, $3.50)
by Deanna James
After just one night of torrid passion and tender need, the dark-
haired, rugged lord could not deny that Moira, with her precious
beaty, was born to be a princess. But how could he grant her
freedom when he himself was a prisoner of her love?

*Available wherever paperbacks are sold, or order direct from the
Publisher. Send cover price plus 50¢ per copy for mailing and
handling to Zebra Books, 475 Park Avenue South, New York,
N.Y. 10016. DO NOT SEND CASH.*

YOU WILL ALSO WANT TO
READ THESE CAPTIVATING HISTORICAL ROMANCES!

TEXAS FLAME (1013, $2.95)
by Catherine Creel
Amanda's journey west through an uncivilized haven of outlaws
and Indians leads her to handsome Luke Cameron, as wild and
untamed as the land itself, whose burning passion would consume
her own!

RAPTURE'S RAGE (1121, $3.50)
by Bobbie Walton
Renee's dazzling looks brought her many suitors, but she only
had eyes for Marshall. Though he vowed never to love a woman
again—he couldn't deny his desire!

SAVAGE DESIRE (1120, $3.50)
by Constance O'Banyon
Mara knew it was fate that brought her and virile Tajarez
together. But destiny would not allow them to savor the joys of
love. They would only be bound by SAVAGE DESIRE.

TEXAS RAPTURE (1195, $3.50)
by Jalynn Friends
With her ripe, sensuous body and wicked green eyes, Laura Karell
could only captivate Logan. How could he know that she was
truly innocent? All Logan had to do was convince her of his
love—and bring her the unrelenting joys of TEXAS RAPTURE.

*Available wherever paperbacks are sold, or order direct from the
Publisher. Send cover price plus 50¢ per copy for mailing and
handling to Zebra Books, 475 Park Avenue South, New York,
N.Y. 10016. DO NOT SEND CASH.*